Up the Bright River

Up the Bright River

The Worlds of Philip José Farmer

Edited by Gary K. Wolfe

Subterranean Press 2010

First Edition

ISBN
978-1-59606-329-7

Subterranean Press
PO Box 190106
Burton, MI 48519

www.subterraneanpress.com

Acknowledgments

"Attitudes" originally appeared in *The Magazine of Fantasy and Science Fiction* in 1953 and was reprinted in *Father to the Stars* (1981).

"How Deep the Grooves" originally appeared in *Amazing Stories* in 1963 and was reprinted in *Down in the Black Gang and Other Stories* (1971).

"The Blasphemers" originally appeared in *Galaxy* in 1964 and was reprinted in *Down in the Black Gang and Other Stories* (1971).

"A Bowl Bigger Than Earth" originally appeared in *Worlds of If* in 1967 and was reprinted in *Down in the Black Gang and Other Stories* (1971).

"Down in the Black Gang" originally appeared in *Worlds of If* in 1969 and was reprinted in *Down in the Black Gang and Other Stories* (1971).

"The Voice of the Sonar in My Vermiform Appendix" originally appeared in *Quark/2* in 1971 and was reprinted in *The Book of Philip José Farmer* (1973).

"Father's in the Basement" originally appeared in *Orbit 11* in 1972 and was reprinted in *The Book of Philip José Farmer* (1973).

"Toward the Beloved City" originally appeared in *Signs and Wonders* in 1972 and was reprinted in *The Book of Philip José Farmer* (1973).

"Skinburn" originally appeared in *The Magazine of Fantasy and Science Fiction* in 1972 and was reprinted in *The Book of Philip José Farmer* (1973).

"The Sumerian Oath" originally appeared in *Nova 2* in 1972 and was reprinted in *The Book of Philip José Farmer* (1973).

"Extracts from the Memoirs of Lord Greystoke" originally appeared in *Mother Was a Lovely Beast* (1974).

"The Two-Edged Gift" originally appeared in *Continuum I* in 1974 and was reprinted in *Stations of the Nightmare* (1982).

"St. Francis Kisses His Ass Goodbye" originally appeared in *Semiotext(e) SF* in 1989 and was reprinted in *Riders of the Purple Wage* (1992).

"Crossing the Dark River" originally appeared in *Tales of Riverworld* in 1992.

"Up the Bright River" and "Coda" originally appeared in *Quest to Riverworld* in 1993.

Table of Contents

Up The Bright River: The Worlds Of Philip José Farmer

Introduction by Gary K. Wolfe

When Philip José Farmer died in early 2009, the headline of the *New York Times* obituary identified him simply as a "Daring Science Fiction Writer," a description that is likely to have pleased him as much as any of the other encomiums that followed over the next several months. From the very beginning of his career (the appearance of his story "The Lovers" in 1953 remains one of the most spectacular debuts in the history of American science fiction), risk-taking had been his trademark, and he traced his own literary family tree not only to the classic science fiction and pulp writers of his youth, but to famously transgressive writers from Mark Twain, James Joyce, and Henry Miller to Thomas Pynchon, Charles Bukowski, and Charles Willeford. When he moved back from Beverly Hills to Peoria in 1970, not long after having published such controversial novels as *The Image of the Beast, A Feast Unknown,* and *Blown,* he was a little concerned about how the conservative local community would accept him, and this is reflected in one of his many fictional self-portraits, the SF writer Leo Queequeg Tincrowdor, who complains (in "The Two-Edged Gift," included here) that he can't get his books reviewed in the local paper. "I'm just as glad that the paper won't review his books," comments Tincrowdor's wife. "I'm on good terms with our neighbors, but if they found out what he wrote, we'd be ostracized. Fortunately, they don't read science-fiction." Some years later, visiting the Farmers in Peoria, I heard Phil's wife Bette express these same sentiments in almost the same words, while Phil looked on with his characteristically sly grin. He actually seemed to enjoy this odd combination of notoriety and anonymity, sometimes writing outrageous letters to the *Peoria Journal-Star* which either never got published or were severely censored before publication.

Eventually, of course, Peoria did come to celebrate its local celebrity. Perhaps the *Riverworld* and *Dayworld* series in the 1970s and 1980s simply became too big to ignore, or perhaps Peoria itself began to gain a more sophisticated appreciation of even his more controversial titles. When Phil received the Grand Master Award from the Science Fiction Writers of America in 2001, the local library held a "Living Legend" reception including a proclamation from the mayor, and by 2003, when the library hosted a celebration for the 50th anniversary of "The Lovers," it virtually turned into an international conference, with fans arriving from all over the U.S. and Europe. By now there was also a Philip José Farmer website, created by Mike Croteau, who would also begin the print fanzine *Farmerphile* and help to organize a series of annual "Farmercon" mini-conventions in Peoria. In 2006 and 2007, Subterranean Press began its series of Farmer collections, not only bringing back into print classic stories and novels, but introducing a substantial amount of material which had not seen print at all before.

One thing that becomes apparent when you gather together a large number of Farmer readers, as happened at those Peoria conferences and celebrations, is that not all of them are fans of the same Philip José Farmer. There is, to be sure, a core of collectors and devotees who seem equally enamored of all his writing, and there is a substantially larger body of readers who know only the *Riverworld* books, often citing it as one of their seminal experiences in discovering the "mind-blowing" possibilities of science fiction. There are those who will argue that the *World of Tiers* series is conceptually more daring even than Riverworld, and those who mostly enjoy exploring and extending the metafictional playground of his pulp-hero biographies and his "Wold Newton" universe. There are those who prefer Farmer the religious satirist and gadfly, or the adventure writer in the pulp tradition, or the eroticist, or the literary experimentalist, or simply the eclectic SF writer who emerged as one of the genre masters of the 1950s and 1960s. Farmer occupied all these worlds and more, some with greater success than others, and the purpose of the current collection is to celebrate these many worlds. It's always tempting, when a prolific author passes away, to seek the proper pigeonholes, but during his life Farmer famously resisted them; for all his acclaim in science fiction, he decided toward the end of his active career that what he really wanted to write were mysteries. While the selections in *Up the Bright River* feature some of Farmer's most famous creations, few are among his most famous stories (most of which were reprinted in early Subterranean Press collections, and none of which are duplicated here). I hope it will reveal a number of hidden gems that even veteran Farmer readers may have overlooked, but mainly it's a showcase of imaginative worlds, literary preoccupations, and Farmer's capacity for pure entertainment.

Farmer's most famous creation is represented here by the last three Riverworld stories he wrote, "Crossing the Dark River," "Up the Bright River," and "Coda," which appeared in short-lived "shared world" anthologies in 1992 and 1993 and have not since been reprinted. While these may add little new to the mythology of Riverworld itself, they are of particular interest in that they reflect Farmer's growing fascination, in the last decade or two of his life, with his own family history: nearly all of the characters in these stories are his own ancestors. Farmer's broader fascination with religion and religious figures is represented by the earliest story included here, "Attitudes" (1953), the first and I think among the best of the several Father Carmody stories that eventually made up *Father to the Stars,* as well as by "The Blasphemers," a space opera on religious themes; "A Bowl Bigger Than Earth," an unusual version of the afterlife; "Toward the Beloved City," a provocative treatment of the Book of Revelations; and "Saint Francis Kisses His Ass Goodbye," which transports the title figure several centuries into his future (and which quite literally lives up to its title). Farmer's darkly satirical view of doctors and scientists is evident in "The Sumerian Oath," "The Voice of the Sonar in My Vermiform Appendix" (two of his "polytropical paramyths"), and "How Deep the Grooves." The latter is also an example of the SF magazine fiction that Farmer produced regularly in the 1960s and 1970s, as are "Skinburn," "Down in the Black Gang," and "The Two-Edged Gift," although the latter two are also notable for their sharply satirical portraits of Beverly Hills and Peoria. "The Two-Edged Gift," the first of the Paul Eyre stories which eventually constituted *Stations of the Nightmare,* also introduces us to Leo Queequeg Tincrowdor, one of Farmer's fictional alter egos. "Father's in the Basement" is a rare example of Farmer's short horror fiction, though with a characteristically waggish edge (this time satirizing writers themselves). Finally, Farmer's fictional biographies are represented by "Extracts from the Memories of Lord Greystoke," which appeared in Farmer's "feral man" anthology *Mother Was a Lovely Beast* in 1974 as "edited by Philip Jose Farmer." It is, of course, another example of the sort of elaborate paraliterary gamesmanship that Farmer delighted in, and that reveals him as a far more intellectually complex writer than the sometimes slick surfaces of his fiction would at first suggest. Farmer always meant to tell a good tale, but he nearly always meant to provoke as well, and readers who pause to consider the ideas implicit in the stories here, and the assumptions Farmer repeatedly questions, will quickly understand what that phrase "daring science fiction writer" really means.

Attitudes

Roger Tandem crouched behind his pinochle hand as if he were hiding behind a battery of shields. His eyes ran like weasels over the faces of the other players, seated around a table in the lounge of the interstellar liner, *Lady Luck*.

"Father John," he said, "I've got you all figured out. You'll be nice to me, you'll crack jokes, and you'll play pinochle with me, though not for money, of course. You'll even have a beer with me. And, after I begin thinking you're a pretty good guy, you'll lead me gradually to this and that topic. You'll approach them at an angle, slide away when I get annoyed or alarmed, but always circle back. And then, all of a sudden, when I'm not watching, you jerk the lid off hell's flames and invite me to take a look. And you think I'll be so scared I'll jump right back under the wing of Mother Church."

Father John raised his light blue eyes long enough from his cards to say, mildly, "You're right about the last half of your last sentence. As to the rest, who knows?"

"You're smart, Father, with this religious angle. But you'll get no place with me. Know why? It's because you haven't the right attitude."

The eyebrows of the other five players rose as high as they could get. The captain of the *Lady Luck,* Rowds, coughed until he was red in the face and then, sputtering and blowing into a handkerchief, said, "Hang it all, Tandem, what—ah—do you mean by saying that—ah—*he* hasn't got the right attitude?"

Tandem smiled as one who is very sure of himself and replied, "I know you're thinking I've a lot of guts to say that. Here's Roger Tandem, a professional gambler and a collector—and seller—of interstellar *objets d'art,* reproaching a padre. But I've got more to add to that. I not only do not think Father John has the right attitude, I don't think any of you gentlemen have."

Nobody replied. Tandem's lips curved to approximate a sneer, but his fellow-players could not see them because he held his cards in front of his mouth.

"You're all more or less pious," he said. "And why? Because you're afraid to take a chance, that's why. You say to yourself that you're not sure there's life beyond this one, but there just might be. So you decide it's playing safe if you hitch a ride aboard one or another religion. None of you gentlemen belong to the same one, but you all have this in common. You think you have nothing to lose if you profess to believe in this or that god. On the other hand, if you deny one, you might lose out altogether. So, why not profess? It's safer."

He laid his cards down and lit up a cigarette and quickly blew smoke out so it formed a veil before his face.

"I'm not afraid to take a chance. I'm betting big stakes. My so-called eternal soul against the belief that there is nothing beyond this life. Why should I always not do what I want to and thus make myself miserable and hypocritical, when I can enjoy myself thoroughly?"

"That," said Father John Carmody, "is where you may be making a mistake. My opinion is that *you* have the wrong attitude. All of us are betting in a game where there is only one way in which we *can* win. That is by faith. But your method of placing your stakes is not, from my viewpoint, the sensible one. Even if you should be proved correct, you would not know it. How would you collect your wager?"

"I collect it while I live, Father," said Tandem. "That's enough for me. When I'm dead, I don't worry about anyone welshing on me. And I might point out, Father, that you had better have more luck with your faith than you do with your cards. You're not a very good player, you know."

The priest smiled. His round pudgy face was not at all handsome, but, when he was amused, he looked pleasant and likeable. You got the impression he had a tuning fork inside him, and it was shaking him with a mirth he invited you to share.

Tandem liked it except when the laughter seemed to be at his expense. Then his mouth curved into the expression it so often took when his cards hid it.

At that moment a loud voice came over the intercom, and a yellow light began flashing above the entrance to the lounge room. Captain Rowds rose and said, "Ah, pardon me, gentlemen. The—ah—pilot-room wants me. We're about to come out of Translation. Don't forget that we'll be—ah—in free fall as soon as the red light comes on."

The hand was not finished. The cards were put away in a box whose magnetized side would cling to an iron panel set in the table. The players leaned back to wait until the *Lady Luck* came out of Translation and went into free fall for a period of ten minutes while the automatic computer took its bearings.

If they had emerged from no-space at the desired point, they would then continue to their destination by normal space-drive.

Tandem looked around the lounge and sighed. Pickings had been slim during this trip. Most of his time had been spent playing for fun with Father John, Captain Rowds, the Universal Light missionary, and the two sociology professors. It was too bad his companions had no money and thought of themselves as gentlemen. Had they played for keeps, they would have been offended if anyone had insisted on suspending a PK or ESP indicator above the cardtable. And Tandem would, then, have had no second thoughts about using either of those talents. He reasoned that they had been given to him for a purpose. The question of from whom they had come did not shadow his mind.

He'd made some money during the hop from B Velorum to Y Scorpii when he had struck up an acquaintance with a rich young dice-enthusiast, the type who was insulted if you set an alarm on the floor. He was a real gambler. That is, he understood that one PKer could detect when another was using energies supposedly forbidden during a game. But he also understood that, nowadays, one of the most exciting risks was that of running up against somebody who might be as good as you. Or better.

Whatever happened, when two of the "talented" were in a game with a group of non-PKers, neither would divulge that the other was a cheater. Then it became a duel between the two who thought of themselves as the "aristocrats" of gambling. The plebs were left outside in the cold, and possessed neither wisdom nor money at the game's end.

Tandem had had the edge with the rich young man. But, just when he had jockeyed him to the verge of making some big bets, the *Lady Luck* [a misnamed vessel if ever there was one!] had Translated outside their destination, the game had ended, and the sucker had left shortly after.

Now, he was not only getting close to broke, he was, far worse, bored. Even the long argument with Father John—if you could call anything so mild such—no longer titillated him. And now, perhaps, it was that failure to be excited and the vague feeling that the padre had gotten the better of him that made him do what he did. For, as the red light began flashing and the intercom warned the passengers to watch themselves, Tandem unbuckled the belt that held him to the chair. He pushed himself upwards with a slight tap of his foot. As he floated towards the ceiling, he put his hands to his lips in an attitude of prayer and adopted an expression that was a marvelous blend of silliness and saintliness.

"Hey, Father John!" he called. "Look! Joseph of Cupertino! "

There were embarrassed looks and a few nervous laughs from the loungers. Even the apostle of the Universal Light, though the padre's competitor, frowned at what he thought was very bad taste and, in a way, a slight upon his own beliefs.

"Wrong attitude," he muttered, "definitely the wrong attitude."

Father John blinked once before he saw that Tandem was parodying the difficulties that a famous medieval saint had had with involuntary levitations. Far from being offended, however, he calmly took a notebook from his pocket and began writing in it. No matter what the event, he tried to profit from it. Even the devil must be thanked for giving examples. Tandem's antics had inspired him with an idea for an article. If he finished it in time and got it off on a mail-ship, he might have it published in the next issue of his order's periodical.

It would be titled *The Free Fall of Man: Down or Up?*

TANDEM HAD BEEN briefly tempted to get off at the next stop, Wildenwooly. It was a virgin planet that offered much work to its settlers and very few avenues of amusement. Gambling was one. But the trouble with Wildenwooly was that it also did not have many men who had any really big money, and that all were pathologically quick to take offense. Tandem's luck might make them suspicious and, if an indicator were available, it might be used. Nor would it help him much to damp out his powers. The result would be just as extraordinary a streak of bad luck.

Everybody had some PK. The indicators were set too high to register the average energy. Tandem and men like him could not consistently key their output to the normal man's unless they kept a rigid control. And almost always they would get excited during a game, or succumb to temptation, and use an abnormal amount. The result would be their exposure. So, to avoid that, they had to suppress their talent completely. This ended in just as much suspicion. And, while the Woolies could not *prove* that he had been cheating, they might follow their habit of taking the law into their own hands.

As Tandem didn't relish beatings or being ridden out of town on a rail—an unlovely revival of an old American custom—he decided he would stick to the *Lady Luck* until she arrived at Po Chu-I. That was a planet full of Celestials whose pockets bulged with Federation credits and whose eyes were bright with the gleam of their ancient passion for Dame Fortune.

Before the liner got to Po Chu-I, it stopped off at Weizmann and picked up another rich young man. Tandem rubbed his hands and took the sucker for all he could. This was the beauty of the technological age. No matter what the scientific advances, you could find the same old type of human being begging to be fleeced. The rich young man and he located several others who would play with them until the stakes got too high. Tandem's former partners, the captain, the professors, and the two reverends were ignored while he piled up the chips. Unfortunately, just after they took off from Po Chu-I, the rich young man became sullen, argued with him about something unconnected with the gambling, and gave him a black eye.

Tandem did not strike back. He told the rich young man that he would file suit against him in an Earth court for having violated his free will. He had not given anybody permission to strike him. Moreover, he would submit willingly to an injection of Telol. Questioning under the influence of that drug would reveal that he had not been cheating.

For some reason he did not understand, nobody except Father John would speak to Tandem the rest of the trip. And Tandem did not care to talk to the padre. He swore he'd get off at the next stop regardless of what type of world it was.

The *Lady Luck* balked him by setting down upon a planet that was terra incognita as far as Earthmen were concerned. No human settlements had been made there at all. The only reason the liner landed was the need of water to refill its fuel tanks.

Captain Rowds announced to the crew and passengers that they might step out upon the soil of Kubeia and stretch their legs. But they were not to venture beyond the other side of the lake.

"Ah—ladies and gentlemen—ah—it so happens that the Federation Sociological Agent has—ah—made an agreement with the aborigines whereby we may use this area. But we are not to enter into any traffic with the—ah—Kubeians themselves. These people have many peculiar institutions which we—ah—Terrans might offend through—if you will pardon that expression—ignorance. And some of their customs are—ah—if I may so express it, rather—ah—beastly. A word to the wise is—ah—sufficient."

Tandem found out that the ship would take at least four hours for refilling. Therefore, he reasoned, if he cared to do a little exploring, he would have more than enough time. He was determined to get at least a slight view of Kubeia. Their situation inside a little forest-covered valley forbade that. If he were to climb a hill and then a tree, he could see the city of the natives, whose white buildings he had glimpsed from the porthole as the ship sank towards this alien soil. He had no particular interest, really, except that the captain had forbidden it. That, to Tandem, was equal to a command. Even as a child, he had always taken a delicious delight in disobeying his father. And, as an adult, he would not bow to authority.

Head bent slightly downwards, his hand stroking his chin and mouth, he sauntered around the other side of the gigantic liner. There was no one there to order him back. He stepped up his pace. And, at the same time, he heard a voice.

"Wait for me! I'll go with you a way!"

He turned. It was Father John.

Tandem tensed. The priest was smiling, his light blue eyes beaming. And that was the trouble. Tandem did not trust this man because he was altogether too inconsistent. You couldn't predict his behavior. One minute he was smooth as a banana peel; the next, rough as a three-day beard.

The gambler dropped his hand to reveal his half-smile, half-sneer.

"If I ask you to go with me a mile, Father, you must, according to your belief, go with me at least two miles."

"Gladly, son, except that the captain has forbidden it. And, I presume, with good cause."

"Look, Father, what possible harm could come from just sneaking a glance outside? The natives think this area is tabu. They won't bother us. So, why not take a little walk?"

"There is no good reason to disregard the captain. He has complete temporal jurisdiction over the ship, which is his little world. He knows his business; I respect his orders."

"O.K., Father, wrap yourself up in your little robe of submission. You may be safe in it, but you'll never see or enjoy anything outside it. As for me, I'm going to take a chance. Not that it'll be much of one."

"I hope you're right."

"Look, Father, get that woeful expression off your face. I'm just going up the hill a little ways and climb a tree. Then I'm coming right back down. Anything wrong with that?"

"You know whether or not there is."

"Sure, I do," said Tandem, speaking through his fingers, now held over his mouth. "It all depends on your attitude, Father. Walk boldly, be unafraid, don't hide from anything or anybody, and you'll get out of life just what you put in it."

"I'll agree with you that you get out of life just what you put in it. But as to the former part of your statement, I disagree. You're not walking boldly. You're afraid. You're hiding."

Tandem had turned to stride away, but he halted and spun back.

"What do you mean?"

"I mean that you feel you must hide from someone or something all the time. Otherwise, why do you always cover your lips with your hand, or, if not with that, with a shield of playing cards? And when you are forced to expose your face, then you twist into a rictus of contempt for the world. Why?"

"Now it's psychiatry!" snarled Tandem. "You stay here, Father, stuck in your little valley. I'm going to see what the rest of Kubeia has to offer."

"Don't forget. We leave in four hours."

"I have a watch," said Tandem, and he laughed and added, "I'll let it be my conscience."

"Watches run down."

"So do consciences, Father."

Still laughing, Tandem walked off. Halfway up the hill, he paused to peer back between the trees. Father John was standing there, watching, a lone and little black figure. But he must have turned a trifle at just the right angle, for the sun flashed on the crescent of white collar and struck Tandem in the eyes. He blinked and cursed and lit a cigarette and felt much better as the blue curtain drifted up past his face. There was nothing like a good smoke to relax a man.

IT MIGHT HAVE been said of Tandem that he had been looking all his life for black sheep to fleece. Nor did he have any trouble finding them now.

From his spy-post near the top of a great tree, he could look down into the next valley. And there he could see the black sheep. Even on Kubeia.

There was no mistaking the purpose of the crowd gathered into two concentric rings at the bottom of the hill. There was the smaller circle of men inside, all on their knees and regarding intently some object in their center. And behind them stood a greater number of people, also watching intently the thing that resembled, as near as he could tell, a weathercock. Obviously, it wasn't that. He could tell from the attitudes of those around it what its purpose was. And his heart leaped. There was no mistake. He was able to smell a crap game a mile away. This might be a slightly different form than the Terran type, but its essence was the same.

Hastily, he climbed down the tree and began threading through the trunks that covered this hill. A glance at his wrist watch showed him he had three and a half hours left. Moreover, it was inconceivable that Captain Rowds would set off without his passenger. Tandem had to watch this Kubeian game of chance. He wouldn't enter it, of course, because he didn't know the rules and had no local currency with which to buy his way in. He'd just observe a while and then leave.

His heart beat fast; his palms grew moist. This was what he lived for, this tension and uncertainty and excitement. Take a chance. Win or lose. Come on, cubes, roll Daddy a natural!

He grinned to himself. What was he thinking of? He couldn't possibly get into the fun. And there was the possibility that the Kubeians would be so upset by the appearance of an Earthman that the game would break up. He doubted that, though. Gamblers were notoriously blasé. Nothing but cataclysm or the police could tear them away as long as there was money yet to win.

Before he revealed himself, he examined the players. Humanoid, they had brown skins, round heads covered with short coarse auburn hairs, triangular faces innocent of whiskers except for six semi-cartilaginous bristles on their long upper lips, black noses like boxing gloves, black leathery lips, sharp meat-eater's teeth, and well developed chins. A ruff of auburn hairs grew like a boa around their necks.

All were dressed in long black coats and white knee-length breeches. Only one wore a hat. This native seemed to be a ringmaster of some sort, or, as Tandem came to think of him, the Croupier. He was taller and thinner than the others and wore a miter with a big green eyeshade. He stood on one spot, arbitrated disputes about bets, and gave the signal for each play to start. It was the Croupier, Tandem realized, who would govern the temper of the crowd towards the newcomer.

He breathed deeply, adopted the familiar rictus, and stepped out from behind the bush.

He had been right about the attitudes of the Kubeians toward strangers. Those on the outer fringe looked up, widened their somewhat slanting eyes, and pricked up their foxlike ears. But, after glances that assured them he was harmless, they returned to the game. Either they were following a cultural pattern of feigning indifference, or they actually were as adaptable as they seemed to be. Whatever their reasons, he decided to profit by them.

He gently tried to work his way through the throng of spectators and found them quite willing to step aside. Before long he was in the front row. He looked squarely at the Croupier, who gave him an enigmatic but searching glance, and then raised both hands. above his head. Two of his four fingers on each hand were crossed. The crowd gave a single barking cry and imitated his gesture. Then the Croupier dropped his hands; the game went on as if the Terran had always been there. Tandem, after a moment's shrewd study, was convinced that he had found his element and that this was nothing other than a glorified version of Spin-the-Milk-Bottle.

The center of attention was a six-foot-long statue of a Kubeian. Its two arms were extended at right angles on either side, and its legs were held straight out on a line with its body. It was face downward and whirled freely upon its navel, which was stuck on a rod whose other end was cemented firmly into a large block of marble.

The figure's head was painted white. Its legs were black. One arm was red; the other, green. The body was a steel gray.

Tandem's heart accelerated. The statue, he was sure, was platinum.

He watched. A player took hold of one of the arms and crooned a liturgy to it in his exotic tongue, a chant whose tones matched exactly those used by a pleading Terran before he casts his dice. Then, after a signal from the Croupier, he gave the arm a vigorous shove. The figure spun around and around, the sun glancing off it in red and green and black and white and silver flashes. When it began to slow down, the players crouched in breathless anticipation or else held out their arms to it and pleaded invocations that were Galaxy-wide, no matter what the language.

Meanwhile, both the players and the spectators were making side bets. Each had one or more smaller duplicates of the central statue. As it whirled around, they gesticulated at each other, chattered, then tossed their figures up in the air so they revolved around and around. Tandem was sure these statuettes were of platinum, also.

The spinning figure stopped. Its green arm pointed at one of the players. A cry went up from the crowd. Many stepped forward and piled their figurines before the man. He gave the Whirligig—as Tandem now called it—another shove. Again, it spun around and around.

The Earthman had now analyzed the game. You took one of your little whirligigs and tossed it in the air. If one of its limbs or its head sunk into the soft earth, and it happened to be the same color as the big Whirligig's extension when it pointed to you, you collected the statuettes that had landed upon extensions of a different color.

If the Whirligig singled you out, but your statuette had sunk an indicator of another color into the earth, you neither lost nor won but got another try. Otherwise, the person next in line tried his luck.

Tandem rubbed his mental hands. He showed his watch to a neighbor and indicated he'd like to trade it for a whirligig. The naive native, after getting the high sign from the Croupier, readily accepted and seemed quite pleased that he was several thousand credits the loser.

Tandem made several side bets and won. Armed with the whirligigs, he boldly pushed into the inner ring. Once there he coolly exerted his PK to slow the big Whirligig down and stop it at just the right person and on just the right color. He was clever enough not to have it indicate him over a few times; most of his rapidly building fortune was made on side bets. Sometimes, he lost on purpose; sometimes, by chance. He was sure that many of the Kubeians had an unconscious PK that was bound to work for them if enough happened to concentrate on the same color. He could detect little slops of emanations here and there but could not localize them. They were lost in the general shuffle.

It did not matter. The natives would not have his trained talents.

He forgot about that and watched the temper of the crowd. He'd been alone among aliens and had seen them turn ugly when he began to win too steadily. He was ready to start losing so they would cool off, or, if that didn't work, to run. How he expected to make any speed with the weight of his winnings dragging him down, he didn't stop to think. But he was sure that, somehow, he'd come out ahead.

Nothing that he waited for came to pass. The natives lost none of their vaguely vulpine grins, and their rusty-red eyes seemed sincerely friendly. When he won, he was slapped on the back. Some even helped him pile up his whirligigs. He kept an eye on them to make sure they didn't conceal any under their long fuzzy black coats, so much like a Terran preacher's. But, nobody tried to steal.

The afternoon whirled by dizzily in flashing greens and reds and whites and silvers and dull blacks. Not too obviously, the whirligigs at his feet began to build to a small mountain.

Outwardly cool, he was inwardly intoxicated. He was not so far gone that he did not glance occasionally at the watch strapped around the hairy wrist of the Kubeian he had traded it to. Always, he saw that he had plenty of time left to make another killing.

Busy as he was, he noticed also that the crowd of spectators was increasing. This game was like any game of chance anywhere. Let somebody get hot and, through some psychological grapevine that could not be explained, everybody in the neighborhood heard of it. Natives by the dozens were loping through narrow passes into the little valley, pushing the watchers closer to the players, chattering loudly, whistling, applauding with strange barking cries, and building up a mighty stench under the hot sun with the accumulation of sweaty, hairy bodies. Slanting rusty-red eyes gleamed; sharp pointed ears waggled; the auburn hairs of the neckruffs stood up; long red tongues with green bulb-tips licked the thin black-leather lips; everywhere, hands lifted to the skies in a peculiar gesture, each with two of its four fingers crossed.

Tandem did not mind. He had heard—and smelled—crowds like this before. When he was winning, he reveled in it.

Let the Whirligig spin! Let the statuettes soar! And let the wealth pile up at his feet! This was living. This was what even drink and women could not do for him!

There came a time when only four natives were left with any whirligigs before them. It was Tandems turn to spin. He threw his figurine high up, saw it land with its black legs stuck into the soft earth, and stepped forward to give the big figure a whirl. He shot a side-glance at the Croupier and saw tears brightening the rusty eyes.

Tandem was surprised, but he did not try to guess what caused this strange emotion. All he wanted to do was to play, and he had the go-ahead from the native.

But as he laid his hands upon the hard green arm, he heard a cry that shot above the roar of the mob, stilled it, and seized him so he could make no move.

It was Father John's voice, and he was shouting, 'Stop, Tandem! For the love of God, *stop!*"

"WHAT THE HELL are you doing here?" snarled Tandem. "Are you trying to queer the deal?"

"I've come the second mile, son," said Father John. "And a good thing for you, too. One more second, and you would have been lost."

Streams of sweat run down his heavy jowls into his collar, now turning gray with dirt and perspiration. A branch must have raked a three-fingered red furrow across his cheek.

His blue eyes vibrated to the tuning fork deep-buried within his rotund body, but the note was not that of mirth.

"Step back, Carmody," said Tandem. "This is the last spin. Then I'm coming back. Rich!"

"No, you won't. Listen, Tandem, we haven't much time...!"

"Get out of the way! These people might want to take advantage of this and stop the game!"

Father John threw a despairing look towards the sky. At the same time the Croupier left the spot on which he had stood during the game, and advanced with his hand held out towards the padre. Hope replaced despair on Father John's face. Eagerly, he began making a series of gestures directed at the Croupier.

Tandem, though exasperated, could do little else than watch and hope that the meddling officious priest would be sent packing. It irritated him almost to weeping to have complete victory so close and now see it destroyed by this long-nosed puritan.

Father John paid no attention to Tandem. Having snared the Croupier's wet and rusty-red eyes, he then pointed to himself and to Tandem and indicated a circle around them. The Croupier did not change expression. Undaunted at this, Father John then pointed his finger at the natives and described a circle around them. He repeated the maneuvers twice. Abruptly, the slanting eyes widened; the rusty-red gleamed. He rotated his head swiftly, an action which seemed to be his equivalent of nodding yes. Apparently he understood that the padre was indicating that the two humans were in a different class from the Kubeians.

Father John then stabbed his index finger at the Whirligig and followed that by pointing at the Croupier. Again the circle was drawn, this time clearly circumscribing the native and the facedownward statue. Then another circle around the two Earthmen. After which, Father John held up the crucifix hung from his neck so that all could clearly see it.

A single-throated cry rose from the mob. Somehow it held tones of disappointment, not surprise. They pressed forward, but at a bark from the Croupier, they fell back. He himself came forward and eagerly inspected the symbol. When he was done, he looked at Father John for further signs. Tears streamed from his eyes.

"What're you doing, Carmody?" said Tandem harshly. "Is it going to hurt you if I win something valuable?"

"Quiet, man, I've almost got it through their heads. We may be able to call off the game yet. I don't know, though, you're so deep in it now."

"When I get back to Earth or the nearest big port, I'll sue you for interfering with my free will!"

He knew that was an idle threat, for the law would not apply to this case. But it made him feel better to express it.

Father John had not heard him, anyway. He was now struck into the attitude of a crucifixion, arms straight out, legs together, and an agonized expression on his face. As soon as he saw the Croupier rotate his head in comprehension, the padre pointed again at Tandem. The Croupier looked startled; his black boxing-glove nose twitched with some unknown emotion. He shrugged his shoulders in a gesture that could only be interpreted in a Gallic fashion, and he lifted his hands up, palms turned upwards.

Father John smiled; his whole body seemed to hum with the invisible tuning fork inside him. This time, it was a note of relaxation.

"You were lucky, my boy," he said to Tandem, "that, shortly after you left, I remembered an article I had read in the *Interstellar Journal o f Comparative Religions.* This one was written by an anthropologist who had spent some time here on Kubeia, and..."

The Croupier interrupted with some vigorous signs. Evidently Father John had mistaken his meaning.

The priest's lips and jowls sagged, and he groaned. "This fellow has heard of free will, too, Tandem. He insists that you make up your own mind as to whether you care to..."

Tandem did not wait to hear the rest but gave a glad shout.

"Gentlemen, on with the game!"

He scarcely heard the padre's cry of protest as he seized the Whirligig's green arm and gave it a shove that sent it around and around upon its navel. Nor could he have heard any more from Father John, so rapt was he in waiting for the moment when it would slow down to the point where he could begin to exert the tiny shoves or pushes that would bring the black legs pointing straight at him.

Around and around it went, and while it spun, the statuettes of the side-betters flashed in the sun. Fortunes were made or lost among the natives. Tandem stood motionless in a half-crouch, smug in the knowledge that he was not going to lose. The four who faced him did not, individually or collectively, have what he had on the ball. See! Here the Whirligig came, slow, slow, coming around for one more turn. The green arm swept by, then the legs passed him. A little push, a little push would bring them back in their circle, then a small pull, a small pull to keep their speed, and finally, a fraction of a shove to halt them entirely.

This is the way they go. Here they come, long and black with the stylized feet stuck out in the same plane as the legs. Here they come, whoa, whoa, gently, gently...aah!

Hah!

The crowd, which had been holding its breath, released it in a mighty burst, a howl of surprise and disappointment.

And Tandem was still frozen in his crouch, his mind not believing what his eyes saw, and the hairs on the back of his neck prickling as he detected the sudden and irresistible power that had leapt out and swung the legs enough to miss him and make the green arm point at one of his opponents.

It was Father John who shook him and said, "Man, come on. You're wiped out."

Numbly, Tandem watched the weeping Croupier signal to natives who swarmed over his pile of figurines and crated them across the circle to the winner. Now, though he had not realized it, the rules had changed. It was winner take all.

Before they could go, the Croupier stepped up to the padre and handed him one of the statuettes. Father John hesitated, then lifted the chain from around his neck and handed the crucifix to him.

"What's that for?"

"Professional courtesy," said the padre as he steered Tandem by the elbow through the mob of wildly howling and leaping Kubeians. "He's a good man. Not the least jealous."

Tandem did not try to decipher that. His rage, sizzling beneath the crust of numbness, broke loose.

"Damn it, those natives were hiding the power of their PK! But, even so, they'd not have been able to catch me off balance if you hadn't stopped the game when you did and allowed them to gang up on me! It was only pure chance that they happened to be working together! If you hadn't been such a puritanical dog-in-the-manger, I'd have won for sure! I'd be rich! Rich!"

"I take full responsibility. Meanwhile, allow me to ex—Oops, watch it!"

Tandem stumbled and would have fallen flat on his face if Father John had not caught him. Tandem recovered and was angrier than before. He wanted to owe the padre absolutely nothing.

Silent, they made their slow way through the heavy vegetation until they came to a break. Here, at Father John's gentle insistence of hand upon his elbow, Tandem turned. He was looking through an avenue in the trees at a fill view of the valley.

"You see, Roger Tandem, I had read this article in the *Journal*. It was titled 'Attitudes,' and a good thing for you, for our previous talk about wrong attitudes brought it back to my mind. I decided then and there, to—if you will pardon the seeming egotism of the statement—to go the second mile. Or a third, if need be.

"You see, Roger, when you saw these people, you interpreted the scene in terms of the signs and symbols you are used to. You saw these natives around a device that seemed clearly to be for gambling. You saw further evidences: people on their knees, feverish betting, intent concentration upon the device, and you heard chanting, supplication to Lady Luck, grunts, exclamations, screams of triumph, moans of defeat. You saw a master in charge of ceremonies, the head gambler, the house master.

"What you did not perceive were certain similarities between the postures and sounds adopted during a gambling contest and those that mark the gatherings of certain types of frenetic religious sects in whatever area of the universe you happen to be. They are much the same. Watch the players in a hot crap game and then observe the antics of the less inhibited devout at certain primitive revival meetings. Is there so much difference?"

"What do you mean?"

Father John pointed through the break.

"You almost became a convert."

The winner was standing proudly by the great pile of statuettes at his feet. He seemed to be exulting inwardly in his victory, for he stood straight and silent, his hands by his sides. But not for long. A number of the burly players seized him from behind. His arms were straightened out and tied to a beam of wood. Another beam, at right angles to the first, was applied to his back. His legs, waist, and head were strapped to it. Crucifix-wise, he was picked up and carried forward.

At the same time, the Whirligig was taken off the post.

Even then, Tandem did not see what his fate might have been until the native was poised face down over the post and its sharp point inserted into the navel. Then a worshiper seized the extended arm and pushed.

If the living Whirligig gave any cry of pain, he could not have been heard above the howl of the assembled faithful. Until the tip of the post thrust into the wood beam on his back, he spun, and the mob chanted.

Father John prayed half-aloud.

"If I have interfered, I have done so through love for this man and because I must choose according to the dictates of my heart. I knew that one of them must die, Father, and I did not think that the man was ready. Perhaps the man of this world was not ready, either, but I had no way of knowing that. He was playing with full knowledge of what he must do if he won, and this man Tandem was not. And Tandem is a man like unto myself, Father, and I must presume that, unless I have knowledge of signs to the contrary, I must do my best to save him so that, some day, he may do his best to save himself.

"But if I have erred, I have done so through ignorance and through love."

When Father John was finished, he led Tandem, who was pale and trembling, up the hill.

"The house always wins," said Father John, who was himself a little pale. "That man that you thought was the Croupier was the head priest. The tears you first saw in his eyes were those of joy at making a convert and those you saw later were those of disappointment at losing one. He wanted you to win in this millennia-old ritual-game. If you had, you could have been the first Earthman to be the living representative of their deity, who was sacrificed in that peculiarly painful fashion. And your winnings would have been buried with you, an offering to the god whose living image you became.

"But, as I said, the house never loses. Later, the head priest would have dug them up and added them to his church's treasury."

"Do you mean that all those signals you were making at the Crou—the priest—were to convince him that I…?"

"Belonged to the God of the Upright Cross, yes. Not the God of the Horizontal Cross. And I almost had him convinced until he must have thought of free will, too, and gave you the chance of joining his sect. I, as you have commented, am not so backward about interfering."

Tandem stopped to light a cigarette. His hand shook, but after a few puffs, with the smoke drifting by in blue veils, he felt better.

Squaring his shoulders and lifting his chin, he said, "Look, Father John, if you think that this is going to scare me so I'll jump in under the shadow of Mother Church's wings, you're wrong. So I made a mistake? It was only a half-error, you'll have to admit, for they *were* gambling. And anybody could have been fooled. I didn't need your help, anyway."

"Really?"

"Well, I suppose it was a good thing that you came along….No, it wasn't. I lost; I couldn't have won with those four ganging up on me. So what did I have to lose? I had a good time, and I'm out nothing."

"You lost your watch."

Father John did not seem to have recovered yet from the shadow that had fallen over him since he had led Tandem away from the valley. The tuning fork inside him hummed deep and black.

"Look, Father," said Tandem, "let's drop all those morals and symbols, huh? No comparisons between my watch and my conscience, huh? You can stretch these things all out of proportion, you know."

He walked fast around the great curve of the ship so he could leave the priest behind. But as he did so, he stopped. A thought that had been roosting in the shadows suddenly hopped into light. He turned and walked back.

"Say, Father, what about those four who were left? I'd have sworn they didn't have enough…"

He stopped. Father John was about 25 yards away, his back turned to him. His shoulders were thrown back a little more than they had been, and there was something in the set of his whole body that showed that the humming fork was beginning to vibrate to a lighter note.

Tandem perceived that only half-consciously. It was what Father John was doing that seized him and demanded all of his attention.

The priest was whirling the statuette up into the air and watching it land upon its black legs. Four times, he repeated. Always, the legs dug into the dirt.

Even from that distance, Tandem could feel the power.

How Deep the Grooves

Always in control of himself, Doctor James Carroad lowered his voice.

He said, "You will submit to this test. We must impress the Secretary. The fact that we're willing to use our own unborn baby in the experiment will make that impression a deeper one."

Doctor Jane Carroad, his wife, looked up from the chair in which she sat. Her gaze swept over the tall lean figure in the white scientist's uniform and the two rows of resplendent ribbons and medals on his left chest. She glared into the eyes of her husband.

Scornfully, she said, "You did not want this baby. I did, though now I wonder why. Perhaps, because I wanted to be a mother, no matter what the price. Not to give the State another citizen. But, now we're going to have it, you want to exploit it even before it's born, just as..."

Harshly, he said, "Don't you know what such talk can lead to?"

"Don't worry! I won't tell anyone you didn't desire to add to the State. Nor will I tell anybody how I induced you to have it!"

His face became red, and he said, "You will never again mention that to me! Never again! Understand?"

Jane's neck muscles trembled, but her face was composed. She said, "I'll speak of that, to you, whenever I feel like it. Though, God knows, I'm thoroughly ashamed of it. But I do get a certain sour satisfaction out of knowing that, once in my life, I managed to break down that rigid self-control. I made you act like a normal man, one able to forget himself in his passion for a woman. Doctor Carroad, the great scientist of the State, really forgot himself then."

She gave a short brittle laugh and then settled back in the chair as if she would no longer discuss the matter.

But he would not, could not, let her have the cast word. He said, "I only wanted to see how it felt to throw off all restraints. That was all—an experiment. I didn't care for it; it was disgusting. It'll never happen again."

He looked at his wristwatch and said, "Let's go. We must not make the Secretary wait."

She rose slowly, as if the eight months' burden was at last beginning to drain her strength.

"All right. But I'm submitting our baby to this experiment only under protest. If anything happens to it, a potential citizen..."

He spun around. "A written protest?"

"I've already sent it in."

"You little fool! Do you want to wreck everything I've worked for?"

Tears filled her eyes.

"James! Does the possible harm to our baby mean nothing to you? Only the medals, the promotions, the power?"

"Nonsense! There's no danger! If there were, wouldn't I know it? Come along now!"

But she did not follow him through the door. Instead, she stood with her face against the wall, her shoulders shaking.

A MOMENT LATER, Jason Cramer entered. The young man closed the door behind him and put his arm around her. Without protest, she turned and buried her face in his chest. For a while, she could not talk but could only weep.

Finally, she released herself from his embrace and said, "Why is it, Jason, that every time I need a man to cry against, James is not with me but you are?"

"Because he is the one who makes you cry," he said. "And I love you."

"And James," she said, "loves only himself."

"You didn't give me the proper response, Jane. I said I loved you."

She kissed him, though lightly, and murmured, "I think I love you. But I'm not allowed to. Please forget what I said. I mean it."

She walked away from him. Jason Cramer, after making sure that he had no lipstick on his face or uniform, followed her.

Entering the laboratory, Jane Carroad ignored her husband's glare and sat down in the chair in the middle of the room. Immediately thereafter, the Secretary of Science and two Security bodyguards entered.

The Secretary was a stocky dark man of about fifty. He had very thick black eyebrows that looked like pieces of fur pasted above his eyes. He radiated the assurance that he was master, in control of all in the room. Yet, he did not, as was nervously expected by James Carroad and Jason Cramer, take offense because Jane did not rise from the chair to greet him. He gave her a smile, patted her hand, and said, "Is it true you will bear a male baby?"

"That is what the tests indicate," she said.

"Good. Another valuable citizen. A scientist, perhaps. With its genetic background…"

Annoyed because his wife had occupied the center of the stage for too long, Doctor James Carroad loudly cleared his throat. He said, "Citizens, honored Secretary, I've asked you here for a demonstration because I believe that what I have to show you is of utmost importance to the State's future. I have here the secret of what constitutes a good, or bad, citizen of the State."

He paused for effect, which he was getting, and then continued, "As you know, I—and my associates, of course—have perfected an infallible and swift method whereby an enemy spy or deviationist citizen may be unmasked. This method has been in use for three years. During that time, it has exposed many thousands as espionage agents, as traitors, as potential traitors."

The Secretary looked interested. He also looked at his wristwatch. Doctor Carroad refused to notice; he talked on at the same pace. He could justify any amount of time he took, and he intended to use as much as possible.

"My Department of Electroencephalographic Research first produced the devices delicate enough to detect the so-called rho waves emanated by the human brain. The rho or semantic waves. After ten years of hard work, I correlated the action of the rho waves in a particular human brain with the action of the individual's voice mechanisms. That meant, of course, that we had a device which mankind has long dreamed of. A—pardon the term—mind-reading machine."

Carroad purposely avoided scientific terminology. The Secretary did have a Ph.D. in political science, but he knew very little of any biological science.

Jason Cramer, at a snap of the fingers by Carroad, wheeled a large round shining machine to a spot about two feet in front of Jane. It resembled a weird metallic antelope, for it had a long flexible neck at the end of which was an oval and eyeless head with two prongs like horns. These pointed at Jane's skull. On the side of the machine—Cervus III—was a round glass tube. The oscilloscope.

Carroad said, "We no longer have to attach electrodes to the subject's head. We've made that method obsolete. Cervus' prongs pick up rho waves without direct contact. It is also able to cut out 99.99% of the 'noise' that had hampered us in previous research."

Yes, thought Jane, *and why don't you tell them that it was Jason Cramer who made that possible, instead of allowing them to think it was you?*

At that moment she reached the peak of her hate for him. She wished that the swelling sleeper within her was not Carroad's but Cramer's. And, wishing that, she knew that she must be falling in love with Cramer.

Carroad's voice slashed into her thoughts.

"And so, using the detected rho waves, which can be matched against definite objective words, we get a verbal picture of what is going in the subject's mind at the conscious level."

He gave an order to Cramer, and Cramer twisted a dial on the small control board on the side of Cervus.

"The machine is now set for semantic relations," Carroad said.

"Jane!" he added so sharply that she was startled. "Repeat this sentence after me! Silently!"

He then gave her a much-quoted phrase from one of the speeches of the Secretary himself. She repressed her scorn of him because of his flattery and dutifully concentrated on thinking the phrase. At the same time, she was aware that her tongue was moving in a noiseless lockstep with the thoughts.

The round tube on the side of Cervus glowed and then began flashing with many twisting threads of light.

"The trained eye," said Carroad, "can interpret those waveforms. But we have a surprise for you to whom the patterns are meaningless. We have perfected a means whereby a technician with a minimum of training may operate Cervus."

HE SNAPPED HIS fingers. Cramer shot him a look; his face was expressionless, but Jane knew that Cramer resented Carroad's arrogance.

Nevertheless, Cramer obeyed; he adjusted a dial, pushed down on a toggle switch, rotated another dial.

A voice, tonelessly and tinnily mechanical, issued from a loudspeaker beneath the tube. It repeated the phrase that Carroad had given and that Jane was thinking. It continued the repetition until Cramer, at another fingersnap from Carroad, flicked the toggle switch upward.

"As you have just heard," said Carroad triumphantly, "we have converted the waveforms into audible representations of what the subject is thinking."

The Secretary's brows rose like two caterpillars facing each other, and he said, "Very impressive."

But he managed to give the impression that he was thinking, Is that all?

Carroad smiled. He said, "I have much more. Something that, I'm sure, will please you very much. Now, as you know, this machine—my Cervus—is exposing hundreds of deviationists and enemy agents every year.

"Yet, this is *nothing!*"

He stared fiercely at them, but he had a slight smile on the corners of his lips. Jane, knowing him so well, could feel the radiance of his pride at the fact that the Secretary was leaning forward and his mouth was open.

"I say this is nothing! Catching traitors after they have become deviationist is locking the garage after the car has been stolen. What if we had a system of control whereby our citizens would be *unable* to be anything but unquestioningly loyal to the State?"

The Secretary said, "Aah?"

"I knew you would be far from indifferent," said Carroad.

CARROAD POINTED A finger downwards. Cramer, slowly, his jaws set, twisted the flexible neck of Cervus so that the pronged head pointed directly at Jane's distended stomach. He adjusted controls on the board. Immediately the oscilloscope danced with many intricate figures that were so different from the previous forms that even the untutored eyes of the Secretary could perceive the change.

"Citizens," said Carroad, "for some time after we'd discovered the rho waves in the adult and infant, we searched for their presence in the brain of the unborn child. We had no success for a long time. But that was not because the rho waves did not exist in the embryo. No, it was because we did not have delicate enough instruments. However, a few weeks ago, we succeeded in building one. I experimented upon my unborn child, and I detected weak traces of the rho waves. Thus, I demonstrated that the ability to form words is present, though in undeveloped form, even in the eight-month embryo.

"You're probably wondering what this means. This knowledge does not enable us to make the infant or the unborn speak any sooner. True. But what it does allow us to do is…"

Jane, who had been getting more tense with every word, became rigid. Would he allow this to be done to his own son, his own flesh and blood? Would he permit his child to become a half-robot, an obedient slave to the

State, incapable in certain fields of wielding the power of free will? The factor that most marked men from the beasts and the machine?

Numbly, she knew he would.

"...to probe well-defined areas in the undeveloped mind and there to stamp into it certain inhibitory paths. These inhibitions, preconditioned reflexes, as it were, will not, of course, take effect until the child has learned a language. And developed the concepts of citizen and State.

"But, once that is done, the correlation between the semantic waves and the inhibitions is such that the subject is unable to harbor any doubts about the teachings of the State. Or those who interpret the will of the State for its citizens.

"It is not necessary to perform any direct or physical surgery upon the unborn. The reflexes will be installed by Cervus III within a few minutes. As you see, Cervus cannot only receive; it can also transmit. Place a recording inside that receptacle beneath the speaker, actuate it, and, in a short time, you have traced in the grooves of the brain—if you will pardon an unscientific comparison—the voice of the State."

There was a silence. Jane and Cramer were unsuccessful in hiding their revulsion, but the others did not notice them. The Secretary and his bodyguards were staring at Carroad.

AFTER SEVERAL MINUTES, the Secretary broke the silence. "Doctor Carroad, are you sure that this treatment will not harm the creative abilities of the child? After all, we might make a first-class citizen, in the political sense, out of your child. Yet, we might wreck his potentialities as a first-class scientist. If we do that to our children, we lose out in the technological race. Not to mention the military. We need great generals, too."

"Absolutely not!" replied Carroad, so loudly and flatly that the Secretary was taken aback. "My computations, rechecked at least a dozen times, show there is no danger whatsoever. The only part of the brain affected, a very small area, has nothing to do with the creative functions. To convince you, I am going to perform the first operation upon my own son. Surely, I could do nothing more persuasive than that."

"Yes," said the Secretary, stroking his massive chin. "By the way, can this be done also to the adult?"

"Unfortunately, no," said Carroad.

"Then, we will have to wait a number of years to determine if your theory is correct. And, if we go ahead on the assumption that the theory is correct, and treat every unborn child in the country, we will have spent a tremendous amount of money and time. If you are not correct…"

"I can't be wrong!" said Carroad. His face began to flush, and he shook. Then, suddenly, his face was its normal color, and he was smiling.

Always in control, thought Jane. *Of himself and, if circumstances would allow, of everybody.*

"We don't have to build any extra machines," said Carroad. "A certain amount will be built, anyway, to detect traitors and enemies. These can be used in hospitals, when not in use elsewhere, to condition the unborn. Wait. I will show you how simple, inexpensive, and swift the operation is."

He gestured to Cramer. Cramer, the muscles twitching at the corners of his mouth, looked at Jane. His eyes tried desperately to tell her that he had to obey Carroad's orders. But, if he did, would he be understood, would he be forgiven?

Jane could only sit in the chair with a face as smooth and unmoving as a robot's and allow him to decide for himself without one sign of dissent or consent from her. What, after all, could either do unless they wished to die?

Cramer adjusted the controls.

Even though Jane knew she would feel nothing, she trembled as if a fist were poised to strike.

BRIGHT PEAKS AND valleys danced on the face of the oscilloscope. Carroad, watching them, gave orders to Cramer to move the prongs in minute spirals. When he had located the area he wished, he told Cramer to stop.

"We have just located the exact chain of neurones which are to be altered. You will hear nothing from the speaker because the embryo, of course, has no language. However, to show you some slight portion of Cervus' capabilities, Cramer will stimulate the area responsible for the rho waves before we begin the so-called inhibiting. Watch the 'scope. You'll see the waves go from a regular pulse into a wild dance."

The cyclopean eye of the oscilloscope became a field of crazed lines, leaping like a horde of barefooted and wire-thin fakirs on a bed of hot coals.

And a voice boomed out, *"Nu'sey! Nu'sey! Wanna d'ink!"*

Jane cried out, "God, what was that?"

The Secretary was startled; Cramer's face paled; Carroad was frozen.

But he recovered quickly, and he spoke sharply. "Cramer, you must have shifted the prongs so they picked up Jane's thoughts."

"I—I never touched them."

"Those were not my thoughts," said Jane.

"Something's wrong," said Carroad, needlessly. "Here. I'll do the adjusting."

He bent the prongs a fraction, checked the controls, and then turned the power on again.

The mechanical voice of Cervus spoke again.

"What do you mean? What're you saying? My father is not crazy! He's a great scientist, a hero of the State. What do you mean? Not any more?"

The Secretary leaped up from the chair and shouted above Cervus' voice, "What is this?"

Carroad turned the machine off and said, "I—I don't know."

Jane had never seen him so shaken.

"Well, find out! That's your business!"

Carroad's hand shook; one eye began to twitch. But he bent again to the adjustment of the dials. He directed the exceedingly narrow beam along the area from which the semantic waves originated. Only a high-pitched gabble emerged from the speaker, for Carroad had increased the speed. It was as if he were afraid to hear the normal rate of speech.

Jane's eyes began to widen. A thought was dawning palely, but horribly, on the horizon of her mind. If, by some intuition, she was just beginning to see the truth…But no, that could not be.

But, as Carroad worked, as the beam moved, as the power was raised or lowered, so did the voice, though always the same in tone and speed, change in phrase. Carroad had slowed the speed of detection, and individual words could be heard. And it was obvious that the age level of the speaker was fluctuating. Yet, throughout the swiftly leaping sentences, there was a sameness, an identity of personality. Sometimes, it was a baby just learning the language. At other times, it was an adolescent or young boy,

"Well, man, what is it?" bellowed the Secretary.

The mysterious voice had struck sparks off even his iron nerves.

Jane answered for her husband.

"I'll tell you what it is. It's the voice of my unborn son."

"Jane, you're insane!" said Carroad.

"No, I'm not, though I wish I were."

"God, he's at the window!" boomed the voice. *"And he has a knife! What can I do? What can I do?"*

"Turn that off until I get through talking," said Jane, "Then, you can listen again and see if what I'm saying isn't true."

Carroad stood like a statue, his hand extended towards the toggle switch but not reaching it. Cramer reached past him and flicked the switch.

"James," she said, speaking slowly and with difficulty. "You want to make robots out of everyone. Except, of course, yourself and the State's leaders. But what if I told you that you don't have to do that? That Nature or God or whatever you care to call the Creator, has anticipated you? And done so by several billion years?

"No, don't look at me that way. You'll see what I mean. Now, look. The only one whose thoughts you could possibly have tapped is our son. Yet, it's impossible for an unborn baby to have a knowledge of speech. Nevertheless, you heard thoughts, originated by a boy, seeming to run from the first years of speech up to those of an adolescent. You have to admit that, even if you don't know what it means.

"Well, I do."

Tears running down her cheeks, choking, she said, "Maybe I see the truth where you don't because I'm closer to my baby. It's part of me. Oh, I know you'll say I'm talking like a silly woman. Maybe. Anyway, I think that what we've heard means that we—all of humanity without exception—*are* machines. Not steel and electrical robots, no, but still machines of flesh, engines whose behavior, motives, and very thoughts, conscious or unconscious, spring from the playing of protein tapes in our brains."

"What the hell are you talking about?" said Carroad.

"If I'm right, we are in hell," she said. "Through no fault or choice of ours. Listen to me before you shut your ears because you don't want to hear, can't hear.

"Memories are not recordings of what has happened in our past. Nor do we act as we will. We speak and behave according to our 'memories,' which are not recorded *after* the fact. They're recorded *before* the fact. Our actions are such because our memories tell us to do such. Each of us is set like a clockwork doll. Oh, not independently, but intermeshed, working together, synchronized as a masterclock or masterplan decrees.

"And, all this time, we think we are creatures of free will and chance. But we do not know there isn't such a thing as chance, that all is plotted and foretold, and we are sliding over the world, through time, in predetermined grooves. We, body and mind, are walking recordings. Deep within our cells, a molecular needle follows the grooves, and we follow the needle.

"Somehow, this experiment has ripped the cover from the machine, showed us the tape, stimulated it into working long before it was supposed to."

Suddenly, she began laughing. And, between laughing and gasping, she said, "What am I saying? It can't be an accident. If we have discovered that we're puppets, it's because we're supposed to do so."

"Jane, Jane!" said Carroad. "You're wild, wild! Foolish woman's intuition! You're supposed to be a scientist! Stop talking! Control yourself!"

The Secretary bellowed for silence, and, after a minute, succeeded. He said, "Mrs. Carroad, please continue. We'll get to the bottom of this."

He, too, was pale and wide-eyed. But he had not gotten to his position by refusing to attack.

She ordered Cramer to run the beam again over the previous areas. He was to speed up the process and slow down only when she so directed.

The result was a stream of unintelligibilities. Occasionally, when Cramer slowed Cervus at a gesture from Jane, it broke into a rate of speech they could understand. And, when it did, they trembled. They could not deny that they were speeding over the life thoughts of a growing male named James Carroad, Junior. Even at the velocity at which they traveled and the great jumps in time that the machine had to make in order to cover the track quickly, they could tell that.

After an hour, Jane had Cramer cut off the voice. In the silence, looking at the white and sweating men, she said, "We are getting close to the end? Should we go on?"

Hoarsely, the Secretary shouted, "This is a hoax! I can prove it must be! It's impossible! If we carry the seeds of predeterminism within us, and yet, as now, we discover how to foresee what we shall do, why can't we change the future?"

"I don't know, Mr. Secretary," said Jane. "We'll find out—in time. I can tell you this. If anyone is preset to foretell the future, he'll do so. If no one is, then the problem will go begging. It all depends on Whoever wound us up."

"That's blasphemy!" howled the Secretary, a man noted for his belligerent atheism. But he did not order the voice to stop after Jane told Cramer to start the machine up again.

Cramer ran Cervus at full speed. The words became a staccato of incomprehensibility; the oscilloscope, an almost solid blur. Flickers of blackness told of broad jumps forward, and then the wild intertwined lightning resumed.

Suddenly, the oscilloscope went blank, and the voice was silent.

Jane Carroad said, "Backtrack a little, Jason. And then run it forward at normal speed."

James Carroad had been standing before her, rigid, a figure seemingly made of white metal, his face almost as white as his uniform. Abruptly, he broke into fluidity and lurched out of the laboratory. His motions were broken; his shouts, broken also.

"Won't stay to listen…rot…mysticism…believe this…go insane! Mean… no control…no control…"

And his voice was lost as the door closed behind him.

Jane said, "I don't want to hear this, Jason. But…"

Instantly, the voice boomed, *"God, he's at the window! And he has a knife! What can I do? What can I do? Father, father, I'm your son! He knows it, he knows it, yet he's going to kill me. The window! He's breaking it! Oh, Lord, he's been locked up for nineteen years, ever since he shot and killed my mother and all those men and I was born a Caesarean and I didn't know he'd escape and still want to kill me, though they told me that's all he talked about, raving mad, and…"*

The Blasphemers

I

Twelve thousand ancestors looked down on him.

Jagu stopped for a moment. Despite his scepticism, he could not help being impressed and even a little guilty. Twelve thousand! If there were such things as ghosts, what a might of phantoms was massed in this dark and holy chamber! How intense would be their assembled hatred, focused on him!

He was on the ground floor of the castle and in the Room of the Hero-Fathers. A hundred feet square, it was at this moment lit by a few electric flambeaux. A tremendous fireplace was at one end. In it, in the old days, the greatest enemy of the Wazaga, Siikii of the Uruba clan, had been burned alive after the Battle of Taaluu. Above the mantel were the trophies of that battle: swords, shields, lances, maces and several flintlock blunderbusses.

Beyond this room, deeper in the castle, was a room decorated with the accumulated trophies of a thousand years. Beyond that was another in which the skulls and preserved heads of fallen enemies stared out from niches, above plates bearing their names and the date and place of death. Nowadays, the door to the room was kept locked out of deference to modern sensibilities. It was opened only to historians and anthropologists or during the clan Initiations, the Greeting of the Ghosts.

Three nights ago, Jagu had been locked for twelve hours, all alone in that room.

That was the trouble, thought Jagu, as he turned away and walked softly on four bare paws towards the dark anteroom. The Ghosts, the Hero-Fathers, had not greeted him. There had not been any.

He could not tell his four parents that. It was impossible to acknowledge that his ancestors had scorned him, that they thought him unworthy of the name of *joma*—"man." Not that he thought that the Heroes had scorned him.

What does not exist cannot scorn.

His parents did not know that. They had been elated because he had been one of the few to graduate from the space-navy Academy of Vaagii. They were happy to put their eldest son through the long-awaited initiation into adulthood. But they had not been so happy when he said that he was not yet ready to choose a group-mate from the eligible members of the clan. All four had pleaded with him, threatened him, stormed. He must get married before he left for the stars. He must ensure the perpetuation of their line, leave many eggs in the hatchery before he assumed his duties as a spacer.

Jagu had said no.

Now, he was sneaking out late at night, and he had run the gauntlet of the twelve thousand. But…they were only squares of canvas or wood on which various colored oils had been arranged in different patterns. That was all.

He paused by a tall wall-mirror. The lights behind him shone gloomily in it. He looked like a ghost stepping out of the dark past towards himself, and where his two selves met…

SIX AND A half feet tall he stood. His vertical torso was humanoid. At a distance, and in a dim light, if all but the forward breasts upwards had been hidden, he could have been mistaken for a human being. But his pinkish skin was hidden up to the neck with a golden pile of short curling hairs. The head was very broad and round and massively boned. The cheekbones bulged like bosses on a shield. The jawbone was very thick; the deeply cleft chin was a prow. (The latter was another sore point. His parents did not like it that he had shaved off the goatee.)

The nose was bulbous and covered with tiny bristling blackish hairs. The supraorbital ridges flared out Gothicly. The eyes beneath were large, hazel and rimmed with a half-inch wide circle of brown hair. The ears were shaped like a cat's, and the yellow hair on top of his head stood straight up.

At the base of the spine of his upper torso was a device of bone, a natural universal joint that permitted the upper torso a ninety-degree description forward. The lower torso was quadrupedal, as if he had only half-evolved. The legs and paws were lion-shaped; his long tail was tufted at the end with black hair.

Jagu had the normal vanity of a youth. He thought he was rather good-looking, and he did not mind examining himself. The string of diamonds hanging from around his neck was magnificent, as was also the gold plate at its end. On the plate was a design formed of diamonds in the shape of a lightning streak, his totem.

Though he enjoyed the view, he could not stay there forever. He passed through a doublepointed arch into the anteroom. As he neared the door, he saw a big mound of fur rise and shake itself and slowly form into a six-legged animal with a long bushy tail, a sharp pointed nose, and great round scarlet ears. The rest of the *siygeygey* was, except for the black nose and round black eyes, a chocolate brown.

It rumbled in its massive chest. Then, recognizing Jagu with its nose, it whined a little and wagged its tail.

Jagu patted it and said, "Go back to sleep, Aa. I'm not taking you hunting tonight."

The animal slumped into amorphous shagginess. Jagu pointed the key at the lock and pressed on the end.

Just after dinner, he had deftly removed the key from its hook on the belt of Timo. Since another parent, Washagi, had locked the front door, Timo had not missed the key.

Jagu regretted having to do this, though he did get a thrill out of being a successful pickpocket. But he saw no sense in the custom of refusing a youth his own key until he had become married. He wanted to go out late that night. If he could not get permission, he would go without it.

THE DOOR SWUNG open. He stepped quickly outside, and the door closed.

Ten years ago he would have had to bribe or sneak past the Watcher of the Door. Now doormen were of the past. They could make more money working in the factories. The last of the family retainers had died some years ago; his place was taken by an electronic device.

A full late-summer moon shone at zenith. It cast green-silver nets everywhere and caught shadows gaunt and grotesque. These were the towering diorite statues of the greatest Heroes on the broad lawn, the hundred-odd whose fighting fury had made the name of Wazaga famous.

He did not pause to look at them, for he feared that an awe and dread left over from childhood might influence him. Instead he looked upward, where a score of joma-made satellites raced brightly across the night sky. He thought of the hundreds he could not see, of the space-navy ships patrolling the reaches between the planets of the system, and of the few interstellar ships out there, probing the galaxy.

"What a contrast!" he murmured. "On this earth, dumb stone sculptures rule the minds of a people who can go to the stars!"

He walked into a dark spot at the foot of the castle wall, an opening to a tunnel that led at a sharp slope downward. Formerly this area had been the moat. Then the moat was filled in. Later the excavation was dug and lined with cement. At its end lay the underground garage.

Here Jagu used the key to open the door again, and he entered. He did not hesitate making a choice among the six vehicles. He wanted the long low sleek Firebird. This was last year's model, one electric motor per wheel, one hundred horsepower per motor, stick-controlled, with a bubble-top, holding four passengers. It was painted fiery red.

Jagu lifted the bubble-top and stepped over the low side onto the floor. He squatted down behind the instrument panel, his rump against a thick cushion attached to a vertical steel plate. Then he pulled the bubble down. This was secured by magnetic clamps to the chassis. A separate and small motor provided the power for the electromagnets.

He flicked a toggle switch, and the *on* indicator lit up. The big hydrogen tank was full. He pulled out the sliding panel with its three small sticks and pushed forward on one.

Silently the Firebird rolled forward and up the ramp. As its rear cleared the garage, Jagu pressed a button and the iris of the garage door closed. The Firebird cruised down the driveway, past the stone ancestors and then turned to the right onto the private highway. This led him winding through the forest of *wexa* (scarlet pinoids) for about a mile. Only when he turned onto the public highway, which inclined downwards at this point, did he push the speed-stick forward as far as it would go. The column of the velocity indicator, an instrument like a thermometer, showed 135 mph attained in twenty seconds.

II

HE SHOT UP and over the top of the hill and had to swerve violently to the left to pass a big cargo truck. But there were no approaching lights, and his horn, honking like a goose, answered the truckdriver's furious blasts.

He wished that these were the old days. Then when an aristocrat wanted to travel without obstacle he notified the police. They went ahead to clear the road. Now, to keep the ancient privilege in force would disrupt the heavy flow of commerce. Business came first; so he must take his chances like any one else.

He was not, like his ancestors, immune from arrest if he ran over someone or forced somebody off the road. He was even supposed to obey the speed laws. Usually he did...but tonight he did not feel like it.

He passed a dozen other vehicles, several of them the old internal-combustion type. After traveling for several miles, he slowed enough to turn onto another private road with some screeching of tires and fishtailing.

He drove for a quarter of a mile, then stopped. Here he picked up Alaku. They gave each other a brief kiss. Alaku then jumped into the car beside Jagu and braced his rump against the plate; the bubble closed, the car turned around and they sped away.

Alaku unhooked a flask from his belt, unscrewed the top and offered Jagu a drink. Jagu stuck his tongue out, signifying a negative reply, so Alaku tipped the bottle to his own lips.

After gulping several times he said, "My parents were after me again to know why I didn't pick a mate-group."

"So?"

"So I suggested that I marry you and Fawani and Tuugee. You should have heard the gasping, the choking, seen the red faces, the bristling tails, the flying fingers. And heard the words! I calmed them down somewhat by telling them that I was only joking, of course. Nevertheless, I had to hear a long and hot lecture on the degeneracy of modern youth, its flippancy, its near-blasphemy. On how humor was a very good thing, but there were some things too sacred to joke about. And so on and on. If the lower classes wanted to forget about clan distinctions and marry just anybody, that was to be expected. What with increasing industrialization, and urbanization, mass migrations, modern mobility and so forth, the proletariat couldn't keep the clan lines straight. And it did not matter with them. But with us jorutama, the aristoi, it mattered very much. Where would society, religion, government, etc., be if the great clans let everything slide into chaos? Especially, if our clan, the Two-Fanged Eagles, set a bad example for the rest? You've heard the same thing."

Jagu sucked his breath inwards sharply with assent, and said, "A million times. Only I'm afraid I shocked my parents even more. Questioning marriage lines is bad enough. But to suggest that belief in ancestral ghosts just might—just barely might—*not* be true, might be a hangover from the old superstitious days...well, you've no idea of outraged parenthood until you've hinted at that. I had to undergo a ceremonial purification—an expensive one for the family and a tiring one for me. Also I had to spend four hours locked up in a cell in the dungeon, and I had to listen to sermons and prayers piped into my cell. No way of turning the abominable stuff off. But the chanting did help me to sleep."

"Poor Jagu," said Alaku, and he patted Jagu's arm.

A FEW MINUTES later they hurtled over a hilltop and saw, a mile away at the bottom of the long hill, twin beams of light from a car parked by the roadside.

Jagu pulled up alongside the car. Two got out of it and walked into his Firebird: Fawani and Tuugee. Fawani of the Tree Lion clan and Tuugee of the Split-tongue Dragons. All gave each other a kiss. Then, Jagu drove back to the highway and, in a short time, had it whistling at full speed.

"Where are we meeting tonight?" said Tuugee. "I didn't get the message until late. Fawani phoned, but I had to make small talk and avoid saying anything about tonight. I think my parents are monitoring my calls. The Dragons have always had a reputation for excessive suspiciousness. In this case, they've good reason to be—though I hope they don't know it."

"We're going to the Siikii Monument tonight," said Jagu.

The others gasped. "You mean where the great battle was fought?" said Alaku. "Where our ancestors who fell in that battle are buried? Where..."

"Where the ghosts congregate every night and slay those who dare walk among them?" said Jagu.

"But that's asking for it!" said Fawani.

"So we ask for it," said Jagu. "You don't really believe in all that tripe? Or do you? If so, you'd better get out now. Go home, ask at once for a ritual cleansing, take your beating. What we've done so far has been enough to stir up the ghosts—if any exist."

There was silence for a moment. Then Fawani said, "Pass the bottle, Alaku. I'll drink to defiance to the ghosts and to our everlasting love."

Jagu's laugh was hollow. He said, "A good toast, Fawani. But you'd better drink one to Waatii, the Hero of Speed. We're going to need his blessing, if he exists. Here comes a cop!"

The others turned to see what Jagu had detected in his rearview mirror. About a mile behind them, a yellow light was flashing off and on. Jagu flicked on a switch which brought in outside noises and turned the amplifier control. Now they could hear the barking of the highway patrolman's siren.

"One more ticket, and my parents will take the Firebird away from me," said Jagu. "Hang on."

HE PRESSED A button. A light on the instrument panel lit up to indicate that shields were being lowered over the license plates.

He took the Firebird around a passenger vehicle, his horn blaring, while the approaching beams of another grew larger and larger. Just before collision seemed imminent, while the others in his car had broken into terrified calls to the ghosts of their ancestors to save them, he whipped in front of the car just passed. The cry of tires burning on the pavement came to them, and the gabble of the car they had just missed ramming keened away.

His passengers said nothing; they were too frightened to protest. Besides, they knew that Jagu would pay no attention to them. He would kill them and himself rather than allow them to be caught. And actually it was better to die than be exposed to a public scandal, the recriminations of their parents and the ritual cleansing.

Jagu drove for half a mile and overtook a lumbering semi-trailer. He could not pass on the left, for a string of twin beams, too near, told him that he would have to wait. If he did, the patrolman would be on them. So he passed on the right, on the shoulder of the road. Without slowing.

Fortunately the shoulder was comparatively smooth and wide. Just wide enough for the Firebird: an inch away from the right wheels, the shoulder fell off and began to slope ever more towards the perpendicular. At the bottom of the hill was a creek, silvery in the moonlight. It ran along a heavily wooded slope.

Alaku, looking out the bubble at the nearness of the hill, groaned. Then he lifted the bottle to his lips again. By the time he had taken a few deep swallows, Jagu had pulled around the truck.

Fawani, looking behind him, saw the patrol car pull up behind the truck. Then one beam appeared as the car began to make the same maneuver as Jagu's. But it disappeared; the cop had changed his mind and swung in behind the truck.

"He'll radio ahead," said Fawani. "Do you mean to crash a roadblock?"

"If I have to," said Jagu cheerily. "But the entrance to the Siikii Monument is only a half mile down the road."

"The cop'll know where we turned in," said Alaku.

Jagu switched off the lights, and they sped at 135 mph along the moonlit highway. He began to slow after a few seconds, but they were still traveling at 60 mph when he took the sideroad.

For a moment, all were sure that they were going to overturn—all except Jagu. He had practiced making this turn at least twenty times, and he knew exactly what he could do. He skidded, but he brought the Firebird out of it just in time to keep the rear from sideswiping a large tree. Then he was back on the road and building up speed on the narrow, treelined pavement.

This time he stopped accelerating at 90 mph and drove for a half mile, taking the twists and turns with the ease of much practice and familiarity with this road.

Suddenly he began slowing the car.

In another half mile, he had turned off the road and plunged into what looked to the others like a solid mass of trees. But there was a space between the trees, an aisle just wide enough for the Firebird to pass through without scraping the paint off the sides. And at the end of the dark aisle, another which turned at a forty- five degree angle. Jagu drove the car into the space there and turned off the power.

THEY SAT THERE, breathing heavily, looking off through the trees.

From here they could not see the road itself, but they could see the flashing yellow of the patrol car as it sped down the road toward the Siikii Monument.

"Isn't there danger he'll see the others there?" said Fawani.

"Not if they hid their cars like I told them to," said Jagu. He released the bubble, lifted it and jumped out of the car. Raising the trunk cover in the rear of the car, he said, "Give me a hand. I've got something to fool him when he comes back looking for our tracks on the roadside."

They climbed out and helped him lift a tightly rolled mass of green stuff. Under his orders, they carried it back to the point on the road at which they had turned off. After unrolling the stuff, they spread it out over the car tracks and smoothed it. When they were done the area looked like smooth grass. There were even a few wild flowers—or what looked like wild flowers—sprouting up here and there among the grasses. Presently, from their hiding places behind trees, they saw the patrol car moving slowly back, its searchlight probing along the dirt and grass beside the pavement.

It passed, and soon they could see its lights no more.

Jagu gave the word, and they rolled the counterfeit grass into a tight bundle. Jagu had driven the car backward to the roadside while they were doing that. They placed the roll in the trunk, climbed back in, and Jagu drove off toward the Monument.

As they went along the twisting road, Fawani said, "If we hadn't been driving too fast, we could have avoided all this."

"And missed a lot of fun," said Jagu.

"The rest of you still don't understand," said Alaku. "Jagu doesn't care if we live or die. In fact, I sometimes think he'd just as soon die. Then his problems—and ours—would be over. Besides, he wants to make some sort of gesture at our parents and the society they represent—even if it's only outrunning a cop."

"Alaku's the cool, objective one," said Jagu. "He sits to one side and dissects the situation and the people involved. But, despite his often correct analysis, he never does anything about it. The Eternal Spectator."

"I'm not a leader," said Alaku somewhat coldly. "But I can take as much action as the next person. So far, I've participated quite fully. Have I ever failed to follow you?"

"No," said Jagu. "I apologize. I spoke from the back of my head. You know me; always too impulsive."

"No apology needed," said Alaku, his voice warming.

III

THEN THEY WERE at the gateway to the Siikii Monument. Jagu drove the car past it and under some trees across the road. Other vehicles were parked there. "All seven here," he said.

They recrossed the road to a point about forty yards south of the main gate. Jagu called softly. A voice replied softly; and a moment later a flexible, plastic rope was thrown over the gate.

Jagu was pulled up the twenty-feet high stone wall first, with much difficulty because of the leocentauroid construction of his body. On the other side, he found Ponu of the Greentail Shrike clan waiting for him. They embraced.

After the others had descended and the rope was pulled back over the wall, they walked softly toward the assignation point. The stone statues of their great and glorious ancestors stared down at them. These were dedicated to the fallen of the Battle of Siikii, the last major conflict of the last civil war of their nation. That had occurred one hundred and twenty years before, and the ancestors of some of those assembled tonight had fought and slain each other then. It was this war that had killed off so many of the aristoi that the lower classes had been able to demand certain rights and privileges denied them. It was also this war that had accelerated the growth of the fledgling Industrial Age.

The youths walked past the frowning Heroes and the pillars that marked various heroic exploits during the battle. All but Jagu showed a restraint in the overwhelming presence of the heads. He chattered away in a low but confident voice. Before they had reached the center of the Monument, the others were also talking and even laughing.

Here, in the center, where the battle had been decided, was the most sacred of all sites in this area. Here was the colossal statue of *Joma,* the eponymous ancestor of the joma species.

The statue was carved out of a single mass of diorite and painted with colors that imitated those of the living joma. It had no upper torso nor arms, only the head and neck attached to the quadrupedal body. The holy scriptures of the joma, the Book of Mako, said that Joma had once been like his descendants. But in return for the power of sentience and for the privilege of seeing his young become the dominant species of this world, and eventually of the universe, he had surrendered his arms, become like a crippled beast. Pleased by this sacrifice, Tuu-God had allowed Joma to reproduce parthenogenetically, without the aid of the other three mates. (Since Joma was the surviving member of his kind after Tuu had, in a fit of righteous anger, killed most beings, Joma had no other partners.)

It was here that Jagu had decided to hold the love feast. He could not have picked a place more appropriate to show his contempt for the ghosts and for the beliefs that the entire population of the planet held sacred.

Jagu and his friends greeted those waiting for them. Drinks were passed around along with jests. Ponu was that night's administrator. He had spread the carpets and placed the food and drinks on them—eight carpets, and four joruma sat on each.

As the night passed, and the moon reached its zenith and began to sink, the talking and laughing became louder and thicker. Then Jagu took a large bottle from Ponu, unscrewed the cap and went among the group. He gave each one a large pill from the bottle. Each swallowed it under his watchful eye. They made faces of repulsion, and Fawani almost threw his up. But he managed to keep it down when Jagu threatened to ram it down with his paw if Fawani didn't do the job himself.

After that Jagu made a mock prayer to Mako, a parody of the one that newly married quartets made to their particular household clan-Hero of Fertility. He ended by taking a swig from a bottle of wine and then smashing the bottle against the face of Joma.

An hour later the first round of the love feast had been completed. The participants were resting, getting ready for the next round, and discussing the beauty and the minor disappointments of the last congress.

A whistle blew shrilly.

Jagu sprang to his feet. "The cops!" he said. "All right, everybody, don't panic! Get your headpieces and breastplates. Don't bother to put them on yet. Leave the carpets here; they haven't got any clan insignias on them. Follow me!"

The statue of Joma stood on a small hill in the center of the Monument. It was this advantage in viewing that had determined Jagu's choice of site, in addition to his purpose in making the greatest blasphemy of all. He could see that the main gateway was open, and several cars with beams burning had just come through it. There were three other gates; all but one was also open and cars coming through them. Probably, he thought, that gate had been left closed to lure them toward it. Once over it, they would find the police waiting for them beside the wall.

But if this were a trap, then the police would have observed them hide their cars in the brush. That meant that even if he and his friends eluded the cops, they would all have a long long walk home. A useless walk, because the police would have no trouble determining and finding the owners.

There was a chance that this was not a prepared ambush. The patrolman who had chased them might have been suspicious and brought back other police. They could have climbed the walls, seen the group under Joma and decided to swoop in now. If so, it was also possible that they did not have enough personnel to come in through all the gates.

The unguarded fourth gate could be an escape route.

Almost he decided to make a run for the closed gate. But if he did so, and he was wrong, he would lead his friends to ruin. Whereas he had prepared some time ago a hiding place within the Monument grounds itself.

It would be foolish to take a chance on an unknown when he had something that was nearly one hundred per cent sure.

"Follow me to Ngiizaa!" he said. "Run, but don't panic. If anyone falls or gets into difficulty, call out. We'll stop to help you."

He began running; behind him was the thud of paws and the harsh breathing of stress.

They went down the hill on the side opposite the main gateway and toward the granite statue of the Hero Ngiizaa. Jagu looked around and noted that the other statues should hide them from the approaching policemen. He had chosen Ngiizaa because there was a ring of statues around it, marking where Ngiizaa had fallen inside a pile of his enemy's bodies. It took sixty seconds to get there from the center of the Monument, plenty of time to open the trapdoor at the base of Ngiizaa and for all of them to crowd into the hole beneath.

Over a year ago, Jagu and some of the others, working on moonless or cloudy nights, had dug out the hole. Then they had placed the beams which supported the trapdoor and put sod over it. The trapdoor was solid; he and five others had stood on it to test its weight and make sure that, on the days when crowds came to visit, the door would not betray its presence by bending.

Now he and three others began rolling the sod back. The strip was narrow; it did not take long to do the job. Then, while he held the door up, the others jumped into the hole beneath and went to the back of the hole to make room for those following.

By the time all except himself were in, the police cars had reached the center. Their searchlights began probing the Monument.

He had to drop down and lie motionless while several beams in turn sprayed the circle of statues. When they had passed he leaped up. Alaku, below, held the trapdoor up just far enough for him to squeeze through. He had replaced the sod on top of it.

This was the ticklish part of the whole procedure. No one could be left above to smooth the sod and make sure that the ragged edges did not show. But he did not think that the police could conceive of such a hiding place. When they started to make a search on paw, using their flashlights, they would expect to flush out the members of the party from behind individual statues. Their lights would play swiftly over the grass; they would be looking for youths lying flat on the grass, not for hidden trapdoors.

It was hot and crowded in the hole. Jagu hoped they would not have to wait too long. Zotu had a mild case of claustrophobia. If he started to panic, he'd have to be knocked out for the good of everybody.

The luminous face of his wristwatch showed 15:32. He'd give the cops an hour to search before deciding that the party had somehow gotten over the wall and away. After that, he would lead his friends out of the hole. If the police had not left somebody to watch the road, or if they did not make a determined search of the woods nearby and found the hidden cars, then all would go well. Many ifs...but it was exciting.

A few minutes later, somebody stepped hard on the trapdoor.

Jagu suppressed a groan. If the cop heard the hollow sound...but that was unlikely. They should be shouting at each other.

There was another rap as if somebody were stomping his feet on the trap-door. Then, while he held his breath and hoped the others would not cough or make any other noise, he heard something grate against wood.

The next moment, the door swung up slowly. A harsh voice said, "All right boys. The game's up. Come on out. Don't try anything. We'll shoot you."

IV

Later, in the cell, when he had time to think, Jagu wished that he had resisted. How much better to have been killed than to go through this!

He was in a small cell and alone. He had been there for he did not know how long. There were no windows, his watch had been taken away and he had no one to talk to.

Three meals were given to him through a little swinging door at the bottom of the large door. The tray was bolted to the door, and the food was placed in depressions. There was no cutlery; he had to eat with his fingers. Fifteen minutes after the tray swung inwards, it began to withdraw. No amount of tugging on his part could keep it from moving.

The cell itself was furnished simply. The bed was bolted to the floor and without blankets or pillows. There was a washbowl and an airblower with which to dry himself, and a hole in the floor to receive refuse. The walls were padded. He could not commit suicide if he wished to.

Sometime after the third meal, while he paced back and forth and wondered what punishment he would have to endure, what his companions were going through, what his parents knew and felt, the door opened.

It did so silently; he was not aware of it until he turned to pace back toward it. Two soldiers—not police—entered. Silently they escorted him out of the cell.

Neither were armed, but he had the feeling that they knew all about bare-hand-and-paw-fighting, that they were experienced and that he would get badly hurt if he tried to attack them. He had no such intention. Not until he saw his way clear, anyway. As long as he was inside a building new to him, one that must be equipped with closed-circuit TV and electronic beams, he would be quiet.

Meanwhile...

HE WAS TAKEN down a long corridor and into an elevator.

The elevator was some time rising, but he had no way of telling how many stories they had gone up. Then it stopped, and he was taken down another long hall and then another. Finally they stopped before a door on which was incised, in the florid syllabary of a century ago, *Tagimi Tiipaaroozuu*. Head of Criminal Detection. Arigi, the man responsible for detection and arrest of criminals of stature, conducted his business here. Jagu knew him, for Arigi had been among the elders present at his Initiation. He was a fellow clansman.

Though Jagu's knees shook, he swore he would show no fear. When he was marched in, he knew that he would have to remind himself constantly that he was not afraid. Arigi sat on his haunches behind a huge crescentshaped desk of polished *bini* wood. He had a cold hard face that was made even more unreadable by the dark glasses he wore. On his head was the four-cornered tall-crowned hat of the High Police. His arms were covered with bracelets, most of which had been awarded him by the government for various services. In his right hand was a stiletto with a jeweled handle.

"It may interest you, fledgling," he said in a dry voice, pointing the stiletto at Jagu, "that you are the first of your fellows to be interviewed. The rest are still in their cells, wondering when the trial will commence.

"Tell me," he said so sharply that Jagu could not help flinching, "when did you first decide that the ghosts of your ancestors did not exist? Except as a primitive superstition, figments in the minds of fools?"

Jagu had decided not to deny any accusation that was true. If he were to suffer, so much the worse. But he would not degrade himself by lying or pleading.

"I've always thought so," he said. "When I was a child I may have believed in the existence of the spirits of my ancestors. But I do not remember it."

"And you were intelligent enough not to proclaim this disbelief publicly," said Arigi. He seemed to relax a trifle. But Jagu was sure that Arigi was hoping he too, would relax so that he could spring at him, catch him off guard.

He wondered if his words were being recorded, his image being shown on a screen to his judges. He doubted that his trial for blasphemy would be made public. It would reflect too much discredit and dishonor on his clan, and they were powerful enough to suppress these things. Perhaps they might even have him in here merely to scare him, to make him repent. Then he would be let off with a reprimand or, more likely, be assigned to a desk job. Forever earthbound.

But no, blasphemy was not merely a crime against the people of this planet. It was a spit in the face of his ancestors. Only pain and blood could wipe out that insult; the ghosts would crowd around him while he screamed over a fire and would lap at the blood flowing from his wounds.

ARIGI SMILED AS if he now had Jagu where he wanted him. He said, "Well, at least you're a cool one. You act as a Wazaga should. So far, anyway. Tell me, do all your friends also deny the existence of an afterlife?"

"You will have to ask them that yourself."

"You mean you do not know what they believe?"

"I mean that I will not betray them."

"But you betrayed them the moment you led them to the Siikii Monument to defile the Heroes with your illicit lovemaking and your blasphemous prayers," said Arigi. "You betrayed them the moment you first confided to them your doubts and encouraged them to express theirs. You betrayed them when you bought an unlawful contraceptive from criminals and fed it to your comrades before the orgy."

Jagu stiffened. If no one had talked, how did Arigi know all this?

Arigi smiled again, and he said, "You betrayed them more than you know. For instance, the *weefee* pill you gave them tonight had no potency at all. I had already ordered your source of supply to give you a pill that looked like and tasted like *weefee.* But it had no effect. A fourth of your friends must be pregnant right now. Maybe you, too."

Jagu was shaken, but he tried to hide the effect of Arigi's words. He said, "If you've known about us for a long time, why didn't you arrest us before?"

Arigi leaned his upper torso back and placed his fingers behind his head. He looked at a point above Jagu, as if his thoughts were there. He said slowly, and it seemed irrelevantly, "So far, we joruma have discovered exactly fifty-one planets which can support our type of life. Fifty-one out of an estimated 300,000 in this galaxy alone. Of the ones discovered—all found in the last twenty-five years—twelve were inhabited by a centauroid type of sentient, similar to us, five by a bipedal type, six by very weird sentients indeed. All of these intelligent beings are bisexual or, I should say, have a sexual bipolarity.

"None of them have our quadrupolar sexual makeup. If we extrapolate on what we have so far found, we could say that the centauroid type of body is that most favored by Tuu or, if you prefer, the old pagan Four Parents of Nature. The bipedal form is second. And Tuu alone knows what other exotic beings are scattered throughout the Cosmos.

"We could also speculate that Tuu, for some reason, has favored us with a monopoly on the quadrupolar method of reproduction. At least, we joruma are the only ones encountered so far with that method. Now, what does that suggest to you?"

V

JAGU WAS PUZZLED. This inquisition was not going on the lines he had anticipated. He was not getting a thundering denunciation, a blistering lecture, threats of physical and mental punishment, of death.

What was Arigi leading up to? Perhaps this line of conversation was intended to make him think that he was going to escape. Then Arigi would attack savagely when his defenses were lowered.

"The Book of Mako says that a joma is unique in this universe. That the joruma are fashioned in the shape of Tuu. No other creature in all the world—so said Mako—is favored of Tuu. We are chosen by him to conquer the Cosmos."

"So said Mako," replied Arigi. "Or whoever wrote the book which is supposed to be written by Mako. But I want to know what you think."

Now Jagu thought he knew what Arigi was trying to do to him. He was talking thus, leading him, so he could get him to admit his disbelief. Then Arigi would spring.

But why should Arigi bother? He had all the evidence.

"What do I think?" said Jagu. "I think it rather strange that Tuu should have made so many differing sentient beings—that is, those intelligent enough to have language and to have a word for God in their languages—but only make one in Tuu's image. If he wanted all the planets to be eventually populated by the joruma, why did he create other beings on these planets? All of whom, by the way, think they have been formed in their Maker's image."

The two pairs of Arigi's eyelids had moved inwards so that only a sliver of pale green showed between them. He said, "You know that what you have said is enough to condemn you? That if I submit the evidence to the judges, you could be slowly burned alive? It's true that most blasphemers are killed quickly by being thrown into an intense furnace. But the law still stands. I would be within legal rights if I had you toasted so slowly that it would take you twelve hours or more to die."

"I know," said Jagu. "I had my fun with my friends; I spat at the ghosts. Now I have to pay."

Again Arigi seemed to start talking without relevance to the issue.

"Before Mako died, he said that his ghost would go forth through the Cosmos, and he would place on other worlds a sign that the world was to be the possession of the joruma. Now, this took place 2500 years before space travel. Such a thing was not even dreamed of in his time.

"Yet when we reached the first inhabitable world, we found the sign he promised to leave behind him: The stone statue of Joma, our ancestor. It was carved by Mako to show that he had been there and had staked out this world for the faithful, for the joruma; and five others of the fifty-five so far found have thereon a giant stone statue of Joma.

"Tell me, how do you account for that?"

Jagu said, slowly, "Either Mako's ghost carved the image of Joma out of the native stone, or..."

He paused.

"Or what?"

Jagu opened his mouth, but the words came hard. He swallowed and forced them out.

"Or our spacemen carved those statues themselves," he said.

Arigi's reaction was not what Jagu had expected. Arigi laughed loudly until his face was red. Finally, wheezing, wiping his eyes with a handkerchief, he said, "So! You guessed it! I wonder how many others have? And like you are keeping silent because of fear?"

He blew his nose and then continued, "Not many, I suppose. There are not too many born sceptics such as yourself. Or many as intelligent."

He looked curiously at Jagu. "You aren't happy to find yourself right? What's the matter?"

"I don't know. Maybe, though I disbelieved, I'd always hoped that my faith could be re-established. How much easier for me if it could be! If our spaceships had found the statues of Mako waiting for them, I'd have no choice but to believe..."

"No, you wouldn't," said Arigi sharply.

Jagu stared. "I wouldn't?"

"No! If all the evidence pointed toward the reality of Mako as a ghost, if the evidence were overwhelming, you still would not have believed. You would have found some rationalization for your disbelief. You would have said that the correct explanation or interpretation just wasn't available. And you would have continued to reject the idea of the ghost."

"Why?" said Jagu. "I'm a reasonable person; I'm rational. I think scientifically."

"Oh, sure," said Arigi. "But you were born an agnostic, a sceptic. You had the temperament of the disbeliever in the womb. Only by a violent perversion of your innate character could you have accepted religion. Most people are born believers; some are not. It's that simple."

"You mean," said Jagu, "that reality doesn't have a thing to do with it? That I think as I do, not because I have reasoned my way through the dark labyrinth of religion, but because my temperament made me think so?"

"That's an accurate statement."

"But—but—" said Jagu, "what you're saying is that there is no Truth! That the most ignorant peasant and fervent believer of ghosts has as much basis to his claims as I have to mine."

"Truth? There are truths and truths. You fall off a high cliff, and you accelerate at such and such a velocity until you hit the ground. Water, if not dammed, flows, downward. These are truths no one argues about. Temperament does not matter in physical matters. But in the realm of metaphysics, truth is an affair of natal prejudice. That is all."

JAGU HAD NOT been shaken by the thought of the fire and the death that waited for him. Now he was trembling, and outraged. Later he would be depressed. Arigi's cynicism made his look like a child's.

Arigi said, "The enlightened members—pardon me—the born sceptics of the aristoi have not believed in the existence of ghosts for some time. In a land crowded with the granite images of their illustrious ancestors, and crowded with worshippers of these sculptured stones, we laugh. But silently. Or only among ourselves. Many of us even doubt the existence of God.

"But we aren't fools. We suppress any show of public scepticism. After all, the fabric of our society is woven from the threads of our religion. It's an excellent means for keeping the people in line or for justifying our rule over them.

"Now, haven't you detected a certain pattern in the finding of the statues of Mako on the interstellar planes? In the particular type of planet on which the statues are?"

Jagu spoke slowly to control the shakiness of his voice.

"The images are not found on those planets populated by sentients technologically equal to us. Only on those planets with no sentients or with sentients having an inferior technology."

"Very good!" said Arigi. "You can see that that is no coincidence. We aren't about to wage war on beings who are able to retaliate effectively. Not yet, anyway. Now, I'll tell you why I revealed this to you—rather, confirmed your suspicions. Ever since we have had a faster-than-light drive, our interstellar exploratory ships have been manned with crews of a certain type. All are aristocrats, and all are disbelievers. They have had no compunction about chiseling statues out of the native rock on the appropriate planets."

"Why do they have to do this?" said Jagu.

"To establish a principle. To justify us. Some day, another sentient of equal, maybe superior, technological development will try to claim one of our planets for its own. When that day comes, we want our warriors and the people at home to be fired with a religious frenzy."

"You want me and my comrades to do this work for you?"

"For yourselves, too," said Arigi. "You young ones will have to take the reins of government after we're dead. And there's another factor. We're recruiting you because we need replacements. This is dangerous work. Every now and then, a ship is lost. Just lost. Leaves port and is never heard of again. We need new interstellar spacers. We need you and your friends now. What do you say?"

"Is there a choice?" asked Jagu. "If we turn down your offer, what happens to us?"

"An accident," said Arigi. "We can't have a trial and execution. Not even in secret. Too much chance of dishonoring ancient and honorable clans."

"Very well. I accept. I can't speak *for* my friends, but I'll speak *to* them."

"I'm sure they'll see the light," said Arigi dryly.

VI

A FEW DAYS later, Jagu flew to the school for advanced space-navy officers.

He and his friends began to take numerous training trips on ships that operated within the confines of the solar system. A year passed, and then they made three trips to nearby planetary systems under the tutelage of veterans. On the final voyage and the combat exercises that went with it, the veterans acted only as observers.

There was another ceremony. A new interstellar destroyer was commissioned and christened the *Paajaa,* and Jagu was given a captain's redstone to wear on the brim of his hat. The rest of the group also got various insignias of lesser ranks, for the craft was to be manned entirely by them.

Before leaving on the maiden voyage of the *Paajaa,* Jagu was summoned for one more interview with Arigi. By now Jagu knew that Arigi held more power than the public guessed. He was not only head of the planetary police system, he also was responsible for all military security systems.

Arigi welcomed Jagu as a member of the inner circle. He asked him to sit down and gave him a glass of *kusuto.* It was vintage of the best, thirty years old.

"You have added honor and luster to our clan," said Arigi. "The Wazaga can be proud of you. You were not given the captainship merely because you are a Wazaga, you know. A stellar ship is too expensive and important to be entrusted to a youth whose main ability is affiliation with a ruling group. You are a captain because you deserve the rank."

He sniffed at the bouquet of the wine and took a small sip.

Then he put the glass down, squinted at Jagu and said, "In a few days you will receive official orders to make your first exploratory voyage. Your ship will have enough fuel and supplies for a four-year trip, but you will be ordered to return at the end of two and a half, circumstances permitting. During that one and a quarter year, you will try to locate inhabitable planets. If any planet has sentients with a technology with space travel restricted to its system and atomic power, you will note its present development and its potential resistance to future attack by us. If the sentients have interstellar travel, you will observe as much as possible but will not place your ship in danger of attack. And you will return, after making the observations, directly and at full speed to us.

"If the sentients have an inferior technology, you will locate a site easily observable from orbit and will erect or carve an image of Mako there.

"Now! By the time you will have returned, many more eggs will have been hatched here. There will be a larger proportion of natal disbelievers among them than in the few years previously. By the time you are my age, the number of disbelievers will be a great problem. There will be strife, changing mores, doubt, perhaps even bloodshed. Before this occurs, before the change of *Zeitgeist* is on the side of the disbelievers and the faith in the Heroes and in Mako declines, we will have settled colonies on various planets uninhabited by sentients. We will also have wiped out or reduced greatly in number those sentients inferior to us. We will have started populating these with our kind. Because of our method of reproduction, we can populate a planet faster than any other sentient. And that is well, since we will need these colonies to aid us in the wars that will come.

"It is inevitable that we will have to fight cultures equal or perhaps even superior to ours. When that comes, we will have established the pattern—that we have a spiritual right to take anything we want. By then the weakened belief in the religion of our fathers will not affect our fighting zeal. We will be replacing it with another belief. Our right to conquest.

"Meanwhile, of course, I will be doing my best to suppress any resistance to our official religion. Those infidels among the aristoi will be indoctrinated in the proper attitude: a conscious hypocrisy. Those who nobly refuse will be dealt with in one way or another. The disbelievers among the lower classes will also be eliminated. They will be branded as criminals.

"But, of course, they can only fight the *Zeitgeist* so long. Then it takes over. By that time, I will have joined my ancestors, and my work will be done."

He smiled wryly and said, "I will be a ghost, perhaps, with a statue erected to me. However, by then my descendants—except for the inevitable ultrareactionaries—will regard my shrine as a historical or anthropological curiosity. I will have to go hungry among the other hungry ghosts—unhonored, unfed, wailing with weakness and impotent anger."

Jagu wondered if Arigi did not more than half-mean those words. He also wondered if Arigi was not as self-deceiving as those he laughed at. He was making his own, personal mythology to replace the old.

After all, what evidence did he really have to support his thesis that believers were born, not made?

A week later, he was on the *Paajaa* and had given the order to take it off. Another week, and his natal star was only one among many, a tiny glow. He was headed for the faroff and the unknown.

A year later, thirty stars later, they found two inhabitable planets. The second, like the first, rotated around a star of the Ao-U type. Unlike the first, it was the third planet from the star and it had sentients.

The *Paajaa* went into orbit in the upper atmosphere, and the telescopes were turned on the surface. The powers of magnification of the telescopes were so great that the spacers could see as distinctly as if they had been poised only twenty feet above the ground.

The sentients were bipedal and comparatively hairless except for thick growths on their heads or, among the males, on the faces. The majority covered their bodies with a variety of garments. Like the joruma, their skin colors and hair types varied; the darker ones were mainly in the equatorial zone.

Thousands of photographs were made during the orbitings of the *Paajaa*. Those taken of the groups that wore little or no clothing made it evident that these bipedals had only two sexes.

Another fact was determined. These sentients had no technology to be compared to the joruma's. They did not even have aircraft, except for a few balloons. Their main propulsive power was the steam engine. Steam drove engines of iron on iron tracks and paddlewheels or screws on ships. There were many sailships, also. The most formidable weapons were cannons and simple breech loading rifles.

The aborigines were roughly at about the same stage the joruma had been about a century and a half ago.

VII

ON THEIR THREE-HUNDREDTH orbit, Alaku made a shattering discovery.

He was looking at the scene projected on a large screen by a telescope when he cried out loudly. Those nearby came running, and they stopped when they saw what he was staring at. They too cried out.

By the time Jagu arrived, the scene was out of the telescope's reach. But he listened to their descriptions, and he ordered that the photos made be brought to him at once.

He looked at the photos, and he said, keeping his face immobile so that the others could not understand how shocked he was, "We'll have to go down and see for ourselves."

Four of them went down on the launch while the ship, in stationary orbit, stayed overhead. Their destination was on a rocky plateau about five miles southeast of the nearest city. The city was on the west bank of a great river that created a ribbon of greenery in the middle of the desert that covered much of the northern half of the continent. It was night, but a full moon shone in a cloudless sky. It illuminated brightly the three huge pyramids of stone and the object that had upset the crew of the *Paajaa* so much.

This lay in the center of a large quarry.

After hiding their ship in a deep and narrow ravine, the four proceeded in a small halftrack. A minute later, Jagu halted it, and all got out to look.

There was silence for a while. Then Jagu, speaking slowly as if hesitant to commit himself, said, "It seems to be Joma."

"It's ancient," said Alaku. "Very ancient. If Mako made this, he must have done so immediately after dying. He must have come straight here."

"Don't jump to conclusions," said Jagu. "I was going to say that another ship had gotten here before us. But we know no ship has been sent to this sector. However..."

"However what?" said Alaku.

"As you said, it's ancient. Look at the ripples in the stone. They must have been made by erosion from blowing sand. Look at the face. It's shattered. Still, the natives of long ago could have made this. It's very possible."

Silent again, they re-entered the halftrack and began to drive slowly around the enormous statue.

"It faces the east," said Alaku. "Just as Mako said the statues of Joma would."

"Many primitive sentients on many worlds face their gods, their temples and their dead towards the east," said Jagu. "It's natural to regard the rising sun as the recurrent symbol of immortality."

Fawani said, "This maybe the biggest reproduction of Joma. But it's not the only one on this world. The photos showed others. They too must be ancient. Perhaps it's only coincidence. The natives themselves made them. They're figures, symbols of their religion."

"Or," said Alaku, "the natives founded a religion that was based on Joma after Mako came here and carved this statue out of the rock. He may even have given them our religion. So, as you saw, they set up a temple before Joma. I'm sure that's what the ruins in front of the breasts were. They made other smaller images of Joma. Then ages later they ceased to believe in Joma...just as we are ceasing to believe. Yet the testimony to the truth was before their mocking eyes..."

Jagu knew they could not determine the truth no matter how long they speculated among themselves. The thing to do was to locate somebody who did know.

HE TURNED THE halftrack towards the city.

There were isolated houses on its outskirts. Before he had gone a mile, he found what he was looking for. A party of natives were headed towards him. All were riding beasts that looked very much like the *gapo* of the deserts of his own planet, except that these had only four legs and one hump.

The gapoids scattered in a panic; some threw their riders. The joruma shot these with gasdriven darts, the tips of which were coated with a paralyzing drug. After tearing the robes from his victims to make sure he had a specimen of each sex (for he knew that the zoologists at home would want to examine them) the joruma chose a male and a female. These were loaded into the half-track, which then returned to the launch. In a few minutes, the launch was rising towards the *Paajaa*.

Back on the ship, the sleepers were placed on beds within a locked room. Jagu inspected them and, for the thousandth time, wondered if the joruma were not designed by Tuu to be superior. Perhaps they were really made in Tuu's image. These bipedals seemed to be so scrawny and weak and so inefficient, sexually speaking. One sex could never hatch an egg or bear young. This fault halved the species' chances of reproducing. Moreover, he thought, preserving humor even in his semi-stunned condition, it cut out three-quarters of the fun.

Maybe the other sentients were, as some theologians had theorized, experiments on Tuu's part. Or maybe Tuu had meant for non-joruma to be inferior.

Let the theologians speculate. He had a far more important and immediate enigma to solve. Also he had Alaku to worry about.

Alaku, the cool one, he whose only permanent passion was intellectualism, the agnostic, was by far the most shaken.

Jagu remembered Arigi's words. You believe what you want to believe. The metaphysical cannot be denied or affirmed in terms of the physical.

"It's a judgment," said Alaku. "We thought we were so clever and our fathers so ignorant and superstitious. But Mako knew that some day we would come here and find the truth. He knew it before our great-great-great-great-grandfathers were born."

"We have two natives," said Jagu. "We'll learn their language. From them we may discover who did carve out Joma—I mean that statue that seems to resemble Joma."

"How will they know?" said Alaku, looking desperate. "They will have only the words of their ancestors as testimony, just as we have the words of ours."

This was the last time Jagu talked to Alaku.

Shortly thereafter, Alaku failed to appear for his turn of duty on the bridge. Jagu called him over the intercom. Receiving no answer, he went to Alaku's cabin. The door was locked, but it yielded to the master key. Alaku lay on the floor, his skin blue from cyanide.

He left no note behind. None was needed.

The entire crew was saddened and depressed. Alaku, despite a certain aloofness, had been loved. The many eggs he had fathered in them, and the eggs they had fathered in him, were in the cryogenic tank, waiting to be quick-thawed when they returned to their home.

A few hours later, the two natives killed each other. The bigger one strangled the other. But before that the veins of the strangler's wrists had been bitten into and opened by the other. After the smaller had died, the other had exercised violently to stimulate the bleeding.

Almost, Jagu decided to turn around and capture some more sentients from the same area. But he could not force himself to do that. To return and see Joma again, the awe-inspiring ancient being of stone...who knew but what more might go mad? He could be among them.

For several ship-days, he paced back and forth on the bridge. Or he lay in his bed in his cabin, staring at the bulkhead.

Finally, one third-watch, Jagu went onto the bridge. Fawani, the closest of all to him, was also on the bridge, carrying out his slight duties as pilot. He did not seem surprised to see Jagu; Jagu often came here when he was supposed to be sleeping.

"It has been a long time since we were together," said Fawani. "The statue on that Tuu-forsaken planet and Alaku's suicide...they have killed love. They have killed everything except wonder about one question."

"I don't wonder. I *know* that it was made by the natives. I know because that's the only way it could be."

"But there's no way of proving it, is there?" said Fawani.

"No," replied Jagu. "So before we get back home, long before, we must make up our minds to act."

"What do you mean?"

"We have several avenues of action. One, report exactly what we have seen. Let the authorities do the thinking for us, let them decide what to do. Two, forget about having discovered the second planet. Report only the first planet. Three, don't go home. Find a planet suitable for colonization, one so far away it may not be found by other joruma ships for hundreds of years, maybe longer.

"All three are dangerous," continued Jagu. "You don't know Arigi as I do. He will refuse to believe in the coincidence because the mathematical chances against it are too high. He will also refuse to believe that Mako did it. He will conclude that we made those statues to perpetrate a monstrous hoax."

"But how could he believe such a thing?"

"I couldn't blame him," said Jagu, "because he knows our past record. He might think that we did it just to raise hell. Or even that the long voyage unbalanced us, that we became converted, backslid to superstition, committed a pious fraud to convince him and others like him. It doesn't matter. He'll think we did it. He has to think that or admit his whole philosophy of life is wrong.

"If we try to get rid of all evidence, the photos, the logbook, we run a risk of someone talking. I think it'd be a certainty. We belong to the species that can't keep its mouth shut. Or somebody else may go mad and babble the truth.

"Personally I think that we should try the third alternative. Go far out into an unknown sector, so far that we can't return. This will put us beyond the range of any ships now built. If, in the future, one should find us, we can always say we had an accident, that the ship couldn't return."

"But what if we reach the end of our fuel, and we still have found no suitable planet?" said Fawani.

"It's a long chance, but the best we have," said Jagu.

He pointed at the lower lefthand corner of a starmap on a bulkhead. "There are quite a few Ao-U stars there," he said. "If I gave the order to you now, at this moment to head the ship toward them—would you obey my order?"

"I don't know what to think," said Fawani. "I do know that we could spend the rest of our long voyage home arguing about the best course of action. And still be undecided by the time we let down on earth. I trust you, Jagu, because I believe in you."

"Believe?" said Jagu. He smiled. "Are there also born believers in others? And those men born to be believed in? Perhaps. But what about the rest of the crew? Will they as unhesitatingly follow me?"

"Talk to them," said Fawani. "Tell them what you told me. They will do as I did. I won't even wait for the outcome. I'll turn the ship now. They won't need to know that until after they've decided to do so—provided you talk to them before I'm relieved."

"Very well. Turn it around. Head it in that general direction. We'll pick out a particular star later. We'll find one or die trying. We'll begin life anew. And we don't teach our children anything about the ghosts of longdead heroes."

"Turn about it is," said Fawani. He busied himself with the controls and with inserting various cards in the computer. Then, he said, "But can man exist in a religious vacuum? What will we tell them to replace the old beliefs?"

"They'll believe what they want to believe," said Jagu wearily. "Anyway, we've a long time to think about that."

HE WAS SILENT while he looked out at the stars. He thought about the planet they had just left. The sentients there would never know what gratitude they owed to him, Jagu.

If he had returned to base and told his story, the Navy—no matter what happened to Jagu and his crew—would go to that planet. And they would proceed to capture specimens and would determine their reaction to a number of laboratory-created diseases. Within a few years only the naturally resistant of the natives would be left alive. Their planet would be open to colonization by the joruma.

Now the bipedals had a period of grace. If they developed space travel and atomic power soon enough, the next joruma ship would declare them off-limits.

Who knew? His own descendants might regret this decision. Some day, the sons of those sentients who had been spared by his action might come to the very planet on which his, Jagu's, sons would be living. They might even attack and destroy or enslave the joruma.

That was another chance he and his descendants would have to take.

He pressed the button that would awaken the sleepers and summon those on watch. Now he must begin talking.

He knew that they all would be troubled until the day they died. Yet, he swore to himself, their sons would not know of it. They would be free of the past and its doubts and its fears.

They would be free.

A Bowl Bigger than Earth

I

No squeeze. No pain.

Death has a wide pelvis, he thought—much later, when he had time to reflect.

Now he was screaming.

He had had an impression of awakening from his deathbed, of being shot outwards over the edge of a bowl bigger than Earth seen from a space capsule. Sprawling outwards, he landed on his hands and knees on a gentle slope. So gentle it was. He did not tear his hands and knees but slid smoothly onward and downward on the great curve. The material on which he accelerated looked much like brass and felt frictionless. Though he did not think of it then—he was too panic-stricken to do anything but react—he knew later that the brassy stuff had even less resistance than oil become a solid. And the brass, or whatever it was, formed a solid seamless sheet.

The only break was in the center, where the sheet ended. There, far ahead and far below, the bowl curved briefly upward.

Gathering speed, he slipped along the gigantic chute. He tried to stay on his hands and knees; but, when he twisted his body to see behind him, he shifted his weight. Over he went onto his side. Squawling, he thrashed around, and he tried to dig his nails into the brass. No use. He met no resistance, and he began spinning around, around. He did see, during his whirlings, the rim from which he had been shoved. But he could see only the rim itself and, beyond, the blue cloudless sky.

Overhead was the sun, looking just like the Terrestrial sun.

He rolled over on his back and succeeded during the maneuver in stopping the rotations. He also managed to see his own body. He began screaming again, the first terror driven out and replaced by—or added to as a higher harmonic—the terror of finding himself in a sexless body.

Smooth. Projectionless. Hairless. His legs hairless, too. No navel. His skin a dark brown-like an Apache's.

Morfiks screamed and screamed, and he gripped his face and the top of his head. Then he screamed higher and higher. The face was not the one he knew (the ridge of bone above the eyes and the broken nose were not there), and his head was smooth as an egg.

He fainted.

LATER, ALTHOUGH IT could not have been much later, he came to his senses. Overhead was the bright sun and beneath him was the cool nonfriction.

He turned his face to one side, saw the same brass and had no sensation of sliding because he had no reference point. For a moment he thought he might be at the end of his descent. But on lifting his head he saw that the bottom of the bowl was closer, that it was rushing at him.

His heart was leaping in his chest as if trying to batter itself to a second death. But it did not fail. It just drove the blood through his ears until he could hear its roar even above the air rushing by.

He lowered his head until its back was supported by the brass, and he closed his eyes against the sun. Never in all his life (lives?) had he felt so helpless. More helpless than a newborn babe, who does not know he is helpless and who cannot think and who will be taken care of if he cries.

He had screamed, but no one was running to take care of him.

Downward he slipped, brass-yellow curving away on both sides of him, no sensation of heat against his back where the skin should have burned off a long time ago and his muscles should now be burning.

The incline began to be less downward, to straighten out. He shot across a flat space which he had no means of estimating because he was going too fast.

The flatness gave away to a curving upwards. He felt that he was slowing down; he hoped so. If he continued at the same rate of speed, he would shoot far out and over the center of the bowl.

Here it came! The rim!

He went up with just enough velocity to rise perhaps seven feet above the edge. Then, falling, he glimpsed a city of brass beyond the people gathered on the shore of a river but lost sight of these in the green waters rushing up towards him directly below.

He bellowed in anguish, tried to straighten out, and flailed his arms and legs. In vain. The water struck him on his left side. Half-stunned, he plunged into the cool and dark waters.

By the time he had broken the surface again, he had regained his senses. There was only one thing to do. Behind him, the brassy wall reared at least thirty feet straight up. He had to swim to the shore, which was about four hundred yards away.

What if he had not been able to swim? What if he chose to drown now rather than face the unknown on the beach?

A boat was his answer. A flatbottomed boat of brass rowed with brass oars by a brown-skinned man (man?). In the bow stood a similar creature (similar? exactly alike) extending a long pole of brass.

The manlike thing in the bow called out, "Grab hold, and I'll pull you in."

Morfiks replied with an obscenity and began swimming toward the beach. The fellow with the pole howled, "A trouble-maker, heh? We'll have no antisocial actions here, citizen!"

He brought the butt of the pole down with all his strength.

It was then that Morfiks found that he was relatively invulnerable. The pole, even if made of material as light as aluminum and hollow, should have stunned him and cut his scalp open. But it had bounced off with much less effect than the fall into the river.

"Come into the boat," said the poleman. *"Or nobody here will like you."*

II

It was this threat that cowed Morfiks. After climbing into the boat, he sat down on the bench in front of the rower and examined the two. No doubt of it. They were twins. Same height (both were sitting now) as himself. Hairless, except for long curling black eyelashes. Same features. High foreheads. Smooth hairless brows. Straight noses. Full lips. Well developed chins. Regular, almost classical features, delicate, looking both feminine and masculine. Their eyes were the same shade of dark brown. Their skins were heavily tanned. Their bodies were slimly built and quite human except for the disconcerting lack of sex, navel and nipples on the masculine chests.

"Where am I?" said Morfiks. "In the fourth dimension?"

He had read about that in the Sunday supplements and some of the more easily digesteds.

"Or in Hell?" he added, which would have been his first question if he had been in his Terrestrial body. Nothing that had happened so far made him think he was in Heaven.

The pole rapped him in the mouth, and he thought that either the poleman was pulling his punches or else his new flesh was less sensitive than his Terrestrial. The last must be it. His lips felt almost as numb as when the dentist gave him novocaine before pulling a tooth. And his meager buttocks did not hurt from sitting on the hard brass.

Moreover, he had all his teeth. There were no fillings or bridges in his mouth.

"You will not use *that* word," said the poleman. "It's not nice, and it's not true. The protectors do not like that word and will take one hundred per cent effective measures to punish anybody responsible for offending the public taste with it."

"You mean the word beginning with H?" said Morfiks cautiously.

"You're catching on fast, citizen."

"What do you call this...place?"

"Home. Just plain home. Allow me to introduce myself. I'm one of the official greeters. I have no name; nobody here does. Citizen is good enough for me and for you. However, being a greeter doesn't make me one whit better than you, citizen. It's just my job, that's all. We all have jobs here, all equally important. We're all on the same level, citizen. No cause for envy or strife."

"No name?" Morfiks said.

"Forget that nonsense. A name means you're trying to set yourself apart. Now, you wouldn't think it was nice if somebody thought he was better than you because he had a name that was big in We-know-where, would you? Of course not."

"I'm here for...how long?" Morfiks said.

"Who knows?"

"Forever?" Morfiks said dismally.

THE END OF the pole butted into his lips. His head rocked back, but he did not hurt much.

"Just think of the present, citizen. Because that is all that exists. The past doesn't exist; the future can't. Only the present exists."

"There's no future?"

Again, the butt of the pole.

"Forget that word. We use it on the river when we're breaking in immigrants. But once on the shore, we're through with it. Here, we're practical. We don't indulge in fantasy."

"I get your message," Morfiks said. He damped the impulse to leap at the poleman's throat. Better to wait until he found out what the setup was, what a man could or could not get away with.

The rower said, "Coming ashore, citizens."

Morfiks noticed that the two had voices exactly alike, and he supposed his own was the same as theirs. But he had a secret triumph. His voice would sound different to himself; he had that much edge on the bastards.

The boat nudged onto the beach, and Morfiks followed the other two onto the sand. He looked quickly behind him and now saw that there were many boats up and down the river. Here and there a body shot up over the rim of the brassy cliff and tumbled down into the waters as he had a few minutes ago.

Beyond the lip of the cliff rose the swell of the brass slide down which he had hurtled. The slide extended so far that he could not see the human figures that undoubtedly must be standing on the edge where he had stood and must just now be in the act of being pushed from behind. Five miles away, at least, five miles he had slid.

A colossal building project, he thought.

Beyond the city of brass rose another incline. He understood now that he had been mistaken in believing the city was in the middle of a bowl. As far as he could see, there was the river and the city and the cliffs and slides on both sides. And he supposed that there was another river on the other side of the city.

The city reminded him of the suburban tract in which he had lived on Earth. Rows on rows of square brass houses, exactly alike, facing each other across twenty-foot wide streets. Each house was about twelve feet wide. Each had a flat roof and a door in front and back, a strip of windows which circled the house like a transparent belt. There were no yards. A space of two feet separated each house from its neighbor.

A person stepped out of the crowd standing on the beach. This one differed from the others only in having a band of some black metal around the biceps of its right arm.

"Officer of the Day," it said in a voice exactly like the two in the boat. "Your turn will come to act in this capacity. No favorites here."

It was then that Morfiks recognized the possibilities of individualism in voice, of recognizing others. Even if everybody had identical dimensions in larynges and the resonating chambers of palate and nasal passages, they must retain their habits of intonation and choice of pitch and words. Also, despite identical bodies and legs, they must keep some of their peculiar gestures and methods of walking.

"Any complaints about treatment so far?" said the O.D:

"Yes," said Morfiks. "This jerk hit me three times with its pole."

"Only because we love it," said the poleman. "We struck it—oh, very lightly!—to correct its ways. As a father—pardon the word—punishes a child he loves. Or an older brother his little brother. We are all brothers..."

"We are guilty of antisocial behavior," said the O.D. sternly. "We're very very sorry, but we must report this incident to the Protectors. Believe us, it hurt us..."

"Worse than it hurts us," said the poleman wearily. "We know."

"We'll have to add cynicism to the charge," said the O.D. "K.P. for several months if we know the Protectors. Should anybody be guilty again—"

The O.D. told Morfiks to walk with it, and it briefed Morfiks as they went through the streets. These were made of a pale violet rubbery substance only slightly warm to the feet despite the sun beating down upon it. Morfiks would be given his own home. He was lord and master there and could do whatever he wished in it as long as he did not break any rules of public morality.

"You mean I can invite anybody I want to and can keep out anybody I want to?"

"Well, you can invite anybody you want. But don't throw anybody out who comes in uninvited. This is, unless the uninvited behaves antisocially. In which case, notify the O.D., and we'll notify a Protector."

"How can I be master of my house if I can't choose my guests?" Morfiks said.

"'The citizen doesn't understand," said the O.D. "A citizen should not want to keep another citizen out of his house. Doing so is saying that a citizen doesn't love all citizens as brothers and sisters. It's not nice. We want to be nice, don't we?"

Morfiks replied that he had always been known as a nice guy, and he continued to listen to the O.D. But, on passing an area where a large field coated with the violet rubber broke the monotonous rows of houses; he said, "Looks like a children's playground with all those swings, seesaws, games, trampolines. Where are the kids? And how—"

"Only the Protectors know what happens to the children who come from We-Know-Where," said the O.D. "It's better, much, much better, not to ask them about it. In fact, it's very good not to see or talk to a Protector.

"No, the playgrounds are for the amusement of us citizens. However, the Protectors have been thinking about taking them down. Too many citizens quarrel about who gets to use them, instead of amicably arranging precedence and turns. They actually dare to fight each other even if fighting's forbidden. And they manage, somehow, to hurt each other. We don't want anybody to get hurt, do we?"

"I guess not. What do you do for entertainment, otherwise?"

"First things first, citizen. We don't like to use any of the personal pronouns except we, of course, and *us* and *our* and *ours. I, me, they, you* all differentiate. Better to forget personal differences here, heh? After all, we're just one big happy family, heh?"

"Sure," Morfiks said. "But there must be times when a citizen has to point out somebody. How do I—we—identify someone guilty of, say, antisocial behavior?"

"It doesn't matter," said the O.D. "Point out anyone. Yourself—if you'll pardon the word—for instance. We all share in the punishment, so it makes no difference."

"You mean *I* have to be punished for someone else's crime? That isn't *fair!*"

"It may not seem so to us at first," said the O.D. "But consider. We're brothers, not only under the skin but on the skin. If a crime is committed, the guilt is shared by all because, actually, all are responsible. And if punishment is given to all, then all will try to prevent crime. Simple, isn't it? And fair, too."

"But you—we—said that the poleman would be given K.P. Does that mean we all go on K.P.?"

"We did not commit a felony, only a misdemeanor. If we do it again, we are a felon. And we suffer. It's the only nice thing to do, to share, right?"

MORFIKS DID NOT like it. He was the one hit in the teeth, so why should he, the victim, have to take the punishment of the aggressor?

But he said nothing. He had gotten far on We-Know-Where by keeping his mouth shut. It paid off; everybody had thought he was a nice guy. And he *was* a nice guy.

There did seem to be one fallacy in the setup. If being a stool pigeon meant you, too, suffered, why turn anybody in? Wouldn't it be smarter to keep quiet and inflict the punishment yourself on the aggressor?

"Don't do it, citizen," said the O.D.

Morfiks gasped.

The O.D. smiled and said, "No, we can't read minds. But every immigrant thinks the same thing when told about the system. Keeping quiet only results in double punishment. The Protectors—whom this citizen has never seen face to face and doesn't want to—have some means of monitoring our behavior. They know when we've been antisocial. The offender is, of course, given a certain amount of time in which to confess the injury. After that..."

To keep himself from bursting into outraged denunciation of the system, Morfiks asked more questions.

Yes, he would be confined to this neighborhood. If he traveled outside it, he might find himself in an area where his language was not spoken. That would result in his feeling inferior and different because he was a foreigner. Or, worse, superior. Anyway, why travel? Any place looked like every place.

Yes, he was free to discuss any subject as long as it did not concern We-Know-Where. Talking of that place led to discussions of—forgive the term—*one's* former identity and prestige. Besides, controversial subjects might arise and so lead to antisocial behavior.

Yes, this place was not constructed, physically, like We-Knew-Where. The sun might be a small body; some eggheads had estimated it to be only a mile wide. The run orbited around the strip, which was composed of the slides, two rivers and the city between the rivers, all of which hung in space. There was some speculation that this place was in a pocket universe the dimensions of which were probably not more than fifty miles wide and twenty high. It was shaped like an intestine, closed at one end and open at the other to infinity—maybe.

At this point, the O.D. cautioned Morfiks about the perils of intellectual speculation. This could be a misdemeanor or felony. In any event, eggheadedness was to be avoided. Pretending to be brainier than your neighbor, to question the unquestionable, was unegalitarian.

"There's no worry about that," Morfiks said. "If there's anything hateful and despicable, it's eggheadedness."

"Congratulations on skill in avoiding the personal," said the O.D. "We'll get along fine here."

III

THEY ENTERED AN immense building in which citizens were sitting on brass benches and eating off brass tables running the length of the building. The O.D, told Morfiks to sit down and eat. Afterwards, Morfiks could get to his new home, No. 12634, by asking directions. The O.D. left, and a citizen on K.P.

served Morfiks soup in a big brass bowl, a small steak, bread and butter, salad with garlic dressing and a pitcher of water. The utensils and cup were of brass.

He wondered where the food came from, but before he could ask, he was informed by a citizen on his right that he was not holding the spoon properly. After a few minutes of instruction and observation, Morfiks found himself able to master etiquette as practiced here.

"Having the same table manners as everybody else makes a citizen a part of the group," said the instructor. "If a citizen eats differently, then a citizen is impolite. Impoliteness is antisocial. Get it?"

"Got it," said Morfiks.

After eating, he asked the citizen where he could locate No. 12634.

"We'll show us," said the citizen. "We live near that number."

Together, they walked out of the hall and down the street. The sun was near the horizon now. Time must go faster, he thought, for it did not seem to him that he had been here for more than a few hours. Maybe the Protectors sent the sun around faster so the days would be shorter.

They came to No. 12634, and Morfiks' guide preceded him through swinging batwing doors into a large room with luminescent walls. There was a wide couchbed of the violet rubbery substance, several chairs cut out of solid blocks of the same stuff and a brass table in the center of the room. In one corner was a cubicle with a door. He investigated and found it to be the toilet. Besides the usual sanitary arrangements, the cubicle contained a shower, soap and four cups. There were no towels.

"After a shower, step outside, dry off in the sun," the guide said.

It looked at Morfiks for such a long time that Morfiks began to get nervous. Finally, the guide said, "I'll take a chance you're a pretty good Joe. What was your name on Earth?"

"John Smith," said Morfiks.

"Play it cool, then," the guide said. "But you were a man? A male?"

Morfiks nodded, and the guide said, "I was a girl. A woman, I mean. My name was Billie."

"Why tell me this?" he demanded suspiciously.

Billie came close to Morfiks and put her hands on his shoulders.

"Listen, Johnny boy," she whispered. "Those bastards think they got us behind the eight ball by putting us into these neuter bodies. But don't you believe it. There's more than one way of skinning a cat, if you know what I mean."

"I don't," Morfiks said.

Billie came even closer; her nose almost touched his. A face in a mirror.

"Inside, you're just the same," said Billie. "That's one thing They can't change without changing you so much you're no longer the same person. If They do that, They aren't punishing the same person, are They? So, you wouldn't exist any more, would you? And being here wouldn't be fair, would it?"

"I don't get it," Morfiks said. He took a step backwards; Billie took a step forwards.

"What I mean is, you and me, we're still male and female inside. When They, whoever They are, stripped off our old bodies, They had to leave us our brains and nervous systems, didn't They? Otherwise, we'd not be ourselves, right? They fitted our nervous systems into these bodies, made a few adjustments here and there, like shortening or increasing nerve paths to take care of a stature different than the one you had on Earth. Or pumping something inside our skulls to take care of brains being too small for the skulls They gave us."

"Yeah, yeah," Morfiks said. He knew what Billie was going to propose, or he thought he did. He was breathing hard; a tingle was running over his skin; a warmth was spreading out from the pit of his stomach.

"Well," said Billie, "I always heard that it was all in your head. And that's true. Of course, there's only so much you can do, and maybe it isn't as good as it was on You-Know-Where. But it's better than nothing. Besides, like they say, none of it's bad. It's all good, some is just better than others."

"You mean?"

"Just close your eyes," Billie crooned, "and imagine I'm a woman. I'll tell you how I looked, how I was stacked. And you think about it. Then you tell me how you looked, don't hold anything back, no need to be bashful here, describe everything down to the last detail. And I'll imagine how you were."

"Think it'll work?" Morfiks said.

Billie, her eyes closed, softly sang, "I know it will, baby. I've been around some since I came here."

"Yeah, but what about the punishment?"

Billie half-opened her eyes and said, scornfully, "Don't believe all that jazz, Johnny boy. Besides, even if They do catch you, it's worth it. Believe me, it's worth it."

"If only I thought I could put one over on Them," Morfiks said. "It'd be worth taking any risk."

Billie's answer was to kiss him. Morfiks, though he had to repress revulsion, responded. After all, it was only the bald head that made Billie look like a half-man.

They struggled fiercely and desperately; their kisses were as deep as possible.

SUDDENLY MORFIKS PUSHED Billie away from him.

"It's worse than nothing," he panted. "I think something's going to happen, but it never quite does. It's no use. Now I feel awful."

Billie came towards him again, saying, "Don't give up so easy, honey. Rome wasn't erected in a day. Believe me, you can do it. But you got to have faith."

"No, I'm licked," Morfiks said. "Maybe if you did look like a woman, instead of just a carbon copy of me. Then...no, that wouldn't be any good. I'm just not designed for the job; neither are you. They got us where it hurts."

Billie lost her half-smile; her face twisted.

"Where it hurts!" she shrilled. "Let me tell you, Buster, if you can't get your kicks being a man here, you can by hurting somebody! That's about all that's left!"

"What do you mean?" Morfiks said.

Billie laughed loudly and long. When she mastered herself, she said, "I'll tell you one good thing about looking like everybody else. Nobody knows what you really are inside. Or what you were on Earth. Well, I'll tell you about myself.

"I was a man!"

Morfiks sputtered. His fists clenched. He walked towards Billie.

But he did not strike her...him...it.

Instead, he smiled, and he said, "Well, let me tell you something. My real name was Juanita."

Billie became pale, then red.

"You...you!"

THE NEXT FEW days, Morfiks spent four hours each morning on the building of new houses. It was easy work. The walls and sections of the roof were brought in on wagons of brass pulled by citizens. Supervised by foremen, the laborers raised the walls, secured the bottoms to the brass foundation of the city with a quick-drying glue and then fastened the walls together by gluing down strips of the violet stuff at the corners of the walls.

Morfiks took his turn being a foreman for one day after he had gotten enough experience. He asked a citizen where the material for the houses and the rubber and the glue came from.

"And where's the food grown?"

The citizen looked around to make sure no one could hear them.

"The original brass sheets and rubber are supposed to have originated from the blind end of this universe," he said. "It's spontaneously created, flows like lava from a volcano."

"How can that be?" Morfiks said.

The citizen shrugged. "How should I know? But if you remember one of the theories of creation back on You-Know-Where, matter was supposed to be continuously created out of nothing. So if hydrogen atoms can be formed from nothing, why not brass and rubber lava?"

"But brass and rubber are organized configurations of elements and compounds!"

"So what? The structure of this universe orders it."

"And the food?"

"It's brought up on dumbwaiters through shafts which lead down to the underside. The peasants live there, citizen, and grow food and raise some kind of cattle and poultry."

"Gee, I'd like that," Morfiks said. "Couldn't I get a transfer down there? I'd like to work with the soil. It'd be much more interesting than this."

"If you were supposed to be a peasant, you'd have been transformed down there to begin with," the citizen said. "No, you're a citydweller, brother, and you'll stay one. You predetermined that, you know, in You-Know-Where."

"I had obligations," Morfiks said. "What'd you expect me to do, shirk them?"

"I don't expect nothing except to get out of here some day."

"You mean we can get out? How? How?"

"Not so loud with that *you,*" the citizen growled. "Yeah, or so we heard, anyway. We never saw a corpse but we heard about some of us dying. It isn't easy, though."

"Tell me how I can do it," Morfiks said. He grabbed the citizen's arm but the citizen tore himself loose and walked away swiftly.

Morfiks started to follow him, then could not identify him because he had mingled with a dozen others.

In the afternoons, Morfiks spent his time playing shuffleboard, badminton, swimming or sometimes playing bridge. The brass plastic cards consisted of two thicknesses glued together. The backs were blank, and the fronts were punched with codes indicating the suits and values. Then, after the evening meals in the communal halls, there were always neighborhood committee meetings. These were to settle any disputes among the local citizens. Morfiks could see no sense in them other than devices to keep the attendants busy and tire them out so that they would be ready to go to bed. After hours of wrangling and speech-making, the disputants were always told that the fault lay equally on both sides. They were to forgive each other, shake hands and make up. Nothing was really settled, and Morfiks was sure that the disputants still burned with resentments despite their protestations that all was now well with them.

What Morfiks found particularly interesting was the public prayer—if it could be called that—said by an O.D. before each meeting. It contained hints about the origins and reasons for this place and this life but was not specific enough to satisfy his curiosity.

"Glory be to the Protectors, who give us this life. Blessed be liberty, equality and fraternity. Praise be to security, conformity and certainty. None of these did we have on We-Know-Where, O Protectors, though we desired them mightily and strove always without success to attain them. Now we have them because we strove; inevitably we came here, glory be! For this cosmos was prepared for us and when we left that vale of slippery, slidery chaos, we squeezed through the walls and were formed in the template of passage, given these bodies, sexless, sinless, suitable. O Mighty Protectors, invisible but everywhere, we know that We-Know-Where is the pristine cosmos, the basic world, dirty, many-aspected, chaos under the form of seeming order, evil but necessary. The egg of creation, rotten but generative. Now, O Protectors, we are shaped forever in that which we cried for on that other unhappy universe..."

There was more but most of it was a repetition in different words. Morfiks, sitting in the brass pews, his head bowed, looked up at the smooth hemisphere of the ceiling and walls and the platform on which the O.D. stood. If he understood the O.D., he was bound here forever, immortal, each day like the next, each month an almost unvarying image of the preceding, year after year, century after century, millennia after millennia.

"Stability, Unseen but Everfelt Protectors. Stability! A place for everyone and everyone in a place!"

The O.D. was saying that there were such things as souls, a configuration of energy which exactly duplicated the body of the person when he had existed on We-Know-Where. It was indetectible by instruments there and so had been denied by many. But when one died there, the configuration was released from the attraction of the body, was somehow pushed from one universe into the next.

There were billions of these, all existing within the same space as the original universe but polarized and at angles to it. A "soul" went to that universe for which it had the most attraction.

Indeed, the universe to which it traveled had actually been created by men and women. The total cumulative effect of desire for just such a place had generated this place.

If Morfiks interpreted the vague statements of the O.D. correctly, the structure of this universe was such that when a "soul" or cohesive energy configuration came through the "walls," it naturally took the shape in which all citizens found themselves. It was like hot plastic being poured into a mold.

Morfiks dared question a citizen who claimed to have been here for a hundred years. "The O.D. said all questions have been settled, everything is explained. What's explained? I don't understand any more about the origins or reasons for things here than I did on We-Know-Where."

"So what's new?" the citizen said. "How can you understand the un-understandable? The main difference here is that you don't ask questions. There are many answers, all true, to one question, and this place is one answer. So quit bugging me. You trying to get me—uh, us—into trouble? Hey, O.D.!"

Morfiks hurried off and lost himself in a crowd before he could be identified. He burned with resentment at the implications of this world. Why should he be here? Sure, on We-Know-Where he had stayed with one company for 20 years, he had been a good family man, a pal to his kids, a faithful husband, a pillar of the best church in the neighborhood, had paid off his mortgages, joined the Lions, Elk, and Moose and the Masonic Lodge, the PTA, the Kiwanis, the Junior Chamber of Commerce and been a hard worker for the Democrats. His father before him had been a Democrat, and though he had had many misgivings about some of the policies, he had always followed the party line. Anyway, he was a right-wing Democrat, which made him practically the same thing as a left-wing Republican. He read the *Reader's Digest, Look, Life, Time, Wall Street Journal, Saturday Evening Post,* and had always tried to keep up with the bestsellers as recommended by the local newspaper reviewer. All this, not because he ready wanted it but because he felt that he owed it to his wife and kids and for the good of society. He had hoped that when he went "over yonder" he would be rewarded with a life with more freedom, with a number of unlimited avenues for the things he really wanted to do.

What were those things? He didn't remember now, but he was sure that they were not what was available here.

"There's been a mistake," he thought. "I don't belong here. Everything's all screwed up. I shouldn't be here. This is an error on somebody's part. I got to get out. But how can I get out of here any more than I could get out of We-Know-Where? There the only way out was suicide and I couldn't take that, my family would have been disgraced. Besides, I didn't feel like it.

"And here I can't kill myself. My body's too tough and there's nothing, no way for me to commit suicide. Drowning? That won't work. The river's too well guarded, and if you did slip by the guards long enough to drown, you'd be dragged out in no time at all and resuscitated. And then punished."

IV

ON THE FOURTH night, what he had been dreading happened. His punishment. He woke up in the middle of the night with a dull toothache. As the night went on, the ache became sharper. By dawn, he wanted to scream.

Suddenly, the batwings on his doorway flew open, and one of his neighbors (he presumed) stood in the room. He/she was breathing hard and holding his/her hand to his/her jaw.

"Did you do it?" said the neighbor in a shrill voice.

"Do what?" Morfiks said, rising from the couch-bed.

"Antisocial act," the intruder said. "If the culprit confesses, the pain will cease. After a while, that is."

"Did you do it?" Morfiks said. For all he knew, he might be talking to Billie again.

"Not me. Listen, newcomers often—always—commit crimes because of a mistaken notion a crime can't be detected. But the crime is always found out."

"There are newcomers who aren't born criminals," Morfiks said. Despite his pain, he intended to keep control too.

"Then you, and I mean *you*, won't confess?"

"The pain must be breaking some people apart," said Morfiks. "Otherwise, some wouldn't be using the second person singular."

"Singular, hell!" the citizen said, breaking two tabus with two words. "Okay, so it doesn't make much difference if you or me or the poor devil down the street did it. But I got a way of beating the game."

"And so bringing down more punishment on us?"

"No! Listen, I was a dental assistant on We-Know-Where. I know for a fact that you can forget one pain if you have a greater."

Morfiks laughed as much as his tooth would permit him, and he said, "So, what's the advantage there?"

The citizen smiled as much as his toothache would permit. "What I'm going to propose will hurt you. But it'll end up in a real kick. You'll enjoy your pain, get a big thrill out of it."

"How's that?" Morfiks said, thinking that the citizen talked too much like Billie.

"Our flesh is tough so we can't hurt each other too easily. But we can be hurt if we try hard enough. It takes perseverance, but then what doesn't that's worthwhile?"

The citizen shoved Morfiks onto the couch, and, before Morfiks could protest, he was chewing on his leg.

"You do the same to me," the citizen mumbled between bites. "I'm telling you, it's great! You've never had anything like it before."

Morfiks stared down at the bald head and the vigorously working jaws. He could feel a little pain, and his toothache did seem to have eased.

He said, "Never had anything like what?"

"Like blood," the citizen said. "After you've been doing this long enough, you'll get drunk on it."

"I don't know. There, uh, seems something wrong about this."

THE CITIZEN STOPPED gnawing.

"You're a greenhorn! Look at it this way. The protectors tell us to love one another. So you should love me. And you can show your love by helping me get rid of this toothache. And I can do the same for you. After a while, you'll be like all of us. You won't give a damn; you'll do anything to stop the pain."

Morfiks got into position and bit down hard. The flesh felt rubbery. Then he stopped and said, "Won't we get another toothache tomorrow because of what we're doing now?"

"We'll get an ache somewhere. But forget about tomorrow."

"Yeah," Morfiks said. He was beginning to feel more pain in his leg. "Yeah. Anyway, we can always plead we were just being social."

The citizen laughed and said, "How social can you get, huh?"

Morfiks moaned as his crushed nerves and muscles began to bleed. After a while, he was screaming between his teeth, but he kept biting. If he was being hurt, he was going to hurt the citizen even worse.

And what the hell, he was beginning to feel a reasonable facsimile to that which he had known up there on We-Know-Where.

Down in the Black Gang

I'm telling you this because I need your love. Just as you need mine, though you don't know it—yet. And because I can't make love to you as a human makes love to a human.

You'll know why when I've told you the true story. The story I first told was a lie.

You must know I'm not human, even if I do look just like one. Do humans sweat quicksilver?

You must know I can't make love to you. If you were Subsahara Sue, you'd have no trouble. But they'll be watching Sue, so I won't dare go near. No, I didn't mean that I prefer her. It's just...I don't want to get into subtleties. Anyway, Sue might turn me in, and if I'm caught, I'll be keelhauled. Let me tell you, keelhauling is no fun.

I need love almost as much as I need a hiding place. That's why I'm telling you. You, the first human to know. I need love. And forgiveness. Only, as you'll see...never mind...I'll tell you all about me. I have much explaining to do, and you may hate me.

Don't.

I need love.

The Rooster Rowdy had caused the trouble almost 2500 Earth-years ago.

I didn't know anything about it. None of the crew knew anything about it. You see, communication is instantaneous, but perception is no faster than light.

You don't see? Maybe you will as I go along.

The instruments on The Bridge had indicated nothing and would not for I-don't-want-to-tell-you-how-many-years. If the Quartermaster—let's call him

The Filamentous Wafter—had not been prowling that particular deck, hunting down ratio fixers, nobody would've known about it until it was too late.

As it was, it still might be too late.

The first I knew of the trouble was when the call came from The Bridge. *Directly.*

"Hello, engine room MWST4! Hello, engine room MWST4!"

Five minutes earlier, the call would not have been able to get through. The electric sparks, microwaves, and hot mercury drops—spinning like tops—would have warped transmission. They were flying all over inside our tent. Five hundred years had passed since Subsahara Sue and I had seen each other. Although we both worked in the same continent, my territory was the Berber-Semitic area, and Sue's was all the rest of Africa.

After finally getting permission to have leave together, we'd signed in at a Libyan seaside hotel. We spent most of our time on the beach, inside our tent, which was made of a material to confine the more explosive byproducts of our lovemaking. During half a millennium, we'd dormantized our attraction—notice I say, attraction, not love, if that'll make you feel any better—but even in dormancy attraction accumulates a trickle charge and 500 years builds up a hell of a lot of static. However, there's a large amount of resistance to overcome, and I'd been oscillating and Sue resonating for hours before our nodes touched.

The tourists on the beach must have wondered where the thunder was coming from on that cloudless day.

Afterwards, Sue and I lay quietly to make sure that no one had been alarmed enough to investigate our tent. When we talked, we talked about personal matters first, what we'd been doing, our loneliness, and so on. Then we talked shop. We chattered about philiac thrust/phobiac weight efficiency ratios, toleration tare, grief drag, heliovalves, and so on, and ended up by reminiscing about crewmen.

She said, "Who's in charge of cosmic bleedoff?"

The intercom bleeped.

"Hello, engine room MWST4! Hello, engine room MWST4!"

Groaning, I turned on the intercom, which looked just like a portable TV (for the benefit of humans). The "head" and part of the "shoulders" of The First Mate filled most of the screen, even though the camera must have been several thousand miles away. Behind him was a small part of The Bridge and a piece of abyss-black shadow edged by a peculiar white light. The Captain's tail.

That was all I cared to see of The Captain at any time. I'll never forget having to look at a closeup of his "mouth" when he chewed me—not literally, thank the stars—in A. H. 45. I have to admit that I deserved that savaging. I was lucky not to get keelhauled.

Oh, how I goofed up the Mahomet Follow-up! The black gangs all over The Ship had to sweat and slave, all leaves cancelled, until proper thrust could be generated.

The First Mate, seeing the mercury drip off me, roared, "Mecca Mike! What the bilge have you been doing? You oscillating at a time like this? You sleeping at the post again? You neglecting your duty *again?*"

"Sir, I'm on leave," I said. "So I couldn't be guilty of neglecting my duty. Besides, sir, I don't know what you mean by *again.* I was never courtmartialed, sir, and..."

"Silence!" he bellowed. Behind him, the tail of The Captain twitched, and I started to oscillate negatively.

"Why didn't you answer the all-stations alarm?"

"It didn't get through," I said. I added, weakly, "There must have been too much static and stuff."

The First Mate saw Subsahara Sue trying to hide behind me. He yelled, "So *there* you are! Why didn't you answer your phone?"

"Sir, I left it in the hotel," Sue said. "Since we'd be together, we decided we'd just take Mike's phone, and..."

"No wonder both of you are still in the black gang! No more excuses, now! Listen, while I tell you loud and clear!"

The Rooster Rowdy was responsible for the emergency.

I was surprised when I heard The First Mate mention him. I'd thought he was dead or had run away so far into the lower decks that he'd never be found until The Ship docked. He was one of the ring-leaders—in fact, he was The First Mate then—in the Great Mutiny 100,000 Earth-years ago. He was the only one to escape alive after The Captain and his faithfuls mopped up on the mutineers. And the Rooster Rowdy had been running, or hiding, ever since. Or so we thought.

He was called Rooster for very good reasons. His mounting lust had driven him out of hiding, and he'd tried to rape The Crystalline Sexapod.

A moment ago, I told you Sue had asked me who was in charge of cosmic bleedoff. I would have told her that The Crystalline Sexapod was in charge if we hadn't been interrupted. The Sexapod had her station at that moment inside a quasar galaxy, where she had just finished setting up the structure of a new heliovalve. The Rooster Rowdy was near enough to sense her, and he came galloping in, galactic light bouncing off the trillion trillion facets of his spinning three-organ body, and he rammed through sextillions of sextillions of stellar masses and gases and just ruined the galaxy, just ruined it.

The Crystalline Sexapod put up a good fight for her virtue, which was the same thing as her life—I haven't time to go into biological-moral details—but in the process she completed the wreckage of the galaxy and so wrecked the heliovalve and wasted a century and a half of time. She took off for the lower decks, where, for all anybody knew, she might still be running with the Rooster Rowdy hot (2500° F) after her.

The wrecked heliovalve meant that there was no bleedoff of phobiac drag in that sector or in a quarter of all of the sectors, since this valve was the master valve in a new set-up intended to increase efficiency of bleedoff by 32.7 percent. And that really messed up our velocity.

Fortunately, The Quartermaster happened to be in the lower decks, where he was hunting ratio fixers. A ratio fixer, I'll explain, is a creature that lives in the interstices between ratios. Thus, it's compelled to be moving on, can't stay in one place long, otherwise it'll lose its foothold and fall. If it stands still very long, one of the quotients—analogous to a human foot—dwindles, and the other expands. The ratio fixer, like any form of life, wants security, so it tries to fix ratios (freeze them). Its efforts to keep from falling messes up proportions and causes The Ship's bulkheads and sometimes even the hull to buckle.

The Ship's shape, size, and mass are in a constant state of flux, but generally controlled flux. And if these are changed without The Bridge finding out about them in time, the vectors of velocity, direction, etcetera, are changed.

Using human analogies, ratio fixers might be compared to the rats in a ship. Or, better, to barnacles on a hull. Or maybe to both.

The Quartermaster had caught one and was choking it with its filaments when it caught sight of the wrecked heliovalve and of The Rooster Rowdy chasing The Sexapod through a hatchway into the depths. He notified The Bridge at once, and the all-stations alarm went out.

Now I understood why The First Mate was talking directly to me instead of the message being filtered down through sub-to-the-2nd-power officers and petty officers. With this emergency, it would take a long time for an order from The Captain to reach every engine room if it went through normal procedure.

But I had not, of course, understood completely. Or at all. I just thought I did because I was too awed and stunned to be thinking properly.

The Mate thundered, "In the name of The Port! You better not foul this one up!"

"I'll do my best, sir, as always," I said. Then, "Foul what one up, sir?"

"Idiot! Nincompoop! I'm not speaking directly to you just to give you a pep talk! A Thrust Potential has been detected in your engine room!"

"A Thr-Thr-Thrust Po-Po-Potential! In this area? But—"

"Imbecile! Not in *your* area, what is it, the Semitic? But it's your specialty! According to the message, it's in the Southern California area, wherever in bilge that is!"

"But what do I have to do with that, sir?"

"Stoker, if we weren't in such a mess, and if the Thrust Potential wasn't so promising, and if I didn't have to contact 10,000 other promising TP areas, I'd have you up here on The Bridge and flay you alive! You don't ask questions while I'm talking! Remember that, Stoker!"

"Yes, sir," I said humbly.

The First Mate then became very business-like. Aside from a few numbskulls, coprolite-heads, and other terms, he addressed me as one entrusted with a great task and with the abilities to carry it out. That is, if I had learned anything from experience. He did remind me that I had not only screwed up the Mahomet Follow-up, I had blown the whole Ancient Egyptian Monotheist Deal.

(I was called Ikhnaton Ike and Pharaoh Phil by my chief engineer for a long time afterwards.)

The First Mate was, however, kind enough to say that I had shown much skill in the Follow-up to the Burning Bush Business.

Beware The First Mate when he's kind. I said to myself, "What's he working up to?"

I soon found out. It was the last thing I'd expected. It was a transfer to the Southern California area and a promotion to engineer, first class. I was staggered. The chief engineer and several engineer's mates and a number of very competent stokers operated in that area. In fact, there were more black gang members there than in any area of Earth.

"The chief engineer's had a breakdown," The First Mate said, although he did not have to explain anything. "He's on his way to sick bay now. This report says there's something about that area that generates psychic collapse. A distortion of psychomagnetic lines of force. However, as you know, or should know, you ignoramus, this kind of field also compensates by generating thrust-potential impulses. The Northeast section of this—what's it called? U.S.A.—has a similar distortion. Both are danger areas for our engines. But, on the other hand, you don't get anything good from a safe neutral area."

"Thanks for the elementary lecture," I said inside my head, which was a safe, though not neutral, place for my retort.

A few minutes later, I had finished saying a sorrowful good-bye to Sue and was checking out of the hotel.

"Why should you be transferred to Beverly Hills, California?" Sue said. "It may be largely Jewish in population, but the citizens are basically English speakers. They don't think Semitically, like your Arabs, Abyssinians, and Israelis."

"That's not the only puzzling thing," I said. "The Thrust Potential is non-Semitic. That is, it's not even descended from Semitic speakers."

The engineers and stokers in that area must all have become somewhat unstable, too. Otherwise, they surely would have been used. The thinking of The Bridge was, Let's shoot in Mecca Mike. He's fouled up, but he also had some great successes. Perhaps this time he'll come through. He's the best we have, anyway, The Dock preserve us!

The First Mate told me that I had better come through. Or else...

There would be officers watching my work, but they wouldn't interfere unless I was obviously ruining an "engine" beyond repair.

If I came through, if I developed the badly needed Thrust Potential, I'd be promoted. Probably to chief engineer.

The situation for The Ship was much worse than I'd guessed. Otherwise, they'd have let me take an airliner. But orders were to get me to California with utmost speed. I drove into the Libyan countryside during the daylight. At noon the saucer-shaped vehicle landed, picked me up, and took off at 30 G. It socked into its base fifty miles west of Phoenix, Arizona, with Air Force jets scrambling from Luke Field. They neither saw the ship nor the base, of course, and I drove into Phoenix in what looked like a 1965 Buick and took a plane into Los Angeles.

Coming down over Los Angeles must have been disheartening to the other passengers. They saw the great greenish-gray tentacles, the exhaled poison, hanging over the big complex. I had my special "glasses" on, and what I saw was encouraging, at least momentarily. Down them, in the blackness which is phobias drag, were a dozen fairly large sparks and one huge spark. That big spark, I knew, must be in Beverly Hills.

There, if all went well—it seldom does—was the potential to develop a thrust which, combined with the thrusts in existence and with those being developed on other worlds, would, hopefully, cancel the drag caused by the wrecking of the bleedoff heliovalve. And so the vitally needed velocity would be ours.

Can anything good come out of Nazareth?

Can anything good be in Beverly Hills?

History has answered the first question. The future would answer the second.

I told the taxi driver at the airport to take me to a street which angled south off of Wilshire between Doheny Drive and Beverly Drive. This was lined with dry-looking maples. The block where the taxi let me off was, in a sense, in the "slums" of Beverly Bills. Relatively speaking, of course. Both sides of the street in this block were occupied by apartment buildings, some only five years old and others about 25 to 35 years old. The apartments in the new buildings rented from $350 to $650 a month and so were considered low-rent in Beverly Bills. The apartments in the old buildings averaged about $135 a month.

My Thrust Potential, my TP, was in the second story of an older building. I had the cab park across the street from it, and I went inside a newer, more expensive apartment building. This had a VACANCY, 1 BDRM, FURN., NO PETS, NO CHILDREN sign on the lawn. I put down three months' rent in cash, which upset Mrs. Klugel, the landlady. She had always dealt in checks. I signed the lease and then went back to the taxi to get my bags.

My second-story apartment was almost directly across the street from my TP and almost as high as her apartment. I carried my three bags up to it. One was full of clothes, the second full of money, and the third crammed with my equipment. Mrs. Klugel stood in the vestibule. She was a heavy short woman about 65 with orange-dyed hair, a nose like a cucumber, and a clown's mouth. Her black-rimmed eyes widened as I went lightly up the staircase with a huge bag in each hand and one under my arm. "So you're a strong man in some act already?" she said.

I replied that I was not a strong man, professionally, that is. I was a writer who intended to write a novel about Hollywood.

"So why don't you live in Hollywood?"

"By Hollywood, I mean this whole area around here," I said, sweeping my hand around.

She was such a lonely old lady, she was difficult to get rid of. I said I had work to do, and I would talk to her later. As soon as she shut the door, I readjusted the antigrav belt around my waist under my shirt. My two thousand pounds of dense metal-shot protein would have buckled the floor if I hadn't had the belt operating. Then I took out my equipment and set it up.

I was nervous; quicksilver beaded from me and fell onto the floor. I made a mental note to clean up the stuff before I left the apartment. Mrs. Klugel looked as if she'd snoop around during my absences, and it certainly would be difficult to explain mercury drops on the floor.

The set-up for my work was this. Across the street, in the 25-year-old run-down building, were four apartments. My concern was the upper story on the right side, facing the street. But I soon found out that the apartment just below was also to be intimately involved.

The apartment upstairs was reached by climbing a steep series of steps, carpeted with frayed and faded material. A long hall at the top of the stairs ran the length of the building, ending in a bathroom at its far end. Off the hallway, starting next to the bathroom, were doors leading to a bedroom, another bedroom, the doorway to the back entrance, the doorway to a tiny utility room, and the doorway to the living room. The utility room and living room connected to the kitchen.

The back bedroom was occupied by Diana, the 20-year-old divorced mother, and her 20-month-old child, Pam. The grandparents, Tom and Claudia Bonder, slept in the other bedroom. Tom also did his writing in this room. Claudia was 45 and Tom was 49.

When I looked through the spec-analyzers, via the tap-beam, I saw the baby, Pam, as the bright light I had seen coming in over Los Angeles. She was the big Thrust Potential.

Sometimes the light was dimmed. Not because its source was weakened. No. It darkened because of the hatred pouring out of the grandfather.

This black cataract was, seemingly, directed mainly at the people in the apartment below. If hatred were water, it would have drowned the people below. And, if they were what Tom Bonder said they were, they deserved drowning, if not worse.

Tom Bonder's hatred, like most hatreds, was not, however, simple.

None of the hatreds in that building, or in any of the buildings in Beverly Hills, and believe me, there were hatreds in every building, were simple.

I digress. Back to that particular building.

Watching that building was like watching the Northern Lights during a meteor shower on the Fourth of July. I ignored the pyrotechnic displays of the tenants on the other side of the building. They had little to do with the "stoking" and the follow-up.

Tom Bonder, ah, there was a splendid spectacle! Although he had been depressed in his youth, at which time he must have radiated heavy-drag black, like smoke from Vesuvius, he had semi-converted his youthful depression into middle-aged anger. Reversed the usual course of psychic events, you might say. Now he looked like Vesuvius in eruption.

Bonder, the grandfather, was determined not to fail as a grandfather just because he had failed as a father, husband, lover, son, teacher, writer—and you name it.

And truly, he had failed, but not as badly as he thought, or, I should say, desired, since he lusted for defeat. Rage poured out of him day and night, even when, especially when, he was sleeping.

What most infuriated him was the uproar beating upwards day and night from the Festigs downstairs. The Festigs were a father, 40 years old, a mother,

28, and a daughter, Lisa, two. From the time they arose, anywhere from 9:30 to 11:30, until they went to bed, midnight or 1:00, or later, the mother was shouting and bellowing and singing and clapping her hands sharply and the little girl was screaming with glee but usually wailing or screeching with frustration and anger. The father was silent most of the time; but he was like an old sunken Spanish galleon, buried in black silt, with his treasures, his pieces-of-eight and silver ingots and gold crosses, spilled out of a breach in the hull and only occasionally revealed when the currents dredged away some mud. Oh, he was depressed, depressed, which is to say he was a very angry man indeed. The bleak heavy stuff flowed from Myron Festig like a Niagara fouled with sewage. But sometimes, out of boredom, as he sat on his chair in the living room, he groaned mightily, and the groan went up and out the windows and into the windows of the apartment upstairs.

And Tom Bonder would jump when he heard the groan and would quit muttering and raging under his breath. He would be silent, as one lion may fall silent for a moment when he hears the roar of another from far away.

The screaming joys and buzzsaw tantrums were enough for the Bonders (not to mention the next-door neighbors) to endure. But the child also had the peculiar habit of stomping her feet if she ran or walked. The sound vibrated up through the walls and the floors and through the bed and into the pillow-covered ears of Tom Border. Even if he managed to get to sleep, he would be awakened a dozen times by the footstompings or by the screams and the bellows.

He would sit up and curse. Sometimes, he would loosen his grip on his fear of violence and would shout out of the window: "Quiet down, down there, you barbarians, illiterate swine! We have to get up early to go to work! We're not on relief, you bloodsucking inconsiderate parasites!"

The reference to relief, if nothing else, should have turned Myron Festig's depression into rage, because the Festigs were one of the few people in Beverly Hills living on relief. The relief came from the county welfare and from money borrowed from Mrs. Festig's mother and doctor brothers. Occasionally, Myron sold a cartoon or took a temporary job. But he was very sensitive about the welfare money, and he would have been astounded to learn that the Bonders knew about it. The Borders, however, had been informed about this by the manager's wife.

Rachel Festig, the wife and mother, was revealed in the analyzer as intermittent flashes of white, which were philiac thrust, with much yellow, that is, deeply repressed rage sublimated as sacrificial or martyred love. And there was the chlorine-gas green of self-poisonous self-worship.

But there was the bright white light of the Bonder baby, Pam. Now that I was near it, I saw it split into two, as a star seen by the naked eye will become a double star in the telescope. The lesser star, as it were, radiated from Lisa Festig. All infants, unless they're born psychotic, have this thrust. Lisa's, unfortunately, was waning, and its brightness would be almost entirely gone in a year or so. Her mother's love was extinguishing it in a dozen ways.

But the far brighter white, the almost blinding Thrust Potential, radiated from the Bonder granddaughter. She was a beautiful, strong, healthy, good-humored, intelligent, extremely active, and very loving baby. She was more than enough to cause her grandparents to love her beyond normal grandparental love. But they had reason to especially cherish this baby. The father had dropped out of sight in West Venice, not that anybody was looking for him.

Furthermore, both Claudia and Tom felt that they had been psychically distorted by their parents and that they, in turn, had psychically bent their daughter, Diana. But Pam was not going to be fouled up, neurotic, nearneurotic, unhappy, desolate, and so on. At the moment, both the elder Borders were going to psychoanalysts to get their psyches hammered out straight on the anvil of the couch.

Neither the daughter nor Mrs. Bonder, though they figured significantly and were to be used by me, were as important in my plans as Tom Bonder.

Why? Because he was an atheist who had never been able to shake himself free of his desire to know a God, a hardheaded pragmatist who lusted for mysticism as an alcoholic lusts for the bottle he has renounced, a scoffer of religions whose eyes became teary whenever he watched the hoakiest, most putridly sentimental religious movies on TV with Bing Crosby, Barry Fitzgerald and Humphrey Bogart as priests. This, plus the tiniest spark of what, for a better term, is called pre-TP, and his rage, made me choose him. As a matter of fact, he was the main tool I had for the only plan I had.

Rachel Festig thought of herself as the Great Mother. Tom Bonder agreed with that to the extent that he thought she was a Big Mother. Rachel's idea of a mother was a woman with enormous breasts dripping the milk of kindness, compassion, and, occasionally, passion. The Great Mother also had a well-rounded belly, wide hips, thick thighs, and hands white with baking flour. The Great Mother spent every waking moment with the child to the exclusion of everything else except cooking and some loving with the husband to keep him contented.

Now there was a Mother!

Myron needed to be dependent, to be, at 40, an invertebrate, a waxingly fat invertebrate. Yet he wanted to be a world-famous cartoonist, a picture-satirist of the modern age, especially in its psychic sicknesses. Recently, in a burst of backbone, he had stayed up all night for several weeks, and completed an entire book of cartoons about group therapy. He knew the subject well, since he was a participant in a group and also had private sessions once a week. Both were paid for by arrangement with the county and his brother-in-law, the doctor.

The cartoon book was published and sold well locally, then the excitement died down and he subsided into a great roll of unbonestiffened protoplasm. Repression blackened him onto nacre. He gained a hunger for food instead of fame, and so he ate and swelled.

Torn Bonder worked daytimes as an electronic technician at a space industry plant in Huntington Beach, and evenings and weekends he wrote fast-action private-eye novels for paperback publishers and an occasional paperback western.

He loathed his technician job and wanted to go into full-time fiction writing. However, he was having enough trouble writing part-time now because of the uproar downstairs.

I used the tap-beam and sight-beam to listen and look into the apartments and also to eavesdrop on Bonder's sessions with the analyst. I knew he ascribed his problems to a too-early and too-harsh toilet training, to a guilt caused by conflict between his childhood curiosity about sex and his parents' harsh repression of it and so on. His main problem throughout most of his life had been a rigid control over himself. He thought himself a coward because he had always avoided violence, but he was finding out in therapy that he feared that he might become too violent and lose his self-control.

Fortunately, he was now getting rid of some of his anger in little daily spurts, but, unfortunately, not swiftly enough.

He was always on the verge of going berserk.

Berserk! That was the key to my "stoking."

The Ship must have been losing speed even worse than we of the crew had been told. About six months after I got into Beverly Hills, I received a call from The First Mate again.

"How's the set-up coming along?"

"As well as can be expected," I said. "You know you can't stoke too fast, sir. The engine might overheat or blow."

"I know that, you cabin-boy reject!" he bellowed so loudly that I turned the volume down. Old Mrs. Klugel quite often kept her ear pressed to the tenants' doors.

I said, "I'll use more pressure, sir, beat it'll have to be delicately applied. I sure wouldn't want to wreck this little engine. Her nimbus looks as if she could provide enormous thrust, if she's brought along properly."

"Three hours you get," The First Mate said. "Then we have to have 1,000,000 T units."

Three hours of Ship's time was 30 Earth-years. Even if I got the stoking done quickly, I had a hell of a lot of hard mercury-sweating work in the next 30 years. I promised I'd do my best, and The First Mate said that that had better be better than good enough, and he signed off.

Tom Bonder and Myron Festig were working themselves closer to that condition I'd been working for. The Festig child was stomping her feet and screaming all day and until one in the morning, and the inability to get sleep was putting black circles around Tom Bonder's eyes. And red halos of wrath around him.

Myron Festig was deep in the sludge pit of despond. His latest cartoon had been turned down by *Playboy.* He had just been fired from a job as a cheese salesman. His mother-in-law was threatening to visit them for a long time. His brother-in-law, the doctor, was needling him because he wasn't making a steady income, aside from welfare payments. And Rachel, his wife, when not chewing him out for his inability to hold a job, was crying that they should have another baby. They needed a son; she would deliver him a boy to make him proud.

The last thing Myron wanted was another mouth to stuff, and, though he dared not say it, another noisy mouth and big heavy feet to distract him from his cartooning.

Tom Bonder would have agreed with this. He was, he told his wife, slowly being herded to suicide or homicide. He could not take much more of this. And more frequently, as if in jest, he would open a drawer in the kitchen and take out a hand-axe, which he had brought with him when he moved from the Midwest. And he would say, "One more night of thumping from Little Miss Buffalo Stampede, one more night of bellowing 'Myron!' or 'Rachel', and I go downstairs and chop up the whole swinish bunch!"

Isis wife and daughter would grin, nervously, and tell him he shouldn't even joke like that.

"I'm fantasizing!" he'd cry. "My headshrinker says it's good therapy to imagine slaughtering them, very healthy! It relieves the tensions! As long as I can fantasize, I won't take action! But when I can't fantasize, beware! Chop! Chop! Off with their heads! Blood will flow!" And he would swing the axe while he grinned.

Sometimes, exasperated beyond endurance, he would stomp his foot on the floor to advise the Festigs that their uproar was intolerable. Sometimes, the Festigs would quiet down for a while. More often, they ignored the hints from above or even increased the volume. And, once, Myron Festig, enraged that anyone should dare to object to his family's activities (and also taking out against the Bonders the rage he felt against himself and his family) slammed his foot angrily against the floor and cried out.

Mr. Bonder, startled at first, then doubly enraged, slammed his foot back. Both men then waited to see what would happen. Nothing, however, followed.

And this and other events or nonevents are difficult to explain. Why didn't Tom Bonder just go down and have a talk with the Festigs? Why didn't he communicate directly, face to face, with words and expressions?

I've watched human beings for a million years (my body was shaped like a ground ape's then), and I still don't know exactly why they do or don't do certain things.

Bonder's overt problem was communication. Rather, the lack thereof. He kept too rigid a control over himself to talk freely. Which may be why he turned to writing.

He probably did not go down to tell the Festigs haw they were disturbing him because, to him, even a little anger meant a greater one would inevitably follow, and he could not endure the thought of this. And so he avoided a direct confrontation.

Yet, he was getting more and more angry every day; his safety valve was stuck, and his boilers were about to blow.

I can tell by your expression what you're thinking. Why don't we build "engines" which will automatically put out the required thrust?

If this were possible, it would have been done long ago.

The structure of the universe, that is, of The Ship, requires, for reasons unknown to me, that philiac thrust be generated only by sentient beings with free will. Automatons can't love. If love is built into, or programmed into, the automaton, the love means nothing in terms of thrust. It's a pseudolove, and so a pseudothrust results, and this is no thrust at all.

No. Life has to be created on viable planets, and it must evolve until it brings forth a sentient being. And this being may then be manipulated, pulled and pushed, given suggestions and laws, and so forth. But the blazing white thrust is not easy to come by, and the black drag is always there. It's a hideous problem to solve. And hideous means often have to be used.

And so, obeying my orders, I speeded up the stoking. Far faster than I liked. Fortunately, a number of events occurring about the same time three months later helped me, and everything converged on one day, a Thursday.

The evening before, Myron Festig had gone on the Joseph Beans TV Show to get publicity for his group-therapy cartoon book, although he had been warned not to do so. As a result, he was stingingly insulted by Beans and his doltish audience, was called sick and was told that group therapy was a mess of mumbo-jumbo. Myron was smarting severely from the savage putdown.

On the next day, Tom Bonder was two and a half hours late getting home. The motor of his car had burned out. This was the climax to the increasing, almost unendurable, frustration and nerve-shredding caused by the two-hour five-day-a-week round-trip from Beverly Hills to Huntington Beach and back on the freeway. In addition, his request for a transfer to the nearby Santa Monica plant was lost somewhere on the great paper highway of interdepartmental affairs of the astronautics company, and the entire request would have to be initiated again in triplicate.

Two days before, Myron Festig had been fired from another job. He'd made several mistakes in giving change to customers because he was thinking of ideas for cartoons.

Tom Bonder found his wife did not want to listen to his tale of trouble with the car. She had had a setback in therapy and was also upset about some slights her employer had given her.

After tapping in on Myron's account to his wife of how he lost his job, I made an anonymous phone call to the welfare office and told them that Myron Festig had been working without reporting the fact to them. They had called Myron to come down and explain himself.

Myron Festig's brother-in-law, the doctor, wanted part of his loan back. But the Festigs were broke.

Tom Bonder, on coming home, was received with a letter of rejection. The editor to whom he had sent his latest private-eye thriller had turned it down with a number of nasty remarks. Now Bonder wouldn't be able to pay all of next month's bills.

Myron Festig's mother, the day before, had called him and begged him, for the hundredth time, to accept his aged father's offer to become his junior partner in his business. He should quit being a nogoodnik "artist" who couldn't support his wife and child. Or, for that matter, himself.

Moreover, and this as much as anything sent him skiing out of control on the slopes of despair, his psychiatrist had gone on a two-weeks' vacation in Mexico.

And, that very morning, Myron got word that one of the therapy group, a lovely young woman whom Myron was becoming very fond of, had killed herself with a .45 automatic.

Tom Bonder flushed the toilet, and it filled up and ran all over the bathroom floor. Bonder suppressed his desire to yell out obscenities and denunciations of his landlord because he did not want to upset his granddaughter, and he called the plumber. This incident was the latest in a long series of blown fuses in the old and overloaded electrical circuits and the backing of dirty waters in the old and deteriorating plumbing.

Rachel Festig told Myron that he had to get another job and quickly. Or she was going to work, and he could stay home to take care of the child. Myron sat in the big worn easy chair and just looked at her, as if he were an oyster with five o'clock shadow and she were a strange fish he was trying to identify. Rachel became hysterical and raved for an hour (I could hear her across the street through my open window, I didn't need my tap-beam) about the psychic damage to Lisa if her mother left her to go to work. Myron was so silent and unresponsive that she became frightened.

The plumbers finally left. The baby, who had been awakened by their activities, finally went back to sleep. Tom Bonder sat down at his desk in the crowded bedroom to start writing a story for a mystery magazine. If he wrote it quickly enough and the editors did not dawdle reading it, and bought it, and then did not dawdle in sending his money, he might have enough to pay next month's bills. He wrote two paragraphs, using his pencil so that the typewriter wouldn't wake up the baby.

The thumping of Lisa's feet and her screaming as she ran back and forth from room to room disturbed him even more than usual. But he clamped his mental teeth and wrote on.

Then Rachel began to march along behind Lisa, and she sang loudly (she always said she could have been a great singer if she hadn't married Myron), and she clapped her hands over and over.

It was now nine p.m. The baby stirred in her crib. Then, after some especially heavy crashing of Lisa's feet, Pam cried out. Tom's daughter came into the back bedroom and tried to quiet her down.

Tom Bonder reared up from his desk, his flailing hand scattering papers onto the floor. He stalked into the kitchen and opened a bottom drawer. As usual, it stuck, and he had to get down on his knees and yank at it. This time, he did not mutter something about fixing it someday.

He took out the hand-axe and walked through the front room, hoping his wife would see it.

She curled her lip and said, "Don't be more of an ass than God made you, Tom. You're not scaring anybody with that."

And then, "Why aren't you writing? You said you couldn't talk to me because you had to write."

He glared at her and said nothing. The reasons for his anger were so obvious and justified that she must be deliberately baiting him because of her own turmoiled feelings.

Finally, he grunted, "That menagerie downstairs."

"Well, if you have to fantasize, you don't have to hold that axe. It makes me nervous. Put it away."

He went back into the kitchen. At that moment, I phoned.

His wife said, "Get the phone. If anybody wants me, I'm out to the store. I don't feel like talking to anyone tonight, except you, and you won't talk to me."

Violently, he picked up the phone and said, harshly, "Hello!"

I was watching the whole scene directly on the tap-beam, of course, and at the same time was displaying the Festigs' front room on a viewer.

I mimicked Myron Festig's voice. "This is Myron. Would you please be more quiet up there? We can't think with all that noise."

Tom Bonder yelled an obscenity and slammed down the phone. He whirled, ran out into the hall, and charged down the steps with the axe still in his hand.

Rachel and Lisa had stopped their noisy parade, and Myron had risen from his chair at the thunder on the staircase.

I had started to dial the Festigs' number as soon as I'd finished with Tom Bonder. The phone rang when Bonder reached the bottom of the steps. Myron, who was closest to the phone, answered.

I mimicked the voice of Myron's mother. I said, "Myron! If you don't go into business with your father at once, I'll never ever have anything any more to do with you, my only son! God help me! What did I ever do to deserve a son like you? Don't you love your aged parents?" And I hung up.

Tom Bonder was standing outside the Festigs' door with the axe raised when I ran out of my apartment building. I was wearing a policeman's uniform, and I was ready for Mrs. Klugel if she should see me. I meant to tell her I was going to a costume ball.

She did not, however, come out of her room since her favorite TV show was on.

I walked swiftly across the street, and not until I got on the sidewalk did Tom Bonder see me.

He could have been beating on the door with his axe in a maniac effort to get inside and kill the Festigs. But his abnormally powerful self-control had, as I'd hoped, reasserted itself. He had discharged much of his anger by the obscenity, the energy of aggression in charging down the stairs, and the mere act of raising the axe to strife the door. Now he stood like the Tin Woodman when the rain rusted his joints, motionless, his eyes on the door, his right arm in the air with his axe in his hand.

I coughed; he broke loose. He whirled and saw the uniform by the nearby street light. My face was in the shadows.

I said, "Good-evening," and started back across the street as if I were going home after work. I heard the door slam and knew that Tom Bonder had run back into his apartment and doubtless was shaking with reaction from his anger and from relief at his narrow escape from being caught in the act by a policeman.

Once in my apartment, I used the tap-beams to observe the situation. Tom Bonder had opened the door and tossed the axe onto the floor in front of the Festigs' door.

It was his obscure way of communicating. Quit driving me crazy with your swinish uproar, or the next time...

I'm sure that the dropping of the axe before the Festigs was, at the same time, an offer of peace. Here is the axe which I have brandished at you. I no longer want it; you may have it.

And there was a third facet to this seemingly simple but actually complicated gesture, as there is to almost every human gesture. He knew well, from what Rachel had told his daughter, and from what he had observed and heard, that Myron was on as high and thin a tightrope as he. So, the flinging down of the axe meant also: Pick it up and use it.

Tom Bonder did not realize this consciously, of course.

I had thought that Tom Bonder might do just what he had done. I knew him well enough to chance that he would. If he had acted otherwise, then I would have had to set up another situation.

Myron opened the door; he must have heard the thump of the hatchet and Bonder's steps as he went back up the stairs. He picked it up after staring at it for a full minute and returned to his easy chair. He sat down and put the axe on his lap. His fat fingers played with the wooden handle and a thumb felt along the edge of the head.

Rachel walked over to him and bent over so her face was only about three inches from his. She shouted at him; her mouth worked and worked.

I didn't know what she was saying because I had shut off the audio of their beam. I was forcing myself to watch, but I didn't want to hear.

This was the first time I had cut off the sound during a "stoking". At that moment, I didn't think about what I was doing or why. Later, I knew that this was the first overt reflection of something that had been troubling me for a long long time.

All the elements of the situation (I'm talking about the Festigs, now) had worked together to make Myron do what he did. But the final element, the fuse, was that Rachel looked remarkably like his mother and at that moment was acting and talking remarkably like her.

The black clouds which usually poured out of him had been slowly turning a bright red at their bases. Now the red crept up the clouds, like columns of mercury in a bank of thermometers seen through smoke. Suddenly, the red exploded, shot through the black, overwhelmed the black, dissolved it in scarlet, and filled the room with a glare.

Myron seemed to come up out of the chair like a missile from its launching pad. He pushed Rachel with one hand so hard that she staggered back halfway across the room, her mouth open, jelled in the middle of whatever she had been screaming.

He stepped forward and swung.

I forced myself to watch as he went towards the child.

When Myron Festig was through with the two, and he took a long time, or so it seemed to me, he ran into the kitchen. A moment later, he came back out of the kitchen door with a huge butcher knife held before him with both hands, the point against the solar plexus. He charged across the room, slammed into the wall and rammed its hilt into the wall. The autopsy report was to state that the point had driven into his backbone.

I turned the audio back on then, although I could hear well enough through my apartment window. A siren was whooping some blocks away. The porchlight had been turned on, and the manager, his wife, and juvenile daughter were standing outside the Festigs' door. Presently, the door to the Bonders' apartment opened, and Mrs. Bonder came out. Tom Bonder and Diana followed a minute later.

The manager opened the door to the Festigs' apartment. Tom Bonder looked into the front room between the manager and the side of the doorway.

He swayed, then stepped back until he bumped into Mrs. Bonder. The blood was splashed over the walls, the floors, and the furniture. There were even spots of it on the ceiling.

The broken handle of the axe lay in a pool of blood.

I turned the beam away from the Festigs and watched Tom Bonder. He was on his knees, his arms dangling, hands spread open stiffly, his head thrown back, and his eyes rolled up. His mouth moved silently.

Then there was a cry. Pam, the baby, had gotten out of her crib and was standing at the top of the steps and looking down at the half-open door to the porch and crying for her mother. Diana ran up to her and held her in her arms and soothed her.

At the cry, Tom Bonder shook. No nimbus except the gray of sleep or trance or semi-consciousness had welled from him. But then a finger of white, a slim shaft of brightness, extended from his head. In a minute, he was enveloped in a starry blaze. He was on his feet and taking Mrs. Bonder by the hand and going up the steps. The police car stopped before the building. The siren died, but the red light on top of the car kept flashing.

I packed my stuff in my three bags and went out the back entrance. It was now highly probable that Tom Bonder would take the course I had planned. And, since he was a highly imaginative man, he would influence his granddaughter, who, being a Thrust Potential, would naturally incline toward the religious and the mystical. And toward love. And those in charge of her development would see that she came into prominence and then into greatness in later life. And, after the almost inevitable martyrdom, they would bring about the proper followup. Or try to.

They would. I wouldn't.

I was through. I had had enough of murder, suffering and bloodshed. A million, many millions, of Festigs haunted me. Somehow, and I know the crewmen and officers say it's impossible, I'd grown a heart. Or I'd had it given to me, in the same way the Tin Woodman got his heart.

I'd had enough. Too much. That is why I deserted and why I've been hiding for all these years. And why I've managed to get three others of the black gang to desert, too.

Now we're being hunted down. The hunters and the hunted are not known by you humans. You engines, so they call you.

But I fled here, and I met you, and I fell in love with you, not in a quite-human way, of course. Now you know who and what I am. But don't turn away. Don't make me leave you.

I love you, even if I can't make love to you.

Help me. I'm a mutineer, but unlike The Rooster Rowdy, I'm interested in mutinying because of you humans, not because I want to be first, to be The Captain.

We must take over. Somehow, there has to be a better way to run The Ship!

The Voice of the Sonar in My Vermiform Appendix

A POLYTROPICAL PARAMYTH

Whiteness blinked within Barnes. The whiteness was like a traffic signal light from which the red plastic lens had fallen.

It was his resonance again. There was too much whiteness around him. The laboratory walls and ceiling were fishbelly white. The floor was penguin-breast pseudo-marble. The two doctors wore white.

But Miss Mbama, the technician, though she, too, wore white, was black. This was why Barnes kept turning his revolvable chair to stay zeroed in on her. Then the bursts of whiteness in his brain were reduced in brightness and frequency.

Miss Mbama (née Kurtz) was a tall well-built young woman with a towering bush of *au naturel* hair and West African Bush Negro features modified by some alpine bush Bavarian ancestors. She was good-looking and should have been used to stares. But his embarrassed her. Her expression told that she was thinking of asking him why he rotated like a weathercock with her always the wind. But he had decided not to answer her. He was tired of explaining that he could not explain.

Electrodes were taped to his scalp, over his heart, and over his appendix. (He wore only pajama pants.) Wires ran from the electrodes to the instruments on the far side of the room. The cathode ray tubes flashed squiggles, dots, sine waves, square waves, and complex Lissajous figures.

One instrument was emitting: ping! ping! ping! Like the sounds the super-submarine in the old *Journey to the Bottom of the Sea* TV show emitted as it cruised fifty miles under the surface in search of the giant sentient roaring radish.

There was a submarine of sorts inside him—shades of *Fantastic Voyage* and the saving teardrop!—a tiny vessel which carried a sonar transceiver.

From another instrument issued a woman's voice speaking a language which had baffled the greatest linguists of the world.

Doctor Neinstein leaned over Barnes. His white jacket cut off Barnes's view of Mbama, and the whiteness resonated blindingly inside Barnes. Between flashes, he could, however, see quite clearly.

"I hate to cut it out," Doctor Neinstein said. "I loathe the very idea. You can see how upset I am. I always am happiest when cutting. But we're losing a priceless opportunity, a unique chance, to study it. However, the welfare of the patient comes first, or so they taught us in medical school."

A reporter, also dressed in white (he wanted to be the twenty-first century Mark Twain), stepped up to Barnes. He thrust a microphone between doctor and patient.

"A few final comments, Mr. Barnes. How's it feel to be the only man in the world to have an appendix and then lose it?"

Barnes snarled, "That isn't my only claim to fame, Scoop. Shove off."

"Thank you, Mr. Barnes. For those who've just tuned in, this is Doctor Neinstein's laboratory in the Johns Hopkins Medicopsychic Annex, donated by the philanthropist recluse, Heward Howes, after Doctor Neinstein performed an operation on him. The nature of the operation is still unknown. But it is common knowledge that Heward Howes now eats only newspapers, that his bathroom is in a bank vault, and that the government is concerned about the flood of counterfeit hundred-dollar bills whose source is apparently Las Vegas. But enough of this idle chatter, folks.

"Our subject today is Mr. Barnes, the most famous patient of the twenty-first century—so far. For the benefit of those who, through some incredible bad luck, have missed the case of Mr. Barnes, he is the only person in the world who still has genes responsible for growing an appendix. As you know, genetic control has eliminated the useless and often dangerously diseased appendix from the entire human population for fifty years. But, due to a purely mechanical oversight..."

"...and a drunken lab assistant," Barnes said.

"...he was born with the genes..."

"Stand back, journalistic dog!" Doctor Neinstein snarled.

"Quack! Butcher! You're interfering with the freedom of the press!"

Doctor Neinstein nodded at his distinguished colleague, Doctor Grosstete, who pulled a lever projecting from the floor behind a dressing screen in the far corner. Scoop's yell rose from the trapdoor like the mercury in a thermometer in the mouth of a malarial patient.

"Hmm. G in *altissimo,"* Doctor Grosstete said. "Scoop was in the wrong profession, but then I guess he knows that now."

There was a faint splash and then the bellowing of hunger-mad crocodiles.

Doctor Grosstete shook his head. "Opera's loss. But in the ecology of things..."

"Nothing must interfere with the march of medical science," Doctor Neinstein said. For once, the mournful lines of his face were winched up into a smile. But the strain was too great, and the fissures catenaried again. He bent over Barnes and applied a stethoscope to the bare skin of the right lower quadrant of the abdomen.

"You must have a theory by now explaining why a woman's voice is coming from the sonar," Barnes said.

Neinstein jerked the thumb of his free hand at the screen which showed a sequence of what looked like hieroglyphs.

"Observe the video representation of the voice. I'd say there is a very small ancient Egyptian female riding inside that device. Or on top of it. We'll not know until we cut it out. It refuses to obey our commands to return. Doubtless, some circuit has malfunctioned."

"It refuses?" Barnes said.

"Forgive the pathetic fallacy."

Barnes's eyebrows rose. Here was a physician who read more than medical literature. Or was the phrase an echo of a humanities course which the good doctor had had to endure?

"Of course, linguistics is not my profession. So you must not pay any attention to my theory."

Here was a medical doctor who admitted he was not omniscient.

"What about the white flashes I get? Those are in your proper province. I'd say they reflect my idiosyncratic resonances, so to speak."

"Tut, tut, Mr. Barnes. You're a layman. No theories, please."

"But all these phenomena are inside me! I'm originating them! Who is better qualified to theorize than I?"

Neinstein hummed an unrecognizable and discordant tune, causing Grosstete, the opera buff, to shudder. He tapped his foot, did a little shuffle-off-to-Buffalo without releasing the stethoscope, looked at his wristwatch, and listened to the sounds coming up from the tiny prowling U-boat.

Barnes said, "You'll have to abandon your original theory that I was insane. You're all hearing the voice and seeing it on the crt. Even if no one so far has seen the flashes in my head. Unless you think the voice is a mass illusion? Or is the correct term a hallucination?"

Doctor Grosstete said, "Listen! I could have sworn she was reciting from Aida! *Never fading, endless love!* But no! She's not speaking Italian. And I don't understand a single word."

Mbama went by on Barnes's left, and he followed her with his eyes as far as he could. The pulses of white faded reluctantly like the noise of popcorn in a cooling pan.

"Miss Mbama does look remarkably like Queen Nefertiti, except for her skin color, of course," Barnes said.

"Aida was Ethiopian, not Egyptian," Doctor Grosstete said. "Please remember that, if you don't want to be embarrassed in a musical group. Both Egyptians and Ethiopians are Caucasians, by the way. Or largely so."

"Get your program here," Barnes said. "You can't tell your race without a program."

"I was only trying to help," Grosstete said. He walked away, looking like Doctor Cyclops with a bellyache.

Two men entered the laboratory. Both wore white. One was red; one, yellow. Doctors Big Bear and Chew. The red linguist said, "How!" He attached a tiny recorder to Barnes's abdomen. The yellow linguist asked Neinstein for a thousand pardons, but would he please stand out of the way?

Big Bear's dark broad big-nosed face hung before Barnes. He saw him as an afterimage for several seconds. He was standing on the edge of a great plain with tall yellow-brown grass and half-naked men wearing feathers and riding painted ponies in the distance, and nearby was a herd of great dark-furred dark-eyed round-humped bison. The voice in his ears had become a man's, chanting in a language which was a mixture of fricatives and sadness.

The scene vanished. The woman's voice returned.

Big Bear had left to talk to Doctor Neinstein, who was looking very indignant. Chew stood before Barnes, who saw a landscape as if he were looking out of the window of a jet taking off. Pagodas, rice fields, kites flying over green hills, a drunken poet walking along the edge of a blue brook.

Why was it he got pictures from red and yellow but not from black and white? Black was the absence of color, and white was a mixture of all colors. This meant that, in reality, blacks were uncolored people and whites (of the lighter variety) were the colored folks. Except that whites were not white, they were pink or brown. Some were, anyway. And blacks were not black, they were brown.

Not that that had anything to do with his getting pulses of white from his resonance, his inner tuning fork, unexplainedly aberrating now. He also, now he thought about it, must get pulses off black in between the white when he looked at Miss Mbama. But he did not see these. Black was a signal, but just not there, just as, in an electronic circuit, a pulse could mean yes or 1, and a non-pulse could mean no or zero. Or vice versa, depending on the code you used.

Barnes told Chew what he had been thinking. Chew told Barnes to pick up his feet and hang onto the chair. He whirled Barnes around many times in the revolving chair while the wires wrapped themselves around Barnes and the chair. Then Chew rotated him swiftly to his original position with the wires hanging loose. The pulses of different colors and flashes of landscapes scared Barnes. He seemed to have flown from the laboratory into an alien kaleidoscopic world.

The voice was a high-pitched gabble until the chair stopped whirling.

He described everything to Chew.

"Perhaps there is something to your theory of resonances," Chew said. "It's quasimystical, but that doesn't mean it can't describe certain phenomena, or be used to describe them, anyway. If a man had a way to determine what truly sets him to vibrating, what wave lengths he is tuned to, down under all the inhibitions and wounds, then he would have no trouble being happy.

"But you did not have this superresonance until you got sick. So what good is it to you or to anybody?"

"I'm like a TV antenna. Turn me in a particular direction, and I get a particular frequency. But I may only pick up a fuzzy image and audio, or a ghost. Turn me another direction, and I receive a strong frequency. Strong to me; weak to you."

Barnes swiveled on the chair to point directly at Mbama.

"How about a date tonight, Mbama?" he said. Her name was a murmur of immemorial elms, of drowsy bees, or something from Tennyson. At the same time, the woman's voice from the sonar became even drippier with honey and with the suggestion of silk sliding over silk. And the hieroglyphs on the cathode ray tubes bent and shot little arrows at each other.

"Thanks for the invitation," she said. "You're a nice guy, but my boy friend wouldn't like it. Besides, you aren't going any place for a week or more, remember? You'll be in bed."

"If you and your friend should ever split..."

"I don't believe in mixed dating."

"Pull your feet up again," Doctor Neinstein said. "Close your eyes. If some linguist can whirl you around, I certainly can. But I'll take the experiment further than he did."

Barnes drew his legs up and closed his eyes. He opened them a minute later because he felt the chair turning. But no one was standing close enough to have turned the chair.

Mbama was obeying. Neinstein's signals. She was walking only a few feet from him in a circle around him. And he and the chair were rotating to track her.

Neinstein made a strangling sound.

"Telekinesis," Chew said.

"Walk back this way," Barnes said to Mbama. He closed his eyes again. The chair turned.

"I don't even have to see her," Barnes said, opening his eyes. Mbama stopped walking. The chair overtracked, then returned so that Barnes's nose pointed along a line that bisected her.

"I have to go to lunch," Mbama said. She walked through the door. Barnes rose, stripped off the electrodes, and followed her, picking up his pajama top as he went out.

Neinstein shouted, "Where do you think you're going? You're scheduled for surgery shortly after lunch. Our lunch, not yours. Don't you dare eat anything. Do you want another enema, maybe an upper colonic? Your appendix may burst at any moment. Just because you don't feel any pain, don't think…! Where *are you* going?"

Barnes did not answer. The pinging and the voice of the woman were coming, not from the machines, which had been disconnected, but from inside him. They contended in his ears. But the white pulses were gone.

An hour later, Miss Mbama returned. She looked frightened. Barnes staggered in after her and collapsed into the chair. Doctor Neinstein ordered that he go to the emergency room immediately.

"No, just give me first aid here," Barnes said. "I hurt a lot of places, but the worst is in my appendix. And he didn't even touch me there."

"Who's he?" Neinstein said, applying alcohol to the cut on Barnes's temple.

"Miss Mbama's boy friend, who's no boy but a man and a big one. Ouch! It didn't do any good to try to explain that I couldn't help following her. That I was, literally, swept off my feet. That I'm a human radar sending out pulses and getting back strange images. And when I started to talk about psychophysical resonances, he hit me in the mouth. I think I got some loose teeth."

Neinstein touched Barnes's abdomen, and Barnes winced.

"Oh, by the way, I got plenty of referents for you linguists," he said. "I'm seeing what the voice is talking about, if it is a voice. Miss Mbama's boy friend jarred something besides my teeth loose. I got a neural connection I didn't have before."

"Sometimes kicking a malfunctioning TV set helps," Grosstete said.

Chew and Big Bear stuck electrodes on Barnes's body and adjusted the dials of several instruments. Peaks, and valleys, ditches, arrows, skyrockets shot across the faces of the tubes and then rearranged themselves into the outlines of Egyptian-type hieroglyphs.

Barnes described the words coinciding with the images.

"It's like an archaeologist with scuba gear swimming through the halls of a palace, or, perhaps, a tomb in sunken Atlantis. The beam of light he's shining on the murals picks out the hieroglyphs one by one. They swim out of darkness and then back into it. They're figures, abstract or stylized birds and bees and animal-men, and there are strange figures which seem to be purely alphabetical mingled with these."

Big Bear and Chew agreed that the so-called voice was actually a series of highly modulated sonar signals. They were registering the differing depths and ridges on the wall of his vermiform appendix as the tiny bloodmarine cruised up and down.

Hours went by. The linguists sweated over sound and visual referent. Everybody had coffee and sandwiches, except Barnes, who had nothing, and Doctor Grosstete, who drank grain alcohol. Neinstein talked on the phone three times, twice to postpone the operation and once to tell an angry editor he did not know where his reporter was.

Suddenly, Big Bear shouted, "Eureka!"

Then, "Champollion!"

Then, "Ventris!"

He held up a long piece of paper covered with phonetic symbols, codes for the hieroglyphs, and some exclamation marks.

"There's the hieroglyphs for *this* and for a copula, and there's one for the definite article and that one, that means *secret,* every time so far. Let's see. THIS IS THE SECRET OF THE...UNIVERSE? COSMOS? THE GREAT BEGETTER? THIS IS THE WORD THAT EXPLAINS ALL. READ, O READER, LITTLE MAN. THIS IS THE WORD..."

"Don't be afraid, man! Say the word!" Chew said.

"That's all there is!" Barnes said, and he groaned.

"There's only a gap, a crack...a corruption. The word is gone. The infection has eaten if up!"

He bent over, clutching at his abdomen.

"We must operate!" Neinstein said.

"McBurney's incision or the right rectus?" Doctor Grosstete said.

"Both! This is The Last Appendectomy! We'll make it a double show! Are all the guests in the amphitheater? Are the TV crews ready? Let us cut, Doctor Grosstete!"

Two hours later, Barnes awoke. He was in a bed in the laboratory. Mbama and two nurses were standing by.

The voice and the pingings were gone. The pulses and the visions were fled. Mbama walked by, and she was only a good-looking black girl.

Neinstein straightened up from the microscope. "The sonar is only a machine. There is no Egyptian queen riding in it. Or on it."

Grosstete said, "The tissue slides reveal many microscopic indentations and alto reliefs on the inner walls of the appendix. But nothing that looks like hieroglyphs. Of course, decay has set in so deeply..."

Barnes groaned and mumbled, "I've been carrying the secret of the universe. The key to it, anyway. All knowledge was inside me all my life. If we'd been one day sooner, we would know it All."

"We shouldn't have eliminated the appendix from man!" Doctor Grosstete shouted. "God was trying to tell us something!"

"Tut, tut, Doctor! You're getting emotional!" Doctor Neinstein said, and he drank a glass of urine from the specimens on Miss Mbama's table. "Bah! Too much sugar in that coffee, Mbama! Yes, Doctor, no medical man, should get upset over anything connected with his ancient and honorable profession—with the possible exception of unpaid bills. Let us use Occam's *razor.*"

Grosstete felt his cheeks. "What?"

"It was coincidence that the irregularities on Barnes's appendix reflected the sonar pulses in such a manner that the hieroglyphs and a woman's voice seemed to be reproduced. A highly improbable—but not absolutely impossible—coincidence."

Barnes said, "You don't think that, in the past, appendixes became diseased to indicate that the messages were ripe? And that if only doctors had known enough to look, they would have seen...?"

"Tut, tut, my dear sir, don't say it. See The Word? The anesthesia has not worn off yet. After all, life is not a science fiction story with everything exhaustively, and exhaustingly, explained at the end. Even we medical men have our little mysteries."

"Then I was just plain sick, and that was all there was to it?"

"Occam's razor, my dear sir. Cut until you have only the simplest explanation left, the bare bone, as it were. Excellent, that! Old Occam had to have been a physician to invent that beautiful philosophical tool."

Barnes looked at Miss Mbama as she walked sway, swaying.

"We have two kidneys. Why only one appendix?"

Father's In The Basement

Nowadays, Gothic has degenerated into a word meaning a shuddery tale wherein a lovely young woman, not too bright, is trapped in a huge shuddery old mansion with a handsome young man, sometimes middle-aged, who's suffering from the delusion he's Lord Byron or Rochester (not Jack Benny's). Also in the house are various other creatures, an old housekeeper or butler who is usually evil, or a young and handsome housekeeper who is usually evil, out to get the heroine and the hero in one way or another, a lost will, a mad wife locked up in a room in one wing of the crumbling castle, and various kindly victims.

In the old days, it meant a long novel, usually in three volumes, always taking place in an old castle or monastery with secret passages in the walls, ghosts, vampires, poisoners, trapdoors, and various monsters.

This Gothic isn't like any of the above.

THE TYPEWRITER HAD clattered for three and a half days. It must have stopped now and then, but never when Millie was awake. She had fallen asleep perhaps five times during that period, though something always aroused her after fifteen minutes or so of troubled dreams.

Perhaps it was the silence that hooked her and drew her up out of the thick waters. As soon as she became fully conscious, however, she heard the clicking of the typewriter start up.

The upper part of the house was almost always clean and neat. Millie was only eleven, but she was the only female in the household, her mother having died when Millie was nine. Millie never cleaned the basement because her father forbade it.

The big basement room was his province. There he kept all his reference books, and there he wrote at a long desk. This room and the adjoining furnace-utility room constituted her father's country (he even did the washing), and if it was a mess to others, it was order to him. He could reach into the chaos and pluck out anything he wanted with no hesitation.

Her father was a free-lance writer, a maker of literary soups, a potboiler cook. He wrote short stories and articles for men's and women's magazines under male or female names, science fiction novels, trade magazine articles, and an occasional Gothic. Sometimes he got a commission to write a novel based on a screenplay.

"I'm the poor man's Frederick Faust," her father had said many times. "I won't be remembered ten years from now. Not by anyone who counts. I want to be remembered, baby, to be reprinted through the years as a classic, to be written of, talked of, as a great writer. And so..."

And so, on the left side of his desk, in a file basket, was half a manuscript, three hundred pages. Pop had been working on it, on and off, mostly off, for fifteen years. It was to be his masterpiece, the one book that would transcend all his hackwork, the book that would make the public cry "Wow!" the one book by him that would establish him as a Master ("Capital M, baby!") It would put his name in the *Encyclopaedia Brittanica;* he would not take up much space in it; a paragraph was all he asked.

He had patted her hand and said, "And so when you tell people your name, they'll say, 'You aren't the daughter of the great Brady X. Donaldson? You are? Fantastic! And what was he really like, your father?"'

And then, reaching out and stroking her pointed chin, he had said, "I hope you can be proud of having a father who wrote at least one great book, baby. But of course, you'll be famous in your own right. You have unique abilities, and don't you ever forget it. A kid with your talents has to grow up into a famous person. I only wish that I could be around...."

He did not go on. Neither of them cared to talk about his heart "infraction," as he insisted on calling it.

She had not commented on his remark about her "abilities." He was not aware of their true breadth and depth, nor did she want him to be aware.

The phone rang. Millie got up out of the chair and walked back and forth in the living room. The typewriter had not even hesitated when the phone rang. Her father was stopping for nothing, and he might not even have heard the phone, so intent was he. This was the only chance he would ever get to finish his Work ("Capital W, baby!"), and he would sit at his desk until it was done. Yet she knew that he could go on like this only so long before falling apart.

She knew who was calling. It was Mrs. Coombs, the secretary of Mr. Appleton, the principal of Dashwood Grade School. Mrs. Coombs had called every day. The first day, Millie had told Mrs. Coombs that she was sick. No, her father could not come to the phone because he had a very deadly schedule to meet. Millie had opened the door to the basement and turned the receiver of the phone so that Mrs. Coombs could hear the heavy and unceasing typing.

Millie spoke through her nose and gave a little cough now and then, but Mrs. Coombs's voice betrayed disbelief.

"My father knows I have this cold, and so he doesn't see why he should be bothered telling anybody that I have it. He knows I have it. No, it's not bad enough to go to the doctor for it. No, my father will not come to the one now. You wouldn't like it if he had to came to the phone now. You can be sure of that.

"No, I can't promise you he'll call before five, Mrs. Coombs. He doesn't want to stop while he's going good, and I doubt very much he'll be stopping at five. Or for some time after, if I know my father. In fact, Mrs. Coombs, I can't promise anything, except that he won't stop until he's ready to stop."

Mrs. Coombs had made some important-sounding noises, but she finally said she'd call back tomorrow. That is, she would unless Millie was at school in the morning, with a note from her father, or unless her father called in to say that she was still sick.

The second day, Mrs. Coombs had phoned again, and Millie had let the ringing go on until she could stand it no longer.

"I'm sorry, Mrs. Coombs, but I feel lots worse. And my father didn't call in, and won't, because he is still typing. Here, I'll hold the phone to the door so you can hear him."

Millie waited until Mrs. Coombs seemed to have run down.

"Yes, I can appreciate your position, Mrs. Coombs, but he won't come, and I won't ask him to. He has so little time left, you know, and he has to finish this one book, and he isn't listening to any such thing as common sense or...No, Mrs. Coombs, I'm not trying to play on your sympathies with his talk about his heart trouble.

"Father is going to sit there until he's done. He said this is his lifework, his only chance for immortality. He doesn't believe in life after death, you know. He says that a man's only chance for immortality is in the deeds he does or the works of art he produces.

"Yes, I know it's a peculiar situation, and he's a peculiar man, and I should be at school."

And you, Mrs. Coombs, she thought, you think I'm a very peculiar little girl, and you don't really care that I'm not at school today. In fact, you like it that I'm not there because you get the chills every time you see me.

"Yes, Mrs. Coombs, I know you'll have to take some action, and I don't blame you for it. You'll send somebody out to check; you have to do it because the rules say you have to, not because you think I'm lying.

"But you can hear my father typing, can't you? You surely don't think that's a recording of a typist, do you?"

She shouldn't have said that, because now Mrs. Coombs would be thinking exactly that.

She went into the kitchen and made more coffee. Pop had forbidden her coffee until she was fourteen, but she needed it to keep going. Besides, he wouldn't know anything about it. He had told her, just before he had felt the first pain, that he could finish the Work in eighty-four to ninety-six hours if he were uninterrupted and did not have to stop because of exhaustion or another attack.

"I've got it all composed up here," he had said, pointing a finger at his temple. "It's just a matter of sitting down and staying down, and that's what I'm going to do, come hell or high water, come infraction or infarction. In ten minutes, I'm going down into my burrow, and I'm not coming back up until I'm finished."

"But, Pop," Millie had said, "I don't see how you can. Exercise or excitement is what brings on an attack...."

"I got my pills, and I'll rest if I have to and take longer," he had said. "So it takes two weeks? But I don't think it will. Listen, Millie," and he had taken her hand in his and looked into her eyes as if they were binoculars pointing into a fourth dimension, "I'm depending on you more than on my pills or even on myself. You'll not let anybody or anything interfere, will you? I know I shouldn't ask you to stay home from school, but this is more important than school. I really need you. I can't afford to put this off any longer. I don't have the time. You know that."

He released her hand and started toward the basement door, saying, "This is it; here goes," when his face had twisted and he had grabbed his chest.

But that had not stopped him.

The phone rang. It was, she knew, Mrs. Coombs again.

Mrs. Coombs's voice was as thin as river ice in late March.

"You tell your father that officers will be on their way to your house within a few minutes. They'll have a warrant to enter."

"You're causing a lot of trouble and for no good reason;" Millie said. "Just because you don't like me...."

"Well, I never!" Mrs. Coombs said. "You know very well that I'm doing what I have to and, in fact, I've been overly lenient in this case. There's no reason in the world why your father can't come to the phone...."

"I told you he had to finish his novel," Millie said. "That's all the reason he needs."

She hung up the phone and then stood by the door for a moment, listening to the typing below. She turned and looked through the kitchen door at the clock on the wall. It was almost twelve. She doubted that anybody would come during the lunch hour, despite what Mrs. Coombs said. That gave her—her father, rather—another hour. And then she would see what she could do.

She tried to eat but could get down only half the liverwurst and lettuce sandwich. She wrapped the other half and put it back into the refrigerator. She looked at herself in the small mirror near the wall clock. She, who could not afford to lose an ounce, had shed pounds during the past three and a half days As if they were on scales, her cheekbones had risen while her eyes had sunk. The dark brown irises and the bloodshot whites of her eyes looked like two fried eggs with ketchup that someone had thrown against a wall.

She smiled slightly at the thought, but it hurt her to see her face. She looked like a witch and always would.

"But you're only eleven!" her father had boomed at her. "Is it a tragedy at eleven because the boys haven't asked you for a date yet? My God, when I was eleven, we didn't ask girls for dates. We hated girls!"

Yet his Great Work started with the first-love agonies of a boy of eleven, and he had admitted long ago that the boy was himself.

Millie sighed again and left the mirror. She cleaned the front room but did not use the vacuum cleaner because she wanted to hear the typewriter keys. The hour passed, and the doorbell rang.

She sat down in a chair. The doorbell rang again and again. Then there was silence for a minute, followed by a fist pounding on the door.

Millie got up from the chair but went to the door at the top of the basement steps and opened it. She breathed deeply, made a face, went down the wooden steps and around the corner at the bottom and looked down the long room with its white-painted cement blocks and pine paneling. She could not see her father because a tall and broad dark-mahogany bookcase in the middle of the room formed the back of what he called his office. The chair and desk were on the other side, but she could see the file basket on the edge of the desk.

Her practiced eye told her that the basket held almost five hundred pages, not counting the carbon copies.

The typewriter clattered away. After a while, she went back up the steps and across to the front door. She opened the peephole and looked through. Two of the three looked as if they could be plainclothesmen. The third was the tall, beefy, red-faced truant officer.

"Hello, Mr. Tavistock," she said through the peephole, "What can I do for you?"

"You can open the door and let me in to talk to your father," he growled. "Maybe he can explain what's been going on, since you won't."

"I told Mrs. Coombs all about it," Millie said. "She's a complete ass, making all this fuss about nothing."

"That's no way for a lady to talk, Millie," Mr. Tavistock said. "Especially an eleven-year-old. Open the door. I got a warrant."

He waved a paper in his huge hand.

"My father'll have you in court for trampling on his civil rights," Millie said. "I'll come to school tomorrow. I promise. But not today. My father mustn't be bothered."

"Let me in now, or we break the door down!" Mr. Tavistock shouted. "There's something funny going on, Millie, otherwise your father would've contacted the school long ago!"

"You people always think there's something funny about me, that all!" Millie shouted back.

"Yeah, and Mrs. Coombs fell down over the wastebasket and wrenched her back right after she phoned you," Tavistock said. "Are you going to open that door?"

It would take them only a minute or so to kick the door open even if she chained it. She might as well let them in. Still, two more minutes might be all that were needed.

She reached for the knob and then dropped her hand. The typing had stopped.

She walked to the top of the basement steps.

"Pop! Are you through?"

She heard the squeaking of the swivel chair, then a shuffling sound. The house shook, and there was a crash as someone struck the door with his body. A few seconds later, another crash was followed by the bang of the door against the inner wall. Mr. Tavistock said, "All right, boys! I'll lead the way!"

He sounded as if he were raiding a den of bank robbers, she thought.

She went around the corner to the front room and said, "I think my father is through."

"In more ways than one, Millie," Mr. Tavistock said.

She turned away and walked back around the corner, through the door and out onto the landing. Her father was standing at the bottom of the steps. His color was very bad and he looked as if he had gained much weight, though she knew that that was impossible.

He looked up at her from deeply sunken eyes, and he lifted the immense pile of sheets with his two hands.

"All done, Pop?" Millie said, her voice breaking.

He nodded slowly.

Millie heard the three men come up behind her. Mr. Tavistock leaned over her and said, "Whew!"

Millie turned and pushed at him. "Get out of my way! He's finished it!"

Mr. Tavistock glared, but he moved to one side. She walked to a chair and sat down heavily. One of the detectives said, "You look awful, Millie. You look like you haven't slept for a week."

"I don't think I'll ever be able to sleep," she said. She breathed deeply and allowed her muscles to go loose. Her head lolled as if she had given up control over everything inside her.

There was a thumping noise from the basement, Mr. Tavistock cried out, "He's fainted!" The shoes of the three men banged on the steps as they ran down. A moment later Mr. Tavistock gave another cry. Then all three men began talking at once.

Millie closed her eyes and wished she could quit trembling. Some time later, she heard the footsteps. She did not want to open her eyes, but there was no use putting it off.

Mr. Tavistock was pale and shaking. He said, "My God! He looks, he smells like…"

One of the detectives said. "His fingertips are worn off, the bones are sticking out, but there wasn't any bleeding."

"I got him through," Millie said. "He finished it. That's all that counts."

Toward the Beloved City

The western sky was as red as if it had broken a vein. In a sense, it had, Kelvin Norris thought.

The Earth had broken open, too, and it was this which had created the bloody sunsets. The Pacific and Mediterranean coasts had shaken many times with a violence unknown since the days of creation. Old volcanoes had spouted, and new ones had reared up. It would be twenty years before all the dust would settle. It would have been a hundred years if it had not been for the great nightly rains, rains which nevertheless did not succeed in making the atmosphere wet, at least, not along the Mediterranean coast. By noon the air was as dry as an old camel bone, and at sunset the sky was red with light reflected from the dust that would not die.

A thousand years would have to pass before the dust of human affairs would settle. Meanwhile, this land was tawny and broken, like the body of a dead lion torn by hyenas. And the sun, rising after last night's violent rain, had been another lion. But it lived, and its breath turned the skin of men and women to leather and burned the bones of the dead to white. Even now, sinking toward the horizon, it lapped greedily at the moisture in Kelvin Norris's skin.

He was riding a horse, the only one he had seen alive since he and his party had landed near the submerged city of Tunis. There were many bones of horses and other animals, killed in the quakes or by tidal waves or bombings or gunfights or by disease or by starving men, for food. Bones of men also lay everywhere. The crows and ravens and kites were, however, numerous, though swiftly losing their fat now. Kelvin knew the taste of their stringy carrion-smelling flesh very well.

The party had traveled on foot from the California mountains across the continent, had built from wreckage a small sailing ship with an auxiliary engine, sailed across the Atlantic to England and from there down along the newly created coasts of France and Portugal, through the straits of Gibraltar (past the great tumbled rock), and then had been wrecked by a storm, on the shore of what was left of Tunisia.

Three days ago, Anna Silvich had shot a scrawny goat that had kept them from collapsing with hunger. Then Kelvin had found the white stallion, which was amazingly sleek and healthy. Its presence, so well-fed, in these bleak and deserted environs, seemed a miracle. Some of the party said that it *was* a miracle. Perhaps this was the very horse on which the rider called Faithful and True had led the hosts of Heaven to victory over the Beast and the Antichrist.

But Kelvin said that he did not think that was likely, though it could be one of the horses ridden by one of the hosts that had followed the Faithful and True into the final battle. However, if a miracle were to be performed, if would be just as easy to transport them, teleport them rather, in the closing of an eye, the scratching of a nose, instead of letting them slog along by boat and foot. But this was not to be; they were alone. He hastened to add as the others frowned, that he meant that the party would never be alone, of course, in the sense that He was always with them. What he had meant was that they could not just sit down and expect some sort of celestial welfare.

That morning, Kelvin had taken a rifle and thirty bullets, all he had for a .32 caliber gun, a goatskin waterbag containing distilled water (which became red-colored two hours afterward), and a leather sling and some stones, and had ridden into the hills. The countryside here had been stripped by the cataclysms, but, in the past three years, some plants had re-established themselves. There were still hares and rodents and lizards and the little desert foxes in this area. He hoped to get some of these with his sling. The .32 was for protection only or in case he should, by some chance, find larger game.

He had tied the horse to a bush and had gone on foot into the tumbled and deeply fissured hills. He smashed a lizard with a stone from his sling and dropped it into the bag hanging from his belt. A few minutes later, he killed a raven with a stone. And then, under a deep shelf of rock, he found the ashes of a recent fire and some thoroughly scraped sheep and rat bones. There were no tracks in this rocky wilderness for him to follow, but he went down three long fissures searching for signs of the fire builder. Reluctantly, he gave up looking and returned to the place where he had tied the horse. His tightening belly and his weakness told him that he would have to give permission for the horse to be butchered. It would hurt him to kill such a fine animal, but the party would then have plenty of meat for a few days.

The ringing of iron shoes on rocks warned him before he left the mouth of the fissure. Crouching, he looked around a boulder. A woman with short curly auburn hair, dressed in a ragged and dirty green coverall, was riding his horse away.

He did not want to shoot her or to make the horse bolt because of the shot. He put the rifle down and ran out after her while he took a stone from the bag at his belt and fitted it into the sling. She turned her head to look behind her just as the stone gave her a glancing blow on her back, near the spine. She screamed and fell forward off the horse; it reared and then galloped off.

Kelvin approached her with the rifle pointed at her. She seemed to be armed with only a knife, but he had learned long ago not to trust to appearances. At the moment, she did not look as if she could use a hidden weapon, even if she had one. She was sitting up, leaning on one arm, and groaning. The skin on her arms and legs and on one side of her face was torn.

"Any broken bones?" he said.

She shook her head and moaned, "Oh, no! But I think you almost broke my back. It really hurts."

"I'm sorry," he said, "but you were stealing my horse. Now, take out your knife slowly and throw it over to one side. Gently."

She obeyed and then slowly got to her feet. At his orders, she stripped and turned around twice. so that he could make sure that she had no weapons taped to her. After he inspected the coverall, he threw it back to her, and she put it back on.

"Have you got anything to eat?" she said.

"The dinner ran away," he said. "What's your name and what are you doing here? And are you a Christian?"

There had been a time when he would not have asked that last question. He had assumed that all those who had bowed to the Beast and allowed it to put its mark on them had been killed either during the series of cataclysms that had almost wrecked the Earth or during the war afterward. But it had long been evident that he had misread the Revelation of John.

"I'm Dana Webster of Beverly, Yorkshire, and I was in a party which was going to the beloved city. But they're all dead now, mostly of starvation, though some were killed by heathens. I found the horse, and I took it because I wanted to get away from whomever owned it, far away, where I could eat the horse without worrying about being tracked down."

She did have a slight English accent, he noted. And her remark about the heathens implied that she was Christian. But she could retract the statement, or rationalize it, if it turned out that she had given the wrong answer. After all, she had no way of knowing that he was really a Christian.

He handed her his canteen, and she drank deeply before giving it back. "It tastes wonderful, even if it does look like blood," she said. "Do you suppose it'll ever get its natural color back? I mean, its lack of color."

"I don't know," he said.

"There's a lot we don't know, isn't there?"

"We'll know when we get to the beloved city," he said. "Let's go."

She turned and walked ahead of him. He carried the rifle in the crook of his elbow, but he was ready to use it at any time. They trudged along silently while the sun dropped through its pool of red. Once, he thought he saw the east begin to lighten, and he stopped, giving a soft cry. She halted and then turned slowly so that he would not misinterpret her movement.

"What is it?" She said.

"I thought…I hoped…no…I was mistaken. I thought that the east was beginning to light up with His glory and that He was surely coming. But my nerves were playing tricks on me. Nerves plus hunger."

"Even if you saw a glory wrapping the world," she said, "how do you know that it would be Him? How could you be certain that it was He and not the Antichrist?"

He goggled at her for a moment and then said, "The Antichrist and the Beast went into the flaming lake!"

"What Beast? I thought the Beast was the world government? You surely don't mean that mythical monster that Gurets was supposed to have locked up in a room in his palace? As for the flaming lake, has anyone ever seen it? I know no one who has. Do you? Actually, all we know is what we've heard by word of mouth or the very little that comes over our radio receivers, supposedly from the beloved city. And where is the beloved city? Well, actually, there isn't any, as the broadcaster admits. There is a site somewhere in what used to be mountainous Israel where the faithful will gather and where the beloved city will be built by the faithful under the supervision of, I presume, angels.

"But how do you know that all this is true or why we're being led, somewhat like sheep into a chute, toward the beloved city? And if there is a flaming lake, and God knows there are plenty all over the world now, how do you know that the Antichrist went into it? Wouldn't the Antichrist, or whoever is supposed to be the Antichrist, have spread this tale about to make the faithful think it was safe to come to Israel?"

"You must be a heathen!" Kelvin said. "Telling a lie like that!"

"Do you see any numbers on my hand?" she said. "And if you looked at my forehead with a polarizer, you wouldn't see any numbers there, either. And if you care to, you can look at my scalp. You won't see any scare there because my head wasn't opened and there's no transceiver there for the Beast to activate any time it wants to press a button."

"We'll see about that when we get to camp," he said.

"I'm not telling lies," she said. "I'm just speculating, as any Christian should. Remember, the Serpent is very cunning and full of guile. What better way to fight those who believe in God than to pose as Christ returned?"

Kelvin did not like the path down which his mind was walking. There should be no more uncertainties; all should be hard and final.

Things were not what he had thought they would be. Not that he was reproaching God even in his thoughts. But things just had not worked out as he had assumed they would. And his assumptions had been based on a lifetime of reading the Scriptures.

"Were you one of those martyred by the Beast?" he said.

Dana Webster had started walking again. She did not stop to reply but slowed down so that he was only a step behind and a step to one side of her.

"Do you mean, was I one of those whose heads were rayed off and who was then, resurrected? No, I wasn't, though I could easily claim to be one and no one could prove that I was lying. Most of my brothers and sisters were killed, but I was lucky. I got away to a hideout up on Mount Skiddaw, in Cumberland. The Beast's search parties were getting close to my cave when the meteorites fell and the quakes started and everything was literally torn to shreds."

"God's intervention," he said. "Without His help, we would all have perished."

"Somebody's intervention."

"What do you mean by *somebody?*"

"Extraterrestrials," she said. "Beings from a planet of some far-off star. Beings far advanced beyond man—in science, at least."

The ideas from her were coming too fast. "Could Extraterrestrials resurrect the dead?" he said.

"I don't know why not," she said. "Scientists have said that we would be able to do it in a hundred years or so, maybe sooner. Of course, that would require some means of recording the total molecular makeup and electromagnetic radiation patterns of an individual. That would someday be possible, according to the scientists. And then, using the recordings, the dead person could be duplicated with an energy-matter converter. This was also theoretically possible."

"But the person would be duplicated, not resurrected," he said. "He would not be the same person!"

"No, but he would think he was."

"What good would that do?"

"How do I know what superbeings have in their superminds? Do you know what's being planned for you by God?"

He was becoming very angry, and he did not wish to be so. He said, "I think we'd better stop talking and save our strength."

"For that matter," she said, "what sense is there in two resurrections or in having a millennium? Why lock up Satan for a thousand years and then release him to lead the heathens against the Christians again, only to lock him up again and then hold the final judgment?"

He did not answer, and she said nothing more for a long time. After an hour, they came down out of the jumbled and shattered hills, and Kelvin saw the white horse eating some long brown grass growing from between tiny cracks in the rocks. They approached slowly while Kelvin called out softly to him. The animal trotted off, however, when Kelvin was only forty feet away from him. He aimed his rifle at it; he could not let this much meat get away now on the slim chance that he might catch it later on.

Dana Webster said, "Don't shoot it! I'll get him!" She called out loudly. The horse wheeled, snorting, and ran up to her and nuzzled her. She patted it and smiled at Kelvin. "I have a feeling for animals," she said. "Rather, there's a good feeling between me and them. An ESP of some sort, sympathetic vibrations, call it what you will."

"Beauty and the beast."

She quit smiling. "The Beast?"

"I didn't mean that. But your power over animals..."

"Don't tell me you believe in witchcraft? Good God! And I'm not swearing when I say that. Don't you believe in love? He feels it. And I feel such a traitor getting him back, because he'll probably be eaten."

An hour later, they led the horse, worn-out from carrying the two humans, into camp near the sea. The sentinels had challenged them, and Kelvin had given the proper countersigns. They passed them and entered a depression on a jagged but low hill. All around them was the mouth-watering odor of frying fish. The four men who had put out into the red-tinged waters, in the small, lightweight, collapsible boat had been fortunate. Or blessed by God. They had not expected to catch anything at all, because the fish life had been frighteningly depleted. When St. John had predicted that a third of the seas would be destroyed, he had underestimated. Rather, underpredicted.

Dana Webster pointed at the thirteen large fish frying in the dural pans over the fires. She said, "Does that mean we won't have to slaughter the horse?"

"Not now, anyway," he said.

"I'm so glad."

Kelvin was glad, too, but he was not impressed by her love for it. He had known too many butchers of children who were very much concerned about humane treatment for dogs and cats.

The men and women waiting for them were lean and dark with the sun and wind and were ridged, as if they were pieces of mahogany carved by windblown sand. They shone with something of a great strength derived from certainty. They had been through the persecutions and the cataclysms and the battles against the slaves of the Beast after the Beast's power had been broken by the cataclysms. "Blessed and holy is he who shares in the first resurrection! Over such the second death has no power, but they shall be priests of God and of Christ and they shall reign with him a thousand years."

However, Kelvin thought, the statement that the second death will have no power over them apparently meant that those who had resisted the Beast for love of God would not be judged again. But they could die, and those who died would not return to the Earth until the thousand years had passed. And then they would rise with the other dead in their new bodies and witness the final judgment. It was then that those faithful who had died before the time of the Beast would be given new bodies and the others would go to whatever fate awaited them. The Alpha and Omega, the final kingdom, would come.

All this had gone into the shaping of their bodies and the expression of face and eye. They were saints now, and nothing could ever change that. But saints could go hungry and thirsty and get very tired and become discouraged. And they would kill if they must.

There were no children here nor had any of the party seen anyone under seven during their journey across the continent and the seas. Their time would come at the end of the millennium.

"What do we have here?" Anna Silvich said.

Anna was a tall gray-eyed blonde who would have been beautiful under softer conditions. Now her flesh was pared away so that the bones seemed very near and the white skin was dark and cracked. Despite this, Kelvin had felt very attracted to her. He intended to ask her to be his wife after they reached the beloved city. He could have married her before this, if she would have him, since any of the party could conduct the ceremony. They were all priests now. But he did not want to do anything that would take his mind off the most important object: getting to the beloved city.

"We have here one who claims she is a Christian," Kelvin said.

Anna took a pencil-shaped plastic object from her shirt-pocket, pointed it at Dana Webster's forehead, and slid a section of the object forward.

"See?" Webster said. "I don't have the mark of the Beast."

Anna stepped forward and seized the woman's hair and pulled her head down. Kelvin started to protest against the unnecessary roughness, but he decided not to. He would see how Webster reacted; perhaps she might get angry enough to trip herself up. Anna released the woman's hair and said, "No scars there. But that doesn't mean anything. If I had a microscope or even a magnifying glass..."

Dana Webster said nothing but looked scornful. If she were upset or angry about her treatment, however, she did not allow it to interfere with her appetite. She ate the fish and the biscuits and canned peaches. The latter two items had been found in the ruins of a house by Sherborn, a little man who had a nose for buried or concealed food.

Kelvin had given the prayer of thankfulness before they ate, but he felt he should say more afterward. "God has been good and given us enough today to restore our strength. We can face tomorrow with the certain knowledge that He will provide more. It's evident from today's catch that there are still fish in the Mediterranean. There must be enough to keep us fed until we get to the beloved city."

Dana Webster, he noticed, said amen to that just as the others did. That could mean nothing except that she was playing her role of Christian, if she was indeed playing. She could be sincere. On the other hand, there were her remarks while they were traveling campward. He asked her what she had meant by *Extraterrestrials.*

She looked around at the dark faces with their protruding cheekbones and hollow cheeks and the darkly rimmed but fire-bright eyes. "I should have kept these doubts—or, rather, speculations to myself," she said. "I should've waited until we got to the beloved city. Then everything would be straightened out. One way or another. Of course, by then it might be too late for us. I hate to say anything about this because you'll think I'm a heathen. But I have a mind, and I must speak it. Isn't that the Christian way?"

"We're not slaves of the Beast, if that's what you mean," Anna said. "We won't kill somebody because they differ somewhat from us on certain theological matters. Of course, we won't listen to blasphemy. But then you won't blaspheme if you're a Christian."

"It's easy to see you don't like me, Anna Silvich," Webster said. "Of course, that doesn't mean you're not a Christian, you can love mankind but dislike a particular person for one or another reason. Even if she is a fellow believer. Still, that doesn't mean that you're excused from examining yourself and finding out why you can't love me."

Anna said, with only a slight quaver of anger, "Yes, I don't like you. There is something about you...some...odor...."

"Of brimstone, I suppose?" Dana Webster said.

"God forgive me if I'm wrong," Anna said. "But you know what we've all been through. The betrayals, the spies, the prisons, seeing our children and mates tortured and then beheaded, our supposed friends turning their backs on us or turning us in, the terrible, terrible things done to us. But you know this, whether you're what you say you are or a Judas. However, you are right in reproaching me for one thing. I shouldn't say you stink of the devil unless I really have proof. But..."

"But you have said so and therefore you've stained me in everybody's thoughts," Dana said. "Couldn't you have waited until you were certain, instead of maliciously, and most unchristianly, stigmatizing me?"

"Somehow, we've strayed from the original question," Kelvin said. "What do you mean, Dana, by *Extraterrestrials?*"

She looked around at the faces in the firelight and then at the shadows outside as if there were things in the shadows. "I know you won't even want to consider what I'm going to speculate about. You're too tired in body and mind, too numb with the horrors of the persecution and the cataclysms and the battles that followed, to think about one more battle, or series of battles. But do I have to remind you that men have been looking for the apocalypse for two thousand years? And that there have been many times when men claimed that it was not only at hand but had actually begun?"

"There have been times when men who spoke with authority, or seeming authority, proclaimed that the end of the world was at hand. But they were all mistaken, deceived by themselves or by the Enemy. Which may be the same. I mean, the Enemy may be the enemy within ourselves, not an entity, a unique person with an objective existence outside of us. The point is, what if we're being fooled again? Not self-deceived, as in the past, but deceived by an outside agency? By Extraterrestrials who are using weapons against Earth, weapons which far surpass ours? And now we're being asked to gather at the so-called beloved city, asked to come in and surrender. Why? Perhaps we're to form the basis of the future slave population for these beings?"

There was a long silence afterward. Anna Silvich broke it by crying, "You have convicted yourself, woman! You are trying to put doubts into our hearts, to destroy our faith! You are a heathen!"

Kelvin held his hands up for silence, and, when that did not work, shouted at Anna and the others to shut up. When the uproar had died, he said, "What evidence do you have that your Extraterrestrials exist, Dana?"

"Exactly the same evidence you have that this is the beginning of the millennium," she said. "The difference is my interpretation. Try to look at the situation, and our theories, objectively. And remember, that the Antichrist fooled many, probably including some right here, when he claimed to be Christ. He has been exposed and, supposedly, defeated for all time. Or, at least until the final battle a thousand years from now. But think. Could it be Satan himself who was trying his final trick on us? Or could it be that Extraterrestrials who knew of the longing of the faithful for the millennium have caused this pseudomillennium to occur? And..."

"Or perhaps it is Satan who is using the Extraterrestrials?" Anna said scornfully.

"It could be," Dana Webster said.

"Just a minute," Kelvin said. "I can't for the life of me, the soul of me, I should say, imagine why these Extraterrestrials should bring the faithful back to life? What reason could they have to do that?"

"Have you seen any of the resurrected?" Dana Webster said. "Is there anybody in this group who has seen one of them? Or, perhaps, some among you were killed and then brought back to life?"

Kelvin said, "It's true that no one here was restored to life. But it is not true that none of us have seen a resurrected person. I myself talked with a man who had been killed for his faith, though he was given the chance to deny God and become a slave of the Beast after seeing his wife and children raped and tortured and then beheaded. But he refused and so he was roasted over the fire and his head cut off. But he awoke at the bottom of the grave which had been opened for him, and he crawled out and was with a number of others who had been brought back to life. His wife and children were not among them, but he was sure that he would find them. I had no reason to doubt him, since I had known him from childhood."

"What do you think of that, Webster?" Anna said.

"But you did not see him killed, nor did you see him resurrected, isn't that right?" Webster said. "How do you know that he did not in actuality deny God and become a slave of the Beast? How do you know that his story about his resurrection was not a lie, that he wasn't lying so he could pass himself off as a Christian, since he had fallen among Christians? Indeed, it would be wise of the Enemy, whether Satan or Extraterrestrial, to send out spies with these lying stories so they could deceive the Christians."

Kelvin had to admit to himself that he had no proof of his friend's story and that what Webster postulated could be true. But he did not think that she was right. Some things had to be taken on faith. On the other hand, the Antichrist had fooled many, including himself at first. He gestured impatiently and said, "All this talk! We'll take you with us to the city and, when we get there, we'll find out the truth about everything."

"Why take her along?" Anna said. "She's convicted herself out of her own mouth with her lies, and she'll be an extra mouth to feed...."

"Anna!" Kelvin said. "That's not loving..."

"The time has come and gone for loving your enemies!" Anna said. "The new times are here; there is no room for tolerance of heathens. And we can't take her along, because she'll be lying to us with her tales of Extraterrestrials and other subtleties designed to make us fall into error! And we haven't anyone to ask what we should do with her. We have to make up our own minds and act on our decision, hard though it may seem."

Dana Webster gave a little start. Even by the firelight, she could be seen to pale. She pouted past Anna and said, quietly but with a tremor in her voice, "Why don't you ask him what to do?"

They spun around, their hands going for their weapons. But the tall man in white robes and with short hair as white as newly washed wool had his hands high up in the air so they could see he was unarmed. He was smiling; his teeth were very white in the firelight, and his eyes were shining with the reflected light. The eyes of no human being shone like those; they were like a lion's. Nor could any human being have crept by the sentinels and appeared so suddenly. The breeze, which Kelvin had suddenly felt just before Webster had spoken, must have been the air displaced by the emergence of this man...person...from nowhere. Kelvin felt his skin grow cold over his scalp and the back of his neck. He was scared, yet he was glad. At least someone to tell them what was happening and what they must do had come.

The man slowly lowered his hands. He was very handsome and very clean and had a beautiful well-proportioned body, quite in contrast to the ragged, dirty, scruffy bunch, scarred and skinny and stinking. The man slowly opened his robes so that they could see that he had no concealed weapons beneath them. They could also see that he was sexless. And, now that Kelvin was coming out of the shock of the sudden appearance, he saw that *he* was a misnomer. The being's features were effeminate. But the total impression the being gave was more masculine than feminine, and so Kelvin continued to think of the person as he.

He said, "You may call me Jones. I'll take up only a few minutes of your time."

Kelvin recognized the deep rich voice. It was the same voice that came to them from time to time, over their transistor receivers. It was the voice that had told the faithful all over the world to start out for the beloved city. It had also told a little about what was expected from the faithful when they did get to the beloved city. Only one thing was clear. The new citizens would have much hard work to do for a long, long time.

"We would be honored, and very happy, if you would stay for more than a few minutes...Mr. Jones," Kelvin said. "We have many questions. We also have a crucial problem here."

The angel looked at Dana Webster, but he did not lose his smile. "I don't know what your problem is with her, but I'm sure you'll do the right thing," he said. "As for your questions, most of them will have to wait. I'm busy just now. We have a thousand years to get ready for, and that will pass quickly enough for those who will live through it."

It was difficult to get up enough courage to argue with an angel, but Kelvin had not survived because of lack of courage. He said, "Why do we have to get to the beloved city on our own? We've suffered enough, I would think, and several of our party have been killed by heathens or in accidents. That doesn't seem to jibe with what we read in St. John the Divine...."

Jones raised a long slim hand on the back of which were many white woolly hairs. He said, still smiling, "I don't know the answer to that, any more than I know why there is a first death and then a second death or why all the heathens weren't killed or why they will flourish and propagate once more. Some of whom, by the way, will be your children and grandchildren to the two hundred and fiftieth generation, to your sorrow, though not to your everlasting sorrow. Don't ask me why. I know more than you, but I don't know everything. I am content to wait until the obscurities and ambiguities and seeming paradoxes are straightened out. And you will have to wait. Unless you are killed, of course, and spared the thousand years of struggle."

"We are as subject as ever to the whims of chance!" Kelvin said. "I thought..."

"You thought you'd have everything programmed, everything certain and easy," Jones said. "Well, God has always dealt with this world on a statistical basis, excepting certain people and events. And, generally speaking, He will continue to do so until the second death. Then, my friend, He will deal with every bit of matter in this world, and the souls that inhabit certain material forms, on a specific and individual basis. And that will be the difference between the world as it has been, and the new, unfluctuating, and unchanging world as it will be after the second death. Not that He is not aware of every atom now and what it is doing. But in the unchanging time to come, He will have His hand upon all matter and all souls, and nothing will evolve or change. You might say that, up to now, and until the thousand years are over, He has respected Heisenberg's principle of uncertainty." Jones looked at each intently, still smiling, and then said, "Actually, I'm here in my office—one of many—of requisitioner. I'm taking your horse, which is needed at the city."

"Why don't you just create some horses and leave this one with us?" Anna said. "We need it for food."

"There's other food to be had," Jones said. "This horse is destined to be the father of many hundreds of thousands. As far as I know, the only new creations will be after the second death, when you fortunate ones will be given new bodies. Something like the one I'm using."

That answered one question. There would be no sex in the new Earth and the new Heaven. And why should there be? There would be no more babies, and the ecstasy of beholding God's face would far transcend any fleshly delights. Despite this, Kelvin felt a panic. He would be castrated. Then he told himself that he would have to get over that reaction. There would be compensations which would make the loss of his sex seem trivial and, perhaps, a cause for rejoicing. Nor would he be any less a man, that is, a human being.

Anna said, loudly, "There is one thing you should know so you can report it to your superiors, even if you won't do anything about it here!"

Jones raised his woolly white eyebrows and said, "Superiors? I have only two, and I won't have to report to them. They know what's going on at every second."

Anna was checked, but she rallied after a moment's silence. She said, "Forgive me if I'm presuming. But you should know that this woman here claims that all this, that is, the events of the past four years, have been caused by Extraterrestrials! She says we're being fooled! It's all a trick of things from outer space or whatever they come from! What do you say to that?"

Jones smiled and said, "Well, angels *are* Extraterrestrial beings, though not all Extraterrestrials are angels. As I said, it's your problem. You're grown up now, though still, of course, children of God. I go now. God bless you." Jones mounted the horse and rode out of sight down a defile. Kelvin climbed up onto the shoulder of a high hill to watch him ride out. He heard the bang, like a large balloon exploding, as the air rushed in to fill the vacuum deft by a suddenly unoccupied space.

After five minutes, he climbed back down.

"If he wanted the horse, why didn't he just take it?" Anna said; "Surely he could have done it without leaving the city."

"Perhaps teleportation requires that the teleporter has to be physically present to do the work." Dana said.

"Teleportation?" Anna said. "That was an angel, you fool. Angels don't have to resort to teleportation."

"Teleportation is only a term used to describe a phenomenon," Dana said. "It's the same whether it's brought about by an angel or an Extraterrestrial."

"And you're a heathen," Anna said. "That angel must think we're a fine bunch of featherbrains if we can't see what's so obvious. He was laughing at us because we were so stupid."

"He could have been laughing because I told you the truth and you wouldn't believe it," Dana Webster said.

"And if he was one of your creatures from outer space, why didn't he just wipe us out," Anna said, "or just teleport us to the city? It would be so easy for him."

"I don't know," Dana Webster said. "Maybe they're giving us some sort of test so they can decide where to assign us for some sort of job. Those who survive the terrible journey to the city get some sort of booby prize. Or become the studs and mares of a new breed of superslaves. I don't know."

The effect of her words was stronger than Kelvin liked. Too many looked as if they were seriously considering her speculations.

It rained heavily that night, as it had for almost every night for three years. Everybody was soaked, but no one came down with colds or pneumonia or any respiratory disease yet, many had been subject to colds and allergic to pollen or suffering from various degrees of emphysema before the cataclysms had begun. Something had rid them of all diseases, in fact, and Kelvin pointed this out that morning. He indicated it as evidence that they would all be free of body infirmities and ailments, and would not age for a thousand years. Yet microorganisms continued to do their work on dead bodies. Meat got spoiled; dead animals, and humans, rotted. Surely, this discrimination was God-given. Why should the Enemy, or Extraterrestrials, give human beings immunity from disease?

"I don't know," Dana Webster said. "We'll find out. Also, have the heathens been given this same immunity? If they have, then surely God is not responsible for the immunity, that is, He is not responsible for the dispensation of immunity. He, of course, is primarily responsible for anything that happens, in that it can't happen unless He permits it."

Kelvin expected her to bring up the question of why a good God would permit evil in the first place, but she did not push that time-waster on them.

The days and nights, the burning under the sun and the cold soaking at night, went on and on. A thousand miles of desert along the sea behind them and another thousand to go.

Dana Webster had more than done her share. She was a genius at catching lizards and finding large quantities of locusts and stunning birds and the little desert foxes with her slings. The items she brought to the community pot were not attractive, but they were nutritious and filled the belly. Even Anna had to admit that the party had eaten better since Webster joined them. But Anna also pointed out that Webster's very gift at hunting could be due to a strange power she had over animals. And who knew but that this was because she was herself one of the slaves of the Beast. Ex-slaves rather, since the Beast was now in the lake of burning brimstone. But the ex-slaves were still dedicated to evil, of course.

Kelvin had become irritated at Dana Webster's attitude, since he was now very attracted to her. In fact, he told himself during a fit of honesty, he was in love with her. He did not tell Dana, of course, because he could never marry her if she were a heathen. There had been a time when Christians had married heathens, but that must never be again. There was no doubt anymore about the line between good and evil. That is, as far as marriage went, there was no doubt about the lines. But there was still doubt about the honesty and the motives of people. And he was not sure what Dana Webster was. Sometimes, she talked so close to blasphemy that he felt repelled. Or uneasy. And he was uneasy because she seemed to be making some sense. At other times, he, thought that she was truly a Christian but one who did not trust appearances and so was perhaps oversuspicious. But, in this world of untrustworthy appearances, could a person be overly suspicious?

Whatever the truth, he now yearned for this woman as he had yearned for none, not even Anna, since his wife had betrayed him. Was there something still evil in him, something that attracted him to women who had enlisted for Satan? But he had been attracted to Anna, and surely she was not on the Enemy's side? Nor did he have any proof that Dana was with the Enemy.

It did not seem likely that some residue of evil still lay deep within him. He had refused to go along with the Beast, and he had survived the cataclysms and the overthrow of the Beast, and so the second death had no power over him. He had been judged once and for all.

But could it be that he still needed refining, that there were elements of evil in him, and that the thousand years were to be used to purge him? Was that why the millennium must be? So that the surviving Christians could be purged of all evil? What, then, would purge those who had died and who would arise at the second judgment and be given new bodies? Why did they not have to go through the fire of a thousand years?

One night, Dana, who had been silent about her theories of the reality of the situation for a long time, proposed a new theory. "Those prophets who came closest to predicting the future as it really develops are those whose minds have an inborn computer. They don't truly prophesy, in the sense that they can actually look into the future. No, their minds, unconsciously, of course, compute the highest probabilities, and it is the most likely course of events that they predict. Or choose, rather. Your true prophet has a gift which is not a clairvoyance but is the selection of what is most probable. He sees the *in potentio* as actualized, though vaguely and in large general terms. His vision must necessarily be cast into symbolic images because he can't understand what he sees. He can't because he is a creature of the present, and the future contains many unfamiliar things."

"But John saw what was revealed by God," Anna said. "God would not reveal a probability; He would show only a certainty."

Dana shrugged and said, "Sometimes, a prophet will get two probable futures mixed up, he'll not be able to differentiate between the most likely and the next most likely. He sees the future as one, but in reality he is witnessing a part of one probable future inserted in the continuum of another probable future. That is why, perhaps, John saw two resurrections, the millennium, and so forth. He saw two or more futures all mixed up. Only true events will straighten out what future is really the most probable. Do you follow me?"

"And I suppose he may have seen Extraterrestrials and thought they were angels?" Anna said.

"It's possible."

Anna stood up and cried, "She is saying all these confusing things to lead us astray!"

"But you can't be led astray," Dana Webster said. "Only the heathen can now be led astray."

"Not if your theory is right," Anna said, and then she stared at Webster in an obvious confusion.

The entire party was upset. The next night, seeing that the situation had not improved, even though Dana had refused to talk about her theories anymore, Kelvin held a conference. After he had Dana taken to one side, he said to the others, "We may be saints, but we're certainly not behaving as such. Now, I've heard some of you, especially Anna, say that Dana should he killed. You don't even want just to kick her out of our party, because she might then find some heathens and lead them to attack us. Or because she may be the mother of heathens, and such should not be allowed to breed.

"Anna, would you be the one to shoot her in cold blood if we decided that she should die?"

"It wouldn't be in cold blood!"Anna said.

"Would it be in hate then? With an unchristian desire to shed blood?"

"At one time," Anna said, "it would have been a sin to hate. But the first death has come, and the old order has passed away, and the new one has come. There is no more returning of lost sheep to the field. Once a heathen, always a heathen. That is the way it is now."

"The old order will not pass away until after the second death," Kelvin said. "I quote you Revelation 21:4: 'Now God's home is with men? He will live with them and they shall be His people. God himself will be with them....He will wipe away all tears from their eyes. There will be no more death, no more grief, crying, or pain. The old things have disappeared.' And don't forget what John says in 20:13, '...and all were judged according to what they had done.' If we kill Dana Webster, we will be judged by what we have done, which will be, in my opinion, murder."

"But you said we won't be judged again!" Anna said. "And remember what that angel said. Whatever we do, will be the right thing!"

Kelvin was silent for a while. Everything was so tangled and shadowy, not bright and straight as it was supposed to be after the Beast had been put away. Or had they misunderstood the real meaning of the Revelation. What was it supposed to be? John had not said so or even implied it. Kelvin, like so many, had just assumed it.

It was then that Anna said that they would all starve if Dana Webster had to be fed, and that she should be killed before she could say another word. of her blasphemous speculations.

"We have eaten better since Dana joined us," Kelvin said. "You know that to be true, Anna, so why do you lie? Listen, all of you, whatever else is not clear in this hot and dusty world, two things are. It is by these two that we must live, and by these two that we must die. One is, love God. The other is, love your fellow man. As long as Dana claims to be a Christian, then we must treat her as one until we get proof to the contrary."

"Many of us were delivered into the hands of the torturer and the butcher because of that," Anna said.

"So be it," Kelvin said. "But that is the way it must be. We take her along to the beloved city, and when we're there, then we'll find out."

Anna walked away. Others were not happy about his decision but, in these hard and dangerous times, there was no room for committee action. Like it or not; survival depended upon the quick rule of one good man.

Dana, smiling, though still pale, came up to him and kissed him on the lips. Kelvin felt a spasm of desire for her, but he pushed her away, though gently. He could not marry her now, or perhaps, ever. Not until they got to the city would he find out what was or was not permitted. And if he allowed his desire to overrule his good sense and he married her now, the group would believe, perhaps rightly, that he had put his self above the good of the whole.

Nevertheless, he did not get to sleep easily that night, and he found himself straining through the darkness toward Dana, as if his soul itself were trying to lift his body up and propel it through the air to her. The rains fell, and he huddled under the shelf of rock and wished he had her warm body inside the blanket with him. After a while, he prayed himself to sleep.

He awoke to shouting, screams, curses, the sound of the edge of steel striking flesh, and then shots from those of his party who had awakened in time.

Kelvin got off one shot, saw the dark figure before him fall, and something struck his head. He awoke shortly after dawn with a headache like a hot stone in his brain. His hands were tied behind him, and his feet were hobbled. Six of the attackers, all in ragged black and gold uniforms of the soldiers of the Beast, were standing over the survivors of his party. Little Jessica Crenwell lay on her back, unconscious and groaning, and apparently not long for life. Dana Webster rose from beside Crenwell and walked toward him. She seemed unhurt. And she carried a rifle.

He suppressed a groan and said, "So Anna was right."

But she was not, as he had expected, pleased.

"I had nothing to do with these," she said, gesturing at the sullen-faced heathen. "At least, I did not tell them to attack. They have ruined my plans to enter your beloved city with your party. Now I'll have to find another party of fools or somehow manage to convince the city's guardians that I am what I claim to be. And that won't be easy."

"I don't understand," he said, wincing from the pain involved in talking. "If you meant to palm yourself off as a Christian, why did you argue so vehemently that this was a false apocalypse? Why your theory of the Extraterrestrials?"

She smiled then, and she said, "Long before we reached the city, I would have pretended to have converted wholly to your way of thinking. I would have repented my errors. You would then accept me far more easily, because I would have seemed to have been confused and hurt by my traumatic experiences but would have been cured, shown the right way. And then you wouldn't have had much hesitation about marrying me, would you?"

"To be honest, no. I would have rejoiced at your change and leaped at the chance to marry you. But I would have done so only if you had made it plain that you really wanted me."

"And I would have arranged it so that you would not have been able to hold out," she said. "And then, as your wife, as one of the faithful band I would have started planting my little seeds of doubt here and there, watering them on the sly, and all the time determining the weaknesses and the strengths of the city for the day when we attack."

"We?"

"We have been chosen by the new rulers of Earth as the favored executives, the herders of the swine. We were approached before all this began, told what would happen, and given our duties. And it was all as they said it would be. They are your true prophets, my friend, not some old half-crazy man on an island. They knew that the stresses inside the Earth would bring on the greatest quakes the Earth has ever known, and they knew that a group of large asteroids was heading for the Earth. Why shouldn't they, since they launched the asteroids ages ago, and since they have devices to store up energy in the Earth and to trigger it off whenever they care to do so"

"They?" Kelvin said, and he felt the stone in his brain become bigger and hotter.

"They are from a planet which orbits a star in Andromeda. They are the true rulers of this universe, or destined to be such. They can travel through interstellar space at speeds far exceeding those of light. But there is another race which has the same powers, and an evil race which has been the eon-long enemy of the Andromedans."

Kelvin groaned, partly from the agony in his head and partly from the agony in his soul.

"Your story sounds vaguely familiar," he said. "And I'm not referring to the science fiction stories we used to read before the Beast suppressed them."

"It's in the Bible," she said, "but in a rather distorted form. I wasn't lying when I said that some men could compute the most probable future. To some extent, that is, on a broad and unspecific scale, of course. However, the Arcturans were going to seize Earth and take over when the Andromedans struck. The Arcturans are those you think of as angels. They are the ones preparing to build the beloved city, which will be a fortress to hold Earth—they think."

Kelvin said, "Satan may be locked up, but surely his aides are loose. But they won't be able to do anything really drastic for a long, long time. Not for a thousand years."

She laughed and said, "You still insist on believing your old cast-off myth?"

"It is you who believe in the myth, though it is new," he said. "You have to rationalize. You have to believe that the evil spirits are not spirits but beings from another star. And they, of course, must be the good ones, because no one really allies himself with what he admits is an evil cause. No, somehow, the cause must be a good one, no matter what evil it does. And we Christians, of course, are the evil ones. The Enemy has to think of himself as good."

The other heathens were walking toward him. They held knives and cigarette lighters.

Dana Webster said, "I must go now. I have work to do. I leave you to these. They'd be angry if I frustrated them by killing you. I need them, so they'll get their way now. I'm sorry, in a way, since I don't like torture. But there are times when it must be used."

"That's the difference between me and you, between us and your kind," Kelvin said. "I pity you, Dana Webster, I pity you from the deepest part of my being. I wish even now that you could see the light, that you could love God, know God as I know Him. But it is too late. The thousand years have started, and your end is foretold.

"And if I scream, *when* I scream, I should say, and if I beg for mercy from these things that have no mercy, and if I scream at them to get it over with—well, no matter how long it seems, it will be over. And then I will arise in a new body, and the old order will have passed away, and there will be no death any longer or any grief or pain."

"You nauseating egotistic fool!" she said.

"'Time will tell which of us is a fool," he said. "But time has already told which of us is for man and God."

As death came, a smile passed, fleetingly, over his face—a smile Dana Webster would not, indeed, could not understand.

Skinburn

"Your skin tingles every time you step outdoors?" Dr. Mills said. "And when you stand under the skylight in your apartment? But only now and then when you're standing in front of the window, even if the sunlight falls on you?"

"Yes," Dent Lane said. "It doesn't matter whether or not it's night or day, the skies are cloudy or clear, or the skylight is open or closed. The tingling is strongest on the exposed parts of my body, my face and hands or whatever. But the tingling spreads from the exposed skin to all over my body, though it's much weaker under my clothes. And the tingling eventually arouses vaguely erotic feelings."

The dermatologist walked around him. When he had completed his circuit, he said, "Don't you ever tan?"

"No, I just peel and blister. I usually avoid burning by staying out of the sun as much as possible. But that isn't doing me any good now, as you can see. I look as if I'd been on the beach all day. That makes me rather conspicuous, you know. In my work, you can't word to be conspicuous."

The doctor said, "I know."

He meant that he was aware that Lane was a private detective. What he did not know was that Lane was working on a case for a federal government agency. CACO—Coordinating Authority for Cathedric Organizations—was short of competent help. It had hired, after suitable security checks, a number of civilian agents. CACO would have hired only the best, of course, and Lane was among these.

Lane hesitated and then said, "I keep getting these phone calls."

The doctor said nothing. Lane said, "There's nobody at the other end. He, or she, hangs up just as soon as I pick the phone up."

"You think the skinburn and the phone calls are related?"

"I don't know. But I'm putting all unusual phenomena into one box. The calls started a week after I'd had a final talk with a lady who'd been chasing me and wouldn't quit. She has a Ph.D. in bioelectronics and is a big shot in the astronautics industry. She's brilliant, charming, and witty, when she wants to be, but very plain in face and plane in body and very nasty when frustrated. And so..."

He was, he realized, talking too much about someone who worked in a top-secret field. Moreover, why would Mills want to hear the sad story of Dr. Sue Brackwell's unrequited love for Kent Lane, private eye? She had been hung up on him for some obscure psychological reason and, in her more rational moments, had admitted that they could never make it as man and wife, or even as man and lover, for more than a month, if that. But she was not, outside of the laboratory, always rational, and she would not take no from her own good sense or from him. Not until he had gotten downright vicious over the phone two years ago.

Three weeks ago, she had called him again. But she had said nothing to disturb him. After about five minutes of light chitchat about this and that, including reports on their health, she had said good-bye, making it sound like an *ave atque vale,* and had hung up. Perhaps she had wanted to find out for herself if the sound of his voice still thrilled her. Who knew?

Lane became aware that the doctor was waiting for him to finish the sentence. He said, "The thing is, these phone calls occurred at first when I was under the skylight and making love. So I moved the bed to a corner where nobody could possibly see it from the upper stories of the Parmenter Building next door.

"After that, the phone started ringing whenever I took a woman into my apartment, even if it was just for a cup of coffee. It'd be ringing before I'd get the door open, and it'd ring at approximately three-minute intervals thereafter. I changed my phone number twice, but it didn't do any good. And if I went to the woman's apartment instead, her phone started ringing."

"You think this lady scientist is making these calls?"

"Never! It's not her style. It must be a coincidence that the calls started so soon after our final conversation."

"Did your women also hear the phone?"

Lane smiled and said, "Audiohallucinations? No. They heard the phone ringing, too. One of them solved the problem by tearing her phone out. But I solved mine by putting in a phone jack and disconnecting the phone when I had in mind another sort of connection."

"That's all very interesting, but I fail to see what it has to do with your skin problem."

"Phone calls aside," Lane said, "could the tingling, the peeling and blistering, and the mild erotic reaction be psychosomatic?"

"I'm not qualified to say," Mills said. "I can, however, give you the name of a doctor whose specialty is recommending various specialists."

Lane looked at his wristwatch. Rhoda should be about done with her hairdresser. He said, "So far, I'm convinced I need a dermatologist, not a shrink. I was told you're the best skin doctor in Washington and perhaps the best on the East Coast."

"The world, actually," Dr. Mills said. "I'm sorry. I can do nothing for you at this time. But I do hope you'll inform me of new developments. I've never had such a puzzling, and, therefore, interesting, case."

Lane used the phone in the ground-floor lobby to call his fiancée's hairdresser. He was told that Rhoda had just left but that she would pick him up across the street from the doctor's building.

He got out of the building just in time to see Rhoda drive his MG around the corner, through a stoplight, and into the path of a pickup truck. Rhoda, thrown out by the impact (she was careless about using her safety belt), landed in front of a Cadillac. Despite its locked brakes, it slid on over her stomach.

Lane had seen much as an adviser in Vietnam and as a member of the San Francisco and Brooklyn police departments. He thought he was tough, but the violent and bloody deaths of Leona and Rhoda within four months was too much. He stood motionless, noting only that the tingling was getting warmer and spreading over his body. There was no erotic reaction, or, if there were, he was too numb to feel it. He stood there until a policeman got the nearest doctor, who happened to be Mills, to come out and look at him. Mills gave Lane a mild sedative, and the cop sent him home in a taxi. But Lane was at the morgue as hour later, identified Rhoda, and then went to the precinct station to answer some questions.

He went home prepared to drink himself to sleep, but he found two CACO agents, Daniels and Lyons, waiting for him. They seemed to have known about Rhoda's death almost as quickly as he, and so he knew that they had been shadowing him or Rhoda, he answered some of their questions and then told them that the idea that Leona and Rhoda might be spies was not worth a second's consideration. Besides, if they were working for SKIZO, or some other outfit, why would SKIZO, or whoever, kill their own agents?

"Or did CACO kill them?" Lane said.

The two looked at him as if he were unspeakably stupid.

"All right," Lane said. "But there's absolutely no evidence to indicate that their deaths were caused by anything but pure accident. I know it's quite a coincidence..."

Daniels said, "CACO had both under surveillance, of course. But CACO saw nothing significant in the two women's behavior. However, that in itself is suspicious, you know. Negative evidence demands a positive inquiry."

"That maxim demands the investigation of the entire world," Lane said.

"Nevertheless," Lyons said, "SKIZO must've spotted you by now. They'd have to be blind not to. Why in hell don't you stay out from under sunlamps?"

"It's a skin problem," Lane said, "As you must know, since you've undoubtedly bugged Dr. Mill's office."

"Yeah, we know," Daniels said. "Frankly, Lane, we got two tough alternatives to consider. Either you're going psycho, or else SKIZO is on to you. Either way..."

"You're thinking in two-valued terms only," Lane said. "Have you considered that a third party, one with no connection at all with SKIZO, has entered the picture?"

Daniels cracked his huge knuckles and said, "Like who?"

"Like whom, you mean. How would I know? But you'll have to admit that it's not only possible but highly probable."

Daniels stood up. Lyons jumped up. Daniels said, "We don't have to admit anything. Come along with us, Lane."

If CACO thought he was lying, CACO would see to it that he was never seen again. CACO was mistaken about him, of course, but CACO, like doctors, buried mistakes.

On leaving the apartment building, Lane immediately felt the warm tingling on his face and hands and, a few seconds later, the spreading of the warmth to his crotch. He forgot about that a moment later when Daniels shoved him as he started to get into the back seat of the CACO automobile. He turned and said, "Keep your dirty hands off me, Daniels! Push me, and I may just walk off. You might have to shoot me to stop me, and you wouldn't want to do that in broad daylight, would you?"

"Try it and find out," Daniels said. "Now shut up and get in or get knocked in. You know we're being observed. Maybe that's why you're making a scene."

Lane got into the back seat with Lyons, and Daniels drove them away. It was a hot June afternoon, and evidently the CACO budget did not provide for cars with air-conditioning. They rode with the windows down while Lyons and Daniels asked him questions. Lane answered all truthfully, if not fully, but he was not concentrating on his replies. He noticed that when he hung his hand out of the window, it felt warm and tingling.

Fifteen minutes later, the big steel doors of an underground garage clanged shut behind him. He was interrogated in a small room below the garage.

Electrodes were attached to his head and body, and various machines with large staring lenses were fixed on him while he was asked a series of questions. He never found out what the interpreters of the machines' graphs and meters thought about his reactions to the questions. Just as the electrodes were being detached, Smith, the man who had hired Lane for CACO, entered. Smith had a peculiar expression. He called the interrogators to one side and spoke to them in a low voice. Lane caught something about "a telephone call." A minute later, he was told he could go home. But he was to keep in touch, or, rather, keep himself available for CACO. For the time being, he was suspended from service.

Lane wanted to tell Smith that he was quitting CACO, but he had no desire to be "detained" again. Nobody quit CACO; it let its employees go only when it felt like it.

Lane went home in a taxi and had just started to pour himself a drink when the doorman called up.

"Feds, Mr. Lane. They got proper ID's."

Lane sighed, downed his Scotch and, a few minutes. later, opened the door. Lyons and two others, all holding .45 automatic pistols, were in the hall.

Lyons had a bandage around his head and some Band-Aids on one cheek and his chin. Both eyes were bloodshot.

"You're under arrest, Lane," Lyons said.

In the chair in the interrogation room, attached once again to various machines, Lane answered everything a dozen times over. Smith personally conducted the questioning, perhaps because he wanted to make sure that Lyons did not attack Lane.

It took Lane ten hours to piece together what had happened from occasional comments by Smith and Lyons. Daniels and Lyons had followed Lane when he had been released from CACO HQ. Trailing Lane by a block, Daniels had driven through a stoplight and into the path of a hot rod doing fifty miles an hour. Daniels had been killed. Lyons had escaped with minor injuries to the body but a large one to the psyche. For no logical reason, he blamed Lane for the accident.

After the interrogation, Lane was taken to a small padded room, given a TV dinner, and locked in. Naked, he lay down on the padded floor and slept. Three hours later, two men woke him up and handed him his clothes and then conducted him to Smith's office.

"I don't know what to do with you," Smith said. "Apparently, you're not lying. Or else you've been conditioned somehow to give the proper—or perhaps I should say, improper—responses and reactions. It's possible, you know, to fool the machines, what with all the conscious control of brain waves, blood pressure, and so on being taught at universities and by private individuals."

"Yes, but you know that I haven't had any such training," Lane said. "Your security checks show that."

Smith grunted and looked sour.

"I can only conclude," he said, "from the data that I have, that you are involved in counterespionage activity."

Lane opened his mouth to protest, but Smith continued, "Innocently, however. For some reason, you have become the object of interest, perhaps even concern, to some foreign outfit, probably Commie, most probably SKIZO, CACO's worst enemy. Or else you are the focus of some wildly improbable coincidences."

Lane couldn't think of anything to say to that. Smith said, "You were released the first time because I got a phone call from a high authority, a very high authority, telling me to let you go. By telling, I mean ordering. No reasons given. That authority doesn't have to give reasons.

"But I made the routine checkback, and I found out that the authority was fake. Somebody had pretended to be him. And the code words and the voice were exactly right. So, somehow, somebody, probably SKIZO, has cracked our code and can duplicate voices so exactly that even a voiceprint check can't tell the difference between the fake and the genuine. That's scary, Lane."

Lane nodded to indicate that he agreed it was scary. He said, "Whoever is doing this must have a damn good reason to reveal that he knows all this stuff. Why would a foreign agent show such a good hand just to get me out of your clutches—uh, custody? I can't do anyone, foreign agent or not, any good. And by revealing that they know the code words and can duplicate voices, they lose a lot. Now the code words will be changed, and the voices will be double-checked."

Smith drummed his fingers on the desktop and then said, "Yes, we know, But this extraordinary dermal sensitivity...these automobile accidents..."

"What did Lyons report about his accident?"

"He was unaware of anything wrong until Daniels failed to slow down on approaching the stoplight. He hesitated to say anything, because Daniels did not like backseat drivers, although Lyons was, as a matter of fact, in the front seat. Finally, he was unable to keep silent, but it was too late. Daniels looked up at the signal and said, 'What in hell you talking about?' and then the other car hit them."

Lane said, "Apparently Daniels thought the signal was green."

"Possibly. But I believe that there is some connection between the phone calls you got while with your women and the one I got from the supposed high authority."

"How could there be?" Lane said. "Why would this, this person, call me up just to ruin my lovemaking?"

Smith's face was as smooth as the face on a painting, but his fingers drummed a tattoo of desperation. No wonder. A case which could not even give birth to a hypothesis, let alone a theory, was the ultimate in frustration.

"I'm letting you go again, only this time you'll be covered with my agents like the North Pole is with snow in January," Smith said.

Lane did not thank him. He took a taxi back to his apartment, again feeling the tingling and warmth and mildly erotic sensations on the way to the taxi and on the way out of it.

In his rooms, he contemplated his future. He was no longer drawing pay from CACO, and CACO would not permit him to go to work for anybody else until this case was cleared up. In fact, Smith did not want him to leave his apartment unless it was absolutely necessary. Lane was to stay in it and force the unknown agency to come to him. So how was he to support himself? He had enough money to pay the rent for another month and buy food for two weeks. Then he would be eligible for welfare. He could defy Smith and get a job at nondetective work, say, a carryout boy at a grocery store or a car salesman. He had experience in both fields. But times were bad, and jobs of any kind were scarce.

Lane became angry. If CACO was keeping him from working, then it should be paying him. He phoned Smith, and, after a twelve-minute delay, during which Smith was undoubtedly checking back that it was really Lane, phoning, Smith answered.

"I should pay you for doing nothing? How could I justify that on the budget I got?"

"That's your problem."

Lane looked up, because he had carried the phone under the skylight and his neck had started tingling. Whoever was observing him at this moment had to be doing it from the Parmenter Building. He called Smith back and, after a ten-minute delay, got him.

"Whoever's laying a tap-in beam on me is doing it from any of the floors above the tenth. I don't think he could angle in from a lower floor."

"I know," Smith said. "I've had men in the Parmenter Building since yesterday. I don't overlook anything, Lane."

Lane had intended to ask him why he had overlooked the fact that they were undoubtedly being overheard at this moment. He did not do, so because it struck him that Smith wanted their conversations to be bugged. He was keen to appear overconfident so that SKIZO, or whoever it was, would move again. Lane was the cheese in the trap. However, anybody who threatened Lane seemed to get hurt or killed, and Smith, from Lane's viewpoint, was threatening him.

During the next four days, Lane read Volume IV of the Durants' *The Story of Civilization,* drank more than he should have, exercised, and spent a half hour each day, nude, under the skylight. The result of this exposure was that the skin burned and peeled all over his body. But the sexual titillation accompanying the dermal heat made the pain worth it. If the sensations got stronger each day, he'd be embarrassing himself, and possibly his observers, within a week.

He wondered if the men at the other end of the beam (or beams) had any idea of the gratuitous sexuality their subject felt. They probably thought that he was just a horny man with horny thoughts. But he knew that his reaction was unique, a result of something peculiar in his metabolism of his pigment or his whatever. Others, including Smith, had been under the skylight, and none had felt anything unusual.

The men investigating the Parmenter Building had detected nothing suspicious beyond the fact that there was nothing suspicious.

On the seventh day, Lane phoned Smith. "I can't take this submarine existence any longer. And I have to get a job or starve. So, I'm leaving. If your storm troopers try to stop me, I'll resist. And you can't afford to have a big stink raised."

In the struggle that followed, Lane and the two CACO agents staggered into the area beneath the skylight. Lane went down, as he knew he would, but he felt that be had to make some resistance or lose his right to call himself a man. He stared up into the skylight while his hands were cuffed. He was not surprised when the phone rang, though he could not have given a reasonable explanation of why he expected it.

A third agent, just entering, answered. He talked for a moment, then turned and said, "Smith says to let him go. And we're to come on home. Something sure made him change his mind."

Lane started for the door after his handcuffs were unlocked. The phone rang again. The same man as before answered it. Then he shouted at Lane to stop, but Lane kept on going, only to be halted by two men stationed at the elevator.

Lane's phone was being monitored by CACO agents in the basement of the apartment building. They had called up to report that Smith had not given that order. In fact; no one had actually called in from outside the building. The call had come from somewhere within the building.

Smith showed up fifteen minutes later to conduct the search throughout the building. Two hours later, the agents were told to quit looking. Whoever had made that call imitating Smith's voice and giving the new code words had managed, somehow, to get out of the building unobserved.

"SKIZO, or whoever it is, must be using a machine to simulate my voice," Smith said. "No human throat could do it well enough to match voiceprints."

Voices!

Lane straightened up so swiftly that the men on each side of him grabbed his arms.

Dr. Sue Brackwell!

Had he really talked to her that last time, or was someone imitating her voice, too? He could not guess why; the mysterious Whoever could be using her voice to advance whatever plans he had. Sue had said that she just wanted to talk for old times' sake. Whoever was imitating her might have been trying to get something out of him, something that would be a clue to…to what? He just did not know.

And it was possible that this Whoever had talked to Sue Brackwell, imitating his, Lane's voice.

Lane did not want to get her into trouble, but he could not afford to leave any possible avenue of investigation closed. He spoke to Smith about it as they went down the elevator. Smith listened intently, but he only said, "We'll see."

Glumly, Lane sat on the back seat between two men, also glum, as the car traveled through the streets of Washington. He looked out the window and through the smog saw a billboard advertising a rerun of *The Egg and I.* A block later, he saw another billboard, advertising a well-known brand of beer. SKY-BLUE WATERS, the sign said, and he wished he were in the land of sky-blue waters, fishing and drinking beer.

Again, he straightened up so swiftly that the two men grabbed him.

"Take it easy," he said. He slumped back down, and they removed their hands. The two advertisements had been a sort of free association test, provided only because the car had driven clown this route and not some other it might easily have taken. The result of the conjunction of the two billboards might or might not be validly linked up with the other circuits that had been forming in the unconscious part of his mind. But he now had a hypothesis. It could be developed into a theory which could be tested against the facts. That is, it could be if he were given a chance to try it.

Smith heard him out, but he had only one comment. "You're thinking of the wildest things you can so you'll throw us off the track."

"What track?" Lane said. He did not argue. He knew that Smith would go down the trail he had opened up. Smith could not afford to ignore anything, even the most farfetched of ideas.

Lane spent a week in the padded cell. Once, Smith entered to talk to him. The conversation was brief.

"I can't find any evidence to support your theory," Smith said.

"Is that because even CACO can't get access to certain classified documents and projects at Lackalas Astronautics?" Lane said.

"Yeah. I was asked what my need to know was, and I couldn't tell them what I really was trying to find out. The next thing I'd know, I'd be in a padded cell with regular sessions with a shrink."

"And so, because you're afraid of asking questions that might arouse suspicions of your sanity, you'll let the matter drop?"

"There's no way of finding out if your crazy theory has any basis."

"Love will find a way," Lane said.

Smith snorted, spun around, and walked out.

That was at 11 A.M. At 12:03, Lane looked at his wristwatch (since he was. no longer compelled to go naked) and noted that lunch was late. A few minutes afterward, an Air Force jet fighter on a routine flight over Washington suddenly dived down and hit CACO HQ at close to 1000 mph. It struck the massive stone building at the end opposite Lane's cell. Even so, it tore through the fortress-like outer walls and five rooms before stopping.

Lane, in the second subfloor, would not have been hit if the wreck had traveled entirely through the building. However, flames began to sweep through, and guards unlocked his door and got him outside just in time. On orders transmitted via radio, his escorts put him into a car to take him across the city to another CACO base. Lane was stiff with shock, but he reacted quickly enough when the car started to go through a red light. He was down on the floor and braced when the car and the huge Diesel met. The others were not killed. They were not, however, in any condition to stop him. Ten minutes later, he was in his apartment.

Dr. Sue Brackwell was waiting for him under the skylight. She had no clothes on; even her glasses were off. She looked very beautiful; it was not until much later that he remembered that she had never been beautiful or even passably pretty. He could not blame his shock for behaving the way he did, because the tingling and the warmth dissolved that. He became very alive, so much so that he loaned sufficient life to the thing that he pulled down to the floor. Somewhere in him existed the knowledge that "she" had prepared this for him and that no man might ever experience this certain event again. But the knowledge was so far off that it influenced him not at all.

Besides, as he had told Smith, love would find a way. He was not the one who had fallen in love. Not at first. Now, he felt as if he were in love, but many men, and women, feel that way during this time.

Smith and four others broke into the apartment just in time to rescue Lane. He was lying on the floor and was as naked and red as a newborn baby. Smith yelled at him, but he seemed to be deaf. It was evident that he was galloping with all possible speed in a race between a third-degree burn and an orgasm. He obviously had a partner, but Smith could neither see nor hear her.

The orgasm might have won if Smith had not thrown a big pan of cold water on Lane.

Two days afterward, Lane's doctor permitted Smith to enter the hospital room to see his much-bandaged and somewhat-sedated patient. Smith handed him a newspaper turned to page two. Lane read the article, which was short and all about EVE. EVE—Ever Vigilant Eye—had been a stationary-orbit surveillance satellite which had been sent up over the East Coast two years ago. EVE had exploded for unknown reasons, and the accident was being investigated.

"That's all the public was told," Smith said. "I finally got through to Brackwell and the other bigwigs connected with EVE. But either they were under orders to tell me as little as possible or else they don't have all the facts themselves. In any event, it's more than just a coincidence that she—EVE, I mean—blew up just as we were taking you to the hospital."

Lane said, "I'll answer some of your questions before you ask them. One, you couldn't see the holograph because she must've turned it off just before you got in. I don't know whether it was because she heard you coming or because she knew, somehow, that any more contact would kill me. Or maybe her alarms told her that she had better stop for her own good. But it would seem that she didn't stop or else did try to stop but was too late.

"I had a visitor who told me just enough about EVE so I wouldn't let my curiosity carry me into dangerous areas after I got out of here. And it won't. But I can tell you a few things and know it won't get any further.

"I'd figured out that Brackwell was the master designer of the bioelectronics circuit of a spy satellite. I didn't know that the satellite was called EVE or that she had the capability to beam in on ninety thousand individuals simultaneously. Or that the beams enabled her to follow each visually and tap in on their speech vibrations. Or that she could activate phone circuits with a highly variable electromagnetic held projected via the beam.

"My visitor said that I was not, for an instant, to suppose that EVE had somehow attained self-consciousness. That would be impossible. But I wonder.

"I also wonder if a female designer-engineer-scientist could, unconsciously, of course, design female circuits? Is there some psychic influence that goes along with the physical construction of computers and associated circuits? Can the whole be greater than the parts? Is there such a thing as a female gestalt in a machine?"

"I don't go for that metaphysical crap," Smith said.

"What does Brackwell say?"

"She says that EVE was simply malfunctioning."

"Perhaps man is a malfunctioning ape," Lane said. "But could Sue have built her passion for me into EVE? Or given EVE circuits which could evolve emotion? EVE had self-repairing capabilities, you know, and was part protein. I know it sounds crazy. But who, looking at the first apeman, would have extrapolated Helen of Troy?

"And why did she get hung up on me, one out of the ninety thousand she was watching? I had a dermal super-sensitivity to the spy beam. Did this reaction somehow convey to EVE a feeling, or a sense, that we were in rapport? And did she then become jealous? It's obvious that she modulated the beams she'd locked on Leona and Rhoda so that they saw green where the light was really red and did not see oncoming cars at all.

"And she worked her modulated tricks on Daniels and that poor jet pilot, too."

"What about that holograph of Dr. Brackwell?"

"EVE must've been spying on Sue, also, on her own creator, you might say. Or—and I don't want you to look into this, because it won't do any good now—Sue may have set all this up in the machinery, unknown to her colleagues. I don't mean that she put in extra circuits. She couldn't get away with that; they'd be detected immediately, and she'd have to explain them. But she could have put in circuits which had two purposes, the second off which was unknown to her colleagues. I don't know.

"But I do know that it was actually Sue Brackwell who called me that last time and not EVE. And I think that it was this call that put into EVE's mind, if a machine can have a mind in the human sense, to project the much-glamorized holograph of Sue. Unless, of course, my other theory is correct, and Sue herself was responsible for that."

Smith groaned and then said, "They'll never believe me if I put all this in a report. For one thing, will they believe that it was only free association that enabled you to get *eye in the sky* from 'The egg and I' and 'Sky-blue waters'? I doubt it. They'll think you had knowledge you shouldn't have had and you're concealing it with that incredible story. I wouldn't want to be in your shoes. But then, I don't want to be in my shoes.

"But why did EVE blow up? Lackalas says that she could be exploded if a destruct button at control center was pressed. The button, however, was not pressed."

"You dragged me away just in time to save my life. But EVE must have melted some circuits. She died of frustration—in a way, that is."

"What?"

"She was putting out an enormous amount of energy for such a tight beam. She must have overloaded."

Smith guffawed and said, "She was getting a charge out of it, too? Come on!"

Lane said, "Do you have any other explanation?"

The Sumerian Oath

A POLYTROPICAL PARAMYTH

Caught in the Frozen Foods & Ice Cream aisle, with an assassin coming down from each end, Goodbody leaped upon the top of the grocery cart. With the grace and the flair of Doctor Blood (as played by Errol Flynn), Goodbody dived over the top of Ice Cream Cones & Chocolate Syrups. At the same time, the push of his departing feet sent the cart down the aisle into the nearest assassin.

Though Goodbody soared with great aplomb and considerable beauty, he knocked over tall boxes of ice cream cones and fell down on the other side into the Home Hardware & Fix-It-Urself Supplies. The cataract of Goodbody. and wrenches, pliers, screwdrivers, boxes of nails, double sockets, and picture wire startled women customers and caused one to faint into Pet Foods & Bird Cages.

Goodbody dived under a railing and then galloped along the front of the store toward the Liquor Department. A shout caused him to look behind. The fools had actually pulled out their scalpels; they were indeed desperate. It was possible, however, that they did not mean to kill him inside the supermarket. They might be herding him into the parking lot, where others would net him.

He yanked over a pocketbook stand as he went by, whirling it so that *The Valley of The Dolls, The Arrangement, Couples,* and *Purple Sex Thing from the Fleshpot Planet* flew out like the hyperactive fingers of desperately hungry and desperately typing pornographers. The nearest pursuer, waving his scalpel, found that its tip was, embedded in *So You Want To Be a Brain Surgeon?*

How appropriate and how terrible, he thought as he fled through the door. He was the author of that best seller, the royalties of which he could not spend because he might find the AMA agents waiting to pick *him* up if *he* picked up the checks.

In the parking lot, almost as bright as day, a car leaped at him. He soared again, performing three entrechats to gain altitude (reminding him of the days when he had entered the operating amphitheater to the applause of famous surgeons and slack-jawed first-year students). He landed between a Chevy and a Caddy and was off. Tires screamed; doors slammed; feet pounded; voices growled.

"Doctor Goodbody! Halt! We mean no harm! This is for your own good! You're sick, man, sick!"

Cornered in the angle formed by two high walls, he turned to face them. Never let it be said that he would whimper, any more than Doctor Kildare, young god, would have whimpered, even if confronted with a large uncollectable bill.

Six came at him with glittering scalpels, He jerked out his own blade, speedy as Doctor Ehrlich's Magic Bullet. He would go down fighting; they would not get off lightly when they crossed steel with a man whose genius with the cutting edge was surpassed only by that of Doc Savage, now retired.

Herr Doktar Grossfleisch, huge as Laird Cregar when he played the medical student in *The Lodger,* floated forward and cast a hypodermic syringe, .1 caliber. The speed and accuracy with which it traveled would have delighted even crusty (but kindly) old Doctor Gillespie, especially as played by Lionel Barrymore. Goodbody responded with a magnificent parry that sent the syringe soaring over the wall, higher than the legendary intern who drank the embalming fluid.

Two eminent doctors, holding straitjackets before them with one hand and suturing needles with the other, like Roman *retiarii,* advanced. He slashed at them with such speed that five of them cried out with involuntary admiration. They hated themselves afterward for it and would, of course, be reprimanded by the AMA.

Grossfleisch cursed a forbidden curse, for which he would have to pay heavily, though not bloodily. Again her cast a huge syringe with a giant caliber tip, and it sailed over the shoulder of the doctor on Goodbody's left just as Goodbody made a thrust that would have caused Doctor Zorba to go pale with envy. But the needle penetrated Goodbody's extended right arm, and all became as black as the inside of the cabinet of Doctor Caligari.

"Shall we operate, Doctor Cyclops?"

The bright lamp showed six heads in consultation over him. Cyclops' shaven head and thick glasses were not among them. Goodbody had dreamed the words. Coming up from the depths of the dark subconscious, where the only light was the flickering silver of the projector beam on the flickering silver screen, he had brought up with him ancient cherished horrors.

Doctor Grossfleisch, author of *Sponge Counting Techniques* and *Extraordinary Cases of Involved and Involuted Intussusception of the Small Bowel I Have Known,* bent over him. The eyes were as empty and cold as the reflector on the head of a laryngologist. Yet this was the man who had sponsored him, the man who had taught him so much. This was the man who originated the justly famous *When in doubt, cut.*

Doctor Grossfleisch held an ice pick in his goblin-shaped hand.

"Schweinhund! First ve do to you der frontal lobotomy! Den der dissection mitout anesthesia alive yet!"

The ice pick descended toward his eyeball. A door exploded open. A scalpel streaked by Grossfleisch's zeppelin hip and stuck in the operating table, vibrating against Goodbody's strapped arm.

"Halt!"

The six heads turned, and Grossfleisch said, "Ah! Doc. for Leibfremd, world-famous healer and distinguished author of *Der Misunderstood Martyrs: Burke und Hare!* Vhat gifs for zuch a dramatic entrance?"

"Doctor Goodbody must be kept in good health! He is the only man with the genius to perform a brain operation, on our glorious leader, Doctor Inderhaus!"

Goodbody's akin turned cold, and he felt like fainting.

"Zo, our glorious leader has deep tumors of der cuneus and der lingual areas of der brain? Und Goodbody only has der chenius to cut? Mein Gott, how can ve trust him?"

"We stand behind him," Doctor Leibfremd said, "ready to thrust to the ganglia if he makes one false move!"

Goodbody sneered as if he were correcting an intern. "Why should I do this for you when you'll dissect me alive later?"

"Not so!" Leibfremd cried. "Despite your great crimes, we will let you live if you operate successfully on Doctor Inderhaus! Of course, you will be kept a prisoner, but in Grossfleisch's sanatorium, where, need I remind you, the patients live like kings, or, even better, Beverly Hills Physicians!"

"You would allow me to live?"

"You will die a natural death! You will not be touched by a doctor!" Grossfleisch said. "And you will get a professional courtesy discount, too! Ten percent off your bill!"

"Thank you," Goodbody said humbly. But he was thinking of ways to escape even then. The world must know the ghastly truth.

The day of the great operation, the amphitheater was filled with doctors from all over the world: The life of their glorious leader, Doctor

Inderhaus, was at stake, and only the condemned criminal, the Judas, the Benedict Arnold, the Mudd, the Quisling of the medical profession, could save him.

The patient, head shaven, was wheeled in. He shook hands with himself as his colleagues cheered wildly. Tears dripped down his cheeks at this exhibition of love and respect, not unmixed with awe. Then he saw his surgeon approaching, and the benignity of Hyde changed to the hideous face of Jekyll.

Goodbody slipped on his mask and gloves. Grossfleisch held a scalpel to his back, and a man, who looked like Doctor Casey after a hard night with the head nurse, aimed a laser at Goodbody.

"Stand back! Give me room!" Goodbody said. He was icy cold, calm as the surface of a goldfish bowl, his long delicate fingers, which could have been a concert pianist's if he had gone wrong, flexed as if they were snakes smelling blood. A hush fell. Though the audience hated him to a man, despised and loathed him, and longed to spit on him (with no sterilization before or after), they could not help admiring him.

The hours ticked by. Scalpels cut. The scalp was rolled back. Drills growled; saws whined. The top of the skull came out. The keen blades began slicing into the gray wrinkled mass.

"Ach!" Grossfleisch said involuntarily as the forebrain same up like a drawbridge. "Mein Gott! Zuch daringk!"

There was a communal "Ah!" as Goodbody held up the great jellyfish-shaped tumor in his fist. Despite themselves, the doctors gave him a standing ovation that lasted ten minutes.

It was sad, he thought, that the greatest triumph of a series of blazing triumphs the apex of his career, was also his black defeat, the nadir. And then the patient was wheeled out, and the surgeon was seized, stripped, and strapped. Grossfleisch and Ueberpreis, well-known proctologist and author of the notorious article *Did Doctor Watson Poison His Three Wives?,* approached the operating table. They were smiling with an utterly evil coldness and abhorrently sadistic pleasure, like Doctor Mabuses.

The audience leaned forward. They had always felt that both the patient and doctor were better off without employing anesthesia. The physician could determine the patient's reactions much more accurately and quickly if his responses were not dulled.

"Doctor X, I presume?" Goodbody said as he awoke.

"What!" said the nurse, Mrs. Fell.

"A nightmare. I thought my arms and legs had been cut off. Oh!"

"You'll get used to that," the nurse said. "Anytime you need anything, just press that plate with your nose. Don't be bashful. Doctor Grossfleisch said I was to wait on you hand and foot. I mean..."

"I'm not only a basket case but a crazy basket case," he said. "I'm sure that I've been certified insane, haven't I?"

"Well," Mrs. Fell said, "who knows what insane means! One man's looniness is another man's religion. I mean, one man's schizophrenia is another man's manic-depressiveness. Well, you know what I mean!"

It was no use telling her his story, but he had to.

"Don't just dismiss what I'm about to tell you as the ravings of a maniac. Think about it for a long time; look around you. See if what I say doesn't make sense, even if it seems a topsy-turvy sense."

He had one advantage. She was a nurse, and all nurses, by the time they were graduated, loathed doctors. She would be ready to believe the worst about them.

"Every medical doctor takes the oath of Hippocrates. But, before he swears in public, he takes a private, a most arcane, oath. And that oath is much more ancient than that of Hippocrates, who, after all, died in 377 B.C., comparatively recently.

"'The first witch doctor of the Old Stone Age may have given that oath to the second witch doctor. Who knows? But it is recorded, in a place where you will never see it, that the first doctor of the civilized world, the first doctor of the most ancient city-state, that of Sumer, predecessor even of old Egypt, swore in the second doctor.

"The Sumerian oath–scratch my nose, will you, my dear?–required that a medical doctor must never, under any circumstances, reveal anything at all about the true nature of doctors or of the true origin of diseases."

Mrs. Fell listened with only a few interruptions. Then she said, "Doctor Goodbody! Are you seriously trying to tell me that diseases would not exist if it were not for doctors? That doctors manufacture diseases and spread them around? That if it weren't for doctors, we'd all be one hundred percent healthy? That they pick and choose laymen to infect and to cure so they can get good reputations and make money and dampen everybody's suspicions by...by... that's ridiculous!"

The sweat tickled his nose, but he ignored it. "Yes, Mrs. Fell, that's true! And, rarely, but it does happen, a doctor can't take being guilty of mass murder anymore, and he breaks down and tries to tell the truth! And then he's hauled off, declared insane by his colleagues, or dies during an operation, or gets sick and dies, or just disappears!"

"And why weren't you killed?"

"I told you! I saved our glorious leader; the Grand Exalted Iatrogenic Sumerian. They promised me my life, and we don't lie to each other, just to laymen! But they made sure I couldn't escape, and they didn't cut my tongue out because they're sadistic! They get a charge out of me telling my story here, because who's going to believe me, a patient in a puzzle factory? Yes, Mrs. Fell, don't look so shocked! A booby hatch, a nut house! I'm a loony, right? Isn't that what you believe?"

She patted the top of his head. "There, there! I believe you! I'll see what I can do. Only..."

"Yes?"

"My husband is a doctor, and if I thought for one moment that he was in a secret organization...!"

"Don't ask him!" Goodbody said. "Don't say a word to any doctor! Do you want to come down with cancer or infectious hepatitis or have a coronary thrombosis? Or catch a brand-new disease? They invent a new one now and then, just to relieve the boredom, you know!"

It was no use. Mrs. Fell was just going along with him to soothe him.

And that night he was carried into the depths beneath the huge old house, where torches flickered and cold gray stones sweat and little drums beat and shrill goat horns blew and docs with painted faces and red robes and black feathers rattling gourds and thrumming bullroarers administered the Sumerian oath to the graduating class, 1970, of Johns Hopkins. And. they led each young initiate before him and pointed out what would happen if he betrayed his profession.

Extracts from the Memoirs of Lord Greystoke

edited by Philip José Farmer

HOW IT WAS WITH J

I looked out of the cabin window, and there was the ship.

I'd seen ships in pictures, but this was a real sailing ship, an enormous thing of beauty and awe.

I KNEW IT was artificial, but I never thought of it as such. It was a living being, as much alive as an elephant and even stranger than my first sight of an elephant. I never was to get over that deeply ingrained assumption that anything that moved was alive. I've traveled on a hundred ships, driven dozens of automobiles, and piloted scores of airplanes, and I always feel that I am on or in a living being.

And so I waited for the great creature to come to a stop and let the smaller creatures, human beings, from its back. My heart was thudding, I was dry-skinned, my mouth was dry, and I was quivering. At last! To see, not pictures, but the flesh! To face, to talk with, beings of my own kind!

Still, I did not run out to greet them. My experiences with the blacks had taught me that humans might be hostile no matter how friendly I was.

I retreated from the cabin to the bush, and there I spied on them. Presently, a longboat was let down off the davits (I was proud because I knew what *davits* were, though couldn't pronounce the word, of course).

After a while, the boat beached, and some men got out onto the sand. A few minutes later, one of them was murdered during a quarrel.

I was wise to hide in the bush. They were dangerous.

When I saw J* step out of the boat, I was thrilled. I had never seen anything so beautiful except for my foster mother, and that was a completely different kind of beauty, of course. I also got an erection.

This was the normal response of a twenty-year-old human male and of an adult male n'k. B never mentioned this in his novel for several reasons. One, he did not know of it. Two, if he had guessed that it did occur, he could not have described it. Such references were forbidden. He might have said that I was "inflamed with lust," but then the literary conventions required that the hero be "pure in thought and deed." "Purity" required that his mind and body be unconnected with his genitals. Every adult reader knew, of course, that the hero would have an erection, but this was ignored. Or perhaps every adult reader did not know this. The ignorance of sexual matters among the female population of English speakers circa 1909 was amazing. And often tragic.

I did know, from my reading, that the characters in the novels were never described as having genitals nor was the sexual act described except by the most circuitous route. And only the villains were ever "inflamed with lust."

I knew that if I were to display myself to the woman, she would be shocked and repelled. But even if I had done so, I was wearing an antelope-skin loincloth. This was one I'd taken from a black and habitually wore because I *knew* that humans did not expose their genitals. I was mistaken in this, since a number of preliterates, various Sudanese blacks, and Australian aborigines, etc., go completely naked. Or did so at that time.

The males who had first landed seemed to be in control of the woman and her party, so I did not venture out. I was afraid, rightly, that the sailors would try to kill me if I revealed myself. I intended to watch until I got a chance to rescue the woman and her party. I wasn't sure whether or not the sailors intended to butcher their prisoners and eat them. Though none of the novels or histories I'd read had said anything about cannibalism being accepted in human civilization, I assumed that it was tabu. The article on cannibalism in the encyclopedia stated that the custom was prevalent among certain groups of

* I don't know if this stands for Jane, Jean, Jill, June or some other name. "Greystoke" has the annoying, but necessary, habit of using initials only to designate individuals whose identity needs shielding.

African blacks, and I knew that the blacks near the n'k territory were cannibals. Perhaps the practice existed among some groups of whites.

In any event, I did know that rape was common among all groups of men, and I was determined that the woman was not going to be raped. Not unless, of course, she accepted it. I understood that there were certain women, prostitutes or whores, who sold their bodies for use by men. The woman did not seem to be one of those, but then I did not know exactly how one recognized a whore.

I kept a close watch on the tall beautiful blonde with the large grey eyes. Events for the next few days occurred somewhat as B described them, including my posting a warning note on the door of the cabin after it had been ransacked by the mutineers. I was capable by then of writing simple English sentences. Contrary to what B wrote, however, I did not sign my n'k name. This would have been impossible, since I did not know the correlation of n'k sounds with the Latin alphabet. I printed the English translation of one of my n'k names: WHITE BOY. Rather, I gave the translation I preferred. As I've said elsewhere, my name could be translated as Worm, Hairless Boy, and others even more derogatory.

B was also correct when he described me as breaking the neck of a big cat with a full nelson when it tried to get into the cabin window after J and E.* However, the cat was a leopard, not a lioness, and it was an old male. One of the extraordinarily large leopards that existed in that area, it had become a man-eater, preying on the village of blacks. Actually, it was my fault that it was a man-eater, since I had thrown the body of one of the blacks I'd killed to it and so enabled it to acquire a taste for human meat.

On that day when J and E bathed in a pool and J was carried off by Tks, I heard her screaming and tracked the two down. Tks had become king of the tribe after I'd abdicated, but he had been driven out because of his cruelty and his disdain of the tribal laws. He was, I believe, a psychopath. His aberrations may have been caused by being dropped on his head when he was an infant. In any event, he was wandering around when he saw J bathing. He grabbed her and ran off. He did not swing through the trees with her as B described. He was too heavy to have progressed in monkey fashion even if he had been alone. He ran with her in his arms until he got winded and then pushed her ahead of him.

I arrived before he could rape her, and I killed him with my knife. This would have happened sooner or later, since Tks hated me, and I was happy to have it over with. Besides, it made me look good in J's eyes.

---

* J's black mother surrogate, the servant of J's father. J's mother died at J's birth, and E raised her. E was J's chaperone on the treasure-hunting expedition.

She, however, had a short-lived relief. I scooped her up and kissed her all over, as was the n'k custom when making love. This panicked her, and she fought and screamed. I stopped, since I did not want to offend her, though I did not understand why she was so frightened. After I released her, she insisted that we return to the pool so she could put her clothes on. I did not understand her words or gestures, though the gestures were plain enough. I think now that I did not want to understand her. I wanted to keep her for my own, and I was sure that in a short time she would get over her fright.

As B said, I did not return her to the cabin until the next day. She got over her fright somewhat, though my evident tumescent state ensured that she could not relax completely. When night came, I tried to hold her in my arms to keep her warm (also hoping by this to overcome her objections). But she would have none of that. She preferred to sit against the trunk of a tree and shiver all night.

Our relations were not quite as idyllic or as innocent as B portrayed.

Next day, I took her back to the pool, where she donned her clothes. I wanted to watch her, but she made it evident that I must not do so. I did not understand why she was so embarrassed by covering her nakedness. After all, she had been completely naked for twenty-four hours.

NOW THAT I look back on it, I am surprised that J did not become so disgusted with me that she found it impossible to love me. My eating habits must have repulsed her, and my lack of Western toilet training horrified her. But she understood that I was a feral man and that I was in no way responsible for my behavior. She also understood that I was restraining myself from making love to her and so I got some credit as being a basically decent human being.

I wonder what she would have thought if she had known that I'd mated quite often with some of the n'k females? I was unable to tell her about this at that time, and it was just as well. Though she was a liberal-minded woman despite her Victorian conditioning, she might not ever have forgiven me for having three wives. Having had, I should say. When I abdicated the kingship and left the tribe, I also divorced the three females, since I did not want them as companions.

Some years later, I told her about them, and her only response was to laugh and to ask me if I had had any children by them. I answered, truthfully, that I had not.

Since these females had babies by n'k males after I'd left them, it was evident that they were not sterile. I don't know whether it was impossible for a human to fertilize a n'k or whether I am just not very fertile. I've had only one child by J, though we've never used any birth control methods. So I presume that I am at fault.

But, as J has several times remarked, thank goodness virility has nothing to do with fertility.

THE WAY IT WAS WITH O

IN HIS SECOND novel about me, B gives a somewhat bowdlerized and distorted account of my "affair" with O, Countess C. (Lovely woman, she is dead now. After her much older husband died, she remarried and had four children, one of whom I met while he served with the Free French in World War II.)

B says that O and I were alone in her house, though our assignation had, in the beginning, no sexual intent. But we were in each other's arms when her husband, warned by that despicable blackmailer, her brother, entered with intent to kill.

I don't know what would have happened if he had not burst in on us. I myself was not sure what my conduct should be, since I was not sure of the rules in this particular case. I suspect that I would have followed my natural inclinations unless O had said no, and she did not seem likely to do so.

I was neither engaged nor married and was on the rebound from J. As far as I knew, J and I would never see each other again. But I did want to follow the rules of society. The trouble here was that I did not know what the rules were in this particular contest.

Adultery was illegal, but I had observed that humans often did what was illegal and did not consider adultery immoral. At least, not very immoral.

I myself had none of the moral objections to sexual conduct by which humans are supposed to guide themselves. Though adultery is frowned upon by the n'k, everybody practices it. If caught, they suffer physical punishment, not the pangs of conscience or ostracism from society. Once the beating is over, the thing is done.

I was in Paris, and I knew that the rules depended upon the situation. Some French men would kill you if they caught you with their wives. Others accepted it as long as the business was conducted discreetly.

So what, I wondered, was the context of the situation with O? To which group did her husband belong?

While I was wrestling with this problem, O was preparing to disrobe. Whatever her husband's attitude, she was getting ready to mate with me.

I wasn't, as B implied, "loath" to mate. But I did intend to ask her what her husband thought about this.

Then he burst in with a loaded cane and tried to kill me with it. I lost my temper, and I reverted to my normal state of the threatened n'k. If O had not cried out so vehemently, I would have killed him as a terrier kills a rat. But I stopped; and then, cooling off, I felt that I should abide by the human rules. I had made a mistake and must suffer the consequence. Hence, the duel which B describes wherein I refused to fire back at him. Hence, my lie about the seriousness of the intentions of his wife and myself.

A number of B's critics have said that I acted as if I had been born in King Arthur's court. No real human being would have acted as self-sacrificingly as I did. What they overlooked is that I felt obligated to obey the rules because I was not thoroughly human.

Later on, after I had comprehended the extent of the hypocrisy of humans, I would not have behaved so chivalrously. I would have lied to save O, taken the blame, but I would have shot the count in the arm and rendered him hors de combat.

But then I would never have gotten unto the situation in the first place.

HOW I ESCAPED PUBLICITY

If events had been exactly as B described them, the whole world would have been cognizant of me, and nobody would now think of me as a fictional character. The publicity would have turned my life into hell. My only escape would have been to plunge back into the jungle.

D* was well aware of what would happen if my story became known. He was afraid that publicity might destroy me.

My cousin had already inherited the title, and I did not wish to file my claim on it. As B says, I sacrificed my rightful inheritance because I thought that J wished to marry my cousin. I was willing to give up everything if it meant that J would be happy.

I know that this sounds like the noble act of the hero of a romantic novel. But it happened. Perhaps it happened so easily because I had read such novels and thought that I should abide by the rules expressed and implied in them. But I don't really think so. I loved J, and I loathed my cousin because he had, I thought, won out over me. But I did not hate J because she had rejected me. I could understand why she, a highly cultured person, would not want to marry a man raised by beasts. (She thought the n'k were some kind of apes, but even if I had been raised in an Amazonian Indian tribe, she would have hesitated. Or so I thought.)

B says nothing about my difficulties in getting a passport in Port-Gentil* and taking passage to France. But D knew that there would be much trouble when I entered the town unless a suitable story was prepared. Otherwise, the authorities would have thrown me into gaol while they investigated my unauthorized presence in the French territory of Gabon.

While I waited in the jungle outside Libreville, D arranged with some of the bribable authorities to get me a passport. My borrowed identity was that of a Monsieur Jeanne Charles Corday, a Norman trader. Corday's post was far up the Ogouée River, but he was at that time in Port-Gentil. For the sum D promised him, Corday was quite willing to surrender his passport. It was arranged that Corday would be smuggled out of Gabon and back to France at a later date. Corday would then pick up the passport in France as if he had had it all along. By then I was to have assumed a new identity, that of an Englishman.

All this cost D much, but he was quite wealthy and willing to spend much for the man who had saved his life.

As it turned out, after we got to France, D received word that Corday had died of a fever and had been secretly buried by a man in on the deal. So I remained Corday for a long tune. Corday had no relatives and had been out of France for fourteen years so there were no problems in the familial area.

My imperfect French and unfamiliarity with French customs was explained to those authorities not in on the plot as the result of an accident. A blow on the head had impaired my mental functions, and I was returning to France for treatment.

Events transpired somewhat as B has described them. I lived in Paris, studied the English and French languages and the people, read books on many subjects, learning to read while I read, smoked cigarettes, drank absinthe, beat up some thugs who attacked me and then some policemen who tried to arrest me, went through the affair of O and the count, and then traveled to America. There I drove to Wisconsin, saved J from a forest fire, was rejected by J, and received the telegram that told me that the fingerprints on my father's diary were indeed mine. I was the rightful heir to the fortune and the title. Though I must add that I was neither the viscount B said I was nor the duke and earl that F** facetiously said I was.

---

* A town in Gabon, an area on the west coast of equatorial Africa.

** Your editor.

I am titled, and I am descended from viscounts, dukes, and royalty. But I am only a b....[*]

F constructed a highly romantic and grandiose lineage for me in his "biography."[**] He claims to be more of a realistic writer than B, but he is a romantic who clothes his fantasizing with the trappings of reality. He could have told more of the true story in his biography without disclosing my real identity, but he couldn't resist the temptation to gild the lily more than a little. However, I am in Burke's *Peerage,* though not under Greystoke, of course. I am descended from the historical Barons Greystoke and related to the Howards. But that can be said of hundreds of people or, for all I know, thousands.

There was only one way I could have gotten the title and the money without publicity. Nor do I know why B did not tell the real story in his account of how I became....[***] Perhaps he felt the publication of the novel was too close in time to the real events. He may have felt that somebody might have investigated and have been lucky enough to detect the fraud. After all, all one had to do was to reread the English newspapers of a few years back. However, he would not have found that a young English....[****] had been shipwrecked off the coast of Africa and, after some hardships, had been rescued. T's[*****] yacht, contrary to what B said, was only disabled, not sunk.

On the other hand, my father had been on a secret mission for the British government, and when he and his wife disappeared, the government gave out a totally misleading report. So I can't be tracked down through that account.

Even if some determined person did come across the proper clues, he wouldn't find me. I have already faked my death. Nor would he dare make a public accusation. He would be laughed to scorn and undoubtedly sued by my family. B has done me the inestimable favor of establishing once and for all in the minds of the public that I am a purely fictional person.

Half of the events told in B's second novel had their parallel in reality. It is not true that J was abducted by men who would have had to trail me across

* The rest is deleted by Greystoke. B could stand for baron or baronet. If it is the latter, Greystoke would be addressed as Sir, not Lord. Nor would he be a noble. Baronets are a sort of hereditary knights.

** Philip José Farmer, *Tarzan Alive* (New York: Popular Library 1973).

*** Deleted by Greystoke.

****

***** T is Greystoke's cousin.

half of Africa if B's account had been true. Actually, though I did find that lost city, those Cold Lairs inhabited by a few survivors of an ancient Caucasian people, that "rose-red city half as old as time," before I returned to the west coast, I was not to visit it again until some years later.

I did find my cousin* dying on the west coast, and he told me how he had been aware that I was the true heir but had concealed it from J.

After he had died, J told me what would happen if I stepped forth to make my claim. I would never know a moment's privacy while I lived in the civilized world.

"I wouldn't either," J said. "As your wife, I'd be subject to just as much publicity."

"Then I won't claim it," I said.

"No," She said. "You have a right to it."

She looked at her dead fiancé and said, "We've commented on how much you look like him. So..."

My cousin was only an inch shorter than I and had an athlete's physique. His features were much like mine, which wasn't surprising considering that my grandfather and his father were brothers. And he had the same black hair and grey eyes.

"Technically, it's illegal," she said. "But it's not a criminal fraud. You wouldn't be getting anything you aren't entitled to."

So that is why we buried him there and journeyed up the coast to where the rest of the shipwrecked party was. Nobody there who knew my cousin was fooled, of course. But after J had explained what I was going to do and why, they agreed to keep silent. D was the only one from the French ship that rescued us who knew my identity, and he thought that the deception was a splendid idea.

N** remained to be dealt with. He would have been glad to keep silent, too, if I would pay him blackmail. Of that we were all sure. But he had no idea that my cousin had died, and we did not tell him. He was put in the ship's brig and turned over to the French police at Marseilles. I returned to England as my cousin.

We were taking a long chance, though not as long as it might seem at first sight. My cousin had been out of England for a year, taking a sort of Grand Tour before he went to Oxford. He was only nineteen and hence might

* This is not T but WC, Greystoke's nearest relative.

** O's brother, a member of the party but under an assumed name and wanted by the French police.

reasonably be expected to have grown another inch in a year's time. The scars on my forehead and body could be accounted for as a result of the accident to the ship and the jungle hardships. Since I am a gifted mimic, I had no trouble imitating his voice, the timbre of which resembled mine somewhat in any case. His parents were dead, and he had seen no close relatives for years. The servants at the ancestral hall and the villagers nearby were a sticky problem. But they were described to me, their photographs shown, if available, and I was filled in on them by my third cousin, Lord...* He was, as B said, a member of the party, in fact, the owner of the yacht which had sunk. He was marrying J's best friend, and he was very sympathetic when he heard my story. He furnished me with all the information he had about the servants and the villagers.

He also told me as much as he knew about my cousin's friends and his schoolmates. He had gone to Rugby, too, though he was three years ahead of my cousin. He had kept in contact with him after school. They ran in the same circles and belonged to the same clubs.

Still, I was bound to run into friends and relatives of my cousin about whom I would know nothing. So it was thought best to pretend that I had suffered partial amnesia as a result of the shipwreck.

This story got me through a number of difficult situations.

The servants and the villagers must have thought that my African experience had made me rather odd. But if they suspected that I was not who I was supposed to be, they did not bruit it about.

About a year later, N escaped from the French prison. He looked up his old crony in crime, P, and they came to England. Why, I don't know. But somehow they found out that I had taken my cousin's place. They were in a position to blackmail me and would have done so if they had not known that I would kill them regardless of the consequences. Instead, they kidnapped my baby and J and carried them off to Africa. J was to be sold to some desert sultan, and my son was to be raised as a black savage. In this respect, B was correct. But much of the third novel is grossly exaggerated, and many things he describes never happened.

My son died of a jungle fever; N was killed much as B describes. P escaped but was never heard of again, though B used him as a character in the fourth novel. I imagine he died in the jungle shortly after escaping.

And that is how I was able to claim my inheritance with only a few people knowing that I was not my cousin..

* Deleted by Greystoke.

HIS EARLY LIFE IN THE RAIN FOREST

"In the beginning was the Word."

True perhaps for the creation of the world. But not true in any case. In the beginning was a pair of large soft brown breasts with enormous pink nipples. These constitute my earliest memory, which goes back, I believe, to when I was two or three years old. I was not completely weaned until I was about six years old; and when my mother (foster mother, rather) told me I could suckle no more, I went into a screaming rage. I felt that I was no longer loved, that I had been rejected by the only person I loved. She expected this and was prepared. Instead of cuffing me, as she often did when I was misbehaving, she took me into her arms. She explained that I couldn't expect to be treated any longer as a baby, since I was not a baby. I had to become independent of her. She had suckled me for a far longer time than any infant of the tribe was suckled. My playmates were jeering at me because I was still taking her milk, and this added to my burden of being different from the others. I needed to become as much like them as possible. This was one more step toward making them forget my alienness.

Moreover, to nurse me so long, she had given up mating, and while she had no particular desire for any male of the tribe, she was suffering from lack of sexual intercourse. Also, the women and the male elders were urging her to mate again. The tribe needed every infant it could get in order to keep its numbers at a constant level.

That she refused me her breasts did not mean that she no longer loved me. She was doing this for my own good and for the good of the tribe.

None of this except the statement that she still loved me meant anything to me. I would have seen the whole tribe dead before I would have given up the delicious and warm and cozy feeling of suckling. In fact, if I had been big enough and strong enough, I would at that moment have scooped up my mother and run away with her into the forest. And I suppose that if I had been that big and strong, I would have mated with her. There was a diffuse element of sexuality in this suckling. At least, I always got an erection when I suckled. My mother took no especial notice of this, though some of my playmates commented on it. Erections were common among both adults and children of the tribe and accepted with a blaséness that human beings would have regarded as shockingly immoral. Civilized human beings, anyway. There are some preliterate peoples who regard this as natural. Among some peoples of the Sudan area, where the male is naked, if a male should happen to pass by a female and get an erection, the female looks upon it as a compliment. And if no one else is around, the two are liable to go into the bushes.

So it was with the tribe, though there was seldom a chance to commit adultery. Its members felt uneasy when out of sight of the tribe, which is why expulsion was the worst thing that could happen to a member. If he or she could not quickly find another tribe and be adopted to it, he or she just sat down and within a few days grieved themselves to death. This happened far sooner than starvation can account for. The heart was broken and simply quit beating.

I never felt this uneasiness; and if I had been exiled, I would have reacted with rage, not depression. This stemmed from my feeling of alienness, of course, but it was a healthy expression. Better to be mad than sad. Though this feeling of alienness sometimes made me unhappy, it was in the long run a survival factor. Certainly, without it, I could never have spent these days by myself in the cabin teaching myself how to read English. Nor would I have been able to leave the tribe, forever, I thought, when I finally did find people like myself.

I've read Freud and the other great interpreters of the human psyche, Jung, Adler, Sullivan, and so on. On first reading Freud, I believed that every word he said was true. The Oedipal situation seemed to me to be a universal phenomenon. But that was because Freud had certain personal attitudes that coincided with mine. My attitudes came about because of the similarity of his familial situation and mine. I had a mother who was the center of my universe. Or, at least, the only other center of which I was aware. I don't think anybody ever gets over the infant feeling that he is truly the focus of the world. Not completely, anyway. Maturity is a relative state; the most mature are those who have traveled the most distance from that infantile attitude. But nobody has ever gone over the horizon and out of sight of it.

My mother loved only me and I loved only her, outside of ourselves of course. My stepfather hated me, and I knew from an early age that if I didn't kill him first he would kill me. And I was, of course, intensely jealous of him. He was always importuning K'l to mate with him, and though she would always say no, I was afraid that someday she would weaken and say yes. That meant that I'd be sharing her with him, which would have been as traumatic for me as losing an arm or leg or going blind.

Thus we had a sort of *Oedipus Rex* in the jungle, with P/t as King Laius, K'l as Jocasta, and myself as Oedipus. P/t was no king and never would be. But I fantasized from an early age that I would be king someday, which meant that I would have to kill the king, Kck, in combat. Kck tried many times to get K'l to slip away into the bushes with him, and since he knew that she would do so if it were not for me, he hated me almost as much as P/t did. So, in a sense, both P/t and Kck represented King Laius.

I don't want to strain this analogy too far. My readings of Freud and his critics, plus my own observations of many human societies, have convinced me that Freud often applied his own peculiar familial situation as a general principle to all of humanity. I don't think that the majority of male children hate their fathers because of any sexual jealousy. Nor do I think that any but a small minority of female children have penis envy. They might envy the physical superiority and the economic and political benefits that having a penis automatically confer upon the male. There is as much evidence that males might have a vagina envy. That is, very little evidence at all.

On the other hand, Freud did bring the concept of the unconscious mind to its fullest fruition; and he did discover that sexuality is much more diffuse than previously thought, that it pervades and influences most of the elements of human behavior. Sexuality is, in short, a field that stretches far beyond the genital; or, put differently, the genital invades every area of human behavior. The Westerners of his day were loath to accept this, and there are still many who reject this concept.

This rejection is founded on hypocrisy. In fact, society is founded on hypocrisy (among other things). It is my belief that if hypocrisy were eliminated overnight as if it were fecal matter, and people became completely honest, society would fall apart. This dictum applies to all human societies, literate or preliterate.

Hypocrisy has caused much misery and injustice, in fact, the deaths of millions of people over a period of perhaps a million years. But hypocrisy is one of the bonds that keeps human society from collapsing like an old castle a hurricane.

I loathe and abominate hypocrisy; yet, when I am among humans, I have to practice it myself to a certain extent. If I didn't, I wouldn't be able to operate effectively in human society. As it is, I don't operate with a high efficiency. Though I am under no compulsion to be frank when I am disgusted with hypocrites, which means that I can keep silent under most conditions, I seem to radiate disgust. I betray myself in a silent language with certain inflections of stance, gesture, and facial expression; and most humans detect this. They resent it, of course, which makes it difficult to generate any warmth, any feeling of closeness or of equality, between me and most human beings.

As for frankness, I have observed that people who boast of being frank generally are so for one reason. They want to hurt others. They say they are frank because of their love for truth. But they lie to themselves and fail to deceive others with this lie.

I spoke of equality above. There is much talk of equality in human society but very little exists. Human beings have a pecking order just as animals and the subhumans of my tribe have one. Even two individuals of assumed social equality fight on a conscious or unconscious level for a subtly superior position. However, the pecking order is much less rigid in human society than among animals or in any tribe. Among animals the order is usually established in a very short time. It does change but not very often. Death and sickness are the chief operands. In my tribe, the order is somewhat more fluid, and the structure is dual. That is, the females' status is not altogether dependent upon the status of her mate. If she is exceptionally fertile, she may be accorded a higher position than her mate. But this usually results in some male trying to acquire her so he may acquire more status. This sounds contradictory in view of what I've said about the mate of the exceptionally fertile female not gaining status also. But the society of my tribe, like human society, contains a number of contradictory attitudes. If a male can take an exceptionally fertile female away from another male, by physical or verbal means, then this acquisition confers additional status on the male. A male with two females as mates is higher in the pecking order than a male with only one. A male with three females, two of which are infertile or not very productive of infants, has less status than a male with two fertile females. At the same time, his females may have a higher standing in the female pecking order than he has in the male order.

This could result in the females of a lower male having a higher status than the mates of the king. It seldom does because the king is keenly aware that the status of his females is a reflection of his own. The younger and more vigorous of the adult males begin thinking of challenging the king when this occurs. But the king knows this, and so he takes the fertile females away from the lower male. This is not usually done by an open and brutal assault upon the lower male. The king asks the females to become his mates. They have the option of rejecting him, but they seldom do. The females of my tribe are as impressed by social position as are the females of human society.

If the females should refuse the king, the king may then harass the lower male in a hundred different ways. If, for instance, the lower male feels that his particular feeding territory has been invaded by another male, he will appeal to the king to settle the case. The king, though he knows that the claimant's case is just, may decide against him. The king may treat the lower male with an obvious contempt or with open insults which go beyond that determined by the male's position in the pecking order. The rest of the tribe quickly perceive this, and in a short time the male is relegated to an even more inferior position.

The male can then fight the males who are pushing him on down. If he loses, he goes down to the very bottom of the hierarchy. In effect, he has to fight every male above and below him, usually in one day, and even the strongest would tire halfway through this ordeal. So he's doomed to plumb the social abyss unless he challenges the king himself.

Possibly, he might win, in which case he comes out on top. The king doesn't then go to the lowest rank; the king is dead. Most fights between males end when one male confesses that he is beaten, but the battle for kingship is to the death.

Unless the lower male is unusually powerful, or the king is getting old, the lower male usually does not challenge the king. But he is frantic at losing status, and this may cause him to challenge the king. The king knows this, and he also knows that chance or the sheer desperation of the male may result in him (the king) being defeated. So, as often happens in human society, some sort of compromise is worked out. The king takes the fertile females of the lower male but gives the lower male his own infertile or less physically desirable females. The male retains his original status, since it is felt that a male who gets the king's females, even though they were rejected, gains a certain status. This gain cancels the loss of his fertile females.

The pecking order is not as complex or as fluid as that in human society. But it is complex enough that a 50,000-word book could be written about it.

When I say that the king can take or give away females, I do not mean that the females have no say in this. A male can divorce a female, or she him, with a declaration within the hearing of the king and the majority of the tribe. This applies even to the females of the king, though I never saw such an instance.

On the other hand, taking a female is not as simple as among the baboons, for instance. The male cannot take a mate just because he is a physical superior of another male. The female is free to accept or reject. And this is what my mother did. After adopting me, she divorced P/t, and she refused the king's advances. This offended both males. P/t could get no females to become his permanent mates, though I observed that he sometimes talked a female into lying with him when the two were out of sight of the others. This gave me an advantage over him. I would inform him that I'd spied on him. I would threaten to tell the mate of the female if P/t did not cease his persecution of me. P/t would rage, but he feared being beaten up by the cuckolded male and would leave me alone for a long while.

P/t was often beaten up, anyway. He had a bad temper and could not refrain from showing his resentment when the other males shoved him to the rear of the tribal assemblies or transgressed on his small feeding territory. Sometimes, he beat the other male, and it was only this that kept him from going to the very bottom of the order.

It was this bad temper, plus his ugliness, caused by a broken nose, that made the females reject him. Without at least one female as a permanent mate, he could get only so high in the order. This social inferiority thoroughly ruined a disposition that had never been sweet to begin with.

He blamed me for this, but, as B has shown, I didn't take his persecution passively. I gave more than I got; I was a constant torment to him with my tricks. Also, when I was about twelve, I thought of another way to force him to leave me in peace. I had observed that he was in fear when I threatened to tell the tribe about his adulteries. Then it occurred to me to threaten P/t with tales of wholly imaginary adulteries. In other words, I invented the lie.

P/t was so outraged at my first threat that I had to flee through the trees, take to the higher branches where he was too heavy to follow me. After he had cooled off, he realized that I had him in my control. And once more he ignored me, though, after a time he forgot my threat and started to bedevil me. Then I had to threaten him again.

P/t was so outraged because lying was unknown to the tribe. Its members had many human qualities, since they were subhumans or prehumans. But they weren't human enough to have thought of lying. Or intelligent enough, perhaps. He was both angered and shocked when I first proposed my lie. I believe that he never did quite understand what I was doing. Or, if he did, he thought my threat was unnatural, a perversion. It was something monstrous.

So it was, from his viewpoint.

B has recorded that my native intelligence allowed me to invent a number of things new to the tribe. Such as the running noose, the full-nelson, swimming, et al. B did not record my invention of untruth, but this was because he did not know about it.

Later on, when I taught myself to read English from the books I had found in the cabin of my true parents, I discovered that humans abhorred lying. And so, in my effort to become human, I too abhorred lying. After I became acquainted with humans, I found out that this abhorrence is only a pose, a major and indeed vital hypocrisy, of human society. But by then I had ingrained myself too deeply with this abhorrence. I never lie now except when survival demands it. I believe that most humans, excepting compulsive liars, don't lie except when their survival is threatened by the truth, but when they think of survival, they think of survival of their social image, of survival of their emotional and socioeconomic relationships, in fact, of a thousand things that will be endangered if they don't lie. Each individual has his own hierarchy of lying; some lies are permitted, others are forbidden, though if the going gets rough enough, the tabus are quickly shed.

Nor do humans seem to resent lies in the political field. There is a general feeling that all politicians are liars, that, in fact, a man can't be a politician unless he is a liar. I've never been able to understand this attitude. Politicians control the state; and so the welfare of the citizens depends upon being told the truth, both before and after the politician has been elected to office.

I've also never understood why the poor and the oppressed have endured their miserable state for so many thousands of years. They've always outnumbered the wealthy and the oppressors. So why didn't they just rise up and take over the government?

This is why I've never taken any interest in social reform, though I have in individuals who are suffering from poverty and injustice. But that is just because they happened to become personally involved with me.

This attitude has resulted in my being accused of being both an extreme rightist and an extreme leftist. Though by different people, of course. I won't try to change the system myself, since I am well off under it. But I am perfectly willing to grant that the poor and the oppressed should rise in revolution, a bloody one if need be, and take away from the rich and the oppressor.

I know from my reading of history that from time to time the masses have risen up but that usually they were slaughtered. These failures came about only because of disunity and fear among the masses. With a well-planned organization and enough willing to sacrifice themselves (after all, what did they have to lose?), the poor and the oppressed could have revolted successfully several thousand years ago and set up a new system. The male and female servants of the rich, for instance, were in a position to massacre their employers, wipe out the ruling class almost overnight.

But they did none of these things, just turned like rats and bit futilely when their state became so wretched they could no longer endure it. And they died like rats.

On the other hand, how many revolutions succeeded in their aims when they did conquer the ruling class? France got the Terror and then Napoleon I and then Napoleon III. The Russian Revolution wasn't really a revolt of the masses, and a small group got control and has retained it ever since. Are the Russians really better off than they would have been if the Czars were still in power? Are the Chinese better off under the Communists?

Some say they are; some say they aren't. For me the question is academic, since I personally do not care. All I know is that, if the masses under the Communists (or any other ideology) are being oppressed, why don't they do something about it?

D says that I don't understand this because I don't understand human psychology, or sociopoliticoeconomics. He may be right.

K'LS LOVE FOR me resulted in much suffering for her. Because she refused to mate and because she nursed an alien, she went down to the bottom of the social scale. As the saying goes, she had to suck hind tit. When there was a kill and the tribe lined up for meat, she was last in line and lucky to get anything. She had to endure verbal abuse, though she was too powerful for another female to attack her. Also, the tribe had doubts about her mental stability. No sane female would refuse to mate or insist on suckling a being like me. Thus, she must be mad. This belief in her insanity made the females afraid to push her too far. Like most primitive peoples, and they were more primitive than even the Australian aborigine or Digger Indians, they were in awe of anybody who might be "possessed."

K'L WAS LAST in line at the table, but she was intelligent and industrious and so a good food provider. Though it scared her to go far from the vicinity of the tribe, she did so. And hence she foraged ahead of the others. Grubs, worms, eggs, grasshoppers, small rodents, birds, baby antelopes, dead animals, anything that was protein and didn't move fast enough to elude her became part of her diet. Most of her diet consisted of roots, nuts, fruits, and berries, of course, since she was primarily a vegetarian. Many of the roots she ate contained too much siliceous matter for me, and I rejected this from instinct, I suppose. Even when she offered me premasticated vegetable matter, I rejected it. The coarse gritty stuff would in time have worn away my teeth. I did not realize this consciously, but I knew I didn't like the stuff. So, in addition to much mother's milk, I ate many berries, nuts (after she had cracked them open, and fruit and pieces of raw meat from the creatures she caught. In the beginning I could not masticate the raw meat, but K'l chewed these up for me, and these I accepted eagerly.

So, though K'l suffered from a semiostracism, and I suffered too after I became aware of this attitude, we were far from being always unhappy.

Also, that we were alone against the others made us draw much more closely together than the normal mother and child of the tribe.

I sometimes believe in Goethe's theory of elective affinities. Certainly this is the only thing that can account for K'l's fierceness in raising me despite all the objections of the tribe and the abuse she had to take.

I was lucky that it was she and not some other who had lost her infant the same day my parents died. If her baby had not been killed, she would not have wanted to replace it with me. And Kck would have killed me, too, after slaying my father. But, as chance would have it, she wanted me to replace her just-dead infant, and so she snatched me from the cradle and ran off with me. Never mind that I was a queer, even repulsive looking, creature from her viewpoint. She accepted me and from the moment I began suckling, she loved me. So, at least, she told me in afteryears. Even if her love for me at first sight was really an event of retrospect and not of reality, there was no doubt that she soon did come to love me.

Since she had no one else to talk to or to love, she spent all her energies, outside of food-gathering and hunting, on me. She was, for me, a castle with a host of defenders, which is why I had a tremendous sense of security despite my early years of alienation from the other members of the tribe. Her continuous talking to me also resulted in an acceleration of my intelligence. No doubt, I would have outstripped my contemporaries anyway, since a human being is more intelligent and faster talking than the prehumans of my tribe.

It was also my good fortune to have been adopted by a female who was possibly the brightest individual of her people.

DESCRIPTION OF THE N'K

B FIRST HEARD of me when he was living in Chicago. But in the first novel he wrote about me, he pretended that he had learned of me while visiting London. His informant was supposed to have been an official of the British Foreign Service. This man was acquainted with my story because he had access to top secret documents in the Service's files. These supposedly included my father's diary, written in French, which recorded the events that led up to, and included part of, the day on which he was killed by Kck and I was taken from my cradle by K'l.

According to B, the official disclosed my story when he was drunk. When B scoffed at this, the official then showed him documents, though he had no right to reveal these and would have been discharged and possibly gaoled if the Service had known of his act.

The truth is that B was not in London at that time. As far as I know, he has never been in England. His informant was an American who had heard some of my story from an Englishman. Thus B got his facts thirdhand. Nor had his immediate informant seen any documents. If these had been in the Foreign Service files, the Service would have known about my fraud. And it would have felt obligated to expose me.

After B's first novel came out, I realized that someone had talked about me. I knew that the original source of information had to be somebody close to me. It did not take me long to eliminate all but one. I confronted T,* and he confessed that he might have talked about me to an American during one of his alcoholic sprees. T was a splendid man. I liked and respected him very much, except for one facet of his character. Now and then he succumbed to his compulsion and would disappear for days or oven weeks. Poor H** would track him down and bring him home and dry him out. He had enough character, however, not to make a promise he might not be able to keep. He would only say that he would fight against his demon with all the strength he could muster.

As the Americans say, I chewed him out. He was very contrite and shaken up, so much so that he did not drink alcohol for three years. Nor, as far as I know, did he ever say anything of me again while drunk.

Well, he has been dead for many years now, killed while fighting Jerry. He died a hero's death, as they say, and was posthumously awarded Britain's highest medal for valor. I miss him.

B, realizing that his informant had given him the germ of a unique story, wrote a novel. Since he had few facts to begin with, most of the novel is incorrect in its details. It is also considerably romanticized. But he captured the spirit, the essence, of what really happened, and all honor to him for that.

One of the criticisms of B's story was that there were no such creatures as his language-using "great apes." Thus, his novel had to be sheer fantasy, as much modern mythology as Kipling's *The Jungle Book.*

The "great apes" had not been discovered by reputable scientists and hence could not exist.

This criticism came only twelve years after the discovery of the okapi, the existence of which had been scoffed at for years by scientists.

The pygmy elephant and hippopotamus were also supposed to be a mere fable of the natives. But more than one zoo now exhibits them.

There have also been rumors for years of a small maneless spotted lion existing in the forests of Kenya and Uganda. The existence of these is denied, but I have seen them. Whether or not any specimens will ever come to the

---

* Probably Greystoke's third cousin, a baron.

** T's wife, an American, and J's best woman friend.

attention of the scientists is another matter. They were never very numerous, and they may now be extinct.

The point I'm making is that scientists have been wrong. They are perfectly correct in refusing to acknowledge the existence of such creatures until proof is presented of their existence. But too many scientists, and educated laymen, have denied that they could, in fact, exist. And that is an unscientific attitude.

B's critics denied that any unknown species of ape could exist in Africa. They also scoffed at B because his apes ate meat. Chimpanzees and gorillas don't eat meat, they said. Therefore, no apes (even of the mythological variety) are carnivores. It seems to be true that gorillas are pure herbivores in their natural state. But Goodall has shown that chimpanzees in the wild state do eat meat whenever they get a chance; and it is known that baboons, which are monkeys, also eat meat.

The truth is that both B and his critics were half-right and half-wrong.

There is a species of primate which has not been discovered by the scientific community. Or there was, at least. I saw them several times during my childhood and youth, but they may be extinct now. It is this species which has given rise to tales of the Kenyan *agogwe* and the "wild men" observed in the eastern, central, and western areas of Africa. They are about four feet high and very hairy, but they walk upright. Hence, they are not apes, not in a scientific sense. Their pelvic girdles and feet are so similar to men that they would have to be classified as some species of australopithecoid, creatures halfway between ape and man. I doubt that they are the "missing link." It is more probable that they are a cousin of the creature that was in the direct line of man's ancestry.

In any event, I have seen them, though I never had any direct contact with them. They fled my tribe as quickly as they did humans.

My own people are, I believe, another species of hominid or perhaps a giant variety of the *agogwe*. They are not missing links, either, but cousins of man. They are not the great apes described by B, but they do, or did, exist, and it was among them that I was raised.

B was not given any clear description of them and so he visualized them as gorilloids. He had them using a language, which was correct. But in his novels he also attributed language use to the gorillas and monkeys. While it is true that the higher primates can communicate more effectively than the zoologists believe, they do not have a language in the human sense. They use signals, not verbal symbols.

It was lucky for me that the n'k were language users. If I'd been raised by true apes, I would have passed the mental stage beyond which language learning becomes possible. And I would have been not much better than an idiot. Authentic cases of feral humans bear me out in this. If the child has not experienced a human language before the age of five to eight (or perhaps earlier) he becomes incapable of learning language.

So, in a sense, I am not a true feral man. Those who raised me were quite capable linguistically. And their capabilities for learning other things were higher than those of any animals.

B didn't know this. After learning the truth, he was forced to continue the original description in order to be consistent. Not that he cared. He was a storyteller, not an anthropologist.

I have said that my people were possibly a giant variety of paranthropus. Giant is a relative term here, since the tallest was actually only about six feet. Then I'd attained my full growth, I had three inches on the tallest, old Kck.

He didn't like my looking down on him, and this was one more thing to make him hate and fear me.

But he was much stronger; and if it hadn't teen for my father's knife, I would have been killed when he finally challenged me.

The n'k looked hairy, though this was because their body hair grew to four or five-inch length and was as coarse as a chimpanzee's. The numbers of hairs were actually less than that of humans. The breasts of both male and female were innocent of hair; both had short bushy beards and stiff head hairs not more than two inches long.

The n'k head was long and low, bread-loaf-shaped. They had very little forehead, and the supraorbital ridges of the adult male were almost as massive as a gorilla's. A bony crest, like a gorilla's though smaller, ran from the front to the back of the skull of the males. These were necessary to support the massive chewing muscles. The nose was not quite as flat and as wide-nostrilled as a gorilla's. The ears were close to the head and draped exactly like a human's but about one-fourth larger. The jaws were prognathous, about halfway in protrusion between man's and the gorilla's. The lips were not the thin lips of the chimpanzee and the gorilla; they were as fully averted as the average Caucasian's. The teeth were large, fitted for grinding the tough siliceous roots or cracking the nuts which formed a large part of their diet. Contrary to B's description, they did not have the long canines of the gorilla. The teeth were quite hominid, the molars having five cusps in a Y pattern. A primatologist would see at a glance that they belonged to a creature nearer to man than the apes. The palate was not quite as arched as that of the human. The jaws, seen from above, formed a bow shape, unlike the U shape of ape jaws.

The head was carried further forward than that of the human. The pelvis was not as efficiently shaped for walking as the human's. The legs were shorter in proportion to the torso than the human's, and they were less straight. The feet were flat, and there was a wide separation between the big toe and the other toes. The arms were somewhat longer in proportion to the torso than those of a man. The hands were larger and thicker than a man's. The thumb was shorter and thicker in proportion. None of the tribe could come near my manual dexterity.

Their muscles are not only more massive than a human's but superior in quality. Even the smallest female is much stronger than the greatest human weightlifter. The muscles are attached to thick and dense bones. My own skeleton is denser than that of any modern man's. I attribute this to my feral life, to unceasing activity and hard exertion. As I understand it, the bones of the early caveman were also denser due to his exceedingly active life,

Their hair color varies from a dull black to a russet brown. The eyebrows are very bushy and black. Their eyes are russet brown; their skin, coffee with three spoonfuls of cream. Like most rain forest dwellers, they don't have or need many sweat glands. Their body odor differs from that of man. The English language does not contain the vocabulary items needed to describe it accurately. I can only say that to a keen nose it has elements both of the odor of Homo sapiens and of the gorilla with an indescribable element that is unique to them. Their anal excrement is softer but more adhesive than that of Homo sapiens and not nearly as offensive. This, I presume, is because their diet is largely vegetarian. Their urine, curiously enough, reminds me of civet cat urine, yet I would not mistake one for the other.

Unlike the gorilla, they do not foul their own nest. When one has to defecate, he retreats to some distance from the feeding ground. This seems to have nothing to do with modesty. A number of adult males and females and children will retreat at the same time to the same place and there relieve themselves side by side while chatting away unembarrassedly. Nor do they leave the feeding area to urinate.

In going some distance from their feeding or sleeping places to defecate, however, they exhibit a fastidiousness superior to that of the Australian aborigine. The latter will defecate while among a group squatting around a fire and eating.

Their sense of smell is keener than that of Homo sapiens but not nearly as keen as a dog's, whose sense of smell is estimated to be a million times sharper than man's.

B has exaggerated my own olfactory powers. They are not as strong as a n'k's, though they are superior to any human I've ever met. But this is a matter of training. And after I've been in a city for a while, it becomes comparatively deadened. A good thing, too. During my first few days in a city, I become nauseated with the many offensive odors that exude from man and his artifacts.

WIND AND SEX ALONG THE N'K

WHILE I WAS learning to read, I was startled and sometimes shocked. I discovered things that were completely contrary to what the n'k believed and, hence, what I believed.

One of these was that it was the wind that caused trees and their leaves to move. The n'k always believed just the opposite. Trees and grass were living things; and so, when they moved, they caused motion of the air.

Once I had read that the wind was the responsible agent, I saw why. I reproached myself for my stupidity. I should have noticed that if the tree caused the wind, the wind should have flowed out from the tree in all directions. That discovery made me determined that from then on I would be more observant. Nor would I believe anything that had been told me until it was proved.

I was upset again when I learned that there was a direct connection between copulation and reproduction. The n'k did not know this. They believed that rain and lightning fertilized women. The latter caused the birth of exceptionally strong or intelligent individuals.

When I made the discovery about the true origin of the wind, I hastened to tell the n'k. They would not believe me, even after I had offered them proof. In fact, I was scorned and laughed at, and several commented that I was not as bright as I was supposed to be. Indeed, I must be suffering a mental breakdown.

So, when I discovered the link between copulation and fertilization, I kept silent. The n'k did not want to be enlightened. They resented the truth as if it threatened them. In this respect, they are like most humans.

EVERY HUMAN SOCIETY has adopted rules for sexual conduct by which its members are supposed to guide themselves. Conduct which breaks these rules is regarded as unlawful but not perverted, or unlawful and perverted. The former conduct can be broken down into two subclasses. One, that which is regarded with a certain limited tolerance. Two, that which is simply not tolerated, if the conduct becomes known to laymen and police.

My reading of the novels did not help me much in determining exactly what modes of sexual behavior were in what classifications. The *Encyclopaedia Britannica* was of some help, but it had been published in 1885 and was thus far from frank. The most I could find out from my reading was that certain undescribed sexual acts and attitudes were regarded by most people as disgusting and illegal and deserving of long sentences in gaol or even death.

My own sexual attitudes were determined by n'k society. Theirs were at the same time much more rigid and far more liberal than those of any civilized human society.

Much of what was permitted would be regarded as unnatural by Western societies of that day, but any deviation from the rules was regarded as perverted by the n'k. Or I should say would have been regarded so. I never saw or heard of any deviations while I was with the n'k.

Open masturbation among the children was permitted. In fact, if a child did not masturbate, he/she was an object of concern. There must be something wrong with him/her. This included both self- and mutual masturbation.

The males who were unable to get females as mates because of their low position in the pecking order performed self- or mutual masturbation. In their case, however, they did so out of sight of the tribe. Not from any modesty but because they would be objects of derision from the upper class males.

Lawful copulation took place in view of the tribe. The sexual activities of the king were watched closely because any lack of vitality was regarded as a sign of weakening. When this took place, the males considered challenging the king.

Unlawful copulation, that is, adultery, occurred in the bushes, of course. The males were very jealous of their mates. If another male copulated with his mate(s), he was challenging his order in the social scale.

The females could be put into three classes. One included the majority of females, those who took advantage of every opportunity to commit adultery. The second consisted of females who would commit adultery only with males on a higher social plane than their mates. The third, a small minority, were always faithful.

On consideration, there was a fourth class which was a minority of one. This was K'l, my foster mother. During my infancy and childhood and early youth, she refused to take a mate. This was her right, but it caused her to be regarded as perverted. At the same time, it made her more desirable. The males thought that if they could talk her into mating, they would automatically rise in the order.

Of course, this mating would have to be done publicly. And I am not certain that K'l did not now and then succumb to her sexual drive while in the bushes. She must have been very discreet, however, since I had no suspicions that this was occurring. If I had, I would have been very jealous.

Now that I look back on it, I would not blame her if she taken the opportunity to relieve her sexual tensions.

The favorite position of the n'k during copulation was with the female on her back and the male on top. Entry from the rear with the female standing but bent over, braced against a tree, was often performed. The king, Kck, preferred this.

Kissing as sexual foreplay was as common among the n'k as among humans. But kissing involved not only the lips and the breasts. The n'k kissed each other all over. Fellatio and cunnilingus and soixante-neuf were often indulged in, though these were not conducted to the point of climax. Though the n'k knew nothing of the connection between copulation and reproduction, as I have said, they thought that the male must ejaculate within the vagina.

Of course, accidents happened; but when they did, the couple were derided.

Though the lower scale males mutually masturbated or performed fellatio, they were not compulsive homosexuals. If a single male managed to get a permanent mate, he at once ceased any homosexual activities.

Anal intercourse was never performed, at least, not to my knowledge, and if anyone should know, I should. I was often in the trees or behind the bushes, observing the hidden activities of the tribe.

Incidence of sexual activity was much higher than the average in western human society. The king was thought to be approaching senility if he did not copulate with his three or four females at least three times a day. In addition, he was on his good days liable to copulate with three or four other females in the bushes.

I believe that the males of western human society would be capable of this frequency, too, if the social attitudes were different. In Polynesian societies, for instance, when the whites first encountered them, a male was thought senile if he did not copulate with his wife three or four times daily and, in addition, copulated with several of his sisters-in-law. This high sexual activity results, I believe, not from the physical superiority of the Polynesian male to the Western male but from the social attitude toward sex.

The only cases of impotency I saw among the n'k were very old males (forty-five years of age was the equivalent of the human eighty and one young male, Lmp.* And his condition probably resulted from some physical deficiency, though I cannot prove this.

This brief sketch should indicate why I found the human attitudes toward sex ludicrous, incredible, and comicotragical. And it shows why J was so horrified about my attitudes.

But she got over it.

* This is so close to "limp" that Greystoke may be making a little joke.

THE LANGUAGE OF THE N'K

THE ANTHROPOLOGIST GROVER Krantz has studied the fossil skulls of early man (*Homo erectus*) and of his predecessors *Paranthropus* and *Australopithecus*. He speculates that the brain volume which divides man from his forerunners and cousins is 750 cc. The brain volume of modern man averages 1,400 cc. The gorilla's and Australopithecus' is 500 cc. *Homo erectus'* was between 750 and 1,400 cc.

In the late '30s I returned to my native area and looked for n'k skulls. I found three females and five male skulls and measured their capacity. The average for the females was 900 cc and that of the males was 1,200. I also studied the brain of an old male who had died from pneumonia shortly after I rejoined the tribe. I was especially interested in the development of the frontal lobes and of the three primary speech control areas: Broca's, Wernicke's, and the angular gyrus. I also dissected the oral cavity, the larynx, and the pharynx. I did this to compare them to man's and to analyze the anatomical and neural limitations of the n'k in regard to speech.

Krantz says that, at the end of his first year, the human baby's brain is approximately 750 cc. Within six months, the baby begins to talk. Based on this, Krantz suggests that the 750-cc volume is the threshold of the ability to use language. Krantz reconstructed the oral cavities, pharynx, and larynx of *Homo erectus*. Based on these, he concluded that the vocal apparatus of *Homo erectus* was closer to that of a newborn baby's than to an adult of *Homo sapiens*. Consequently, *Homo erectus* had a larynx that was situated higher in the throat than modern man's. This limited the size of the pharynx above it. *Homo erectus'* tongue, consequently, was almost entirely in the mouth; relatively little of it was in the throat. This meant that the tongue of *Homo Erectus* could not act on the pharynx but was limited to varying the size of the mouth in producing speech sounds.

Homo erectus thus did not have a pharynx capable of producing the vowel sounds a (as in father), I (as in machine) and u (as in tool). He also suggested that the three brain areas I mentioned above were less developed than in modern man.

All these limitations, plus the low-slung and heavy jaws, meant that *Homo erectus* had a very limited speech repertoire and probably spoke very slowly.

It would follow from this that the less evolved *Paranthropus* and *Australopithecus* had even more limitations, that his linguistic capabilities were even less than very early man's.

The facts are that the n'k could produce one vowel sound, similar to that found in the English *the* when it precedes a consonant or that of the vowel in *cut*.

This occurred in about one out of ten n'k words. It was, however, unvoiced; that is, it was produced without any vibrations taking place in the vocal bands of the larynx. Nor were the consonants which English speakers voice, *n, l,* and *w,* voiced by the n'k. These were accompanied by a heavy aspiration. But the n'k could control the vocal bands enough to produce a glottal stop. By closing them, they produced a consonant which is found in many human tongues, Danish, Scots, English, Nahuatl, et al. This stop also occurs in standard English, but it has no significance, and most English speakers are not even aware that they produce it.

In addition, the n'k speech contains four click consonants. One of these is similar to that produced by a carriage driver when he is urging his horse to a faster speed or to that which is often spelled *tsk! tsk!*

N'k speech sounds perfectly natural to me, but J and D say that it is weird. The long strings of whispered consonants with no intervening vowels, the clicks, and the glottal stops seem unhuman to J and D. But there is at least one human group, a California Indian tribe, which uses words with whispered consonants and only an occasional vowel, also unvoiced. And the click consonants are common in the Bushman and Hottentot languages found in some Nahuatl dialects.

The brain size of the n'k child doesn't attain 750 cc until he is six years old. This is when he starts to babble, though the babbling is much slower than that of a human baby's and more restricted in the variety of sounds.

I started babbling shortly after K'l adapted me and was speaking as fluently as any adult n'k by the time I was four. This amazed the n'k and compensated in K'l's eyes for my lack of speed in physical development and my lengthy dependence on her. I was also able to talk, literally, five times as fast as the n'k.

If any linguists read this, they may wonder how I was able to voice sounds after I came into contact with humans. Theoretically, since I had had no experience in voicing speech sounds in my formative years, I should, as an adult, have been unable to reproduce them.

But I am a natural mimic. When I eavesdropped on the blacks of the river village, I would try to imitate the sounds of their language. At first, I had little success in vibrating my vocal bands. But I persevered. After a while I was able to imitate perfectly both the unvoiced and voiced sounds of the blacks.

The n'k sounds are:

Vowel: the unvoiced vowel of English *the* or *done,* represented here by e.
Consonants: p, t, k, ', h, s, c, m, n, l, w, */, //, ///,* †

p is the same as in English but is always heavily aspirated that is, followed by a puff of air.

t is like the English t but made by the tip of the tongue higher up.

k is that in *keen* and is always aspirated.

‘ stands for the glottal stop, the catch in the throat called by the Spanish linguists the *saltillo,* the little jump.

F misinterpreted something I said about the glottal stop in n'k and so made an error in the biography he wrote about me. F stated that the n'k regarded the ‘ as a vowel. He should have known better, since he has some knowledge of linguistics. What I said was that B often used a vowel in place of the glottal stop when he spelled out n'k' words. In any case, the n'k had never heard of a vowel or, indeed, of anything connected with phonetics or grammar.

h stands for the fricative *ch* sound in the German *ach* or Scots *loch.*

s is the same as in English.

c stands for the *ch* in *church.*

m is the English *m* but unvoiced.

n equals an English *n* unvoiced.

l is an unvoiced sound halfway between the English *l* and *r.* B used either *l* or *r* in his system of spelling n'k words, I suppose for the sake of variety.

w is like the English but totally unvoiced.

/ stands for a click consonant made by flattening the tip of the tongue against the front teeth and then quickly withdrawing it.

// stands for a click made against the gums above the teeth.

/// stands for a palatal click.

† stand for a click made with the side of the tongue close to the right side of the cheek.

B used b, d, g, and z respectively to represent these clicks. He also used z to represent s sometimes.

Each syllable of n'k consists of two or three consonants or combinations of consonants plus e, e plus consonant, consonant plus e plus consonant, or two consonants plus e.

Each word is a monosyllable, disyllable, or trisyllable, excluding the monosyllable gender prefix.

The stress or accent is lighter than in English but relatively stronger on the second syllable within a word.

Tone, or pitch, is mid-level a declarative phrase and abruptly chopped off at the end of the phrase.

Exclamatory, hortatory, interrogative, and conditional phrases use a rising pitch similar to that in English. This rising pitch is an important grammatical feature. B indicates this in his description of the difference between the phrase, "Do you surrender?" and "I surrender." The former is distinguished by the rising pitch; the latter is a flat "/// //."

Though the n'k speech is about five times as slow as human speech, it has juncture. That is, it has a difference in the speed of transition between the sounds in a word, between words, and between complete phrases. The second is twice as long as the first, and the third is twice as long as the second.

The n'k vocabulary items are few, possibly no more than five hundred. Its grammar is truly primitive and can be quickly described.

The parts of speech are:

Personal names.

Entity indicator: tnt = elephant; w'l = nest; "// = rock; c/// = sky; k' = I; 'sh = wind; mp// = mother.

Attribute indicator: ///e = red; klk = dangerous; s'l = skin; pkt = dead; wn// = beneficial, tasty, healthy; cs† = angry; pks = motionless; 'et = state of possession; tk' = many.

Negator: tn// = no, not.

Action indicator: ///'m = run; /n// = kill; sps = snarl; h'h = laugh; ///tn = looking gloomy.

Temporal indicator: tw' = soon; //p// = sometime in the past; nw/// = dawn; nwk = between dawn and high noon; nl/ = high noon; ns† = between high noon and dusk; nw// = dusk; sink = night.

Locative indicator: wc = there; s's= out of sight; ksw = right; //e' = left; c// = above.

Gender indicator: b' = male; m' = female.

The entity indicator refers to anything that is considered in n'k as an object which is completely separate from other objects. It includes what we would classify as personal pronouns. The n'k is not as conscious of ego differentiation as the human is. At least, that is my impression.

Though he behaves as an individual with self-consciousness, he is not as sharply aware of his aloneness as a human is. *K'* means not only *I* but *we.* Where a human would say *we,* a n'k gestures to indicate that others are part of his *I.* Or he is part of them.

There is no word in n'k corresponding to the human *you* or *they.* The personal name is used instead when addressing an individual; and if *they* is indicated, a gesture indicates this.

Indeed, the *I* is not often used in a phrases though its existence is implicit.

Why do I include the word for *skin* as an attribute indicator, something that humans would call a noun? This is because the skin is classified as an inherent undiscrete part that makes up the whole. It is no more separable than the color of the skin. Thus, my personal name, s'n-t'l, is made up of two attribute indicators.

The word for *mother,* mp//, is not used in the generic sense. A mother is an entity, either my mother or your mother. A n'k could not speak of many mothers. There is no word for father. A *father* is the mate of your mother, and the word used for him is b'-cpm, meaning *he-mate.*

The n'k have no general word to indicate emotion or feeling. The emotions or feelings have to be specific and refer to states invisible to the beholder. If a n'k feels sick, he says, "tn// wn//." That is, "Not healthy," or if he wishes to emphasize it, "k' tn// wn//," or "I am not healthy."

It seems strange to an English speaker to classify a verb, 'et, meaning to *possess,* as an attribute. But this word indicates a nonphysical relationship, an invisible connection between the speaker and the object referred to. No physical action is implied. The relationship referred to is as unchanging as the color of one's eyes. For example, take a sentence translated as, "She is my mother." 'in the first place, no n'k word say *she.* He would use her personal name. If I said this in n,'k, I would say "k'l wc. mp// wc. K' 'et k'l."

Literally, "K'l there. Mother there. I state-of-possession-K'l."

The indefinite plural indicators and the numerical indicators, *many, few* (more than two), and the numbers one through ten are thought of as attributes. Ten is as high as the n'k can count. Anything more is *many.*

An action indicator describes or prescribes movement. Movement includes facial expressions of internal states. To a n'k, rain is not drops falling but an entity that appears from time to time. He would not say, "It is raining." He would say, "Rain here." Or "Rain there." Or "Rain soon."

N'k is uninflected except for the gender prefix, which is always attached to the entity indicator, but to that only.

There is no tense. To indicate the past or future, a temporal indicator is used.

There are no words to indicate aspect, that is, whether the action occurred some time ago and then stopped, occurred in the past and is still operating, is now occurring but will soon stop, is now occurring but will run for a long time.

A n'k phrase seldom consists of more than three words and often only of one. Where gesticulation will suffice, a n'k prefers not to verbalize.

There are no connectives such as *and, but,* or *or.*

N'k has no passive voice, and tone indicates the difference of indicative, subjunctive, imperative, potential, conditional, and obligative modes. Actually, the same tone is used for all but the indicative. The others can be lumped together in the mood of dubiety.

The word order of the most complex phrase is locative indicator-temporal indicator-personal name or entity indicator-attribute indicator-action indicator. The negator is used just before the indicator to which it is most relevant. The attribute indicator is the only one which cannot be used as a complete phrase, though, since personal names often consist of attribute indicators, this is an exception. One n'k can utter another's name to attract his attention.

B has described me in the first novel and in a short story as teaching myself to read English. This is correct. I started off with children's picture books, which my mother (my human mother, of course) had intended to use to teach me to read. I associated the letters of the alphabet with the pictures just as B depicted me. I started with the simplest word-picture books and progressed to the less elementary books. But this was fortuitous. If I had not just happened to pick up the most basic book first, the one that my mother would have used when she started teaching me, I may not have made any progress at all.

One of the things B neglected mentioning when he described my self-education in literacy is punctuation. I had no idea, of course, that these were aids, auxiliaries, for bridging the wide gap between the spoken and the written. I thought they were words too. It took me almost two years to grasp their nature. And I pronounced them, too, giving each a syllabic value.

One of the many features of English that I had trouble with was grasping the distinction between the definite and indefinite article, between "a" or "an" and "the." N'k has neither, but then this lack is nothing special in human languages. Many neither use nor need these articles.

Inflection and conjugation, prepositions and adverbs, and the verb *to be,* caused me much trouble also. These features are totally lacking in n'k; and if I had not been both so curious and intelligent, I might never have understood their use. But I persevered, and I began to comprehend, though, truth to tell, it was not until later after I had been living among English speakers that I fully understood them.

Or I should say, among English and French speakers. After all, French was my first spoken human language.

If anybody other than myself ever reads these words, he or she will probably smile at my egotism when he reads that I call myself intelligent. But this is not egotism. I lack false humility, since I was not raised in a human society. I tell facts as I know them, and the truth is that I have an I.Q. of

197 on the Terman scale. I don't know that this means much; the various I.Q. tests are much subject to criticism. Nor would I have ever succeeded in my self-education if I had not had a tremendous drive to learn. I might not have had this if it lead not been for my feeling of alienation from the tribe. I identified only partially with them, and the discovery that there were others like me in the world made me lust to know everything about them. I intended to find human beings some day and to live with them. I expected to be accepted by them, to dwell with them completely happy. Of course, this was in the early days of my self-education. When I began to read with some fluency the novels and the history books and the *Encyclopaedia Britannica* in any parents' library, I also began to understand that things would not be so simple. It would take more than just being born in a society to be accepted and to be happy.

RELIGION

When I got deep enough into the books, I despaired. Apparently, a man had to have much money (a concept I never understood from just reading about it). A man had to be on guard all the time to keep others from taking his money away. A man had to watch other men to make sure that they did not take his mate away from him. A man might not even want his mate after a while because, inevitably, he and she would be struggling for dominance in familial affairs. Or the mate would be possessed by drives over which she had no control; she might have enough money but not a high enough position in the pecking order. She might be rejected or think she was being rejected by her parents, and she could not rest until she had fulfilled their image of what a daughter should be. And so on. Of course, men were in the same unhappy situation.

Then there were religious conflicts in history and in the novels. I did not understand this at all, perhaps because the religious sense in the n'k was so rudimentary. But I did understand that the religious sense in human beings was highly developed, yet they had no idea of what was true and what wasn't true in their religions. The Christians claimed fiercely that only their religion was true, that they alone had access to divine revelation. Yet the Christians were divided among themselves, calling each ether liars and wicked; and while preaching charity and love and peacefulness, they were killing and torturing each other.

It all seemed simple and clear-cut to me. If you had a creation, then you had a Creator. At least, it seemed obvious to me at first. Later I went through the stage that every person of any intelligence goes through. Who created the Creator? How could the world have come out of nothingness? What existed before time began? Why were suffering, illness, and death inevitable?

If I had been presented with only one explanation of these, if, say, I had only the Bible available, I might have believed a monolithic explanation. But the books told me that there had been many differing explanations; and quite possibly, all were false.

I don't think religious or philosophical issues were worth fighting over or even getting excited about.

I could understand why men schemed and fought for control of land and money and position in the pecking order. Survival is dependent upon these.

But, I asked myself, if man is so intelligent, why hasn't he developed a system where hypocrisy and greed and ruthlessness and oppression are not necessary?

I still ask myself this question, though I know that there isn't any answer. I also know that if there were an answer, it would be rejected by most people. Most humans are not much advanced beyond the n'k when it comes to freeing themselves from their social conditioning. Those who do so generally only seem to do so. They extricate themselves from one set of conditioning only to switch to another. And they do this because of their genetic dispositions. I am convinced that individuals are born Catholics or Methodists or Moslems or Jews, born Tories or Whigs or anarchists. Their genes predetermine them to a certain form of religion or ideology or economics. Some are never able to free themselves from their parents' religion or ideology, and this results in unhappiness for them. Others are able to do so, though their struggles make them unhappy.

As for me, my being an alien, an outsider to both the n'k and the humans, resulted in an unhappiness and confusion in my childhood and youth. But no longer. I am insular. The troubled waters of others affect me only in a physical sense. I am sometimes swept into the difficulties of others, and I have often sided with one group against the other. But the question of which side is morally right or wrong doesn't concern me.

I happen to be a British citizen because circumstances made me so. I was born of British parents, but in my early contacts with civilization I could easily have become a French citizen. Only the fact that my British parentage was established and that this meant I could gain a high position in British society without much effort determined me to be British. If I had been, say, Russian, I might have become Russian and fought for the Russians.

On the other hand, being much more rational and objective than most humans, because I was an outsider, I would have observed that the British society was relatively freer and contained more justice. The conditions of British society were appalling; but compared to those in Russian society, they were less objectionable.

At first sight, American society might seem relatively freer. But it didn't take me long after I'd been in the United States to see that it was a slave society. The whites denied this, of course, but the blacks knew it was a fact. And though the whites thought they were free men and democratic, the fact that they were living in a slave society colored their every thought and action and institution and made them, in a sense, slaves to their slaves. They might not know it, but it did. There can be no truly free men where some citizens are slaves.

This applies not only to ethnic, but to economic, attitudes. The poor are, in fact, slaves, though a white person can get out of that slavery if he is vigorous and intelligent enough. Or ruthless enough.

All human societies are slave societies, some more than others.

To return to my reading.

At first, I could not distinguish between fact and fiction. I thought the novels were true stories. Then I found out that they were only exercises of the imagination. I shouldn't say *only,* since the concept of fiction was new to me. It was, in fact, staggering. The n'k had no fictional stories with which to entertain themselves; any tales they told were of events that had happened in reality.

After I was able to ingest this concept, I still believed that the histories and the sacred books were true. But when I came across references to the Koran and the Book of Mormon and the Christian Science books and the religions of ancient peoples, I saw at once that they couldn't all be true. Somebody was lying. In the end, I concluded that they all were. Or, if one was right, there was no way of finding out which one.

All contained some truths, though even these were distorted.

Then there were the scientists. They denied the claims of the religionists. But scientists had often been wrong and probably still were wrong in many of their conclusions. The scientists were just as prone to dogma and prejudice as the religionists.

The difference between them and the religionists was their method of searching for the truth. Actually, the religionists were no longer searching. They had found the truth, and their searches were only for rationalizations to bolster their claims. The true scientist doubted anything unless it could be proven to be fact. And he still had a mental reservation, because he knew that what seemed established today might be unseated tomorrow.

But though scientists could uncover physical truths, they were as helpless as the religionists in the supernatural or in the cosmogony and cosmology of things and spirits. Nobody could answer my youthful questions nor was anyone ever going to answer them.

Neither deliberately blind faith or highly rationalized faith was for me. I told myself that all religions were, to be blunt, nonsense skillfully arranged to look like sense.

Human economic and political systems were not nonsense. They were machines for the operation of society. But they were all, capitalist, socialist, communist, highly inefficient, and the rationalizations for justifying them were often as transparently false as those used in religion.

That's the way it was and is and probably will be.

The admission of this does not mean that I am cynical or bitter or despairing or depressed. I am not like that "ape-man" in that story by the Czech author,* who killed himself because he could not endure the hypocrisy, greed, and injustice of civilization.

I accept this as the way things are, and I adjust accordingly. I had a very difficult time in my early contacts with humans because I didn't know the rules. People learn the thousand and more subtle laws of social behavior easily because they are brought up from infancy surrounded by adults who know them intimately. The children only have to imitate their examples. Even so, if they are thrust into a segment of society where the rules differ, they make mistakes. And quite often they are incapable of adjusting themselves.

I wasn't entirely innocent when I ventured into civilization, since I had read the novels and histories. But these more often confused than helped me. They gave a partially false picture and, also, the rules had changed somewhat between the time the books were written and the time I experienced society. But I learn quickly. If need be, I can pass as easily for a London dock laborer or a Yorkshire farmer as an English aristocrat. Or, for that matter, skin color and hair aside, for a Masai cattle herder or a Texas rancher.

My ear for sounds and rhythm of a language and my ability at mimicry enable me to do this. Inside of course I am still the "ape-man."

---

* Josef Nesvadba, *The Death of an Apeman,* in *The Lost Face: Best Science Fiction From Czechoslovakia,* Taplinger Publishing Co., 1971.

TIME HAS NO SHADOWS

IN THE BEGINNING was greenness and timelessness.

The rain-forest trees with their thick canopy of vegetation binding them cast few shadows. And time cast no shadow at all.

Those who've read Hudson's *Green Mansions* know that the rain forest is not the same as the bush jungle. Large areas of the latter are often comparatively clear beneath the trees and their connecting many-leveled awnings of branch, vine, and creeper. A twilight and a hush spread through the rain forest; the trunks of the trees soar upward branchless for a hundred feet, looking like the columns of a huge badly lit temple. Most of the forest life, the birds, monkeys, civets, rodents, etc., is in the upper levels; and it is only seldom that a ground-dweller glides through the semidusk.

The n'k's territory was mainly in the rain forest, though part of it was in the bush jungle of the lower ground near the ocean or that along a nearby river.

The silence was often broken by the speech or cries of the n'k but even their language was whispering and quite appropriate for the living temple in which they dwelt.

This can be easily visualized by people who have never been to the rain forest.

But I have never met a person who could truly comprehend my sense of timelessness. On the other hand, I do not truly understand the sense of time which humans have.

I suppose that I have more of it than the n'k, since I am genetically a Homo sapiens. But I don't have much more.

How can I describe something for which no human languages seem to have words?

The preliterate and less technologically advanced peoples perhaps have a somewhat similar attitude. But they, too, are bound to their economics, which is considerably more complicated than that of the n'k. The latter are not even much guided by the sun, which they may not see for days or sometimes weeks except for fleeting appearances through a break in the canopy. The night pales into the semitwilight, and they may or may not rise with dawn. They eat when hungry, which is, however, most of the day. Being primarily root-grubbers, they spend much time digging up roots and stuffing their paunches, which are as big and rounded as those of the gorilla.

They have almost no ritual or ceremony except the feast under the full moon, when the entire tribe dances. If a large animal has been killed, or a member of an enemy tribe of n'k (which doesn't happen often), they eat the body as a climax to the dance. B, by the way, was correct when he said that an earthen drum is pounded by three old females while the tribe dances. I know that some critics have maintained that B got the idea for this from descriptions of chimpanzees pounding on earth or logs with sticks. But they are wrong.

I've asked the n'k why it was always three females who drum, but they didn't know. It is just the custom, they said.

If the tribe happens to be in a completely covered area where the full moon is not visible, the tribe doesn't dance. Nor does it seem to know that it's missing it's monthly event.

The point is that the n'k have no sense of time except when arranging meetings, and that seldom happens. Nor does their sense of tense extend beyond today, the day after today, and a vague past. They don't even have a distinction between the rainy and dry seasons. Gabon gets abundant rain through most of the year, and there is little variation of temperatures.

The essential difference in the attitude toward time between the n'k (and hence mine) and humans is this: humans think of time as a steady flow which can be sectioned by natural or artificial means. The natural is comprised of the sun, the moon, the stars, and the seasons. The artificial is comprised of clocks and calendars.

The n'k think of the sun, moon, and stars as living beings and wouldn't be surprised, though they would be dismayed, if the sun did not appear when it should. They just exist in the now, and the past and the near future are nearby limits to now.

That is the best I can do in trying to explain my original sense of time or lack of it. I'm sure that if some human could look through my mind and eyes, he would be lost and perhaps even scared. He would not know what he was experiencing. The closest he could come to describing it would be to compare it to a nightmare. Dreams are lost in timelessness; things are out of sequence; there is often no causality.

Of course, I became somewhat aware of the concept of time through reading the books in my parents' cabin. But I didn't truly comprehend it until I was in civilization. Even so, I never came to accept time-markers as natural. I went along with clocks because humans lived by them, and I was trying to live by their rules. But I never felt the sense of urgency that accompanies clocks and calendars.

And when I am back in the jungle, it is with relief that I sink back into my natural timelessness. I become one with the beasts and the trees, and I can laze away weeks or months with no thought beyond the now. If I were a true n'k, I would be unable to imagine beyond now.

This was the essential difference between the n'k and me. They had very little imagination, just enough to distinguish them from the beasts. This little difference is, of course, enormous, since it does make them partly human. But I had much imagination. And so I was all human.

Despite this, I am much closer to the n'k than to humans in my sense of time. Perhaps imagination is the ability to comprehend time. The greater the comprehension, the greater the imagination.

The Two-Edged Gift

CHAPTER ONE

Paul Eyre shot a flying saucer.

On this bright morning, he was walking through a farmer's field. Ahead of him was the edge of a woods bisected by a small creek. Riley, the setter, had just stiffened. Nose down, crouched low, seeming to vibrate, he pointed toward the magnet, the invisible quail. Paul Eyre's heart pumped a little faster. Ahead of Riley, a few yards away, was a bush. Behind it should be the covey.

They broke loose with that racket that had made him jump so when he was a novice. It was as if the earth had given violent birth to several tiny planets. But there was not the dozen or so he had expected. Only two. The lead one was much larger than the other, so much larger that he did jump then. He knew as the shotgun roared and kicked that it was not a bird.

The concentrated pattern of his modified choke must have hit the thing squarely. It fell away at a forty-five degree angle instead of dropping as a dead bird drops, and it crashed through the lower branches of a tree on the outskirts of the woods.

Automatically, he had fired the second barrel at the trailing bird. And he had missed it.

The thing had rocketed up like a quail. But it had been dark and about two feet long. Or two feet wide. His finger had squeezed on the trigger even as his mind had squeezed on the revelation that it was not a winged creature.

It wasn't a creature, he thought, but a made thing. More like a huge clay pigeon than anything else.

He looked around. Riley was a white and black streak, running as if a cougar were after him. He made no noise. He seemed to be conserving his breath as if he knew he'd need every atom of oxygen he could get. Behind him was a trail of excrement. Ahead of him, over half a mile up the slope, was a white farmhouse and two dark-red barns.

Roger, Paul's son, had spoken of mines which flew up into the air before exploding. This thing had not been attached to a chain nor had it blown up. It could be a dud. But there had been no blast as it soared up. Perhaps the noise of his shotgun had covered it.

He shook his head. It could not have been anything like that. Unless... Had some vicious person put it in the field just to kill hunters? Senseless violence was on the increase in this God-forsaking country.

The situation was much like that of a car that refused to run. You could think about it all you wanted to and make mental images of what was wrong. But until you opened the hood and looked at the engine, you would not he able to make a definite analysis. So he would open the hood.

He walked forward. The only sound was the northwest wind, gentle here because the woods broke it. The bluejay and the crows that had been so noisy before he had fired were quiet. There was the bluejay, sitting on a tree branch. It seemed frozen with shock.

He was cautious but not afraid, he told himself. He had been afraid only three times in his life. When his father had deserted him, when his mother had died, and when Mavice had said she was leaving him. And these three events had taught him that nothing was as bad as he'd thought it at the time and that it was stupid, illogical to fear. He and his brothers and sisters and mother had gotten along without his father. His mother's death had actually made his life easier. And Mavice had not left him.

"Only the unimaginative, of whom you are the king, have no fear," Tincrowdor had told him. But what did that effete egg-head know of real life or real men?

Nevertheless, he hesitated. He could just walk away, round up the dog, and hunt elsewhere. Or, better, tell Smith that someone had planted a strange mechanical device in his field.

Perhaps, though he did not like to admit it, his sight had betrayed him. Behind his glasses were fifty-four-year-old eyes. He was in good shape, better than most men twenty years younger. Much better than that Tincrowdor, who sat on his tocus all day while he typed away on his crazy stories.

Still, he had been informed by the optometrist that he needed a new prescription. He had not told anyone about this. He hated to admit to anyone that he had a weakness, and that anyone included himself. When he had a chance to get fitted with new lenses, with no one except the doctor the wiser, he'd go. Perhaps he should not have put it off so long.

He resumed walking slowly across the field. Once, he looked toward the farmhouse. Riley, his pace undiminished, was still headed toward it. When he caught Riley, he'd rap him a few on the nose and shame him. If he were ruined by this, he'd get rid of him. He couldn't see feeding something that was useless. The hound ate more than he was worth as it was.

He could imagine what Mavice would say about that. "You're going to retire in eleven years. Would you want us to give you away or send you to the gas chamber because you're useless?"

And he'd say, "But I won't be. I'll be working as hard as ever on my own business after I've retired."

He was ten feet from the wood when the yellow haze drifted out from it.

CHAPTER TWO

He stopped. It couldn't be pollen at this time of the year. And no pollen ever glowed.

Moreover, it was coming with too much force to be driven by the wind. For the second time, he hesitated. The thick yellow luminance looked so much like gas. He thought about the sheep that had been killed in Nevada or Utah when the army nerve gas had escaped. Could—But no…that was ridiculous.

The shimmering haze spread out, and he was in it. For a few seconds, he held his breath. Then he released it and laughed. The stuff blew away from his face and closed in again. Here and there, some bits sparkled. Before he reached the trees, he saw tiny blobs form on the grass, on his hands, and on the gun barrels. They looked like gold-colored mercury. When he ran his hand over the barrels, the stuff accumulated at the ends into two large drops. They ran like mercury into the cup formed by his palm.

Its odor made him wrinkle his nose and snap it to the ground. It smelled like spermatic fluid.

It was then that he noticed that he had not reloaded. He was mildly shocked. He had never missed reloading immediately after firing. In fact, he did it so automatically that he never even thought about it. He was more upset than he had realized.

Abruptly, the haze or fog, or whatever it was, disappeared. He looked around. The grass for about twenty feet behind him was faintly yellow.

He went on. A branch, broken off by the thing, lay before him. Ahead was the dense and silent wood. He pushed through the tangles of thorn bushes, from which he had flushed out so many rabbits. And there was one now, a big buck behind the thorns. It saw him, saw that it was seen, but it did not move. He crouched down to look at it. Its black eyes looked glazed, and its brown fur scintillated here and there with yellowness. It was in the shade, so the sun could not be responsible for the glints.

He poked at it, but it did not move. And now he could see that it was trembling violently.

A few minutes later, he was at the place where the thing would have landed if it had continued its angle of descent. The bushes were undisturbed; the grass, unbent.

An hour passed. He had thoroughly covered the woods on his side of the creek and found nothing. He waded through the waters, which were nowhere deeper than two feet, and started his search through the woods on that side: He saw no yellow mercury, which meant one of two things. Either the thing had not come here or else it had quit expelling the stuff. That is, if the stuff *had* been expelled from it. It might just be a coincidence that the stuff had appeared at the same time the thing had disappeared. A coincidence, however, did not seem likely.

Then he saw a single drop of the mercury, and he knew that it was still… bleeding? He shook his head. Why would he think of that word? Only living creatures could be *wounded.* He had *damaged* it.

He whirled. Something had splashed behind him. Through a small break in the vegetation, he could see something round, flat, and black shooting from the middle of the creek. He had seen it before at a distance and had thought it was the top of a slightly rounded boulder just covered by the creek. His eyes *were* going bad.

He recrossed the creek and followed a trail of water which dwindled away suddenly. He looked up, and something—it—dropped down behind a bush. There was a crashing noise, then silence.

So it was alive. No machine moved like that, unless…

What would Tincrowdor say if he told him that he had seen a flying saucer?

Common sense told him to say nothing to anybody about this. He'd be laughed at, and people would think he was going insane. Or suffering from premature senility, like his father.

The thought seemed to drive him crazy for a minute. Shouting, he plunged through the bushes and the thorn tangles. When he was under the tree from which the thing had dropped, he stopped. His heart was hammering, and he was sweating. There was no impression in the soft moisture-laden ground; nothing indicated that a large heavy object had fallen onto it.

Something moved to the right at the corner of his eye. He turned and shot once, then again. Pieces of bushes flew up, and bits of dark showered. He reloaded—he wasn't about to forget this time—and moved slowly toward the base of the bush at which the thing seemed to have been. But it wasn't there anymore, if it had ever been there.

A few feet further, he suddenly got dizzy. He leaned against a tree. His blood was thrumming in his ear, and the trees and bushes were melting. Perhaps the yellow stuff was some kind of nerve gas.

He decided to get out of the woods. It wasn't fear but logic that had made him change his mind. And no one had seen him retreat.

Near the edge of the woods, he stopped. He no longer felt dizzy, and the world had regained its hardness. It was true that only he would know he had quit, but he wouldn't ever again be able to think of himself as a real man. No, by God—and he told himself he wasn't swearing when he said that—he would see this out.

He turned and saw through the screen of bushes something white move out from behind a tree. It looked like the back of a woman's torso. She wore nothing; he could see the soft white skin and the indentation of the spine. The hips were not visible. Then the back of the head, black hair down to the white shoulders, appeared.

He shouted at the woman, but she paid no attention. When he got to the tree where she had first appeared, he could no longer see her. Some of the grass was still rising, and some leaves had been distorted.

An hour later, Paul Eyre gave up. Had he just thought he'd seen a woman? What would a woman be doing naked in these woods? She couldn't have been with a lover, because she and the man would have gotten out of the woods the first time he'd fired his shotgun.

On the way back, he thought he saw something big and tawny at a distance. He crouched down and opened the bush in front of him. About thirty yards off, going behind an almost solid tangle, was the back of an animal. It was yellowish brown and had a long tufted tail. And if he hadn't known it was impossible, he would have said that it was the rear end of an African lion. No, a lioness.

A moment later, he saw the head of a woman.

She was where the lion would be it if stood up on its hind legs and presented its head.

The woman was in profile, and she was the most beautiful he had ever seen.

He must be suffering from some insidious form of Asiatic flu. That would explain everything. In fact, it was the only explanation.

He was sure of it when he got to the edge of the trees. The field was covered with red flowers and at the other side, which seemed to be miles away, was a glittering green city.

The vision lasted only three or four seconds. The flowers and the city disappeared, and the field, as if it were a rubber band, snapped back to its real dimensions.

He could hear it snap.

Ten minutes later, he was at the farm house.

Riley greeted him by biting him.

CHAPTER THREE

EYRE PARKED THE car in front of his house. The driveway was blocked with a car to which was hitched a boat trailer, a motorcycle lacking a motor, and a Land Rover on top of which was a half-built camper. Behind it was a large garage crammed with machines, tools, supplies, old tires, and outboard motors in the process of being repaired.

Thirteen-thirty-one Wizman Court was in an area which once had been all residential. Now the huge old mansion across the street was a nursing home; the houses next to it had been torn down and buildings for a veterinarian and his kennels were almost completed. Eyre's own house had looked large enough and smart enough when he and Mavice had moved into it twenty years ago. It looked tiny, mean, and decaying now and had looked so for ten years.

Paul Eyre, until this moment, had never noticed that. Though he felt crowded at times, he attributed this to too many people, not the smallness of the house. Once he got rid of his son and daughter, the house would again become comfortable. And the house was paid for. Besides taxes, maintenance; and the utilities, it cost him nothing. If the neighborhood was run down somewhat, so much the better. His neighbors did not complain because he was conducting his own repair business here.

Until now, he had not thought anything about its appearance. It was just a house. But now he noticed that the grass on the tiny lawn was uncut, the wooden shutters needed painting, the driveway was a mess, and the sidewalk was cracked.

He got out of the car and picked up his shotgun and bag with his left hand. The right hand was heavily bandaged. The old ladies sitting on the side porch waved and called out to him, and he waved back at them. They sat like a bunch of ancient crows on a branch. Time was shooting them down, one by one. There was an empty chair at the end of the row, but it would be occupied by a newcomer soon enough. Mr. Ridgley had sat there until last week when he had been observed one afternoon urinating over the railing into the rosebushes below. He was, according to the old ladies, now locked up in his room on the third floor. Eyre looked up and saw a white face with tobacco-stained moustaches pressed against the bars over the window.

He waved. Mr. Ridgley stared. The mouth below the moustaches drooled. Angry, Paul Eyre turned away. His mother had stared out of that window for several weeks, and then she had disappeared. But she had lived to be eighty-six before she had become senile. That was forgivable. What he could not forgive, nor forget, was that his father had only been sixty when his brain had hardened and his reason had slid off it.

He went up the wooden unpainted steps off the side of the front porch. It was no longer just a porch. He had enclosed it and Roger now used it for a bedroom. Roger, as usual, had neglected to make up the bedcouch. Four years in the Marines, including a hitch in Viet Nam, had not made him tidy.

Eyre growled at Roger as he entered the front room. Roger, a tall thin blond youth, was sitting on the sofa and reading a college textbook. He said, "Oh, Mom said she'd do it." He stared at his father's hand. "What happened?"

"Riley went mad, and I had to shoot him."

Mavice, coming in from the kitchen, said, "Oh, my God! You *shot* him!"

Tears ran down Roger's cheeks.

"Why would you do that?"

Paul waved his right hand. "Didn't hear me? He bit me! He was trying for my throat! "

"Why would he do that?" Mavice asked.

"You sound like you don't believe me!" Paul said. "For God's sake, isn't anyone going to ask me how badly he bit me? Or worry that I might get rabies?"

Roger wiped away the tears and looked at the bandages. "You've been to a doctor," he said. "What'd he say about it?"

"Riley's head has been shipped to the state lab," Paul said. "Do you have any idea what it's going to be like if I have to have rabies shots? Anyway, it's fatal! Nobody ever survived rabies!"

Mavice's hand shot to her mouth and from behind it came strangled sounds. Her light blue eyes were enormous.

"Yeah, and horseshoes hung over the door bring good luck," Roger said. "Why don't you come out of the nineteenth century, Dad? Look at something besides outboard motors and the TV. The rate of recovery from rabies is very high."

"So I only had one year of college," Paul said. "Is that any reason for my smartass son to sneer at me? Where would you be if it wasn't for the G.I. Bill?"

"You go to college to get a degree, not an education," Roger said. "You have to educate yourself, all your life."

"For Heaven's sake, you two," Mavice said. "Quit this eternal bickering. And sit down, Paul. Take it easy. You look terrible!"

He jerked his arm away and said, "I'm all right." But he sat down. The mirror behind the sofa had showed him a short, thin but broad-shouldered man with smooth pale brown hair, a high forehead, bushy sandy eyebrows, blue eyes behind octagonal rimless spectacles, a long nose, a thick brown moustache, and a round cleft chin.

His face did look like a mask. Tincrowdor had said that anyone who wore glasses should never sport a moustache. Together, these gave a false-face appearance. That remark had angered him then. Now it reminded him that he was looking forward to seeing Tincrowdor. Maybe he had some answers.

"What about a beer, Dad?" Roger said. He looked contrite.

"That'd help, thanks," Paul said. Roger hurried off to the kitchen while Mavice stood looking down at him. Even when both were standing up, she was still looking down on him. She was at least four inches taller.

"You don't really think Riley had rabies?" she said. "He seemed all right this morning."

"Not really. He wasn't foaming at the mouth or anything like that. Something scared him in the woods, scared him witless, and he attacked me. He didn't know what he was doing."'

Mavice sat down in a chair across the room. Roger brought in the beer. Paul drank it gratefully, though its amber color reminded him of the yellow stuff. He looked at Mavice over the glass. He had always thought she was very good-looking, even if her face was somewhat long. But, remembering the profile of the woman in the woods, he saw that she was very plain indeed, if not ugly. Any woman's face would look bad now that he had seen that glory among the trees.

The front door slammed, and Glenda walked in from the porch. He felt vaguely angry. He always did when he saw her. She had a beautiful face, a feminization of his, and a body which might have matched the face but never would. It was thin and nearly breastless, though she was seventeen. The spine was shaped like a question mark; one shoulder was lower than the other; the legs looked as thin as piston rods.

She stopped and said, "What happened?" Her voice was deep and husky, sexy to those who heard it without seeing her.

Mavice and Roger told her what had taken place. Paul braced himself for a storm of tears and accusations, since she loved Riley dearly. But she said nothing about him. She seemed concerned only about her father. This not only surprised him. It angered him.

Why was he angry? he thought.

And he understood, then, that it was because she was a living reproach. If it weren't for him, she would not be twisted; she'd be a tall straight and beautiful girl. His anger had been his way of keeping this knowledge from himself.

He was amazed that he had not known this before. How could he have been so blind?

He began sweating. He shifted on the sofa as if he could move his body away from the revelation. He felt the beginning of a panic. What had opened his eyes so suddenly? Why had he only now, today, noticed how ugly and mean the house was, how frightened and repulsed he was by the old people across the street, and why Glenda had angered him when he should have shown her nothing but tenderness?

He knew why. Something had happened to him in the woods, and it was probably the stuff which had fallen on him, the stuff expelled by the thing. But how could it have given him this insight? It scared him. It made him feel as if he were losing something very dear.

He almost yielded to the desire to tell them everything. No, they would not believe him. Oh, they'd believe that he had seen those things. But they would think that he was going crazy, and they would be frightened. If he would shoot Riley while in a fit, he might shoot them.

He became even more frightened. Many times, he had imagined doing just this. What if he lost control and the image shifted gears into reality?

He stood up. "I think I'll wash up and then go to bed for a while. I don't feel so good."

This seemed to astonish everybody.

"What's so strange about that?" he said loudly.

"Why, Dad, you've always had to be forced to bed when you've been sick," Glenda said. "You just won't admit that you can get ill, like other people. You act as if you were made of stone, as if microbes bounced off of you."

"That's because I'm not a hyper—a hyper—a what-you-call-it, a goldbricker, like some people," he said.

"A hypochondriac," Glenda and Roger said at the same time.

"Don't look at me when you say that," Mavice said, glaring at him. "You know I have a chronic bladder infection. I'm not faking it. Dr. Wells told you that himself when you called him to find out if I was lying. I was never so embarrassed in all my life."

The shrill voice was coming from a long way off. Glenda was becoming even more crooked, and Roger was getting thinner and taller.

The doorway to the bedroom moved to one side as he tried to get through it. He couldn't make it on two legs, so he got down on all fours. If he was a dog, he'd have a more solid footing, and maybe the doorway would be so confused by the sudden change of identities it would hold still long enough for him to get through it.

He heard Mavice's scream and barked an assurance that he was all right. Then he was protesting to Mavice and Roger that he didn't want to stand up, but they had hoisted him up and were guiding him toward the bed. It didn't matter then, since he had gotten through. Let the doorway move around all it wanted now; he had fooled it. You could teach an old dog new tricks.

Later, he heard Mavice's voice drilling through the closed door. Here he was, trying to sleep off whatever was ailing him, and she was screaming like a parrot. Nothing would ever get her to lower that voice. Too many decibels from a unibelle, he thought. Which was a strange thought, even if he was an engineer. But he wished she would tone down or, even better, shut up. Forever. He knew that it wasn't her fault, since both her parents had been somewhat deaf during her childhood. But they were dead now, and she had no logical reason to keep on screaming as if she were trying to wake the dead.

Why hadn't he ever said anything about it? Because he nourished the resentment, fed it with other resentments. And then, when the anger became too great, he in turn screamed at her. But it was always about other things. He had never told her how grating her voice was.

He sat up suddenly and then got out of bed. He was stronger now, and the doorway was no longer alive. He walked out into the little hall and said, "What are you saying to Morna?"

Mavice looked at him in surprise and put her hand over the receiver. "I'm calling off tonight. You're too sick to have company."

"No, I'm not," he said. "I'm all right. You tell her to come on over as planned."

Mavice's penciled eyebrows rose. "All right, but if I'd insisted they come, you would have gotten mad at me."

"I got work to do," he said, and headed toward the rear exit.

"With that bandage on your hand?" Mavice said.

He threw both hands up into the air and went into the living room. Roger was sitting in a chair and holding a textbook while watching TV.

"How can you study freshman calculus while Matt Dillon is shooting up the place?" Paul Eyre said.

"Every time a gun goes off and a redskin bites the dust, another equation becomes clear," Roger said.

"What the hell does that mean?"

"I don't know what it means," Roger said calmly. "I just know it works."

"I don't understand you," Paul said. "When I was studying I had to have absolute quiet."

"Didn't you listen to the radio while you were hitting the books?"

Paul seemed surprised.

"No."

"Well, I was raised this way," Roger said. "All my friends were. Maybe we learned how to handle two or more things simultaneously. Maybe that's where the generation gap is. We take in many different things at once and see the connections among them. But you only saw one thing at a time."

"So that makes you better than us?"

"Different, anyway," Roger said. "Dad, you ought to read MacLuhan. But then..."

"But then what?"

"But you never read anything but the local newspaper, sports magazines, and stuff connected with your work."

"I don't have time," Paul said. "I'm holding down a job at Trackless and working eight hours a day on my own business. You know that."

"Leo Tincrowdor used to do that, and he read three books a week. But then he wants to know."

"Yeah, he knows so much, but if his car breaks down, can he fix it himself? No, he has to call in an expensive mechanic. Or get me to do it for him for nothing."

"Nobody's perfect," Roger said. "Anyway, he's more interested in finding out how the universe works and why our society is breaking down and what can be done to repair it."

"It wouldn't be breaking down if people like him weren't trying to break it down!"

"You would have said the same thing a hundred years ago," Roger said. "You think things are in a mess now; you should read about the world in 1874. The good old days. My history professor—"

Paul strode from the room and into the kitchen. He never drank more than two beers a day, but today was different. And *how* it was different. The top of the can popped open, reminding him of the sound when the field had snapped back to normalcy. Now *there* was a connection which Roger, nobody else in the world, in fact, would have made. He wished he had stayed home to catch up on his work instead of indulging himself in a quail hunt.

CHAPTER FOUR

AT SEVEN, THE Tincrowdors walked in. Usually, Paul kept them waiting, since he always had to finish up on a motor in the garage. By the time he had washed up, Leo had had several drinks and Morna and Mavice were engaged in one of their fast-moving female conversations. Leo was happy enough talking to Roger or Glenda or, if neither were there, happy to be silent. He did not seem to resent Paul's always showing up late. Paul suspected that he would have been content if he never showed up. Yet, he always greeted him with a smile. If he had been drinking much, he also had some comment which sounded funny but which concealed a joke at Paul's expense.

Tonight, however, Paul was in the living room when they arrived. He jumped up and kissed Morna enthusiastically. He always kissed good-looking women if they would let him; it gave him a sense of innocent infidelity, outside of the sheer pleasure of kissing. Morna had to bend down a little, like Mavice, but she put more warmth into it than Mavice. Yet she was always, well, often, chewing him out in defense of her friend, Mavice.

Leo Queequeg Tincrowdor enclosed Paul's hand with his over-sized one and squeezed. He was a six footer with heavy bones and a body that had once been muscular but now was turning to fat. His once auburn hair was white and thinning. Below protruding bars of bone, his strange leaf-green eyes, the balls bloodshot, looked at and through Paul. His cheeks were high and red. His beard was a mixture of gray, black, and red. He had a deep voice the effect of which was lessened by a tendency to slur when drinking. And Paul had only seen him twice when he hadn't been drinking. He pushed ahead of him a balloon of bourbon. When he had money, it was Walter's Special Reserve. When he was broke, it was cheap whiskey cut with lemon juice. Evidently, he had recently received a story check. The balloon had an expensive odor.

"Sit down, Leo." Ritualistically, Eyre asked, "What'll it be? Beer or whiskey?"

Ritualistically, Tincrowdor answered, "Bourbon. I only drink beer when I can't get anything better."

When Paul returned with six ounces of Old Kentucky Delight on ice, he found Tincrowdor handing out two of his latest softcovers to Roger and Glenda. He felt a thrust of jealousy as they exclaimed over the gifts. How could the kids enjoy that trash?

"What's this?" he said, handing Leo his drink and then taking the book from Glenda. The cover showed a white man in a cage surrounded by some green-skinned women, all naked, reaching through the bars for the man. In the background was a mountain vaguely resembling a lion with a woman's head. On top of the head was a white Grecian temple with small figures, holding knives around another figure stretched out on an altar.

"Sphinxes Without Secrets," Leo said. "It's about a spaceman who lands on a planet inhabited by women. The males died off centuries before, mostly from heartbreak. A chemist, a women's lib type, had put a substance in the central food plant which made the men unable to have erections."

"What?" Mavice said. She laughed, but her face went red.

"It's an old idea," Leo said. He sipped the bourbon and shuddered. "But I extrapolate to a degree nobody else has ever done before. Or is capable of doing. It's very realistic. Too much so for the *Busiris Journal-Star.* Their reviewer not only refused to write a review, he sent me a nasty letter. Nothing libelous. Old Potts doesn't have the guts for that."

"If there weren't any men, how could they have babies?" Paul said.

"Chemically induced parthenogenesis. Virgin birth caused by chemicals. It's been done with rabbits and theoretically could be done with humans. I don't doubt that the Swedes have done it, but they're keeping quiet about it. They have no desire to be martyrs."

"That's blasphemy!" Paul said. His face felt hot, and he had a momentary image of himself throwing Tincrowdor out on his rear. "There's only been one virgin birth, and that was divinely inspired."

"Inspired? That sounds like a blow job," Tincrowdor said. "No, I apologize for that remark. When among the aborigines, respect their religion. However, I will point out that if Jesus was the result of parthenogenesis, he should have been a woman. All parthenogenetically stimulated offspring are females. Females only carry the X chromosome, you know. Or do you? It's the male's Y chromosome that determines that the baby be a male."

"But God is, by the definition of God, allpowerful," Glenda said. "So why couldn't He have, uh, inserted a sort of spiritual Y chromosome?"

Tincrowdor laughed and said, "Very good, Glenda. You'd make an excellent science-fiction author, God help you."

"Anyway, every culture has its deviates, and this lesbian society was no exception. So a few perverts were not repulsed by the spaceman. Instead, he was to them a most desirable sex object."

"How could a woman who wanted a man instead of a woman be a deviate?" Paul said.

"Deviation is determined by what the culture considers normal. When we were kids, going down was considered by almost everybody to be a perversion, and you could get put in jail for twenty years or more if caught doing it. But in our lifetime, we've seen this attitude change. By 2010, anything between consenting adults will be acceptable. But there are still millions in this country who think the only God-favored way is for the woman to lie on her back with the man on top. And would you believe it, there are millions who won't undress in front of each other or keep a light on during intercourse. These sexual dinosaurs, for that's what they are, will be extinct in another fifty years. Could I have another drink?"

Paul Eyre glared at his wife. She must have been confiding in Morna. Tincrowdor had made it obvious that he was talking about the Eyres. Was nothing sacred anymore?

Nor did he like this kind of talk before Glenda.

He said, "Roger, will you get him another whiskey?"

Roger left reluctantly. Mavice said, "So what happened to the spaceman?"

"He was a homosexual and wanted nothing to do with the woman who let him out of his cage. Scorned, she turned him in to the priestesses, and they sacrificed him. However, he was stuffed and put in a museum alongside a gorilla-type ape. Due to complaints from the Decency League, he was eventually fitted with a skirt to hide his nauseating genitals."

"What does the title mean?" Mavice said.

"That's from Oscar Wilde, who said that women were sphinxes without secrets."

"I like *that!*" Mavice said.

"Oscar Wilde was a queer," Morna said. "What would he know about women?"

"Being half-female, he knew more about them than most men," Tincrowdor said.

Paul wanted to get away from that subject. He leaned over and took the other book from Glenda. "*Osiris On Crutches.* What does that mean? Or maybe I'm better off if I don't ask."

"Osiris was an ancient Egyptian god. His evil brother, Set, tore him apart and scattered the pieces all over earth. But Osiris' wife, Isis, and his son, Horus, collected the pieces and put them back together again and revivified him. My book tells the story in detail. For a long time, Osiris was missing a leg, so he hopped around earth on crutches looking for it. That wasn't the only thing he was missing. His nose couldn't be found, either, so Isis stuck his penis over his nasal cavity. This explains why Osiris is sometimes depicted as being ibis-headed. The ibis was a bird with a long beak. An early Pharoah thought this was obscene and so ordered all artists to change the penis into a beak.

"Anyway, after many adventures, Osiris found his leg but wished he hadn't. He got a lot more sympathy as a cripple. He found his nose, too, but the tribe that had it refused to give it up. Since it was a piece of a divine being, they'd made a god of it. It was giving them good crops, both of wheat and babies, and it was dispensing excellent, if somewhat nasal, oracles.

"Osiris blasted them with floods and lightning bolts, and so scared them into returning his nose. But he would have been better off if he hadn't interfered with their religious customs. His nose elongated and swelled when he was sexually excited, which was most of the time, since he was a god. And he breathed through his penis.

"For heaven's sake!" Paul said. "That's pornography! No wonder Potts won't review your books!"

"They said the same thing about Aristophanes, Rabelais, and Joyce," Tincrowdor said.

"I'm just as glad that the paper won't review his books," Morna said. "It would be so embarrassing. I'm on good terms with our neighbors, but if they found out what he wrote, we'd be ostracized. Fortunately, they don't read science-fiction."

Leo was silent for a moment, and then he looked at Paul's bandaged hand. "Morna said your dog bit you today. You had to shoot him."

He made it sound like an accusation.

"It was terrible," Mavice said. "Roger cried."

"Tears over a dog from a man who's booby-trapped cans of food to blow up infants," Tincrowdor said.

Roger handed him his drink and said, "Those same little kids were the ones tossing grenades in our trucks!"

"Yeah, I know," Tincrowdor said. "Don't criticize a man unless you've walked a mile in his G.I. boots. I shot some twelve-year-olds in World War II. But they were shooting at me. I suppose the principle's the same. It's the practice I don't like. Did you ever see your victims, Roger? After the explosions, I mean."

"No, I'm not morbid," Roger said.

"I saw mine. I'll never forget them."

"You better lay off the booze," Morna said. "You've been insulting and now you're going to get sloppy sentimental."

"Advice from the world's champion insulter," Tincrowdor said. "She calls it being frank. Does it hurt, Paul? The bite, I mean."

"You're the first person who's asked me that," Paul said. "My family's more concerned about the dog than me."

"That's not true!" Mavice said. "I'm terribly worried about rabies!"

"If he starts foaming at the mouth, shoot him," Tincrowdor said.

"That's not funny!" Morns said. "I saw a kid that'd been bit by a dog when I was working in the hospital. He didn't get rabies, but the vaccination made him suffer terribly: Don't you worry, Paul. There's not much chance Riley had hydrophobia. He hadn't had any contact with other animals. Maybe the post-mortem will show he had a tumor on his brain. Or something."

"Maybe he just didn't like Paul," Tincrowdor said.

Paul understood that Tincrowdor was speaking not only for the dog but for himself.

"I once wrote a short story called *The Vaccinators from Vega.* The Vegans appeared one day in a great fleet with weapons against which Earth was powerless. The Vegans were bipedal but hairy and had bad breaths because they ate only meat. They were, in fact, descended from dogs, not apes. They had big black eyes soft with love, and they were delighted because we had so many telephone poles. And they had come to save the universe, not to conquer our planet. They said a terrible disease would soon spread throughout the galaxy, but they would be able to immunize everybody. The Earthlings objected against forcible vaccination, but the Vegans pointed out that the Earthlings themselves had provided the precedent.

"After they had given everybody a shot, they departed, taking with them some of the terrestrial artifacts they thought valuable. These weren't our great works of art or sports cars or atom bombs. They took fire hydrants and flea powder. Ten weeks later all members of homo sapiens dropped dead. The Vegans hadn't told us that *we* were the dreaded disease. Mankind was too close to interstellar travel."

"Don't you ever write anything good about people?" Paul said.

"The people get the kind of science-fiction writer they deserve."

At least, that's what Paul thought he said. Tincrowdor was getting more unintelligible with every sip.

"Sure, I've written a number of stories about good people. They always get killed. Look at what happened to Jesus. Anyway, one of my stories is a glorification of mankind. It's entitled *The Hole in the Coolth.* God is walking around in the Garden in the coolth of the evening. He's just driven Adam and Eve out of Eden, and He's wondering if He shouldn't have killed them instead. You see, there are no animals in the world outside. They're all in the Garden, very contented. The Garden is a small place, but there's no worry about the beasts getting too numerous. God's ecosystem is perfect; the births just balance the deaths.

"But now there's nothing except accident, disease, and murder to check the growth of human population. No sabertooth cats or poisonous snakes. No sheep, pigs, or cattle, either. That means that mankind will be vegetarians, and if they want protein they'll have to eat nuts. In a short time they'll have spread out over the earth, and since they won't discover agriculture for another two thousand years, they'll eat all the nuts. Then they'll look over the fence around the Garden and see all those four-footed edibles there. There goes the neighborhood. The Garden will be ruined; the flowers all tromped flat; the animals exterminated in an orgy of carnivorousness. Maybe He should change His mind and burn them with a couple of lightning strokes. He needs the practice anyway."

"Another thing that bothers God is that He can't stop thinking about Eve. God receives the emotions of all his creatures, as if he's a sort of spiritual radio set. When an elephant is constipated, He feels its agony. When a baboon has been rejected by its pack, He feels its loneliness and sadness. When a wolf kills a fawn, He feels the horror of the little deer and the gladness of the wolf. He also tastes the deliciousness of the meat as it goes down the wolf's mouth. And He appreciates the animals' feelings for sex.

"But human beings have a higher form of sex. It involves psychology, too, and this is so much better. On the other hand, due to psychology, it's often much inferior. But Adam and Eve haven't existed long enough to get their psyches too messed up. So God, as a sort of mental peeping tom, enjoys Adam's and Eve's coupling. Qualitatively, Adam and Eve are so far ahead of the other creations, there's no comparison.

"When Adam takes Eve in his arms, God does too. But in this eternal triangle, no cuckolding is involved. Besides, God had made Eve first.

"But when Adam and Eve were run out of Eden, God decided to dampen the power of His reception from them. He'll stay tuned in, but He'll be getting only faint signals. That means He won't be getting full ecstasy of their mating. On the other hand, He won't be suffering so much because of their grief and loneliness. The two are deep in Africa and heading south, and the signals are getting weaker. About the only thing He can pick up is a feeling of sadness. Still, He sees Eve in His mind's eye, and He knows He's missing a lot. But He refuses to apply more of the divine juice. Better He should forget them for a while.

"He's walking along the fence, thinking these thoughts, when He feels a draft. The cold air of the world outside is blowing into the pleasant warm air of the Garden. This should not be, so God investigates. And he finds a hole dug under the golden, jewel-studded fence that rings Eden. He's astounded, because the hole has been dug from the Garden side. Somebody has gotten *out* of the Garden, and He doesn't understand this at all. He'd understand if somebody tried to get *in*. But *out!*

"A few minutes later, or maybe it was a thousand years later, since God, when deep in thought, isn't aware of the passage of time, he receives a change of feeling from Adam and Eve. They're joyous, and the grief at being kicked out of Eden is definitely less.

"God walks out of Eden and down into Africa to find out what's made the change. He could be there in a nanosecond, but He prefers to walk. He finds Adam and Eve in a cave and two dogs and their pups standing guard at the entrance. The dogs snarl and bark at Him before they recognize Him. God pets them, looks inside the cave, and sees Adam and Eve with their children, Cain, Abel and a couple of baby girls. It was their sisters who would become Cain and Abel's wives, you know. But that's another story.

"God was touched. If human beings could gain the affections of dogs so much that they would leave the delights of Eden, literally dig their way out just to be with human, then humans must have something worthwhile. So He returned to the Garden and told the angel with the flaming sword to drive the other animals out.

"It'll be a mess," the angel said.

"'Yes, I know,' God said. 'But if there aren't other animals around, those poor dogs will starve to death. They've got nothing but nuts to eat.'"

Paul and Mavice were shocked by such blasphemy. Roger and Glenda laughed. There was a tinge of embarrassment in their laughter, but it was caused by their parents' reaction.

Morna had laughed, but she said, "That's the man I have to live with! And when he's telling you about Osiris and God, he's telling you about himself!"

There was silence for a moment. Paul decided that now was his chance. "Listen, Leo, I had a dream this afternoon. It may be a great idea for you."

"O.K.," Tincrowdor said. He looked weary.

"You didn't sleep this afternoon," Mavice said. "You weren't in bed for more than a few minutes."

"I know if I slept or if I didn't. The dream must've been caused by what happened this morning. But it's wild. I dreamt I was hunting quail, just like

I did this morning. I was on the same field, and Riley had just taken a point, like he did this morning. But from then on..."

Leo said nothing until Paul was finished. He asked Roger to fill his glass again. For a moment he twiddled his thumbs, and then he said, "The most amazing thing about your dream is that you dreamed it. It is too rich in imaginative details for you."

Paul opened his mouth to protest, but Tincrowdor held up his hand for silence.

"Morna has related to me dreams which you told Mavice about. You don't have many—rather, you don't remember many, and those few you do seem to you remarkable. But they're not. They're very poor stuff. You see, the more creative and imaginative a person, the richer and more original his dreams. Yes, I know that you do have a flair for engineering creativity. You're always tinkering around on gadgets you've invented. In fact, you could have become fairly wealthy from some of them. But you either delayed too long applying for a patent, and so someone else beat you to it, or you never got around to building a model of your gadget or never finished it. Someone always got there ahead of you. Which is significant. You should look into why you dillydally and so fail. But then you don't believe in psychoanalysis, do you?"

"What's that got to do with this dream?" Paul said.

"Everything is connected, way down under, where the roots grope and the worms blind about and the gnomes tunnel through crap for gold. Even the silly chatter of Mavice and Morna about dress sizes and recipes and gossip about their friends is meaningful. You listen to them a while, if you can stand it, and you'll see they're not talking about what they seem to be talking about. Behind the mundane messages is a *secret* message, in a code which can be broken down if you work hard at it, and have the talent to understand it. Mostly they're S.O.S.'s, cryptic may-days."

"I like *that!*" Mavice said.

"Up your cryptic!" Morna said.

"What about the dream?" Paul said.

"As a lay analyst, I'm more of a layer—of eggs, unfortunately—than an analyzer. I don't know what your dream *means.* You'd have to go to a psychoanalyst for that, and of course you'd never do that because, one, it costs a lot of money, and two, you'd think people would think you were crazy.

"Well, you are, though suffering from that kind of insanity which is called *normalcy.* What I am interested in are the elements of your dream. The flying saucer, the gaseous golden blood from its wound, the sphinx, and the glittering green city."

"The sphinx?" Paul asked. "You mean the big statue by the pyramids? The lion with a woman's head?"

"Now, that's the Egyptian sphinx, and it's a he, not a she, by the way. I'm talking of the ancient Greek sphinx with a lion's body and lovely woman's breasts and face. Though the one you described seemed more like a leocentaur. It had a woman's trunk which joined the lion's body, lioness', to be exact, where the animal's neck should be."

"I didn't see anything like that!"

"You didn't see the entirety. But it's obvious that she was a leocentaur. Nor did you give her a chance to ask you the question. *What is it that in the morning goes on four legs, in the afternoon on two, and in the evening on three?* Oedipus answered the question and then killed her. You wanted to shoot her before she could open her mouth."

"What was the answer?" Mavice said.

"Man," Glenda said. "Typically anthropocentric and male chauvinistic."

"But these are not ancient times, and I'm sure she had a question relevant to this contemporary age. But you must have read about her sometime, maybe in school. Otherwise, why the image? And about the green city? Have you ever read the Oz books?"

"No, but I had to take Glenda and Roger to see the movie when they were young. Mavice was sick."

"He wouldn't let me see it on TV last month," Glenda said. "He said Judy Garland was an animal."

"She used *drugs!"* Paul said. "Besides, that picture is a lot of nonsense!"

"How like you to equate that poor suffering soul with vermin," Tincrowdor said. "And I suppose your favorite TV series, *Bonanza,* isn't fantasy? Or *The Music Man,* which you love so much? Or most of the stuff you read as the gospel truth in our right-wing rag, the *Busiris Journal-Star?"*

"You're not so smart," Paul said. "You haven't got the slightest idea what my dream means!"

"You're stung," Tincrowdor said. "No, if I was so smart, I'd be charging you twenty-five dollars an hour. However, I wonder if that *was* a dream. You didn't actually *see* all this out in that field? By the way, just where is it? I'd like to go out and investigate."

"You *are* crazy!" Paul said.

"I think we'd better go," Morna said. "Paul has such an awful yellow color."

Paul detested Tincrowdor at that moment and yet he did not want him to leave.

"Just a minute. Don't you think it'd make a great story?"

Tincrowdor sat back down. "Maybe. Let's say the saucer isn't a mechanical vehicle but a living thing. It's from some planet of some far-off star, of course. Martians aren't *de rigeur* anymore. Let's say the saucerperson lands here because it's going to seed this planet. The yellow stuff wasn't its blood but its spores or its eggs. When it's ready to spawn, or lay, it's in a vulnerable position, like a mother sea-turtle when it lays its eggs in the sand of a beach. It's not as mobile as it should be. A hunter comes across it at the critical moment, and he shoots it. The wound opens its womb or whatever, and it prematurely releases the eggs. Then, unable to take off in full flight, it hides. The hunter is a brave man or lacking imagination or both. So he goes into the woods after the saucerperson. It's still capable of projecting false images of itself; its electromagnetic field or whatever it is that enables it to fly through space, stimulates the brain of the alien biped that's hunting it. Images deep in the hunter's unconscious are evoked. The hunter thinks he sees a sphinx and a glittering green city.

"And the hunter has breathed in some of the spore-eggs. This is what the saucerperson desires, since the reproductive cycle is dependent on living hosts. Like sheep liver flukes. The eggs develop in larvae which feed on the host. Or perhaps they're not parasitic but symbiotic. They give the host something beneficial in return for his temporarily housing them. Maybe the incubating stage is a long and complicated one. The host can transmit the eggs or the larvae to other hosts.

"Have you been sneezing yellow, Paul?"

"In time, the larvae will mutate into something, maybe little saucers. Or another intermediate stage, something horrible and inimical. Maybe these take different forms, depending upon the chemistry of the hosts. In any event, in human beings the reaction is not just physical. It's psychosomatic. But the host is doomed, and he is highly infectious. Anybody who comes into contact with him is going to be filled with, become rotten with, the larvae. There's no chance of quarantining the hosts. Not in this age of great mobility. Mankind has invented the locomotive, the automobile, the airplane solely to make the transmission of the deadly larvae easier. At least, that's the viewpoint of the saucerperson.

"Doom, doom, doom!"

"Dumb, dumb, dumb," Morna said. "Come on, Leo, let's go. You'll be snoring like a pig, and I won't be able to get a wink of sleep. He snores terribly when he's been drinking. I could kill him."

"Wait for time to do its work," Tincrowdor said. "I'm slowly killing myself with whiskey. It's the curse of the Celtic race. Booze, not the British, beat us. With which alliteration, I bid you bon voyage. Or von voyage. I'm part German, too."

"What are your Teutonic ancestors responsible for?" Morna said. "Your arrogance?"

CHAPTER FIVE

After the Tincrowdors had left, Mavice said, "You really should get to bed, Paul. You do look peaked. And we have to get up early tomorrow for church."

He didn't reply. His bowels felt as if an octopus had squeezed them in its death agony. He got to the bathroom just in time, but the pain almost yanked a scream from him. Then it was over. He became faint when he saw what was floating in the water. It was small, far too small to have caused such trouble. It was an ovoid about an inch long, and it was a dull yellow. For some reason, he thought of the story of the goose that laid golden eggs.

He began trembling. It was ten minutes or more before he could flush it down, wash, and leave the bathroom. He had a vision of the egg dissolving in the pipes, being treated in the sewage plant, spreading its evil parts throughout the sludge, being transported to farms for fertilizer, being sucked up by the roots of corn, wheat, soy beans, being eaten, being carried around in the bodies of men and animals, being…

In the bedroom, Mavice tried to kiss him goodnight. He turned away. Was he infectious? Had that madman accidentally hit on the truth?

"Don't kiss me then," Mavice shrilled. "You never want to kiss me unless you want to go to bed with me. That's the only time I get any tenderness from you, if you can call it tenderness. But I'm just as glad. I have a bladder infection and you'd hurt me. After all, it's my wifely duty, no matter how sick I am. According to you, anyway."

"Shut up, Mavice," he said. "I'm sick. I don't want you to catch anything."

"Catch what? You said you felt all right. You don't have the flu, do you?"

"I don't know what I got," he said, and he groaned.

"Oh, Lord, I pray it's not the rabies," she said.

"It couldn't be. Morna said rabies doesn't act that fast."

"Then what is it?"

"I don't know," he said, and groaned again. "What is it Leo is so fond of quoting? *Whom the gods wish to destroy, they first make mad?"*

"What's that supposed to mean?" she said, but she softened. She kissed him on the cheek before he could object, and turned over away from him.

He lay awake a long time, and when he did sleep he had fitful dreams. They awoke him often, though he remembered few of them. But there was one of a glittering green city and a thing with a body which was part lioness and part woman and advancing toward him over a field of scarlet flowers.

CHAPTER SIX

Roger Eyre stood up and looked at Leo Tincrowdor. They were standing near the edge of a cornfield just off the Little Rome Road.

"They're the tracks of a big cat all right," he said. "A very big cat. If I didn't know better, I'd say they were a lion's or a tiger's. One that could fly."

"Your major is zoology, so you should know," Tincrowdor said. He looked up at the sky. "It's going to rain. I wish we had time to get casts. Do you think that if we went back to your house and got some plaster...?"

"It's going to be a heavy rain storm. No."

"Damn it, I should have at least brought a camera. But I never dreamed of this. It's objective evidence. Your father isn't crazy, and that dream.... I thought he was telling more than a dream."

"You can't be serious," Roger said.

Tincrowdor pointed at the prints in the mud. "Your father was driving to work when he suddenly pulled the car over just opposite here. Three men in a car a quarter of a mile behind him saw him do it. They knew him, since they work at Trackless, too. They stopped and asked him if his car had broken down. He mumbled a few unintelligible words and then became completely catatonic. Do you think that and these tracks are just coincidence?"

Ten minutes later, they were in the Adler Sanitorium. As they walked down the hall, Tincrowdor said, "I went to Shomi University with Doctor Croker, so I should be able to get more out of him than the average doctor would tell. He thinks my books are a lot of crap, but we're both members of The Baker Street Irregulars and he likes me, and we play poker twice a month. Let me do the talking. Don't say anything about any of this. He might want to lock us up, too."

Mavice, Morna, and Glenda were just coming out of the doctor's office. Tincrowdor told them he would see them in a minute; he wanted a few words with the doctor. He entered and said, "Hi, Jack. Anything cooking on the grange?"

Croker was six-feet three-inches tall, almost too handsome, and looked like a Tarzan who had lately been eating too many bananas. He shook hands with Tincrowdor and said, in a slight English accent, "We can dispense with the private jokes."

"Sorry. Laughter is my defense," Tincrowdor said. "You must really be worried about Paul."

The door opened, and Morna entered. She said, "You gave me the high sign to come back alone, Jack. What's wrong?"

"Promise me you won't say anything to the family. Or to anybody," he said. He gestured at a microscope under which was a slide. "Take a look at that. You first, Morna, since you're a lab tech. Leo wouldn't know what he was seeing."

Morna bent over, made the necessary adjustments, looked for about ten seconds, and then said, "Lord!"

"What is it?" Leo said.

Morna straightened. "I don't know."

"Neither do I," Croker said. "I've been ransacking my books, and it's just as I suspected. There ain't no such thing."

"Like the giraffe," Leo said. "Let me look. I'm not as ignorant as you think."

A few minutes later, he straightened up. "I don't know what those other things are, the orange, red, lilac, deep blue, and purple-blue cells. But I do know that there aren't any organisms shaped like a brick with rounded ends and colored a bright yellow."

"They're not only in his blood; they're in other tissues, too," Croker said. "My tech found them while making a routine test. The things seem to be coated with a waxy substance which doesn't take a stain. I put some specimens in a blood agar culture, and they're thriving, though they're not multiplying. I stayed up all night running other tests. Eyre is a very healthy man, aside from a mental withdrawal. I don't know what to make of it, and to tell you the truth, I'm scared!

"That is why I had him put in isolation, and yet I don't want to alarm anybody. I've got no evidence that he's a danger to anybody. But he's swarming with something completely unknown. It's a hell of a situation, because there's no precedence to follow."

Morna burst into tears. Leo Tincrowdor said, "And if he recovers from his catatonia, there's nothing you can do to keep him here."

"Nothing legal," Croker said.

Morna snuffled, wiped her tears, blew her nose, and said, "Maybe it'll just pass away. Those things will disappear, and it'll be just another of those medical mysteries."

"I doubt it, Pollyanna," Tincrowdor said. "I think this is just the beginning."

"There's more," Croker said. "Epples, the nurse assigned to him, has a face deeply scarred with acne. Had, I should say. She went into his room to check on him, and when she came out, her face was as smooth and as soft as a baby's."

There was a long silence before Tincrowdor said, "You mean, you actually mean, that Paul Eyre performed a miracle? But he wasn't conscious! And—"

"I was staggered, but I am a scientist," Croker said. "Shortly after Epples, near hysteria, told me what happened, I noticed that a wart on my finger had disappeared. I remembered that I'd had it just before I examined Eyre..."

"Oh, come on!" Morna said.

"Yes, I know. But there's more. I've had to reprimand a male nurse, a sadistic apish-looking man named Backers, for unnecessary roughness a number of times. And I've suspected him, though I've had no proof, of outright cruelty in his treatment of some of the more obstreperous patients. I've been watching him for some time, and I would have fired him long ago if it weren't so hard to get help."

"Shortly after Epples had left Eyre and not knowing yet that her scars were gone, she returned to the room. She caught Backers sticking a needle in Eyre's thigh. He said later that he suspected Eyre of faking it, but he had no business being in the room or testing Eyre. Epples started to chew Backers out, but she didn't get a chance to say more than two words. Backers grabbed his heart and keeled over. Epples called me and then gave him mouth-to-mouth treatment until I arrived. I got his heart started with adrenalin. A half hour later, he was able to tell me what happened.

"Now Backers has no history of heart trouble, and the EKG I gave him indicated that his heart is normal. I—"

"Listen," Tincrowdor said, "are you telling me you think Eyre can both cure and kill? With thought projection?"

"I don't know how he does it or why. I'd have thought that Backer's attack was just a coincidence if it hadn't been for Epples' acne and my wart. I put two and two together and decided to try a little experiment. I felt foolish doing it, but a scientist rushes in where fools fear to tread. Or maybe it's the other way around.

"Anyway, I released some of my lab mosquitoes into Eyre's room. And behold, the six which settled on him expecting a free meal fell dead. Just keeled over, like Backers."

There was another long silence. Finally, Morna said, "But if he *can* cure people...?"

"Not *he,*" Croker said. "I think those mysterious yellow microorganisms in his tissues are somehow responsible. I know it seems fantastic, but—"

"But if he can cure," Morna said, "how wonderful! "

"Yes," Leo said, "but if he can also kill, and I say *if,* since he'll have to be tested further before such a power can be admitted as possible, if, I say, he can kill anybody that threatens him, then..."

"Yes?" Croker said.

"Imagine what would happen if he were released. You can't let a man like that loose. Why, when I think of how often I've angered him! It'd be worse than uncaging a hungry tiger on Main Street."

"Exactly," Croker said. "And as long as he's in catatonia, he can't be released. Meanwhile, he is to be in a strict quarantine. After all, he may have a deadly disease. And if you repeat any of this to anybody else, including his family, I'll deny everything. Epples won't say anything, and Backers won't either. I've had to keep him on so I can control him, but he'll keep silent. Do you understand?"

"I understand that he might be here the rest of his life," Tincrowdor said. "For the good of humanity."

St. Francis Kisses His Ass Goodbye

A great mission is made up of many small missions.

Francesco Bernardone, founder in A.D. 1210 of the Friars Minor, the Lesser Brothers, was thinking this as he walked down the steep and winding dirt path halfway up Alverno, a mountain given him by a wealthy admirer. Francesco had refused the gift as a gift; he would not own property, not even his brown woolen robe and the rope used as a belt. He had accepted the mountain as a short-term loan, no interest required.

Behind him ambled the heavily laden ass that was, at the moment, Francesco's small mission, part of a great one. Its nose touched the man in the back now and then, a beast's kiss of affection, though the man had not been near it until he had agreed to take it down to the village for Giovanni the charcoal-burner.

Perhaps the ass also needed to touch its brother, Francesco, for reassurance because the threatening summer storm made it nervous. The dark cloud that always hung near the tip of the peak, though usually brightly rimmed, had swelled like a cobra's hood. Lightning-shot, growling, it was sliding down the firry slopes like a black and fuzzy glacier. The wind was now a hand pushing against his back and snapping the hem of his robe. The storm, like a long-delayed rush of conscience, would soon overtake them; the ass would be terrified by the lightning. Francesco halted and put an arm around the beast's thick neck. Brown eyes looked into a brown eye. The ass's eye was clear with health and innocence; his eyes were clouded with sin and with the disease he had gotten when he had gone to Egypt to convince the Saracens that Jesus was not just one of the prophets, a forerunner, but was unique, the virgin-born son of God, the keeper of the keys to Heaven. He had come back to Italy after the disastrous siege by the Crusaders of Damietta with a great disappointment because his mission had failed, with the friendship of the Saracen king, Malik el-Kamil, and with the malady that blinded him a little more every year and always gave him pain. Brother Pain, who clung to him closer than a blood-brother. And, now that the oncoming clouds had dimmed the light, he could see even less.

He did not know what the ass perceived in his eyes, but he saw one of God's creatures–there were so many, far too many–who needed comfort. Whatever the ass saw, it quit trembling.

"Courage, my brother. If you are struck down, you will be free of your burdens."

Should that happen, he would have to carry the charcoal down the mountain because he had promised Giovanni to deliver the load to the house of Domenico Rivoli, the merchant, and to make sure that someone would bring the ass back up. It would carry food and wine and some money to the burner, his pregnant wife, and his five rib-gaunt children. Francesco could take the charcoal himself, no matter how many trips he had to make, but how could he recompense Giovanni for the animal?

Not one to dwell on possibilities, Francesco plunged on, gripping the ass's halter, and, then, the storm was upon them. He could not see at all. The wind seemed to be trying to tumble him on down the mountain. He was being jerked this way and that by the ass's efforts to tear loose from him. Lightning boomed around him, struck a tree, and dazzled and deafened him. For a moment, he seemed to be sheathed in a bolt, though he knew that he could not have been hit. If he had been, he would not be standing.

Suddenly, he could see. A light from above smote the darkness. It was no lightning. It was a blazing-white spherical mass in which even brighter ribbons turned and lashed out as the mass descended. The ass, braying, trembling again, stood as if transfixed while flame cracked out from its ears, nose, and tail. Sparks and tendrils of brightness shot from Francesco's own body; his fingernails spat fires from their ends.

His lips moving in silent prayer, his eyes shut, he thought that, surely, he was about to be burned alive. Then he opened his eyes. If he was to burned by the Lord, then that was a martyrdom, and he should see it. Still, this was the first time that God had set one of His own faithful afire. Perhaps, this was like Elijah's being borne by God to Heaven in a fiery chariot. Or was that thought a sinful self-exaltation?

When he closed his eyes again despite telling himself to keep them open, he still saw the light. It seemed to fill his body to the end of his toes. The crash of thunder had ceased. Silence had come with the dazzle. At the same time, he felt a slight tugging–not from the halter–within his body. It was as if he was in the middle of a gigantic and hollow magnet, pulling him from every direction. The attraction was slightly more powerful on one side, but which side he did not know.

Then the halter was jerked from his grip. Though he was in terror–or was it ecstasy?–he leaped toward where he thought the beast was. He had promised to get it back to Giovanni, and his promises must be fulfilled even when God–or Satan?–had business with him. His hands flailing, one caught the halter. He grabbed the stiff short mane with the other, and, somehow, scrambled up the load until he was on top of it. He felt the pulling on one side of his body grow stronger. It seemed to him, though he could not see anything except the light, that he and the beast were rising. There flashed through his head–a dark thought in the white light filling his skull–that he was like Mahomet who ascended to Heaven on the winged ass, al-Boraq. That story had been told to him by Sultan Malik himself.

But now he was sitting above a cross, the T formed by the pale stripe across the ass's shoulders and down along its spine. In a sense, he was riding the cross that had ridden him most of life. A great burden he had rejoiced in bearing.

Despite the light, which had not lessened its intensity, he was catching sight of things, brief as lightning flashes but leaving dark, yet somehow burning, afterimages. There was a huge room with many men and women in strange clothes and white coats standing before boxes glowing with many lights and with words in an unknown language, and there were two towering machines in the background which whirled on their axes and shot lightning at each other. That vision was replaced by the dark, big-nosed face of a bearded man in a green turban–something familiar about it–the lips moving with unheard speech. That was gone. Now he saw a great city at night, pulsing with thousands of lights. It was far below him. Pure light banished it. Then it shot out again like a dark jeweled tongue from a mouth formed of light. Now he was closer to it; it was spreading out. Light again. And, once more, the city. He could see buildings with hundreds of well-lit windows, so tall that they would have soared above the Tower of Babel. Enormous machines with stiff unflapping wings flew over them.

He still had the sense of being tugged, though it had suddenly become weaker. He no longer felt airborne. The light was gone. He was in semidarkness. An illumination, feeble compared to that which had filled him, was coming from before him. When he turned his head, he saw a similar illumination behind him. He was in an alley formed by two buildings that went up and up toward a pale night-sky. Around him were a dozen or so figures in bulky clothes. They were staring at this man on the load on top of an ass as if they had appeared out of air, which must be what happened. He was in the middle of a circle formed by a layer of mud six feet across, weeds and bushes sticking at crazy angles out of the dirt which had been transported along with him. He was glad that the air was warm because his robe and he were soaked.

The silence of the journey was gone. The ass was braying loudly; men and women were yelling at him in a foreign language. Now he saw that there were other lights in the alley, flames from the tops of five or six metal barrels spaced out along and next to the two walls. The slight wind brought him odors of long-unwashed bodies and clothes, alcohol, old and fresh piss and shit, decaying teeth, and that stench that rose from the oozing pustules of hopelessness and festering rage.

He was surprised that he could smell all that. He had been immersed in it so long that he scarcely noticed it any more. Perhaps, somehow, his physical and spiritual nostrils had been cleansed during the transit.

Transit to where? This could not be Heaven. Purgatory? Or Hell? He shuddered, then smiled. If, for whatever reason, he had failed to be in God's grace, and there were many reasons why he might have, he could be in Purgatory or Hell. Come either place, he would have work to do.

His own salvation had never been his main concern, though it was a banked fire in his mind. He had stressed to his disciples that the salvation of others was their mission, that that must be brought about by their examples. If they were to be saved, they must not think about it. It must be done by tending to and taking care of others.

That thought was broken off, a branch snapping, when the dim figures swarmed around him, a mass swelled when others joined it from doorways and packing boxes. Before he could protest, he was hauled roughly from the load and cast painfully upon the pavement. The ass, braying, was pulled down on its side away from Francesco. Knives gleamed in the dull light. The beast tore the night with its death screams as the blades plunged into it. Yelling for them to stop, Francesco got to his feet and began pulling off, or trying to pull off, the men around it. Giving up his efforts, he went to the animal, got down on his knees, and lifted the head, heavy as his heart. He kissed it on its nose, felt it quit shaking, and saw that the open eye was fixed.

The deed was done, and he was grieved, though he would have been glad to give these hungry men the beast to eat if it had been his to give. He had no time to dwell on that. Several men grabbed him and ran their hands over him, then shoved him away with angry exclamations. Apparently, they had been searching for money and valuables. A barefooted man who looked as if Famine and Plague were struggling to determine who would first overcome him, holding a big chunk of blood-dripping meat in one hand and a knife in the other, gestured savagely at him, speaking the tongue Francesco did not know. Hoping that he understood the man's signs, Francesco sat down on the pavement, removed the leather sandals, and handed them to the man.

"Take them with my blessings," Francesco said. He stood up. "If you need my robe, you may have that, too."

The man, scowling, talking to himself, had staggered off to one of the barrels by the side of a building. He threw the meat on a metal grillework on the open top, where it began smoking with the other pieces of meat laid there. The man sat down, wiped his bloodied hands on his coat, and fitted the sandals to his feet. By then, the load had been torn apart and most of it thrown by the barrels or added to the fuel in them. Francesco stood in the middle of the alley, nauseated not only by the too-swift events but by the feeling that he was hanging by the soles of his feet from an upside-down surface: The city itself seemed to him to have been turned over, and he was hanging like a fly on a ceiling. Yet, when he jumped slightly to reassure his confused senses that he was not kept from falling by a glue on the bottom of his feet, he came back to the pavement as quickly as he always had.

When he saw some monstrous white thing with two glowing eyes that shot beams of light ahead of it, speeding on the street at the end of the alley, he ignored his nausea and started toward the street. Before he got there, two more of the frightening things went by. But he saw the people within them and knew that they were some kind of self-propelled vehicle. He clung to the corner of the building while others shot by. Was he in a city of wizards and witches? If so, he must indeed be in Hell.

There was more to add to his bewilderment. The buildings along the street were fronted with gigantic panels on which icons of people and animals flashed and many words sprang into light and then disappeared. His mind swirling like the strange many-colored geometric patterns on some of the panels, he stepped back into the alley. He would speak to each of the people there and determine if any spoke Umbrian or Roman Italian or Latin or Provencal, or if any could understand the limited phrases he knew of Arabic, Berber, Aragonese, Catalan, Greek, Turkish, German or English.

He stopped, rigid at the sight of a black woman who was on her knees and holding with one hand the swollen penis of the white man standing above her while she moved her head back and forth along the shaft in her mouth. Her other hand supported a baby sucking at her nipple. In the man's hand was a piece of half-cooked meat. Her payment?

Before Francesco could recover, he heard a loud up-and-down wailing, and a huge vehicle screeched around the corner, making him dive to escape being struck. It stopped, its two beams making noon out of the twilight in the alley, blue and red lights on it flashing, the wailing it made dying down. The man pulled loose from the woman's mouth and ran toward a doorway. Some of the others fled from the barrels; some froze. Doors in the side and rear of the vehicle snapped out and down. Men and women in bright blue uniforms, wearing blue helmets, and holding what had to be weapons, though of a nature that Francesco did not know, sprang shouting from its interior. He, with the other alley people, was shoved with his face against the wall, his outstretched hands against the wall, his legs spread out. He looked around and was cuffed alongside his head with the barrel of a weapon.

But he looked again anyway, and he saw another huge machine, its front a great open mouth, lumber past the first vehicle. It stopped short of the carcass, waited while some uniforms pointed small flashing boxes at the dead ass, then scooped it up with a long broad metal tongue and drew it into the dark maw. The uniforms kicked over the barrels so that the fiery fuel and meat spilled onto the pavement. After this, the uniforms questioned the denizens of the alley but got very little response except some obvious cursing. Francesco could not answer his interrogator, but the uniform just laughed and passed on to the next man. Francesco turned around and, once more, was shocked, this time so much that he was unable for a moment to think coherently.

Three of the alley men were in a stage of activity at a point where they could or would not stop. A man was buggering a tall and very skinny man whose lower garment was around his ankles. He had whiskers that radiated around his face, and in the center of the whiskers was the penis of a man standing before the whiskery man, sliding back and forth rapidly. The uniforms had not touched or questioned them. Evidently, they regarded the spectacle as comic because those standing around were laughing and jeering. But, just as two of the men were screaming with ecstasy, the round top of the second vehicle pointed a long metal tube at the trio, and water shot out of its end. The three were knocked down and rolled over and over until they collided violently with a wall.

The uniforms laughed, then became grim. After the alley people, Francesco among them, had been forced to set the barrels upright again, the hose on top of the machine washed the charcoal and the fuel and the pieces of meat and other trash down the alley until the mass was swallowed by an opening below the curb at the end of the alley. Many of the alley people were struck by the jet.

This distressed Francesco more than anything he had so far seen. It was a great sin to deny food to these hungry unfortunates.

Brother Sun arose a few minutes after the uniforms and their vehicles had left. Cold from the double-soaking despite the warm air, cold also from the transit and the aftermath, very bewildered, Francesco shivered. Not until day had worn on and the air had become hot did he stop quaking. By then, the alley people, looking even more tired, haggard, ugly, and hungry, had dispersed. Later, he would see several of them begging for money. He left the alley to walk on the sidewalk northward through the canyon street. The vehicles, scarce at first, soon became numerous. They jammed the streets as they crawled along, and their honking never stopped. By noon, when people swarmed on the sidewalks, an acrid odor which he had noticed about mid-morning became heavy, and his eyes burned. Then Brother Sun was covered up by his sister clouds. Despite this, the breeze became hotter.

Becoming ever more hungry, he tried vainly to stop some of the pedestrians to beg for bread. They were well-fed and luxuriously dressed, though the clothes of some of the women exposed so much that he was embarrassed. After a while, he got used to that. But his pleas for food were still ignored. He also encountered many crazed people, some beggars, some not, who talked to themselves or shouted loudly at others. These, however, had also populated his own world; he was used to them.

He passed a large building with many broad steps leading up to it and two large stone lions set halfway up the staircase. On the sidewalk near it he stopped by a cart from behind which a man sold food the like of which he had never seen before. Its odors made his mouth water. A man bought a paper sack full of some small puffy white balls and began scattering them for the pigeons abounding here. Francesco asked him for some of the white stuff, but the man turned his back on him.

Passing on, he saw glass-fronted restaurants crammed with customers stuffing themselves. He entered one and got the attention of a servant behind the counter by pointing to his open mouth and rubbing his stomach. A big man grabbed him by the back of his robe and forced him violently, though Francesco did not struggle or protest, back onto the sidewalk.

His belly rumbled. So did the thunder westward. The skies were now black, and the breeze had become a wind that rippled the hems of his robe. It was beginning to cool, though, and the stink that burned his eyes was lessening. The tugging inside him and the feeling of being upside down were still with him, present when be was not too absorbed in the strangeness. He turned to the west and walked until he came to a river. Though thirsty, he did not drink from it. He had often drunk from water that had a bad odor, but this was too strong for him. He went north, then west, then south, then west again, and came to another river, equally malodorous. On both shores were elevated highways, jammed with the everhonking vehicles. The whole city was a din.

Now he did what many of the unfortunates were doing, opening garbage cans and searching therein. He found a half-eaten semicircle of a baked crust of dough with pieces of some strange red vegetable and of meat mixed with cheese. The box underneath it had printed words on it. One of them was PIZZA. Derived from *picca,* meaning *pie?* He devoured that, though it was dry and hard, then dug up another half-eaten item made up of two slices of hard and moldy bread in the middle of which was meat beginning to stink. Nevertheless, he started to bite down on that when a stray dog stopped by him and looked pleadingly at him. Its mangy skin covered a body that seemed more skeleton than flesh. He tossed the bread and meat to the dog, who bolted it. Francesco petted the dog. After that, it followed him for a while but deserted him to investigate an overturned garbage can.

Despite not knowing any of the languages he overheard during his journey through the upside-down city, Francesco had made many interpretations by mid-noon. There were other languages than those issuing from mouths. For instance, the tongue of the city itself, the tongue composed of many tongues just as a great mission was composed of many small ones. Cities were the first machines built by man, social machines, true, but Francesco was especially adept at translating the unspoken languages of cities. The architecture, the artifacts, the art, the music, the traffic, the manners, the expressions of faces and voices, the subtle and the not-so-subtle body movements, the distribution of goods and food, the ways in which the keepers of the law and the breakers of the law (often they were the same) behaved toward each other and toward the citizens upon whom they preyed and who preyed on them, these all formed a great machine which was part organism and part mechanical.

God certainly knew, as did Francesco, that there were enough mechanical artifacts in this city to have provided all of the world that he knew with plenty of them. Aside from the vehicles, there were the blaring mechanical voices in every store and on every street corner and there were the moving and flashing icons that covered the fronts of buildings and were in unnumberable numbers inside the buildings. He did not know the purpose of most. But he understood that the flat cases people wore strapped to their wrists were used to talk at a distance with others and that the many booths on the sidewalks were used for the same purpose.

The whole city was, among other things, a message center. But did these men and women understand the messages, the truth behind the words and images? Did they care if they understood correctly? Did the devices widen the doors for the entrance of the truth? Or did they widen the doors for more lies to enter? Or did they do both?

If both, then the result was that these people were more confused than those of his world. Too much information combined with the inability to separate truth from falsehood was as bad as ignorance. Especially when the disseminators of lies claimed that these were truths. Just as he concluded this, Francesco saw the gaunt man with the whiskery halo-fringe, the buggeree and sucker who had been interrupted in the alley by the uniforms. He was sitting on the sidewalk with his back against a building wall. Francesco could see the scabs, pustules, and blotches covering his face, arms, and the bony legs. He could also see that indefinable expression of the slowly dying. But it was changing into that of those who would soon be able to express nothing. Francesco had seen that too many times not to recognize it.

Now he knew that he was neither in Purgatory or Hell. Whatever else there was in those places, death was not there.

Francesco made his way through the throng, all of whom were ignoring the man, some of whom stepped over his bare legs. He knelt by the man and took his sore-covered hand. It was almost as fleshless as Brother Death's himself. Francesco, though he knew he would not be understood, asked what he could do for him? Did he need to be carried to a sickhouse? Was he hungry? His questions were intended to make the man comprehend that he was with someone who cared for him. There was really nothing that Francesco could du to stave off the irresistible.

The man leaned forward and mumbled something. Francesco took him in his arms and held him while the man's mouth moved against the robe. What was he trying to say? It sounded like *priest.* Suddenly, Francesco knew that the word was some kind of English, though certainly not what he had learned from Brother Haymo of Faversham, his English disciple.

"Prete! Prete!" Francesco said.

For the first time in his life, Francesco felt helpless. He had always been able to do something for those who needed help, but he could not make anyone understand what needed doing now, and he himself could do nothing.

The wind lashed out, even more cool now, and the thunder was closer. A few raindrops fell on his head. Lightning chainlinked the clouds. Then, the blackening clouds tipped over barrels of rain. He and the man were soaked, and the sidewalk was quickly emptied of all but himself and the man he held in his arms. That did not matter since they would not have helped him anyway.

He prayed, "O Lord, this man wishes to confess, to repent, and to be forgiven. Is not the intent good enough for You? What does it matter if no priest is here to hear him? I do not hate him, no matter what he has done. I love him. If I, a mere mortal, one of Your creatures, can love him, how much more must You!"

"He is gone," a deep melodious voice said. Francesco turned his head and looked up through the water blurring his already dimmed vision. As if there were a mirage before him–a dry desert phenomenon beneath the surface of the sea–he saw standing by him a tall man in a green robe and wearing a green turban. Francesco gently released the sagging corpse, wiped the rain from his eyes with his wet sleeve, and stood close to the man. He started. The face was that of the man whom he had glimpsed while in transit to this place. It was handsome and hawk-nosed, its eyebrows thick and dark, looking like transplanted pieces of a lion's mane. The leaf-green eyes in the almost black face were startling.

"It was not easy finding you," the man said. Francesco started again. He had not realized until now that the man was speaking in Provençal.

"Others are looking for you," the man said. "They are frantic to find you, but they do not know what you look like and so will fail. In fact, they do not know if they have transported a man or a woman or an animal or some combination of these. But their indicators make them think that they have picked up at least one human being, possibly more. Unless someone else does for them what they cannot do, they will be responsible for an explosion which will considerably change the face of Earth and might kill all humans and much of the higher forms of animals. We have approximately three hours to prevent this event. If Allah wills..."

So, the man was a Muslim. That thought overrode for a moment the prediction of the cataclysm. Francesco started to ask a question, but the man continued.

"They did not know this would happen until immediately after they had transported you. Their..." He paused, then said, "You would not understand the word. Their...thinking machine...gave a false result because of a slight mathematical error put into the machine by the operator. Slight but reverberating greatly...swelling. To prevent an explosion of any degree, they must send you back. Not only you but all that came with you. That is impossible, but the effect may be considerably reduced if they send back not only you but a mass approximating that which was brought along with you. You will have to estimate that mass for them, describe what did come in with you."

The man stepped into the street and held a hand up. A black vehicle skidded to a stop a few inches before the man. He went to the front left-side window and spoke to the man seated there. A very angry-looking man and woman got out of the back seat a minute later. The green-turbaned man gestured to Francesco to come quickly. Francesco got into the back seat next to him. The vehicle's wheels screamed as it leaped like a rabbit that had just seen a fox. The man spoke a few short words of what had to be English into the small case strapped to his wrist. Numbers flashed on its top.

"There will be no more time travel experiments;" the man said. "The data...the information...has been sent secretly to the government of this country and to those of all nations. The populaces will not be informed until after the explosion, if then. Notifying the people of this city would only cause a panic, and the city could not possibly be evacuated. Even if it could be, the people could not get far enough away unless they went in an airplane...a flying machine. And only a few could get away in time. The people in the project are staying. They will work until the explosion comes, and they hope that its effects, will be considerably reduced, as I said, by sending you back."

Francesco, clinging to a strap above the door, said, "Are you telling me that I have somehow been plucked by satanic powers from my time to a future time?"

"Yes, though the powers are not satanic. Their effect may be, though."

The man pointed out the window by Francesco at a building Francesco could see dimly. But he could make out a tall structure with many spires on the upper half of which was a gigantic panel. Its upper third flashed orange letters, one forming FRANCIS. The lower two-thirds displayed a bright and strange figure, a six-winged and crucified seraph surrounded by roiling light-purple clouds, which in turn were surrounded by swirling, fast-changing, and many-colored geometric figures. Then the vehicle was past it.

"A Catholic church, SAINT FRANCIS OF THE POOR. Attended mainly by the rich." The man chuckled, and he said, "Dedicated to you, Francesco Bernardone of Assisi."

Francesco, who had always felt at ease when events were going too swiftly for others to comprehend, was now numb.

"I was canonized?"

"Yes, but your order started to depart from your ideals, to decay, as it were, before your corpse was cold. Or so it was said."

Francesco bit his lower lip until the blood came, and he dug his fingernails into the palms of his hands until they felt like iron nails being driven in.

"I will *not* change."

"Because you know this? No, you will not."

"When did I die?"

"It would be wise for you not to know."

"But I am going back. Otherwise..."

"Obviously. But what happens here after you do ...that is another matter. The force of the explosion caused by the interaction of matter and temporal energy will be proportional to the amount left here of the matter you brought with you. If, for example, you had held your breath during the transit, then expelled after arriving here, the amount of expelled air–if confined to a small area, and it won't be–would be enough to blow up that church and several blocks around it. What the project people need to know is just how much matter you did bring with you."

Francesco told him what had come in with him and what had happened to it.

"Your sandals, the urine you've pissed out, the dirt surrounding you, the plants and insects in the dirt, the body of the ass left after the butchering, the pieces of meat cooking on the barrels, the smoke from them, and the meat in the bodies of the men who ate it should go back with you. But, of course, they can't. You'll have to estimate an equivalent mass from your memory. The mass can't be exact, but if it's anything near that which was brought in, it will help cancel some of the effects of the mass-temporal energy explosion."

The man thought for a moment. He said, "After I deliver you, I will leave this area. Even I...no time for that now. The northeastern coast will be destroyed and much of the interior country. Many millions will die. But the world will go on."

Francesco said, "You seem to know so much. Why didn't you stop them? At least, warn them."

"I knew no more than they did what would happen. There is only One who is all-wise. I had nothing to do with the project, though I was well informed about it. I was not supposed to be, which is why they were so outraged and furious when I called in and told them I would search for you. They will try to arrest me when I bring you in, though that is stupid because I would be blown to bits along with them. They will not be able to hold me, and you will go back. The world knows when you died. So it is written that you return to your time."

"Not without the ass...an ass," Francesco said.

"What?"

Francesco told him of his promise to Giovanni, the charcoal-burner. "And there must be a load of charcoal, too."

The man spoke again to the case on his wrist, listened, spoke again, listened, then said, "They find it hard to believe that you would rather let the east coast blow up than go back without the donkey. I told them that I doubted that, but it would go easier and faster if they did what you want."

"Is it difficult to obtain an ass and charcoal?"

"No. The ass will come from a nearby zoo...a place where animals are kept. It should arrive soon even if it has to be airlift...brought in a flying machine." He smiled and said, "I told them they should get the biggest ass possible. I suggested that they might substitute the head of the project if for some reason they couldn't get one at the zoo. He fits all your qualifications, aside from being bipedal and lacking long ears."

"Thank you. However, I do not like to go back without even knowing your name."

"Here I am called Kidder."

"Elsewhere...it's not Elijah?"

"I have many names. Some of them are appropriate." Francesco wondered why he had seen Kidder's face during the transit. The forces that had shot him from there to here must have been connected with some psychic–or supernatural–phenomena even if the people who were running the project did not know that. His question, however, was forgotten when the vehicle was caught in slow-moving traffic that did not speed up no matter how long and hard the driver blew the horn. The man talked into his wrist-case again, and, within two minutes, a flying machine appeared at a low altitude above them. It descended, pods on its sides burning at their lower end and emitting a frightening and deafening noise. It landed on a sidewalk, and Francesco and Kidder got into it and were whisked up and away. By then, Francesco was so frozen that he was not scared. The machine landed on top of a high building. He and Kidder got out and were ushered swiftly to an elevator that plunged downwards and stopped suddenly, and then they were hustled along by many white-coated men and women and some uniforms to a great room filled with many machines with flashing lights and fleeting icons and numbers.

Francesco was placed in the center of the room inside a circle marked on the floor. An ass with a burden of charcoal, a large handsome beast, so much better than the poor one that had come with him that he would have to tell Giovanni not to ask questions about it, just be grateful and thank God for it, was led in.

Francesco, his throat dry, said huskily, "*Signore* Kidder, satisfy my curiosity. What is today's date?"

"Seven hundred and eighty years after your birth;" Kidder said. And he was gone, somehow removing himself from the crowd around him and the two uniforms who stood behind him. Francesco cried out to him that he remembered now where he had seen him before the transit. He had been in the camp of Sultan Malik, where Francesco had glimpsed him a few times but had not thought that he was more than one of the Sultan's court. Kidder probably had not heard him. Even if he had been in the crowd, he would not have caught Francesco's words. The two uniforms were shouting too loudly as they tried to force their way through the crowd in search of Kidder.

Then bags of dirt were stacked alongside him and the ass in the center of the circle, and the workers withdrew. The crowd moved back to the walls of the room. They all looked haggard and frightened and white-faced. Francesco felt sorry for them because they knew that they were doomed no matter what happened to him. He blessed them and prayed for them and blessed them again.

The lights flickered; a terrible whining pierced his ears and skull. A great ball of swirling white light descended from a conelike device in the ceiling. It surrounded him, and, though he cried out, he could not hear his own voice. The tugging sensation that had never left him became stronger. He was once more in that limbo in which he saw dimly, again, the men and women in the building and the turbaned head of Kidder.

Then he was in rain and thunder, and the ass was braying loudly beside him. Under his feet was a very thin section of the floor inside the circle.

He no longer felt the tugging, and the world no longer seemed upside down.

It was not long after this that Francesco saw on Mount Alverno the vision of the six-winged and crucified seraph in the skies and that Francesco was blessed–or cursed–with the marks of the nails in his hands (which he tried to conceal as much as possible). And then, seemingly as swift as that transit of which he never spoke, the time came when he was dying. The brothers and sisters were gathered around him, speaking softly, church bells were ringing, and, outside the hut, the rich and the powerful and the poor were standing, praying for him. His blinded eyes were open as if he could see what: the others could not, which indeed he could. He was wondering if the seraph he had seen on the panel on the church front during that wild ride had possibly influenced him, caused him to envision that aweful, painful, yet ecstatic flying figure above the mountain.

Which had come first? His seeing the seraph on that panel in the far future or the splendor in the sky? He would never know. The mysteries of time were beyond him–at this moment.

He wondered about Kidder. Could he be that mysterious Green Man Francesco had heard about from some wise men of the East? He was supposed to have been the secret counsellor of Moses and of many others, and he showed up now and then, here and there, when the need for him was great. But that implied…

That thought faded as another Francesco, an almost transparent Francesco, rose like smoke from his body and stood there looking down at him. Its lips moved, but he could not hear its voice. It kneeled down by him and bent over. Now, he could read the lips.

"Goodbye, Brother Ass," he, the other, said. His body, that creature that he had treated so hard, driven so unmercifully, and to which he had apologized more than once for the burdens he had heaped on it, that was leaving him. No, he was leaving it. Now, he was looking down upon his own dead face. He leaned over and kissed its lips and stood up, happy as never before, and he had always been filled with joy even when hungry and wet and cold and longing vainly for others to have his happiness.

He was ready for whatever might come but hoped that he would have work to do.

Not like that on Earth.

Crossing the Dark River

1

"What? You prescribed lemon juice to cure cholera?"

"What? You had a sure cure for infants who held their breaths until their faces turned blue? And for young females in a hysterical seizure? You stuck your little finger up their anuses? Presto! Changeo! They're rid forever of infantile behavior and the tantrums of the body?"

"What? You're searching for the woman who's supposed to have given birth to a baby somewhere along the River? A baby? In this world where all are sterile and no woman has ever gotten pregnant? You believe that's true? How about buying the Brooklyn Bridge?

"No? Then how about a splinter from the True Cross? Ho! Ho! Ho! And you believe that this baby reproduced by parthenogenesis is Jesus Christ born again to save us Valleydwellers? And you've been traveling up-River to find the infant? Who do you think you are? One of the Three Wise Men? Ho! Ho! Ho!"

And so Doctor Andrew Paxton Davis had not stayed long any place until he had been detained by Ivar the Boneless. He had wandered up the Valley, seldom pausing, just as, on Earth, he had been the peripatetic's peripatetic. During the late 1800s and early 1900s, he had traveled to many cities in the United States. There he had lectured on and practiced his new art of healing and sometimes established colleges of osteopathy. Denver, Colorado; Quincy, Missouri; Pittsburgh, Pennsylvania; Cincinnati, Ohio; LaFayette and Indianapolis, Indiana; Dallas and Corsicana, Texas; Baker City, Oregon; Los Angeles, California, and many other places.

Then he had originated Neuropathy, an eclectic discipline of healing. It combined all the best features of osteopathy, chiropracty, magnetism, homeopathy, and other systems of drugless medicine. He had preached that God-inspired gospel throughout the country. And he had written four thick books that were used by osteopaths and ophthalmologists and read by many laymen throughout the United States.

"From going to and fro in the earth and from walking up and down in it."

That was Satan's answer to God when He said, "Whence comest thou?" That could be said also of Andrew P. Davis. But Davis loathed Satan, and his model was Job, who "was perfect and upright and one that feared God and eschewed evil."

Since Davis had awakened on the Riverworld, he had suffered the torments of Job. Yet he had not faltered in his faith any more than had Job. God must have made this world, but the Great Tempter was here too. To realize that, you just had to look around at the inhabitants.

RIVERWORLDERS DREAMED MOST often about lost Earth. The one exception to this was the nightmare about their mass resurrection, the Day of the Great Shout when all the dead had screamed at one time. What a cry that must have been!

Doctor Andrew Paxton Davis had often awakened moaning, sometimes screaming, from that nightmare. But he had another dream that distressed him even more.

For instance, on this early and still-dark morning of the fifth anniversary of The Day, he had painfully oozed into wakefulness from a Riverworld-inspired nightmare. Not terror but shame and humiliation had written the script for that sleep-drama.

He had gotten his M.D. from Rush Medical College in Chicago in 1867. But, after many years as a physician in the rural areas of Illinois and Indiana, he had become unhappy with the practice. Always a seeker after truth, he had become convinced that the new science and art of healing devised by Dr. Andrew Taylor Still was a breakthrough. Davis had been in the first class (1893) to complete the courses of the newly established American School of Osteopathy in Kirksville, Missouri.

But, ever questioning, ever seeking, he had decided that osteopathy alone was not enough. Hence, his own discipline and his founding of the College of Neuropathy in Los Angeles. When he died at the age of eighty-four of stomach cancer—he also had nightmares about that long agony—he was still the head of a flourishing practice.

However, medical science had improved considerably from his birth in 1835 to his death in 1919. And, from then on, it had accelerated at an incredible velocity. His late-twentieth-century informants made it sound like one of those scientific romances by H.G. Wells.

In the first two years on the Riverworld, he had proudly; at first, anyway, told the doctors he met of his knowledge and accomplishments. He had also confided his belief that the Savior had been born again. So many had laughed at him that he became very reserved about telling any M.D. that he had practiced the healing art. He was almost as reticent about revealing his Quest to laymen. But how could he find the Holy Mother and the Holy Infant unless he told people that he was searching for them?

He had awakened this morning and lain in a sweat not caused by the temperature. After a while, he vaguely remembered a dream preceding the one about the mockery and jeers.

He was outside the tower on top of the hill and just starting to walk down the hill when he heard the king calling him. He turned and looked up through the twilight that enveloped most of his dreams. Ivar the Boneless was staring down at him from the top of the tower. As usual, the king was half smiling. Beside him, Ann Pullen, the queen not only of Ivar's land but of all the bitches in the world, was leaning through a space in the top wall. Her bare breasts were hanging over the top of the stone. Then she lifted one and flipped it at him.

Suddenly, Sharkko the Shyster appeared beside the two. Sharkko, the man who would have been utterly miserable if he could understand how detestable he was. But Sharkko was unable to imagine that anyone could not like him. He had been given solid proof, kicks, slaps, curses, and savage beatings, that he was not loved by all. Yet his mind slid these off and kept his self-image undented and unbreakable.

These three were the most important beings in Davis's life in Ivar's land. He would have liked to have put them in a rocket and fired them off toward the stars. That way, he would keep them from being resurrected somewhere along the River and thus avoid meeting them again. Except in his nightmares, of course.

Later, a few hours after dawn, Davis was walking up the hill to the tower after fishing in the River. He had caught nothing and so was not in a good mood. That was when he met the lunatic gotten up like a clown.

"Doctor Faustroll, we presume?"

The man, who spoke in a strangely even tone, held out an invisible calling card.

Davis glanced down at the tips of the man's thumb and first finger as if they really were holding a card.

"Printed in the letters of fire," the man said. "But you must have a heart on fire to see them. However, imaginary oblongs are best seen in an imaginary unlighted triangle. The darker the place, the brighter the print. As you may have noticed, it's late morning, and the sunlight is quite bright, At least, they seem to be so."

The fellow, like all other insane on Earth, must have been resurrected with all traces erased of any mental illness he had suffered there. But he was crazy again.

His forehead was painted with some kind of mathematical formula. The area around his eyes was painted yellow, and his nose was painted black. A green mustache was painted on his upper lip. His mouth was lipsticked bright-red. On his chest, a large question mark was tattooed in blue. A dried fish was suspended on a cord reaching to his belly. His long, thick, and very black hair was shaped into a sort of bird's nest and held in place by dry gray mud.

And, when the man bent his neck forward, he exposed the upper part of an egg in the nest. Davis could easily see it because the man was shorter than he. It did not roll with the movement of the head. Thus, it must be fixed with fish glue to the top of his head. The wooden and painted pseudo-egg, Davis assumed, was supposed to represent that laid by a cuckoo. Appropriate enough. The stranger was certainly cuckoo.

A large green towel, the clown's only garment, was draped around his hips. The gray cylinder of his grail was near his bare feet. Most people carried a fish-skin bag that held their worldly possessions. This fellow lacked that, and he was not even armed. But he did carry a bamboo fishing pole.

The man said, "While on Earth, we were King Ubu. Here, we are Doctor Faustroll. It's a promotion that we richly deserve. Who knows? We may yet work our way to the top and become God or at least occupy His empty throne. At the moment, we are a pataphysician, D.Pa., at your service. That is not a conventional degree in one sense, but in all senses it is a high degree, including Fahrenheit and Kelvin."

He started to put his imaginary card in an imaginary pocket of an imaginary coat.

Davis said, "I'll take it," and he held out his hand. Humoring the pataphysician, whatever that was, might prevent him from becoming violent.

He moved his hand close to his bare chest to suggest that he was pulling out a card from an inner pocket of his coat. He held it out.

"Andrew Paxton Davis, M.D., Oph.D., N.D., D.O., D.C."

"Where's the rest of the alphabet?" the man said, still keeping his voice even-toned. But he pretended to take the card, read it, and then put it inside his coat.

"I made soup of it," Davis said. His blue eyes seemed to twinkle.

Doctor Faustroll's dark-brown eyes seemed to reflect the twinkle, and he smiled. He said, "Now, if you'll be kind enough to conduct us to the ruler of this place, whatever his or her or its names, we will present ourself or perhaps more than one of our selves and will apply for a position or positions."

Davis was startled. He said, "What? You don't know where you are? The guards did not stop you? How did you get by them?"

Doctor Faustroll indicated an invisible object by his right foot. "We carried ourself through the border in our suitcase. The guards did not see the case. It was midnight and cloudy. Also, they were drowsy."

"It must be a very large case to hold you. All of you?"

"It's very small, but there's enough room for us and our conscience," Doctor Faustroll said. "We take the conscience out of the case only when we intend to use it, which isn't often. Or when it needs airing."

He picked up his grail with one hand and his fishing pole in the other.

Davis hitched up the towel Velcroed to his waist and then grasped the handle of his own grail. His good humor had vanished. He was getting impatient with the fellow, and he did not want to be late for his appointment with the king.

Looking serious, he said, "If I were you, I'd get out of this place as quickly and quietly as possible. If you don't, you'll be working with those wretched people down there."

He pointed at the riverbank. Faustroll turned around to stare at the swarm of sweating, straining, and shouting men and women. Tiny figures at this distance, they were striving to pull or to push a roughly cube-shaped and bungalow-sized block of granite on log rollers into the River. Its forward edge was on two wooden runners, heavily lubricated with fish fat, that dipped into the water.

"They're building a pyramid beneath the surface of the River?" Faustroll said.

"Must you keep up this nonsense?" Davis said. "And why don't you ask me why I'm giving you this advice to scoot out of here as fast as your feet can carry you? If, that is, you're able to do so, which I doubt very much."

"There is no such thing as nonsense," Faustroll said. "In fact, what you call nonsense makes greater sense than what you call sense. Or, perhaps, there is no concrete abstraction that we term sense. But, if there is no sense, then there is also no nonsense. We have spoken. Selah."

2

Davis sighed, and he said, "If you don't mind risking slavery and perhaps torture, come along with me. Don't say I didn't try to warn you."

They had been standing at the edge of the grass-carpeted plain. Now they trudged up the slope of the foothills. Davis, a red-haired man of medium height and build but with abnormally large hands, led the way. The madman was slower because he was observing the whole milieu. Though the mountains towering straight up to 20,000 feet, the mile-wide foothills, and the mile-wide plains on either side of the mile-wide River were typical of most of the Rivervalley, the human activity was not. Many men and women were cutting away large blocks of stone in the vertical face of the mountains and were sliding the blocks down the foothills. The grass in the path of the very heavy weights was crushed, and the earth had sunk in. But the grass was so tough that it had not died out.

Near the lower edge of the foothill were extra oak log rollers for moving the blocks across the plain. Halfway along the plain, several crews were pulling on ropes tied around the blocks while gangs shoved against the rear of the blocks. When these got to the River's edge, they were placed on runners and slid into the water.

As in most areas, the River was shallow for several yards beyond the banks, which were only a few inches above the River. Then the level bottom abruptly became a cliff. That plunged straight down at least a mile before reaching the cold and lightless bottom in which was a multitude of strange forms of fish.

Not only was the bank swarming with people, the River itself was jammed with boats small and large. And two gigantic wooden cranes on the bank were close to being completed.

The other side of the River showed a similar scene. Even as Faustroll watched, a huge stone block on that side slid on runners into the water and disappeared. A huge bubble formed above the roiling water and burst.

Suddenly, Faustroll caught up with Davis.

"We don't leap to quick conclusions," he said, "or even walk to them. But it seems to us that those workers are trying to fill the River. They're not having much success at it."

"Building a dam," Davis said. He quickened his pace. "Ivar and that other fool across the River, King Arpad, plan to dam the stream with all those blocks of stone if it takes them a hundred years. Then they'll be able to keep any boats from slipping through past the guards at night. They'd also tax the merchant boats going up and down the River past this point. Also, Ivar thinks that he'll be able to cut through the mountains to the other side of the Valley. He'll invade the state on the other side and rule it. And the tunnel will be a conduit for trade from the other side. Ivar also has this dream that the tunneling will reveal large deposits of iron.

"Pride goeth before a fall. He'll suffer the fate of the arrogant Nimrod, who built the Tower of Babel thinking that he could conquer the hosts of Heaven."

"How can they cut granite with flint tools?" Faustroll said.

"They can't. But this area was blessed—or cursed—with underground deposits of copper and tin. The only such for thousands of miles either way from here. Ivar and his army of Vikings and Franks grabbed this land three years ago, and that's why he has bronze tools and weapons."

Going up the hill, they heard a loud explosion as rock was blasted with black gunpowder. When they stopped at the top, they heard a loud clanging. Beyond the shallow valley below them was a higher hill on top of which was a large round tower of granite blocks. Circling it at its base was a moat.

Below the two in the valley were the smithies, the molds, and great chunks of tin- and copper-bearing ore and the round bamboo huts with cone-shaped and leaf-thatched roofs in which the workers lived. The din, heat, and stench rolled over the two men in a nauseating wave.

"Men have brought Hell from Earth to this fair place," Faustroll said. "They should be seeking spiritual progress, not material gain and conquest. That, we believe, is why we were placed in this purgatory. Of course, without the science of pataphysics, they won't get far in their quest.

"On the other hand, left or right, we don't know, it may all be accidental. But accidental doesn't necessarily mean meaningless."

Davis snorted his contempt for this remark.

"And just what is pataphysics?" he said.

"Our friend and fellow doctor, let us charge through the breach created by our conversation and assault the definition of pataphysics. It is an almost impossible task since it can't be explained in nonpataphysical terms.

"Pataphysics is the science of the realm beyond metaphysics. It lies as far beyond the metaphysics as metaphysics lies beyond physics—in one direction or another, or perhaps still another.

"Pataphysics is the science of the particular, of laws governing exceptions. You follow us so far?"

Davis only rolled his eyes.

"Pataphysics, pay attention, this may be the heart of the matter, pataphysics is the science of imaginary solutions. But only imaginary solutions are real."

Davis grunted as if struck a soft blow in the stomach.

"For pataphysics, all things are equal," Faustroll continued. "Pataphysics is, in aspect, imperturbable.

"And this, too, is the heart of the matter, one of them anyway. That is, all things are pataphysical. Yet few people practice pataphysics."

"You expect me to understand that?" Davis said.

"Not at once. Perhaps never. Now, the last castle to be conquered. Beyond pataphysics lies nothing. It is the ultimate defense."

"Which means?"

Faustroll ignored that question. He said, "It allows each man or woman to live his own life as an exception, proving no law but his own."

"Anarchy? You're an anarchist?"

"Look about you. This world was made for anarchy. We don't need any government except self-government. Yet men won't permit us to be anarchists—so far."'

"Tell this to Ivar," Davis said. He laughed, then said, "I'd like to see his face when you tell him that."

"Ah, but what about the brain behind that face? If he has a brain?"

"Oh, he has brains! But his motives, man, his motives!"

They descended the hill and then climbed to the top of the next hill, much steeper and higher than the previous ones. The tower drawbridge was down, but many soldiers were by its outer end. Most of them were playing board games or casting dice carved from fish bones. Some were watching wrestling matches and mock duels. Their conical bronze helmets were fitted with nose- and cheek-pieces. A few wore chain-mail armor made of bronze or interlocking wooden rings. All were armed with daggers and swords and many had spears. Their leather bronze-ringed shields were stacked close by them. The wooden racks by these held yew bows and quivers full of bronze-tipped arrows. Some spoke in Esperanto; others, in barbaric tongues.

The sentinels at each end of the drawbridge made no effort to stop the two. Davis said, "I'm the royal osteopath to King Ivar. Since you're with me, they assume you're not to be challenged."

"I like to be challenged," Faustroll said. "By the way, what is an osteopath?"

"You've never heard of osteopathy?" Davis said, raising his reddish eyebrows. "When did you die?"

"All Saints' Day, though I'm no saint in the Catholic sense, in 1907. In Paris, which you may know is in France, who knows how many light-years away?"

Davis said only, "Ah!" That explained the man's madness and decadence. He was French and probably had been a bohemian artist, one of those godless immoral wretches roistering in the dives of Montmartre or the Left Bank or wherever that kind of low life flourished. One of those Dadaists or Cubists or Surrealists, whatever they were called, whose crazed paintings, sculptures, and writings revealed that their makers were rotten with sin and syphilis.

There wasn't any syphilis on this world, but there was plenty of sin.

"My question?" Faustroll said.

"Oh, yes! One, osteopathy is any form of bone disease. Two, it's a system of treatment of ailments and is based on the valid belief that most ailments result from the pressure of displaced bones on nerves and so forth. Osteopaths relieve the traumatic pressure by applying corrective pressure. Of course, there's much more to it than that. Actually, I seldom have to treat the king for anything serious, he's in superb physical health. It could be said that he retains me—enslaves me would be a better term—as the royal masseur."

Faustroll lifted his eyebrows and said, "Bitterness? Discontent? Your soul, it vomits bile?"

Davis did not reply. They had gone through the large foyer and up the stone steps of a narrow winding staircase to the second floor. After passing through a small room, they had stepped into a very large room, two stories high and very cool. Numerous wall slits gave enough light, but pine torches and fish-oil lamps made the room brighter. In the center, on a raised platform, was a long oaken table. Placed along it were high-backed oaken chairs carved with Norse symbols, gods, goddesses, serpents, trolls, monsters, and humans. Other smaller tables were set around the large one, and a huge fireplace was at the western wall. The walls were decorated with shields and weapons and many skulls.

A score or so of men and women were in a line leading to a large man seated in a chair. The oaken shaft of a huge bronze-headed ax leaned against the side of the chair.

"Petitioners and plaintiffs," Davis said in a low voice to Faustroll. "And criminals."

"Ah!" Faustroll murmured. "The Man With the Ax!" He added, "The title of one of our poems."

He pointed at a beautiful bare-breasted blonde sitting in a high-backed chair a few feet from the king's throne.

"She?"

"Queen Ann, the number-one mare in Ivar's stable," Davis said softly. "Don't cross her. She has a hellish temper, the slut."

Ivar the Boneless, son of the semilegendary Ragnar Hairybreeches, who was the premier superhero of the Viking Age, stood up from the chair then. He was at least six feet six inches tall. Since his only garment was a sea-blue towel, his massive arms, chest, legs, and flat corded belly were evident. Despite his bulk, his quick and graceful movements made him seem more pantherish than lionlike.

His only adornment was a wide bronze band around the upper right arm. It bore in alto-relief a valknut, three hunting horns meeting at the mouthpieces to form a triskelion, a three-legged figure. The valknut, the knot of the slain, was the sacred symbol of the greatest of the Norse gods, Odin.

His long, wavy, and red-bronze hair fell to his very broad shoulders. His face would have been called, in Davis's time on Earth, "ruggedly handsome." There was, however, something vulpine about it. Though Davis could not put a verbal finger on the lineaments that made him think of Brer Fox, he always envisioned that character when he saw the king.

Ivar was not the only general in the ninth century A.D. Danish invasion of England. Many native kings ruled there, but the king of Wessex would be the only one whose name would be familiar to twentieth-century English speakers. That was Alfred, whom later generations would call The Great, though his son and grandson were as deserving of that title. Though Alfred had saved Wessex from conquest, he had not kept the Danes from conquering much of the rest of England. Ivar had been the master strategist of the early Dane armies. Later, he had been co-king of Dublin with the great Norwegian conqueror, Olaf the White. But Ivar's dynasty had ruled Dublin for many generations.

As Davis and Faustroll approached the king, Davis said softly, "Don't call him Boneless. Nobody does that to his face without regretting it. You can call him Ivar, though, from what he's told me, it was Yngwaer in the Norse of his time. Languages change; Yngwaer became Ivar. His nickname in Old Norse was The Merciless, but it was close in sound to a word meaning "boneless." Later generations mistranslated the nickname. But don't call him Merciless either.

"If you do, you'll find out why he was called that."

3

DOCTOR DAVIS WAS surprised.

He had been sure that the king would hustle the grotesquely painted and nonsense-talking Frenchman to the slave stockade at once. Instead, Ivar had told Davis to get quarters in the tower for Faustroll, good quarters, not some tiny and miserable room.

"He's been touched by the gods and thus is sacred. And I find him interesting. See that good care is taken of him, and bring him to the feast tonight."

Though this duty was properly the province of the king's steward, Davis did not argue. Nor did he ask Ivar what he meant by referring to the gods. On Earth, Ivar had been a high priest of the Norse god Odin until a few years before he died. Then he had been baptized into the Christian faith. Probably, Davis thought, because the foxlike Dane figured that it couldn't hurt to do that. Ivar was one to make use of all loopholes. But, after being resurrected along the River, the Viking had rejected both religions. However, he was still influenced by both, though far more by his lifelong faith.

Ivar gave his command in his native language, instead of Esperanto. Ivar referred to it as "that monotonously regular, grating, and unsubtle tongue." Davis had learned Old Norse well enough to get by. Two-thirds of its speakers in the kingdom came from Dublin, where Ivar had been king of the Viking stronghold when he had died in 873. But most of these were half-Irish, equally fluent in the Germanic Norse and Keltic Gaelic. Davis could speak the latter, though not as well as he could Norse.

Since the Franks made up one-fourth of the population of Ivar's kingdom, having been resurrected in the same area as the Dane, Davis had some knowledge of that tongue. The Franks came from the time of Chlodowech (died A.D. 511 in Paris), known to later generations as Clovis I. He had been king of the western, or Salian, Franks and conqueror of the northern part of the Roman province of Gaul.

Andrew Davis and Ivar's queen, Ann Pullen, were the only English speakers, except for some slaves, in the kingdom. Davis only talked to her when he could not avoid it. That was not often, because she liked him to give her frequent treatments, during which she did her best to upset him with detailed stories of her many sexual encounters and perversions. And she brazenly insisted that he massage her breasts. Davis had refused to do this and had been backed by Ivar, who seemed amused by the situation.

Ann Pullen had never told Davis that she was aware that he disliked her intensely. Both, however, knew well how each felt about the other. The only barrier keeping her from making him a quarry slave was Ivar. He was fond, though slightly contemptuous, of Davis. On the other hand, he respected the American for his knowledge, especially his medical lore, and he loved to hear Davis's stories of the wonders of his time, the steam iron horses and sailless ships, the telegraph and radio, the automobile, the airplane, the vast fortunes made by American robber barons, and the fantastic plumbing.

What Davis did not tell Ivar was what the late-twentieth century doctors he had met had told him—to his chagrin. That was that much of his treatment of his patients on Earth had been based on false medical information. However, Davis was still convinced that his neuropathic treatments, which involved no drugs, had enormously benefited his patients. Certainly, their recovery rate had been higher than the rate of those who went to conventional M.D.'s. On the other hand, the physicians had admitted that, in the field of psychiatry, the recovery rate of the mentally disturbed patients of African witch doctors was the same as that of psychiatrists' patients. That admission, he thought, either down-valued twentieth-century medicine or up-valued witch doctors.

A few of his informants had admitted that a large number of physically sick people recovered without the help of medical doctors or would have done so without such help.

He explained this to the painted madman on the way to the room, though he was irked because he felt compelled to justify himself. Faustroll did not seem very interested. He only muttered, "Quacks. All quacks. We pataphysicians are the only true healers."

"I still don't know what a pataphysician is," Davis said.

"No verbal explanation is needed. Just observe us, translate our physical motion and verbal expressions into the light of truth, vectors of four-dimensional rotations into photons of veracity."

"Man, you must have a reasonable basis for your theory, and you should be able to express it in clear and logical terms!"

"Red is your face, yet cool is the room."

Davis lifted his hands high above his head. "I give up! I don't know why I pay any attention to what you say! I should know better! Yet..."

"Yet you apprehend, however dimly, that truth flows from us. You do not want to acknowledge that, but you can't help it. That's good. Most of the hairless bipedal apes don't have an inkling, don't respond at all. They're like cockroaches who have lost their antennae and, therefore, can't feel anything until they ram their chitinous heads into the wall. But the shock of the impact numbs even more the feeble organ with which they assumedly think."

Faustroll waved his bamboo fishing pole at Davis, forcing him to step back to keep from being hit on the nose by the bone hook.

"I go now to probe the major liquid body for those who breathe through gills."

Faustroll left the room. Davis muttered, "I hope it's a long time before I see you again."

But Faustroll was like a bad thought that can't be kept out of the mind. Two seconds later, he popped back into the room.

"We don't know what the royal osteopath's history on Earth was," Faustroll said, "or what your quest, your shining grail, was. Our permanent grail is The Truth. But the temporary one, and it may turn out to be that the permanent (if, truly, anything is permanent) grail or desideratum or golden apple is the answer to the question: Who resurrected us, placed us here, and why? Pardon. Not a question but questions. Of course, the answer may be that it doesn't matter at all. Even so, we would like to know."

"And just how will you be able to get answers to those questions here when you couldn't get them on Earth?"

"Perhaps the beings who are responsible for the Riverworld also knew the answers we so desperately sought on Earth. We are convinced that these beings are of flesh and blood, though the flesh may not be protein and the blood may lack hemoglobin. Unlike God, who, if it does exist, is a spirit and thus lacks organs to make sound waves, though It seems to be quite capable of making thunder and lightning and catastrophes and thus should be able to form its own temporary oral parts for talking, these beings must have mouths and tongues and teeth and hands of a sort. Therefore, they can tell us what we wish to know. If we can find them. If they wish to reveal themselves.

"It's our theory, and we've never theorized invalidly, that the River in its twistings and windings forms a colossal hieroglyph. Or ideogram. Thus, if we can follow the entirely of the River and map it, we will have before us that hieroglyph or ideogram. Unlike the ancient Mayan or Egyptian hieroglyphs, it will be instantly understandable. Revelation will come with the light of comprehension, not with the falling of the stars and the moon turning blood-red and the planet cracking in half and the coming of the Beast whose number is 666 and all those delicious images evoked by St. John the Divine."

Davis spoke more hotly than he had intended. "Nonsense! In our first life, faith and faith alone had the answers, faith in the divine work as recorded in the Bible. As on Earth, so here."

"But there is no Holy Scripture here."

"In our minds!" Davis said loudly. "It's recorded here!" And he tapped a fingerpoint against his temple.

"As you know, no afterlife depicted in any religion faintly resembles this one. However, we do not argue. We state the truth and move on, leaving the truth behind us yet also taking it with us. But truth is arrived at when one ceases thinking. That's hard to do, we admit. Yet, if we can think about abandoning thought, we will be able to quit thinking. Thus, with that barrier to mental osmosis removed, the molecules of truth penetrate the diaphragm."

"Lunacy! Sheer lunacy! And blasphemy!"

Faustroll went through the doorway. Over his shoulder, he said, "We go, yet that is an illusion. The memory of this event remains in your mind. Thus, we are still here; we have not left."

Andrew Davis sighed. He sure had a lot to put up with. Why didn't he just take French leave and continue his quest up-River? Why didn't he? He had compelling reasons not to. One, if he were caught sneaking out of Ivar's domain, he'd be a slave and probably flogged. Two, if he did get out of the kingdom's boundaries, he still would not be safe from recapture for several days. The kingdoms for a fifty-mile stretch up the River had an agreement to return slaves to the states from which they had run away. Three, he could take the guaranteed foolproof way of escape. But, to do that, he'd have to kill himself. Then he'd be resurrected far away, but the thought of killing himself was hard to contemplate.

But, though his mind knew that he'd live again, his body didn't. His cells fiercely resisted the idea of suicide; they insisted on survival. Furthermore, he loathed the idea of suicide, though it was not rationally based. As a Christian, he would sin if he killed himself. Was it still a sin on the Riverworld? He doubted that very much. But his lifelong conditioning against it made him act as if it were.

Also, if he did do away with himself, he had a fifty-fifty chance of being translated downstream instead of upstream. If that happened he'd have to travel past territory he'd already covered. And he could be captured and enslaved again by any of hundreds of states before he even got to Ivar's country.

If he awoke far up the River, he might have the goal of his quest behind him. Not until he had come to the end of the River would he know that he had skipped it. Then he would have to retrace his route.

What if the story of the woman who gave birth in the Valley was false? No, he would not consider that. He had not only faith but logic behind his belief. This world was a final test for those who believed in Jesus as their savior. Pass this test, and the next stage would be the true paradise. Or the true Hell.

The Church of the Second Chance had some false doctrines, and it was another trap set by Satan. But the Devil was subtle enough to have planted some true doctrines among the false ones. The Second Chancers did not err in claiming that this world did offer all souls another opportunity to wash off their spiritual filth. What that church overlooked or deliberately ignored was that it also gave Satan a second chance to grab those who had eluded his clutches on Earth.

He looked through the wide, arched, and glassless window. Prom his height, he could see the hills and the plain and the River and the plain, hills, and mountains on the opposite bank. Arpad (died A.D. 907) ruled that twelve-mile-long area. He was the chief of the seven Mongolian tribes, called Magyar, who had left the Don River circa A.D. 889 in what would be Russia and migrated westward to the Pannonian Plains. This was the area that would become Hungary. Arpad had been resurrected among a population that was partly ancient Akkadian, partly Old Stone Age southeast Asiatics, and ten percent of miscellaneous peoples. Though he was a Magyar, a tiny minority in this area, he had became king. That testified to his force of personality and to his ruthless methods.

Arpad was Ivar's ally and also a partner in the dam project. His slaves worked harder and longer and were treated much more harshly than Ivar's. The Norsemen was less severe and more generous with his slaves. He did not want to push them to the point of revolt or of suicide. Arpad's slaves had rebelled twice, and the number of suicides among them was far higher than among Ivar's.

Nor did Ivar trust Arpad. That was to be expected. Ivar trusted no one and had good reason not to rely on the Magyar. His spies had told him that Arpad had boasted, when drunk, which was often, that he would kill Ivar when the dam was finished.

If the Dane planned to jump the gun and slay Arpad first, he had not said so. Though he drank deeply at times, he reined in his tongue. At least, he did so concerning matters of state.

Davis was convinced that one of the two kings was not going to wait for the dam to be completed. Sometime, probably during the next two years, one was going to attack the other. Davis, on the principle that the lesser of two evils was to be preferred, hoped that Ivar would win. Ideally, each would knock the other off. Whichever happened, Davis was going to try to flee the area during the confusion of the battle.

4

He must have been looking through the window longer than he had thought. Faustroll had left the tower and was walking downhill, the fishing pole on his shoulder. And, some paces behind him, was the inevitable spy, a woman named Groa. She, too, carried a fishing pole, and, as Davis watched, she called to the Frenchman. He stopped, and they began talking. A moment later, they were side by side and headed for the River.

Groa was a redheaded beauty, daughter of a ninth-century Norwegian Viking, Thorsteinn the Red, son of Olaf the White and that extraordinary woman, Aud the Deep-Minded. Thorsteinn had been killed in a battle after conquering the northern part of Scotland. It was this event that caused Aud to migrate to Iceland and become ancestress of most Icelanders of the twentieth century.

No doubt, Thorsteinn was somewhere on the River and battling some foe while trying to get power over the foe or else battling to keep a foe from getting power over him. Power had been the main fuel of humankind on Earth. As on Earth, so here. So far. Until the Savior—Savioress?—grew up and worked God's will on His creations.

Groa must have been ordered by Ivar to attach herself to Faustroll. She was to find out if his story was true. Though the king had seemed to accept Faustroll at face value, he would wonder if the fellow had been sent by Arpad to assassinate him. Groa would test him, probe him, and go so far as to lie with him if it was necessary. Perhaps, even if it was not necessary. She was a lusty woman. Then she'd report to Ivar later.

Davis sighed. What a life the afterlife was! Why couldn't everybody live in peace and trust? If they could not all love each other, they could at least be tolerant.

They could not do this for the same reason they had not done so on Earth. It was the nature of *Homo Sapiens.* Of most of men and women, anyway. But... their situation was so different here. It was set up so that none need work hard for food and housing and other necessities. If people could all be pacifists and honest and compassionate, they would need no government by others. The Frenchman was right, though Davis hated admitting it even to himself. Given a new type of people, anarchy could be workable here.

Obviously, Whoever had placed humanity here had designed the Rivervalley so that humans, not having to spend so much time working, had time to advance themselves spiritually. But only those who understood this would advance themselves, change themselves for the better, and go on to whatever stage the Whoevers had built for them.

The Whoevers, however, had to be God. For Davis, there was no doubt or mystery about the identity of the creator of this place. The big mystery was why He had prepared a halfway house for the once-dead instead of the heavenly mansion the Bible had described.

He admitted to himself that the Bible had been very vague about the specifics of the abode of the saved, the saints. It had been much more concrete about the abode of the damned.

He could only accept that God, in His infinite wisdom, knew what he was doing.

Why, as so many complained, had not God given them some reassurance? A sign? A beacon toward which they could go as a moth could fly to the flame? Though that was not the best of comparisons, now he considered it. Anyway, where was the sign, the beacon, the writing in the sky?

Davis knew. It was the birth of a baby to a virgin. In a world where men and women were sterile, one woman had been the exception. She had been impregnated with the Holy Spirit, and she had conceived. God had performed a miracle. The infant, so the story went, was female. At first, hearing this, Davis had been shocked. But, thinking about it calmly and logically, trying to overcome his preconceptions, he had concluded that he should not be upset, not kick against the pricks. On Earth, the Savior had been a male. Here, the Savior was a female. Why not?

God was fair-minded, and who was he to question the Divine Being?

"Davis!" a harsh voice said behind him. He jumped and whirled, his heart beating hard. Standing in the doorway was Sharkko the Shyster, the ever-egregious slave of whom he had dreamed last night.

"Hustle your ass, Davis! The Great Whore of Babylon wants you for a treatment! Right now!"

"I'll tell the queen what you said about her," Davis said. He did not intend to do so, but he wanted to see the loathsome fellow turn pale. Which he did.

"Ah, she won't believe you," the slave said. "She hates your guts. She'd take my word against yours any time. Anyway, I doubt she'd be insulted. She'd think it was a compliment."

"If it wasn't against my nature, I'd boot you in the rear," Davis said.

The slave, his color now restored, snorted. He turned and limped down the hall. Davis left the room. He watched the man as he walked behind him. Though the man had been resurrected in his twenty-five-year-old body, his vision restored to 20/20, he was now a human wreck. His right leg had been broken in several places and reset wrong. His nose had not been reset after the bridge had been shattered. He could not breathe properly because of his nose and some ribs that had also lacked proper resetting. One eye had been knocked out and was not yet fully regrown. His face twisted and leered with a tic.

All of this had resulted from a beating by slaves whose overseer he had been. Unable any longer to endure his bullyings, kicks, and other unjust treatment, they had worked on him late one night and thus worked out their hatred of him. His hut had been too dark for him to identify his attackers, though he, and everybody else, knew his men were the malefactors. If you could fairly call them malefactors. Most people though the deed was justified self-defense.

Ivar thought so, too, after hearing testimony. He decided that Sharkko had broken the rules laid down by the king. These were mainly for the sake of efficiency, not of humanitarianism. But they had been disregarded, and Sharkko's back was bloody from forty lashes with a fish-hide whip. Each of the overseer's slaves had administered a stroke. Ivar, witnessing this, had been highly amused.

Sharkko had then been degraded to a quarry slave. But his injuries had kept him from doing well at the hard work, and he had been made a tower slave after six months. Ivar used him for, among other things, a human bench when he wished to sit down where a chair was unavailable.

The Shyster had been so named by a Terrestrial client who was now a citizen of Ivar's kingdom. From what the client said, he had been cheated by Sharkko and had been unable to find justice in the court. The ex-client was among those who had beaten Sharkko.

The Shyster had been indiscreet enough to tell some cronies that he meant to revenge himself on all who had wronged him. Though Davis did not think that he had earned Sharkko's hatred, he was among those named for some terrible retribution. The Shyster had not been so full of braggadocio that he had said anything about revenging himself on Ivar. He knew what would happen to him if the king heard about such a threat.

Sharkko, hunched over, dragging one foot and mumbling to himself, continued on down the hall. Sharkko was a veritable Caliban, Davis thought, as he followed the monster down the hall to a steep and spiraling staircase.

He felt unusually uneasy. It seemed to him that events were coming to a head, a big, green, and pus-filled boil on the face of this kingdom. The coming conflict between Arpad and Ivar, the arrival of the grotesque and disquieting Faustroll, the increasing tension between himself and the queen, and Sharkko's hatred added up to a situation that could pop open—like a boil—at any time. He could feel it. Though he could not logically predict that the eruption would occur soon, he sensed it.

Or, perhaps, this was caused by his internal conflicts. He himself was ready to break open and out, much as he wanted to wait until the right moment for flight.

The virgin mother and the baby were waiting for him up the River. They did not know it, of course. But he was to play a strong part in the events that would bring on the revelation of the second Savior to this world. Though it might be egotistic to think so, he was sure of it.

He entered the large room where Queen Ann waited for him. She was on the osteopathic table that he had built. But, spread out naked there, she looked as if she were waiting for a lover. Her two attendants giggled when they saw him. They were blacks who had been slaves of an early-twentieth-century Arabian family on Earth. They had been free for only one year after their resurrection. Now they were slaves again.

They should be sympathizing with his plight. Instead, they were amused.

5

"Massage my inner thigh muscles," Ann said. "They're very tight."

She kept talking softly while laughing loudly between sentences. Her remarkably bright and leaf-green eyes never left his face. Though he kept it expressionless, he longed to snarl at her, spit in her face, and then vomit on her. The Jezebel! The Scarlet Women! The Great Whore of Babylon!

"When you're on your back, rotating your pelvis, your legs up in the air for a long time, you put a strain on those muscles," she said. "It's almost an equal strain when I'm on top. Sometimes I have to rest between up-and-downs and hip gyrations. But then I squeeze down on him with my sphincter muscle and so don't really get a rest. It is the sphincter, isn't it, Doctor?"

He knew the human body so well he did not have to see what he was doing. His head turned away from her, his eyes half closed, he kneaded her flesh. How soft her skin was! What a muscle tone! Sometimes, when he was in that drowsy twilight state between dreaming and awakening, he knew his fingers were working on flesh. Not hers, of course. The reflex was caused by a digital memory, as it were, of the thousands of bodies he had treated while on Earth.

"Don't get too close to the king's personal property," she said. "You touch it, and he might cut your hands off."

If he did that, Davis thought, scores of the males in the kingdom would be without hands.

"You're not much of a man," she said. "A real man's tallywhacker would be lifting that towel right off his waist, rip the Velcro apart."

The slave girls giggled though they did not understand English. But they had heard similar phrases in Esperanto for a long time. They knew that she was saying something taunting and demeaning.

Davis envisioned closing his hands around the queen's throat. It wouldn't take long.

Then he prayed, Oh, Lord! Save me from such sinful thoughts!

"Perhaps," he said, "I should massage your knees, too? They seem to be rather stiff."

She frowned and stared hard at him. The she smiled and laughed.

"Oh! You're suggesting…? Yes, do. I have spent a certain amount of time on my knees. But they're on pillows, so it's not so bad. However…"

Instead of flying into a rage, as he had expected, she was amused. She also looked somewhat triumphant, as if goading him into saying something insulting to her, even an innuendo, was a victory. However, she probably did not regard his comments as an insult. The bitch was more likely to think he had complimented her.

What did he care what she thought? To be honest with himself, he cared a lot. Unless she was stopped by Ivar, she could make his life unbearable, torture him, do anything with or to him. Davis had not heard any stories about her being cruel, except for her sexual teasing, which could not be ranked with torture or killing. But he had no guarantee that she might not become so. Especially in her dealings with him.

Ann Pullen was a fellow American, though a nauseating example as far as he was concerned. She had been born about 1632 in Maryland. Her family had been Quakers, but when it converted to Episcopalianism, she had gone to hell. Those were her own words. She had been married four times to tobacco plantation owners in Virginia and Maryland. She had survived them all.

No wonder, Davis thought. She'd wear any man out, if not from her incessant sexual demands and infidelity, then from her TNT temper and willfulness.

Mostly, she had lived in Westmoreland County, Virginia, which was between the Potomac and Rappahannock rivers. In her day, the area had many thick forests and large swamps but no roads. Travel was mainly by river or creek. Nor did the plantations resemble those of a later era. There were no beautiful many-pillared mansions and broad well-kept lawns. The owners' houses were modest, the stables were likely to be made of logs, and chickens and hogs roamed the yards. Pig stealing was common even among the plantation owners. Cash was scarce, the chief currency was tobacco. The people were unusually hot-tempered and litigious, though no one knew why.

By her own testimony, Ann had once been sentenced to ten lashes on her bare shoulders because of her libelous and scandalous speeches against a Mister Presley. She also had once attacked her sister-in-law with bare hands.

It had been recorded in the Order Book of the county in A.D. 1677 that Ann Pullen had encouraged her daughter Jane to become "the most remarkable and notorious whore in the province of Virginie." But Davis had to admit that, in the strict sense of the word, she was not a whore. She fornicated because she liked to do so and never took money.

The Order Book also said that Jane's mother, Ann Pullen, had debauched her own daughter by encouragement to commit adultery and break the whole estate of matrimony.

The daughter's husband, Morgan Jones, had enjoined more than once (as the court had recorded) any man from entertaining or having any manner of dealing with Jane or transporting her out of the county or giving her passage over any river or creek.

It was also recorded that Ann Pullen had declared that Jane had no husband at that time, Jones having died, and she (Ann) did not know why her daughter should not take the pleasure of this world as well as any other woman. Also, Ann did not care who the father of her daughter's child was, provided one William Elmes would take her to England, as he had promised.

Ann was a feminist ahead of her time, a lone pioneer in the movement in the days when it was dangerous to be such. She had also been a libertine, though Davis thought that automatically went with the desire for female equality.

However, such Terrestrial attitudes should not apply on the Riverworld. Even he admitted that, though insisting that there were limits to that viewpoint. Ann had certainly overstepped them. With seven-league boots.

Ivar's kingdom was basically Old Norse. Since women (though not female slaves) in the pre-Christian era had had many more rights than those in the Christian countries, they had even more rights on the Riverworld. In this state, anyway. Theoretically, Ann could divorce Ivar with a simple statement that she wished it, and she could take her property with her. Not half of the kingdom's, that is, the king's. Her grail, her towels, her artifacts, and her slaves were hers.

But divorce didn't seem likely. Ivar was greatly amused by her, even when she became angry at him, and he reveled in her uninhibited and many-talented lovemaking. He knew that she had lovers, but he didn't seem to care. He doubted that she would plot with a lover to assassinate him. She knew well on which side her vagina was buttered.

So Andrew Davis had to suffer the indignities she piled on him. Meanwhile, he dreamed of the divinely begotten infant far up the River. He also tried to think of foolproof ways to escape this land. And how to prevent capture by the other slave-holding states between him and his goal.

Doing his Christian duty, he had tried to pray for Ann. But he sounded so insincere to himself that he knew God would ignore his requests that she be forgiven and be made to see the Light.

When her treatment was over, he left the chamber as he always did. He was angry, frustrated, and sweating, his stomach was boiling, and his hands were shaking.

Oh, Lord, how long must I endure this? Do not, I pray You, continue to subject me to evil and the temptation to curse You as you did Job!

At high noon, the grailstone in the tower courtyard erupted in lightning and thunder. He left the room in which he had been waiting until this happened. To stand in the yard near the stone was to be deafened. Though his grail was full of excellent food and drink, he had no appetite. What he did not eat, he shared with his cronies at the table in the big hall. The cup of brandy and the pack of mingled tobacco and marijuana cigarettes he put aside. He could have kept half of the booze and the coffin nails for himself, but he would give them all to Eysteinn the Chatterer, Ivar's chief tax and tribute collector.

Thus, he paid his taxes at a double rate. That enabled him halfway through the month to pour the daily quota of the liquor down a drain and to shred the cigarettes. He did this secretly because many would have been outraged at this waste. They would report to the king, who would confiscate the extra "goodies" and would punish him.

He had never, during his two lives, tasted any alcohol or smoked. In fact, on Earth, he had not even drunk ice water because of its unhealthy effects. He loathed having to contribute to the king and his vices. But, if he didn't, he would suffer the cat-o'-nine-tails or become a quarry slave. Or both.

That evening, shortly after sunset, he went to the great hall built near the bank. This was where Ivar preferred to eat supper, to drink, and to roister among his cronies and his toadies. (Davis admitted that he was one of the latter. But he had no choice.) The hall was built in the old Viking style, a single huge room with Ivar's table on a platform and at the head of the floor-level tables. The platform had not been used on Earth among the semi-democratic Vikings. It was an innovation adopted by Ivar. The support poles were carved with the heads of humans, gods, beasts, and symbols from the old religion. Among these and often repeated were gold-mining dwarfs, dragons, the Earth-encircling Midgard serpent, stags, bears, valknuts, frost giants, Thor and his hammer, one-eyed Odin with, sometimes, his ravens Hugin and Munin on his shoulders, right-handed swastikas, runic phrases, and Skidbladnir, the magical ship that could be folded and carried in a bag after use.

Tonight, as usual, the men and women drank too much, the talk was fast and furious, boasting and bombast thundered in the hall, people quarreled and sometimes fought. Ivar had forbidden duels to the death because he had lost too many good warriors to them. But the belligerents could go at each other with fists and feet, and the king did not frown on gouging of eyes, crushing of testicles, ripping off of ears, and biting off of noses. Though it took three months, the eyes, noses, and ears would grow again, and the testicles would repair themselves.

Davis had grown used to these nightly gatherings, but he did not tike them. Violence still upset him, and the air stank of tobacco and marijuana smoke and beer and liquor fumes. Also, the sickening odor of farts, followed by loud laughter and thigh-slapping, drifted to him now and then. Queen Ann, who was sitting on Ivar's left, was one of the loudest in her laughter when this form of primitive humor erupted. Tonight she wore a towel around her neck, the ends of which covered her breasts. But she was rather careless about keeping them in place.

Mingled with the other smells was that of the fish caught in the river and fried in one end of the hall.

Davis sat at the king's table because he was the royal osteopath. He would have preferred a table as far away as it could be from this one. That would give him a chance to sneak away after all were too drunk to notice him. Tonight, however, he was interested in watching and occasionally overhearing the conversation of Doctor Faustroll and Ivar the Boneless. The Frenchman sat immediately to the king's right, the most favored chair at the table. He had brought an amazing amount of fish to the feast, far more than any other anglers. Once, during a lessening of the uproar, Davis heard Ivar ask Faustroll about his luck.

"It's not luck," Faustroll lead said. "It's experience and skill. Plus an inborn knack. We survived mainly on fish we caught in the Seine when we lived in Paris."

6

"Paris," Ivar said. "I was with my father, Ragnar, son of Sigurd Hring, when we Danes sailed up the Seine in March, the Franks not expecting Vikings that early in the year. A.D. 845, I've been told. The Frankish ruler, Charles the Bald, split his army into two. I advised my father to attack the smaller force, which we did. We slaughtered them except for one hundred and eleven prisoners. These my father hanged all at once as a sacrifice to Odin on an island in the Seine while the other Frankish army watched us. They must have filled their drawers from horror.

"We went on up to Paris, a much smaller city then than the vast city others have told me about. On Easter Sunday, the Christian's most holy day, we stormed and plundered Paris and killed many worshipers of the Savior. Odin was good to us."

Ivar smiled to match the sarcastic tone of his voice. He did not believe in the gods, pagan or Christian. But Davis, watching him closely, saw the expression on his face and the set of his eyes. They could be showing nostalgia or, perhaps, some unfathomable longing. Davis had seen this expression a score of times before now. Could the ruthless and crafty hungerer for power be longing for something other than he now had? Did he, too, desire to escape this place and its responsibilities and ever-present danger of assassination? Did he, like Davis and Faustroll, have goals that many might think idealistic or romantic? Did he want to shed the restrictions of his situation and be free? After all, a powerful ruler was as much a prisoner as a slave.

"The One-Eyed One blessed us," Ivar said, "though it may just have been coincidence that Charles the Bald was having serious trouble with other Frankish states and with his ambitious brothers. Instead of trying to bar us from going back down the Seine, he paid us seven thousand pounds of silver to leave his kingdom. Which we did, though we did not promise not to come back again later."

Faustroll had so far not interrupted the king, though disgust sometimes flitted across his face. He drank swiftly and deeply, and his cup was never empty. The slave behind him saw to that. He also gave the Frenchman cigarettes after he had smoked up his own supply. The slave was Sharkko, apparently delegated by the king to serve Faustroll tonight. Sharkko was scowling, and, now and then, his lips moved. His words were drowned out by the din, and a good thing, too, Davis thought. Davis could lip-read both English and Esperanto. If Ivar knew what Sharkko was saying, he would have him flogged and then put into the latrine-cleaning gang.

Finally, he banged his wooden cup down, causing those around him, including Ivar, to look startled.

"Your Majesty will pardon us," he said loudly. "But you are still as you were on Earth. You have not progressed one inch spiritually; you are the same bloody barbarous pirate, plenty of offense meant, as the old hypocrite who died in Dublin. But we do not give up hope for you. We know that philosophy in its practical form of pataphysics is the gate to the Truth for you. And, though you at first seem to be a simple savage, we know that you are much more. Our brief conversation in the hall convinced us of that."

Many at the table, including Davis, froze, though they rolled their eyeballs at each other and then gazed at Ivar. Davis expected him to seize the war ax always by his side and lop off Faustroll's head. But the Viking's skin did not redden, and he merely said. "We will talk with you later about this philosophy, which we hope will contain more wisdom and less nonsense than that of the Irish priests, the men in women's skirts."

His "we," Davis knew, was a mimicking and mocking of Faustroll.

Ivar rose then, and silence followed three strokes on a huge bronze gong.

Ivar spoke loudly, his bass voice carrying to all corners of the huge hall.

"The feast is over! We're all going to bed early tonight, though I suppose many of you will not go to sleep until you can no longer get it up!"

The crowd had murmured with surprise and disappointment, but that was followed by laughter at the king's joke. Davis grimaced with disgust. Ann, seeing his expression, smiled broadly.

"We haven't run out of food or drink," Ivar said. "That's not why I'm cutting this short. But it occurred to me a little while ago that tomorrow is the third anniversary of the founding of my kingdom. That was the day when I, a slave of the foul Scots tyrant, Eochaid the Poisonous, rose in revolt with Arpad, also a slave, and with two hundred slaves, most of whom now sit in honored places in this hall. We silently strangled the guards around Eochaid's hall. He and his bodyguards were all sleeping off their drunkenness, safe, they supposed, in their thick-walled hall on a high mound of earth. We burned the log building down and slaughtered those who managed to get out of the fire. All except Eochaid, whom we captured.

"The next day, I gave him the death of the blood eagle as I did on Earth to King Aella of York and King Edmund of East Anglia and some of my other foes whom I sacrificed to Odin."

Davis shuddered. Though he had never seen this singular method of execution, he had heard about it many times. The victim was placed facedown, his spine was cut, and his lungs were pulled out and laid on his back, forming the rough shape of an eagle with outspread wings.

"I have decided that we will go to bed early and get up early tomorrow. The slaves will be given the day off and given plenty of food and drink. Everybody will celebrate. We will all work to collect much fish, and that evening we will start the festivities. There will be games and archery and spear-casting contests and wrestling, and those who have grudges may fight to the death with then enemies if they so wish."

At this, the crowd shouted and screamed.

Ivar lifted his hands for silence, then said, "Go to bed! Tomorrow we enjoy ourselves while we thank whatever gods made this world that we are free of Eochaid's harsh rule and are free men!"

The crowd cheered again and then streamed out of the hall. Davis, the handle of his grail in one hand, was heading for the tower and halfway up the first hill when the even-toned voice of Faustroll rose behind him. "Wait for me! We'll walk the rest of the way with you!"

Davis stopped. Presently, the Frenchman, in no hurry, caught up with him. Heavy fumes of whiskey mixed with fish enveloped him, and his words were somewhat slurred. "*Mon ami? Mia amico!* That which treads on day's heels is beautiful, is it not. The beings that burn in the nocturnal bowl above in their un-Earth patterns, how inspiring! Wise above the wisdom of men, they will have nothing to do with us. But they are generous with their splendor."

"Uhmm," Davis said.

"A most observant remark. Tell me, my friend, what do you think is the real reason behind Ivar's ending the feast?"

"What?"

"I do not trust the goat who leads the woolly ones. Statesmen and politicians, generals and admirals, they seldom reveal their real intentions. The Boneless is up to something his enemies won't like. Nor will his people."

"You're very cynical," Davis said. He looked across the River. The plains and the hills in Arpad's kingdom were dark except for the scattered fires of sentinels. There were also torches on the tops of the bamboo signal towers a half-mile apart and forming a ten-mile-long line.

"Cynical? A synonym for experience. And for one whose eyes have long been open and whose nose is as keen in detecting corruption as the nose of the hairy one some claim is man's best friend. Remember, our leader comes from the land where something is rotten, to paraphrase the Bard of Avon."

They had resumed walking. Davis said, "What did Ivar say to make you suspicious?"

"Nothing and everything. We do not accept anything at face value. The meaning of words and of facial expressions, the hardness of objects, the permanence of the universe, that fire will always burn skin, that a certain cause always leads to a certain result, that what goes up must come down. It isn't always necessarily so."

He swung the cylinder of his grail around to indicate everything.

Davis did not feel like talking about metaphysics or, in fact, anything. Especially not with this fellow, who made no sense. But he accepted Faustroll's invitation to sit down in the tower courtyard and converse for a while. Perhaps he might find out just why Faustroll suspected that Ivar was up to something. Not that it made any difference. What could he do about anything here?

There was a table near a row of torches in wall brackets. They sat down. The Frenchman opened his grail and drew out a metal cup half filled with whiskey. Davis looked at the formula painted on the man's forehead. He had attended lectures on calculus at Rush Medical College, and he was familiar with the markings. But, unless you knew the referents of the symbols, you could never know what they meant or how to use them. He read: - 0 - a - + a + 0 =

Faustroll said, "The significance of the formula? God is the tangential point between zero and infinity."

"Which means?"

Faustroll spoke as if he had memorized this lecture. "God is, by definition, without dimension, but we must be permitted..."

"Is this going to be long?" Davis said.

"Too long for tonight and perhaps for eternity. Besides, we are rather drunk. We can visualize all clearly, but our body is weary and our mind not running on all eight cylinders."

Davis rose, saying, "Tomorrow, then. I'm tired, too."

"Yes, you can understand better our thesis if we have a pen and a piece of paper on which to lay it out."

Davis said good night, leaving the Frenchman sitting at the table and staring into the dark whiskey as if it were a crystal ball displaying his future. He made his way up to his tiny room. It was not until he was at its door that he remembered how astray his conversation with the Frenchman had gone. Faustroll had not told him what he had concluded from his suspicions about Ivar.

He shrugged. Tomorrow he would find out. If, that is, the crazy fellow's tongue did not wander off again. To him, a straight line was not the shortest path between two points. Indeed, he might deny the entire validity of Euclidean geometry.

Davis also had an uneasy feeling that Faustroll's near-psychopathic behavior hid a very keen mind and a knowledge of science, mathematics, and literature far exceeding his own. He could not be dismissed as just another loony.

Davis pushed in the wooden-hinged and lockless door. He looked out through the glassless opening into the darkness lit only by the star-crowded sky. But that light was equal to or surpassed that of Earth's full moon. At first, it seemed peaceful. Everybody except the sentinels had gone to bed. Then he saw the shadows moving in the valley below the tower. As his eyes became more adjusted to the pale light, he saw that a large body of men was in it.

His heart suddenly beat hard. Invaders? No. Now he could see Ivar the Boneless, clad in a conical bronze helmet and a long shirt of mail and carrying a war ax, walking down the hill toward the mass of men. Behind him came his bodyguard and counselors. They, too, were armored and armed. Each wore two scabbards encasing bronze swords, and they carried spears or battle-axes. Some also bore bundles of pine torches or sacks. The containers would, he knew at once, hold gunpowder bombs.

Faustroll had been right. There would be no celebration tomorrow unless it was a victory feast. The king had lied to cover up a military operation. Those not involved—as yet—in the military operation had been lied to. But selected warriors has been told to gather secretly at a certain time.

Suddenly, the starlight was thinly veiled by light clouds. These became darker quickly. Davis could no longer see Ivar or, in fact, any human beings. And now the sound of distant thunder and the first zigzag of lightning appeared to the north.

Soon, the raging rain and the electrical violence that often appeared around midnight would be upon the kingdoms of Ivar and Arpad. Like the wolf on the fold, Davis thought. And Ivar and his army would be like the ancient Assyrians sweeping down from the hills on the Hebrews as that poet—what was his name?—wrote.

But who was Ivar going to assault?

7

THE WIND SPAT raindrops through the window into Davis's face. Another layer of darkness slid in and cut off his view of the men. Thunder rolled closer like a threatening bully. A lightning streak, brief probing of God's lantern beam (looking for an honest man?), noisily lit up the scene. He glimpsed Ivar's group running over the top of the nearest hill to the River. He also saw other dark masses, like giant amoebae, flowing onto the plains from the hills. These were warriors hastening to join Ivar. The larger body of plains dwellers waiting for the king was, as it were, the mother amoeba.

Another blazing and crashing streak, closer this time, revealed a great number of boats in slips that had been empty for a long time. These had to have come in recently from upstream. Just off the bank many vessels: rowboats, dugouts, catamarans, dragonships, and the wide-beamed merchant boats called dromonds. Their sails were furled, and all bristled with spears.

Under cover of the night, Ivar's warriors from every part of the kingdom had slipped down here. Of course, there would be other parties who would attack the opposite bank, Arpad's domain, up-River. The attack had to be against the Magyar's kingdom. Davis did not know why he had wondered what the king was up to. However, Ivar was unpredictable, and it was chancy to bet on any of his next moves.

The secrecy with which the operation had been carried out impressed Davis. He had had no inkling of it, yet he was often in the king's company. This operation, though it involved thousands of men who had somehow not revealed the plans to their female hutmates, had been exceedingly efficient.

But the lightning was going to display the invaders to Arpad's sentinels. Unless, that is, some of Ivar's men had crossed the River earlier and killed the guards.

After a while, the heart of the storm raged over the area within his sight. Now the warriors were grouped on the bank and embarking. So frequent and vivid were the bolts, he could see the invaders moving. They were many-legged clumps the individuals of which were not visible from this distance in the rainy veil.

He gasped. A fleet was putting out from the opposite bank.

A few seconds later, more groups began to gather behind Ivar's forces on the bank. He groaned, and he muttered, "Arpad has pulled a sneak play!" His force had come ashore farther up the River and sneaked along the banks to come up on the Ivarians' flank. And now the Arpadians were charging it. The surprises had been surprised; the fox had been outfoxed. The Magyar was going to grind his former ally between two forces. But that was easier planned than done. Ivar's men on shore, though taken by surprise, had not fled. They were fighting fiercely, and their shore force outnumbered the enemy's. Soon, Ivar's warriors in the boats would join those on the bank. As quickly as the oars could drive the boats, they were driving toward the slips and the open bank. Though the boatmen could not get back to the bank to disembark swiftly, they should be able to get all ashore before the enemy's second force arrived front the opposite bank. And they would overwhelm the ambushers—if Ivar had anything to do with it. He was a very cool and quick thinker. His men, veterans of many battles, did not panic easily.

Meanwhile, Arpad's fleet was about a quarter of a mile from their destination. Its commander, whom Davis assumed was Arpad, not one to hang back behind his army, would be considering two choices. He could order the boats back to his shore and there await the inevitable assault from Ivar's forces. Or Arpad could keep on going straight ahead, hoping that the ambushers would keep Ivar's men entangled long enough for him to land his army.

The rain thickened. Davis saw the conflict now as if through distorted spectacles. And then, five or six minutes later, the downfall began to thin. The worst of the storm had passed over, but thunder and lightning still harried the land. Intermittently, starlight between masses of clouds revealed that a third force had entered the fray. It was a large fleet that must recently have come around the River's bend a half-mile to the north. Davis could not identify who its sailors were. But the only ones liable to come from the north were the men of Thorfinn the Skull-Splitter.

Thorfinn had been on Earth the earl of Orkney Islands and part of northern Scotland. Though a mighty warrior, as his nickname testified, he had died in A.D. 963 in bed. The "straw death," as the Norse called it, was not the fate he wanted. Only men who were killed in battle went to Valhalla, the Hall of the Slain, where the heroes fought each other during the day and those killed were resurrected to fight the next day, where the mead and the food was better than anything on Earth, and where, at night, Odin's Valkyries screwed the drunken heroes' brains out.

But Thorfinn had awakened in the Rivervalley along with everyone else: the brave and the cowardly, the monarchs and the slaves, the honored and the despised, the honest and the crooked, the devout and the hypocrite, the learned and the ignorant, the rich and the poor, and the lucky and the unlucky.

However, the Riverworld was, in many respects, like Valhalla. The dead rose the next day, though seldom in the place where they had died; the drink and the food were marvelous; nonfatal wounds healed quickly; a chopped-off foot or a gouged-out eye grew back again; women with the sexual drive of a Valkyrie abounded. Of course, Valkyries never complained or nagged, but they were mythical, not real.

And what was he, Andrew Paxton Davis, a pacifist, a Christian, and a virtual slave, doing standing here and watching the battle among the heathens? Now, now, now was the time to escape.

He quickly stuffed his few possessions in a fish-skin bag and grabbed the handle of his grail. Like the Arab in the night, I steal away, he thought. Except that I don't have to take the time to fold my tent. He walked out of his room swiftly and sped down the narrow winding steps. He met no one until he got to the courtyard. Then he saw a dark figure ahead of him. He stopped, his heart beating harder than his running accounted for. But a lightning bolt revealed the face of the person who had struck such fear into him.

"Doctor Faustroll!"

The Frenchman tried to bow but had to grip the side of the table to keep from falling on his face.

"Doctor Davis, I presume?" he mumbled.

The American was going to hurry past him but was restrained by a charitable impulse. He said, "There's uproar in Acheron, my good fellow. Now is the time to gain our freedom. Ivar was going to make a sneak attack on Arpad, but Arpad had the same idea about him. There's the devil to pay, and Thorfinn, Ivar's ally, has just shown up. Chaos will reign. We have an excellent chance of getting away during all the commotion."

Faustroll put a hand on his forehead and groaned. Then he said, "Up the River? Our quests for the probably nonexistent?"

"Think, man! Do you want to remain a slave? Now's the time, the only chance we may ever have!"

Faustroll bent to pick up his grail and fishing pole. He groaned again and said, *"La merde primitive!* The devil is using our head as an anvil."

"I'm going," Davis said. "You may come with me or not, as you please."

"Your concern for us is touching," the Frenchman said. "But we really don't have to run. Though we've been in lifelong bondage, we have never been a slave. Unlike the billions of the conventional and the swine-minded, we have been free."

A distant flash faintly illumined Faustroll. His eyes were rolling as if he were trying to see something elusive.

"Stay here, then, and be free in your miserable bonds!" Davis shouted. "I felt it was my duty to tell you what is going on!"

"If it had been love compelling you, it would be different."

"You're the most exasperating man I've ever met!"

"The gadfly has its uses, especially if it is equipped not only with a fore sting but an aft sting."

Davis snorted and walked away. But, by the time he had started down the hill from the tower, he heard Faustroll call out to him.

"Wait for us, my friend, if, indeed, you are that!"

Davis halted. He could not say that he liked the grotesque fellow. But… something in the absurd Frenchman appealed to him. Perhaps, Davis thought, it's the physician in me. The man's mad, and I should take care of him. I might be able to cure him someday.

More likely, it's just that I don't want to be alone. Crazed company is better than none. Sometimes.

The thunder and lightning had rolled on down the Valley. In a few minutes, the bright zigzags and the vast bowling-pin noises would be out of sight and out of ear. Then, as almost always, the downpour would stop as if a valve had been shut. The clouds would disappear within thirty minutes or so after that. And the star-filled sky would shed its pale fire on the pale weapons of the warriors and their dark blood. It would also make it easier for Faustroll and him to be seen.

Now he could faintly hear the frightening sounds of the clash. Shrill screams, deep cries, swords clanging, drums beating, and, now and then, the bellowing of a black gunpowder bomb as it destroyed itself in a burst of light. He also became aware that the tower, in which he had thought was no living soul, was as busy as a disturbed anthill. He turned to look back. Faustroll, panting, was just about to catch up with him. He was silhouetted by the many torches of the many people streaming from the tower.

Among them was Ann Pullen. She had put a heavy towel over her shoulders and a long one around her waist.. But her white face and streaming blond hair were vivid under the flaming brand she held high.

And there was Sharkko walking as fast as his dragging leg would permit him. He carried a grail in one hand, a sword in the other, and a large bag was strapped, to his back.

The others passed Davis on their way down the hill. Apparently, they were going either to join Ivar in the battle or to find a place where they could more closely observe it. The latter, more likely. If they thought that things were going against Ivar, they would be running, too.

Davis grabbed a torch from a slave woman as she passed him. She protested but did not fight him. He held it up and pointed up-River.

"Let's go!"

Easier said than done. Just as they reached the edge of the plain, they were forced to stop. A large body of men, many of them holding torches, jogged by. Davis looked at the round, wooden, leather-covered helmets, the broad dark faces, and the eyes with prominent epicanthic folds. He groaned. Then he said, "More of Arpad's men! They must be a second flanking force!"

These were not Magyars but soldiers from Arpad's ancient Siberian citizens, forming ten percent of the kingdom's population. They looked much more like the American Indians than Eskimos or Chuk-chuks. A group of six or seven men broke off from the mass and trotted toward them. Davis yelled, "Run!" and he fled back up the hill. Behind came the sound of bare feet on the wet grass and wet mud under it. But it was Faustroll.

When he was halfway up the hill, Davis looked behind him. The invaders were no longer in pursuit. Finding that they could not kill the two men easily, they had rejoined the army.

After a while, he and Faustroll quit climbing along the sides of the hill and went down to the edge of the plain. Within ten minutes the starblaze was undimmed by clouds.

"Time to look for a boat," Davis said.

They went slowly and stealthily among the huts. Now and then, they had to go around corpses. Most of these were women, but some had managed to kill invaders before they had been cut down. "The never-ending story," Davis said. "When will they learn to stop killing and raping and looting? Can't they see that it does nothing to advance them? Can't..."

"They didn't see on Earth, why should they here?" Faustroll said. "But perhaps it's a weeding-out process here. We get not just a second chance but many chances. Then, one day, poof! The evil ones and the petty, the malicious, and the hypocritical are gone! Let's hope that that does not mean that nobody is left here. Or, perhaps, that's the way it's going to work out."

He stopped, pointed, and said, "Eureka!"

There were many boats along here, beached or riding at anchor a few feet from the short. They chose a dugout canoe with a small mast. But, just as they were pushing it off the grass into the water, they were startled by a yell behind them.

"Wait! For God's sake, wait! I want to go with you!"

They turned and saw Sharkko hobbling toward them. He was dragging another bag, a large one, behind him. No doubt, Davis thought, it was filled with loot Sharkko had picked up on the way. Despite his fear, his predatory nature had kept the upper hand.

Davis said, "There's not enough room for three."

Panting, Sharkko stopped a few feet from them. "We can take a larger boat."

Then he turned quickly to look down-River. The distant clamor had suddenly become closer. The starlight fell over a dark and indistinct mass advancing from the south. Shouts and clanging of bronze on bronze swelled from it. It stopped moving toward Davis for several minutes. Then the sounds ceased, and the group moved again, more swiftly now.

Whoever the men chasing after those who fled were, they had been killed. But another hue and cry rose from behind the survivors. The men coming toward Davis began to run.

"Get in one of the boats!" Sharkko squalled. "They'll grab them, and we won't have any!"

Davis thought that that was good advice, but he did not intend to take the fellow with him. He resumed helping the Frenchman push the canoe. It slid into the water. But Sharkko had splashed to it, thrown his grail and bags into it, and started to climb in. Davis grabbed the bags and threw them into the water. Sharkko screamed with fury. His fist struck Davis's chin. Stunned, Davis staggered back and fell into the water. When he rose, sputtering, he saw that Sharkko was going after the bags. He got to the boat and threw Sharkko's grail after him. That made the man scream more loudly. Without the grail, Sharkko would either starve to death or have to live from the food he could beg or the fish he could catch.

Faustroll, still standing in the water, was doubled over with laughter.

Davis's anger ebbed and was replaced by a disgust he felt for himself. He hated Sharkko, yet despised himself for hating him and for losing his temper. It was hard to act like a Christian when dealing with such a "sleazebag" (a word he had learned from a late-twentieth-centurian).

But he now had no time to dwell on his own failings. The running men had stopped near him. They seemed out of breath, though that was not the only reason they had halted. They were Ivar and about fifty of his Norse and Frankish warriors and a dozen women. Ann Pullen was one of them. Ivar was bloody though not badly wounded, and the bronze war-ax he waved about dripped red. He seemed to be in favor of making a stand of it against the pursuers. Some of his men were arguing against it. Davis did not know what had happened at first. By listening to them while he was getting into the canoe, he pieced out their situation.

Apparently, the rear attack had caught Ivar by surprise.

But he had rallied his men, and Arpad's had been routed. No sooner was this done than Arpad, leading his fleet, had stormed the shore. In the melee, Ivar had killed Arpad.

"I hewed off his sword arm!" Ivar shouted. "And his forces lost heart and fled. We slaughtered them!"

8

BUT THORFINN THE Skull-Splitter had his own plans. He had sent a part of his army to overrun the west bank. While they were doing that, he had attacked the rear of Arpad's fleet. That was partly responsible for the panic among Arpad's men on the east bank.

Thorfinn had decided then, or perhaps he had long ago decided, to betray Ivar. Thus, he would become master not only of his own kingdom but of Arpad's and Ivar's.

Ivar and his soldiers had not expected betrayal, but they had rallied quickly and had fought furiously. Bud they had been forced to run, and Thorfinn's hounds were baying close to their heels.

Ivar yelled in Norse, "The traitor! The traitor! No faith, no faith! Thorfinn swore by Odin on the oath-ring that we would be as brothers!"

Davis, even in the midst of his anxiety, could not help smiling. From what he knew about Norse kings and their brothers, he was sure that there was nothing unusual about their trying to kill each other. That, in fact, had been typical of most medieval royal kin, whatever their nationality.

Oh, he was among barbarians, and he had been just about to be free of them when the Norris decreed that they should catch up with him. No, he thought, it's not the Norns, the three female Fates of the ancient Scandinavian religion. It's God who's destined this. I've been among the Vikings so long, I'm beginning to think like them.

By now, Ivar had quit raving. In one of the sudden switches of mood that distinguished him, he was laughing at himself.

"After all, Thorfinn only did what I might have done, given the circumstances. Seize the chance turn of events! Get the power! The power!"

Faustroll, now sitting in the canoe, called out, "Your Majesty, true descendant of the great King Ubu! We believe that Power is what motivates almost all of humanity, and Power is responsible for more rationalizations and false justifyings than Religion is, though the two are by no means unconnected! You are a true son of Adam, not to mention of Eve, and perhaps of a fallen angel who saw that the daughters of men were fair and went unto them and lay with them! Go, go, go, our son! Consider Power, worship it, obey its ten thousand commandments! But we are a voice crying in the wilderness! Crying in the jungle fertilized by the never-ending flow of desire for Power in its ten thousand manifestations, the true shit of the true universe!

"Yet somewhere there is the Holy Grail! Seek it, find it, seize it! Be redeemed thereby and by It! In the Grail you have the greatest fountain of Power! But it renders all other Powers powerless!"

Ivar's counselors had been babbling while Faustroll spoke, but they fell silent when their leader lifted his hand. From a distance, not far enough away to damp the writhing of Davis's nerves, came the yells of Thorfinn's men as they ran toward the fugitives.

"For God's sake!" Davis murmured. "Let's get into the boats and get away!"

Ivar shouted, "You are a strange man, Doctor Faustroll! One touched by whatever gods may be! You may have been sent by them! Or by Chance, of which I have heard so much from men of the latter days since I came to this world. Either way, you may have been sent to me. So, instead of slaying you, which would do little good except to get rid of your presence, and I might run into you again, I will go with you! Perhaps..."

He was silent for a moment while the others about him looked more than uneasy. Then he soared, "Into the boats!"

No one protested, though a few of the more aggressive warriors sighed. They scrambled, though not in a panicky manner, into the vessels. Ivar roared orders, assigning each to a particular craft. Davis was commanded, along with Faustroll and Ann Pullen, to get into the largest craft, a single-roasted merchant boat with oarlocks for fourteen rowers. Ivar took the helm while the rowers began pulling and the big sail was unfurled.

He laughed uproariously and said, "The Norns have smiled on me again! These must be the boats Arpad's men used to bring them to this bank for the flanking attack!"

Davis, Pullen, and Faustroll were sitting on a bench just below the helm deck. The Frenchman called up, "Perhaps it's a sign from them that you should leave this area forever!"

"What! And allow the troll-hearted Thorfinn to crow that he defeated Ivar Ragnarsson?"

He shouted in Norse at the warriors who had not yet gotten into a boat. "You there! Helgi, Ketil, Bjorn, Thrand! Push the empty boats into the stream! We will jeer at our enemies while they dance frustrated and furious on the bank and utter threats that will harm us no more than farts against the wind!"

Helgi the Sharp yelled back,

"Boatless will they be.
Boneless makes them bootyless.
Boneheaded Thorfinn,
Bare is your bottom!"

Those within hearing broke into laughter. And Ivar laughed until he choked, which relieved Davis, who had become even more anxious on hearing the stanza. The Dane became very angry when someone slipped up and used the surname he did not care to hear.

"I love the words," Ivar called out. "But, Helgi, your meter is blunted. Wretched. However, considering our haste and that your meter always scans as if it were a newborn foal trying to walk..."

He laughed again for several seconds. Then, recovering, he bellowed, "Row as if Loki's daughter, the hag Hel, clutches your ankles with corpse-cold hands to drag you down into Niflheim! Bend your backs as if you are the bow of Ull and your arms are the god's hundred-league arrows! Row, row, row!"

There might have been rowers as mighty as the Norse, though none was better. However, these men had been in face-to-face battle, and nothing funneled the energy out more swiftly. Nevertheless, they dug in as if they had had a long night's sleep. Their enemies on shore were left far behind. But the starlight glimmered on a large mass along the eastern bank moving up-River. It was about a half-mile behind them. Thorfinn's fleet, part of it, anyway, was hot on their trail. Not so hot, perhaps, since his men would also be battle-weary.

"We make for the kingdom of my brother, Sigurd Snake-in-the-Eye!" Ivar said loudly. "It's a long long way off, but our pursuers will tire before we do. We'll be safe then, and we can loll around, drink all the thickly sugared lichen bar and the grail-given liquor we want. We will also have our fill of the beautiful women there. Or vice versa."

The rowers had no breath to laugh, though some tried. Sigurd was one of the few men Ivar trusted and was probably his only trusted brother. He had been a mighty Viking when young. But, in his middle age, he had hung up his sword and become a peaceful and just ruler of Sjæland, Denmark's largest island. The kingdom he had established since coming to the Riverworld was four hundred miles from Ivar's. He had visited his brother once, and Ivar had visited him twice. Davis had seen Sigurd every time. The slender, wriggly, and red birthmark on the white of his right eye had given him his Terrestrial surname. Though it was gone when he was resurrected, the nickname stuck.

Davis's thoughts were broken by cries behind him. He stood up and looked around the raised helmsman's deck. The boat holding Helgi and three men was passing by a man in the water. Though Davis could not see the swimmer's face, he knew that he had to be Sharkko. Apparently, he was asking to be taken into the boat. But they were laughing as they rowed, and presently, Sharkko, still screaming, was left behind them.

A thrill of sympathy, though fleeting, ran through Davis. Sharkko was a liar, a cheat, a blusterer, a coward, and a bully. Yet the man could not believe that there were people, and they were many, who did not like him. It was pathetic, which was why Davis pitied him at that moment.

He sat down and looked sidewise at Ann, who was sitting near him. A small thin blue towel was draped over her head like a scarf that women wore in church on Earth. She had a strange expression, a mixture of sweetness and longing. Or so it seemed to him, though who knew what the bitch was thinking. Yet she looked like a madonna, mother of the infant Jesus, in a painting Davis had seen in a cathedral.

He wondered if that was what she had looked like when an infant. What had erased that sweetness, that goodness?

Then she turned her head and said, "What in hell are you staring at, you lascivious lout?"

Davis sighed, relishing the moment when he had pitied her because of her lost innocence. And he said, "Not much."

"You may think you can talk to me like that because of the situation," she said. "But I won't forget this."

"Your Majesty is like King Louis XIV of France, of whom someone said that he never forgot anything," he said. He added, under his breath, "And who also said that he never learned anything."

"What?"

Most un-Christian of me, Davis thought. Why can't I learn to turn the other cheek? I should have said nothing to her. The silence of the martyrs.

Later, Ivar transferred the four men from the rear boat to his. By late morning, the lead boat in Thorfinn's fleet was far ahead of the rest of the pack. An hour before high noon, it was within arrow range of Ivar's craft. Ivar turned his vessel around, picked off seven men with his arrows, rammed the enemy, and then boarded him. Davis and Faustroll sat in the boat while the battle raged. Ann Pullen used her woman's bow to wound several men. Whatever she may be, Davis thought, she has courage. But I hope she doesn't turn around and shoot me, too.

Ivar lost six men but killed all of the enemy except those who jumped into the River. Thorfinn's other boats were still out of sight. Ivar took over the enemy's vessel and abandoned his own. He and his crew sailed on while they sang merrily.

By the time they got near to Sigurd's realm, they had passed through at least forty waking nightmares. Or so it seemed to Davis, though the Norse obviously enjoyed it. There was one fight after another and one flight after another. The states for hundreds of miles up-River from Ivar's ex-kingdom and probably down-River, too, were in a state of bloody flux. The invasions of Ivar's land seemed to have had a violent wave effect on others, none of which was very stable. Slaves were revolting, and kings and queens were trying to take advantage of the deteriorating situations to attack each other. Davis believed that only this semi-anarchy enabled Ivar's fleet to get this far. Even so, all but four vessels of the original fleet had been sunk or abandoned. The survivors had lived chiefly on the fish they trolled for while sailing up-River. Now and then, they had been allowed to go ashore and fill their grails. But even when the people seemed peaceful and cooperative, the Vikings were nervous. Behind the smiles of their hosts might be plans to seize the guests as slaves.

"Oh, Lord," Davis prayed, "I beseech you, stop this killing, torturing, robbing, and raping, the heartbreak and the pain, the hatred and viciousness. How long must this go on?"

As long as men permit themselves to do all the horrible deeds, he thought, God wasn't going to interfere. But, if He didn't, then He had a good purpose in His mind.

A few hours past dawn, the fleet arrived at Sigurd's kingdom. Or what had been his. It was obvious that it, too, had been torn apart by the strife that seemed to have been carried by the wind. Men and women capered drunkenly while waving weapons and severed heads. Most of the bamboo huts and wooden buildings were blazing, and bodies lay everywhere. As the fleet drew near the bank, a horde climbed into boats and began paddling or rowing toward Ivar's boats.

"Who are they?" Ivar said. Then, "It doesn't matter. Sail on!"

"What about your brother?" Davis said.

"He may have escaped. I hope so. Whatever happened to him, I can't save him. We are too few."

After that, he was silent for many hours, pacing back and forth on the small afterdeck. He frowned much, and, several times, he smote his breast with an open hand. Once, he startled all on his boats when he threw his head back and howled long and mournfully.

Bjorn the Rough-footed, standing near Davis, shivered and made the sign of Thor's hammer. "The cry of the great wolf Fenris himself comes from his throat," he said. "Ivar acts as if he's about to go berserk! Get ready to defend yourself! Better yet, jump into the River!"

Bart Ivar quit howling, and he stared around as if he had suddenly been transported here from a million miles away. Then he strode to the forward end of the deck, and he called down.

"Osteopath! Clown! Come up here!"

Reluctantly, knowing that the Dane's actions could never be predicted and were often to be dreaded, Davis went up the short ladder with Faustroll. Both halted several feet away from Ivar. Davis did not know what Faustroll was thinking, but he himself was prepared to follow Bjorn's advice.

Ivar looked down at them, his face working with some unreadable expression.

"You two are of lowly rank, but I've observed that even a slave may have more brains than his master. I've heard you speak of your quests, the spirit of which I admit I don't quite understand. But you've intrigued me. Especially when you spoke about the futility and emptiness of always striving to gain more land, more property, and more power. You may be right. I really don't know. But, a few minutes ago, I was seized by some spirit. Perhaps I was touched by whatever god made us, the unknown and nameless god. Whatever strange thing happened, I suddenly felt emptied, my mind and blood pouring out of me. That terrible feeling was quickly gone, and I saw the sense in your wisdom, I also was overwhelmed, for a moment, with the uselessness of all I had done. I saw the weariness of forever fighting to get power and then fighting to keep it or to get even more power. Glory seems golden. But it's really leaden."

He smiled at them, then looked past them toward the north. When he resumed talking, he kept on staring past them. It was as if, Davis thought, Ivar was envisioning something really glorious.

Faustroll murmured softly. "He sees, however dimly, the junction point of zero and infinity."

Davis did not speak, because Ivar was glaring at him and the Frenchman. When Ivar spoke, he wanted your complete attention, no interruptions. But Davis thought, No, it's not that, whatever that means. It's…can't remember the Greek theological term…it means a sudden and totally unexpected reversal—a flipflop—of spirit. Like the reversal of attitude and of goal that Paul of Tarsus experienced on the road to Damascus…he had been fanatically persecuting the Christians…the great light carne even as he was plotting death for all Christians…he fell paralyzed for a while…when he arose, he had become a zealous disciple of Christ. Sudden, unexpected, unpredictable by anyone. Your spirit, hastening you toward the South Pole, turns you around without your will and shoots you toward the North Pole. There were records of similar mystical or psychological reversals of spirit.

He felt awed. It was several seconds before the cold prickling of his skin faded away.

However, he reminded himself, this sudden turnabout was not always for the good. Though it was rare, a flipflop from good to evil occurred. As if Satan, imitating God, also touched a man with his spirit.

"The god did not speak with words," Ivar said. "But he did not have to do so. He said that I should go up the River until I came to its source, no matter how far away that is. There I will find a Power beyond power."

"Always power," Faustroll murmured. He spoke so softly that Davis could barely hear him, and Davis was sure than Ivar could not.

"You, kneader of sore flesh, and you, the mocker of all that men hold to be good sense," Ivar said, "also have your quests. One wants to find the baby born of a virgin. The other hopes to find the truth that has eluded all men from the birth of mankind."

He paused, then said, "Though you are no warriors and have some strange attitudes, you may be the kind of companions I need for the long journey. What do you say?"

His tone implied that he was condescending to give the invitation. Yet he intended it as a compliment.

Faustroll said, "King Ubu and his two fools looking for the Holy Grail? Ah, well, I will be pleased to go with you."

Davis did not hesitate. He said, "Why not? Perhaps we are all seeking the same thing. Or, if we're not, we'll find the same thing."

AUTHOR'S NOTE:

IT'S OBVIOUS THAT the adventures of these three will continue and be concluded in volume 2 of the Riverworld shared-world anthology.

I have a strong sense of historical continuity that was strengthened while I was researching into my genealogy. As of this moment, I have 275 confirmed American ancestors and several thousand European ancestors. So, I thought, why not use some on the Riverworld, where everyone who has lived and died now lives? And I did so.

Thus, every named character in this story, except for Faustroll (Alfred Jarry) and Sharkko, is a direct ancestor of mine. Doctor Andrew P. Davis is my great-great-grandfather (1535-1919). He was an extraordinary man, an eccentric, a quester after the truth, and an innovator. Ann Pullen is my nine-times-great-grandmother. She was, according to the court records, a real hellraiser, spitfire, and liberated woman in an age when it was dangerous for a woman to be so. As for my remote forebears, Ivar the Boneless and the other Viking men and women herein, their living descendants as of 1991 would number many millions. It's reasonable to assume that at least three-quarters or more of my readers will be descended from them.

Up the Bright River

1

Andrew Paxton Davis leaned into the fifteen-mile-an-hour wind. But not too far. He was standing at the end of a fifty-foot-long yew wood gangplank. It was three inches deep and four and a half inches wide. Thirty feet of it was supported by a single forty-five-degree angled beam, the other end of which was attached to the tower structure. Beyond that, the remaining twenty feet formed a sort of diving board. Davis, having ventured out to its end, felt it bend under him.

The ground was three hundred feet below him, but he could clearly hear the roar and screams of the crowd and sometimes fragments of words from an individual. The upturned faces were mostly eager or malicious. Some expressed fear or sympathy for him.

Beyond the end of the board was a twelve-foot gap. Then the projecting end of another gangplank equally long and narrow, began. But his weight bent the end of the plank he stood on and made it five inches lower than the other.

If he could leap from one gangplank to the next he was free. The Emperor had promised that any "criminals" who could do so would be allowed to depart unharmed from the state. Attempting such a feat or refusing to do it was not, however, a choice. All major criminals were sentenced to the ordeal.

The people below were rooting for him or hoping he would fall. Their attitude depended upon which way they had bet.

Behind him, standing on the platform of the tower, the other prisoners shouted encouragement. Davis did not know two of them or what their crimes were. The others were his companions, if you could call them that, who had traveled far together and had been captured by the people of the Western Sun Kingdom. They were the Viking, Ivar the Boneless, the mad Frenchman, Faustroll, and Davis's bane, the beautiful but sluttish Ann Pullen.

Davis had been chosen by the Emperor Pachacuti to jump first. He would just as soon be the last in line. If he refused to leap, he would be thrown off the tower by the guards.

Ivar shouted in Old Norse. Though the wind hurled his words away from his lips, they came from the chest of a giant. Davis heard them as if they were far away.

"Show them you are not afraid! Run bravely and without fear! Run with the fleetness of Hugi, the giant whose name means Thought! Then fly as if you wear the birdskin of Loki! Pray to your god that you will not bring shame to him by hesitating! Nor to us!"

Faustroll's voice was shrill but pierced the wind. He spoke in English.

"It does not matter if you fail and fall, my Philistine friend! One moment of terror, quite cathartic for you and for us, and you will awake tomorrow as whole as ever! Which, if you will pardon my frankness, is not saying much!"

Anal Pullen either said nothing or her voice was snatched away by the wind.

What Faustroll said about him was, excluding the insults, true. He would die today; he would be resurrected at dawn. But he might be far down the River and have to start his journey all over again. That prospect made him quail almost as much as what he must do within the next twenty seconds. He had been given only two minutes to make the attempt.

"Ten feet, Andrew the Red!" Ivar had said when the Emperor pronounced sentence on him. "Ten feet! It is nothing! I will run on the board like a deer and will soar off its end like a hawk and land upon the other board like a lynx pouncing upon its prey!"

Brave words. Though Ivar was six feet six inches tall and was enormously powerful, he weighed over two hundred and thirty pounds. That was a lot of muscle and bone to lift. The heavier the runner, the more the wood would bend down. Not only would he have to leap across, he would have to leap up to attain the end of the other board.

Davis had an advantage in being only five feet six inches high and in weighing only one hundred and forty pounds. But the jumper's degree of courage made a difference. He had seen men and women who might have crossed the gap if fear had not slowed them down.

No hesitation, he told himself. Do it! Get it over with! Give it all you have! But his stomach hurt, and he was quivering.

He prayed to God as he trotted back to the tower and as he turned around to face the gangplank. Fifty feet was not long enough for a good runway. In that distance, he could not reach maximum speed. But that was how it was. No evading it; no excuses. Still praying, he bent down in the starting crouch and then sprang outward with all his strength. The sickness and the quivering were gone, or he was unaware of them. He felt as he had when, in 1845, he was ten years old and competing in a jump across a creek with other farm boys near Bowling Green, Clay County, Indiana. The glory of his healthy young body and intimations of immortality had blazed then.

Now, his spirit and body had become one as they had been one when he had made that winning jump on Earth. He was an arrow aimed at the end of the board beyond the void. The shouts of his companions, the roar of the crowd, and the captain of the guards counting off the seconds remaining became one voice. His bare feet slapped on the wood as they had slapped on the dirt when she had won the contest with his schoolmates. But, then, he had faced only getting wet if he fell short.

The end of the gangplank was coming far more swiftly than he thought possible. Beyond it vas the space he had to travel, a short distance in reality, a long, long one in his mind. And the beam was dipping. Only a few inches, but the slight deviation from the horizontal might defeat him.

He came down hard with his right foot and rose up, up, up. The void was below him. He thought, Oh, God, to whom I have been always faithful, deliver me from this evil! But a rapture, completely unexpected, shot through him. It was as if the hand of God were not only lifting him but enveloping him in the ecstasy few besides the saints knew.

It was worth the price of horror and of death.

2

YESTERDAY, ANDREW PAXTON Davis had also been high above earth. But he was not under any sentence and was not afraid of dying immediately. He was clinging to the railing of a bamboo platform, the crow's nest as it were, while it swayed in the strong wind. He was seasick, though there were no seas on this world.

Bright in the early-morning sun, the city below him creaked as if it were a ship under full sail. He had ascended many staircases and climbed many ladders past many levels to reach the top floor of this sentinel tower, the highest structure of the gigantic skeletal building that was also a city. Though he had stood here for only two minutes, he felt as if he had endured an hour of watch on a vessel during a violent storm. Yet the view was certainly peaceful and undisturbed. The storm was within himself.

Northward, the River ran for thirty miles before turning left to go around the shoulder of the mountain range. That marked the upper border of this kingdom. Southward, twenty miles away, the River came from around another bend. That was the lower border of this small yet mighty monarchy. The Inca Pachacuti ruled both sides of the River within these borders, and he was disobeyed only at the risk of torture, slavery, or death.

Just past the edge of the City on the north was the Temple of the Sun, a flat-topped pyramid a hundred and fifty feet high and made of stone, earth, and wood. Below Davis was the Scaffolding City, the City of Many Bridges, the City Swaying in the Wind, the Airy Domain of Pachacuti Inca Yupanqui, who had ruled on Earth from A.D. 1438 to 1471. The Peruvians of that time knew him as the great conqueror and Emperor Pachacuti.

The City that Pachacuti had built was like none known on Earth and was, perhaps, unique on the Riverworld. The view from the top level of the high-most sentinel tower would have made most people ecstatic. It made Davis feel like throwing up.

The Incan sentinel was grinning. His teeth were brown from chewing the grail-provided cocoa leaf. He had seen Davis here many times and was enjoying his plight. Once, the guard had asked Davis why he came here if the place always made him ill. Davis had replied that at least here he could get away from the even more sickening citizens of the City.

But, suddenly inspired, he had added, "The higher I get from the ground, the closer I am to the Ultimate Reality, the Truth. Up here, I may be able to see the Light."

The watchman had looked puzzled and somewhat fearful. He had moved away from Davis as far as he could get. What Davis did not tell him was that it was not only the height and the swaying that made him nauseous. He was also sick with longing to see a child who might not be and may never have been. But he would not admit that that could be the reality. He was certain that, somewhere up the River, was a woman who had borne a baby in a world where no woman, so far, had conceived. Moreover, Davis was certain that the baby was of virgin birth and that it was the reincarnation of Jesus.

From below came, faintly, the voices of the people chattering away in Kishwa, Aymara, Samnite, Bronze Age Chinese, and a dozen other languages, the tinkling of windblown bundles of mica shards, the shrillnesses of whistles and flutes, and the deep booming of drums. All these floated upward, wrapped in the odor of frying fish.

Except for the temple and the city, the plains and foothills looked like most other areas along the River. The mushroom-shaped grailstones, the conical-roofed bamboo huts, the fishing boats, the large oar-and-sail war or merchant vessels, the people moving around on the plains bordering the River, were nothing unusual. But the city and the temple were extraordinary enough to bring men and women from far-off places up and down the River. Like Earth tourists, they were gawkers who had to pay a price for admission. Their dried fish; wooden, fishbone, flint, and chart tools and weapons; rings and statuettes; containers of booze, cigarettes, dreamgum, and ochre enriched the kingdom. Even the slaves enjoyed the bounty to some extent.

Presently, as Davis stood there, looking northward toward the invisible Light, the face of a man appeared just above the platform. He hoisted himself up from the ladder with powerful arms and stood erect. He towered over Davis and the sentinel. His shoulder-length hair was bronze-red; his eyes were large and light blue; his face was craggy yet handsome. He wore a kilt made of a blue towel, a necklace of colored fish bones, and a cap decorated with wooden pieces carved into the semblance of feathers. His tanned humanskin belt held a large stone ax.

Despite his savage appearance, he, too, had a quest. During the flight from his former kingdom, he seemed to have been seized with a revelation. At least, he had said so to Davis. What it was, he kept to himself. Davis had not been able to tell that the illumination or whatever it was had changed his character for the better. But Ivar was determined to travel to the end of the River. Where, Davis supposed, the Viking thought that he would find the beings who had made this planet and resurrected the dead of Earth. And they would reveal the Ultimate Reality, the Truth.

Ivar the Boneless spoke to Davis in the Old Norse of the early-ninth-century Vikings. “Here you are, Andrew the Red, the Massager, enjoying the view and your sickness. Have you seen the Light?”

“Not with my eyes,” Davis said. “But my heart sees it.”

“What the heart sees, the eye sees,” Ivar said.

He was now standing by Davis, his huge hands squeezing on the railing bar, his massive legs braced on the slowly rocking platform. Though he looked at the north of the Rivervalley, he was not trying to see Davis’s Light. Nor was he looking for his own Light. As always when here, he was planning an escape route while seeing the entire kingdom spread out before him. Being the general of one of the Inca’s regiments was not enough to detain a man who had been a king on Earth and in the Valley.

"We've tarried here far too long," he growled. "The source of the River beckons, and we have many a mile to go."

Davis looked anxiously at the sentinel. Though the Aymara did not understand Ivar's language, he still might report to the Inca that the two had been conversing in a suspicious manner. Pachacuti would then demand that Davis and Ivar tell him what they had said. If he was not satisfied with their answers, he would torture them to get the truth out of them. Suspicion floated through this land like a fever-breeding miasma. Hence, it was full of spies.

As Ivar had once said, a man could not fart without the Inca hearing about it.

"I go up-River tonight," Ivar said. "You may come along with me, though you are not a great warrior. Yet, you have some cunning, you have been useful in frays, and you do have a strong reason to leave this place. I tell you this because I can trust you not to betray me if you decide to stay behind. That is praise, since few may be trusted."

"Thank you," Davis said. His tone hinted at sarcasm, but he knew that the Viking was, according to his lights, being complimentary. "I will go with you, as you knew I would. What are your plans? And why tonight? What makes it different from all the others?"

"Nothing is different. My patience is gone. I'm weary of waiting for events to open the way. I'll make my own event."

"Besides," Davis said, "the Inca is too interested in Ann. If you wait much longer, he will make her one of his concubines. I assume that she's going with us."

"Correct."

"And Faustroll?"

"The crazed one may stay here or go with us as he wishes. You will ask him if he cares to accompany us. Warn him to stay sober. If he is drunk, he will be left behind, most probably as a corpse."

Davis and Ivar talked in low tones as Ivar revealed his plans. Then the Viking climbed down from the crow's nest. Davis stayed awhile so that the sentinel would not think that they had been conspiring and were eager to begin their wicked work against the Inca.

At noon, Davis was by a grailstone on the edge of the River. After the top of the stone erupted in lightning and thunder, he waited until an overseer handed him his big cylindrical grail. He went off to eat from its offerings, walking slowly and looking for Faustroll in the crowd. He did not have much time for this. His appointment with the Inca was within the hour, and that bloody-minded pagan accepted no excuses for lateness from his subjects.

After several minutes, Davis saw the Frenchman, who was sitting cross-legged on the ground. He was eating and at the same time talking to some friends. Faustroll's appearance was no longer so grotesque. He had washed out of his black hair the glue and mud forming a nest in the center of which was a wooden cuckoo egg. His hair now hung dawn past his shoulders. He no longer had a painted mustache and he had also removed the painted mathematical formula from his forehead. He spoke only occasionally in the even-stressed words once distinguishing all of his speech. The change in him had encouraged Davis to believe that Faustroll was beginning to recover his sanity.

But his fishing pole was always at hand, and he still called himself "we." He insisted that using "I" made an artificial distinction between subject and object, that everybody was part of one body called humanity and that this body was only a small part of the even vaster universe.

"We" included the "Great Ubu," that is, God, and also anything that did not exist but could be named, and also the past, present, and future. This triad he considered to be indivisible.

Faustroll had irked, angered, and repulsed Davis. But, for some reason, Davis also felt a sort of fondness for him and was, despite himself, fascinated by Faustroll. Perhaps that was because the Frenchman was also looking for the Ultimate Reality, the Truth. However, their concepts of these differed greatly.

Davis waited until Faustroll happened to look at him. He signaled with a hand raised level with his forehead, his fingers waggling. Faustroll nodded slightly to acknowledge the signal, but he continued his animated talk in Esperanto. After a few minutes, he rose, stretched, and said that he was going fishing. Fortunately, no one offered to go with him. The two met by the very edge of the River.

"What do we have in mind?" the Frenchman said, speaking in English.

"Ivar is going to leave tonight. I'm going with him, and so is Ann Pullen. You're invited. But you must not get drunk."

"What? Surely, we are jesting!"

"We are not amused," Davis said.

"We are sometimes intoxicated, but we are never drunk."

"Come off it," Davis said. "No clowning around tonight. Ivar said he'd kill you if you're drunk, and that's no empty threat. And you know what'll happen to us if we get caught. Are you coming with us or not?"

"We never leave a place. On the other hand we are never in one place. That would be too mundane and scarcely to be tolerated. Yes, we will accompany us, though the answer to the Great Question, the uncompleted side of the formula, may be here in this minute metropolis of uncertainty and instability, not, as we hope, far up the River."

"Here's what Ivar proposes," Davis said.

Faustroll listened without interrupting, something he rarely did, then nodded. "We believe that that is as good a plan as any and perhaps better than most. Which is not to say that it has any merit at all."

"Very well. We'll meet at midnight at the Rock of Many Faces."

Davis paused, then said, "I do not know why Ivar insists on bringing Ann Pullen along. She's a troublemaker and a slut."

"Ah! We hate her so much, we must love her!"

"Nonsense!" Davis said. "She's contemptible, wicked, vicious, the lowest of the low. She makes the Great Whore of Babylon look like a saint."

Faustroll laughed. "We believe that she is a soul who had and has the strength of intellect and character to free herself of the bonds, limits, and restrictions imposed upon women by men since time began or, perhaps, shortly before that. She snaps her fingers under the puissant but pinched proboscis of the god you worship and the puny pinched penises of the men who worship him. She..."

"You will burn in hell as surely as a struck match burns," Davis said, his blue eyes slitted, his hands clenched.

"Many matches do not light because they are deficient in the wherewithal of combustion. But we agree with the dying words of the immortal Rabelais: 'Curtain! The farce is finished! I am setting out to seek a vast perhaps.' If we die the death of forever, so be it. There are not enough fires in Hell to burn all of us away."

Davis opened his arms wide and held out his hands, indicating hopelessness. "I pray that the good Lord will make you see the errors of your ways before it is too late for you."

"We thank you for the kind thought, if it is kind."

"You're impenetrable," Davis said.

"No. Expenetrating."

Faustroll walked off, leaving Davis to figure out what he meant.

But Davis hurried away to be on time for his daily appointment. Just as he had been the royal masseur for Ivar the Boneless, when Ivar was king of an area far to the south of this state, so Davis was now premier masseur for Pachacuti. His job angered and frustrated him because he had been on Earth an M.D., a very good one, and then an osteopath. He had traveled to many places in the U.S.A., lecturing and founding many osteopathic colleges. When he was getting old, he had founded and headed a college in Los Angeles based on his eclectic discipline, neuropathy. That used the best theories and techniques of drugless therapy: osteopathy, chiropractic, Hahnemanism, and others. When he had died in 1919 at the age of eighty-four, his college was still flourishing. He was sure that it would grow and would found new branches throughout the world. But late-twentieth-centurians he had met had said that they had never heard of him or of the college.

Seven years ago, Ivar had been forced to flee from his kingdom because of treachery by an ally, Thorfinn the Skull-Splitter. Davis, Faustroll, and Ann Pullen had gone with Ivar. They did not know what to expect from Thorfinn, but they assumed that they would not like it.

After many fights, enslavements, and escapes while going up the River, they had been captured by the Incans. And here they were, enduring what they must and plotting to get freedom someday.

Ivar was as patient as a fox watching a toothsome hen, but his patience had been eroded away. Just why the Viking had not taken off by himself, Davis did not know. He would be burdened by them—from his viewpoint, anyway. But an unanalyzable magnetism kept the four together. At the same time that they were attracted to each other, they also were repulsed. They revolved about each other in intricate orbits that would have given an astronomer a headache to figure out.

About ten minutes by the sand clock before his scheduled appearance, Davis was in the building housing the Inca's court. This was a four-walled and roofed structure sitting on the intersection of many beams a hundred feet above the ground. The skeletal city creaked, groaned, and swayed around, above, and below them. It was noisy outside the building and only a trifle less so inside. Though the Inca sat on a bamboo throne on a dais while he listened to his petitioners, the people around him talked loudly to each other. Davis had threaded his way through them and now stood a few feet from the dais. Presently, the Inca would rise, a fishskin drum would boom three times, and he would retire to a small room with the woman he had chosen to honor with his royal lust. Afterward, Davis would massage the royal body.

Pachacuti was a short and dark man with a hawk nose, high cheekbones, and thick lips. Around the hips of his short squat body a long green towel served as a kilt, and a red towel, edged in blue, was draped over his shoulders as a cape. His headpiece was a turban-towel secured by a circlet of oak from which sprouted long varicolored fake feathers made of carved wood.

If Pachacuti had been naked, Davis often thought, he would not have looked like a monarch. Very few unclothed kings would be. In fact, even now, he was no more distinguished in appearance than any of his subjects. But his manner and bearing were certainly imperial.

Who was the woman who would share the royal couch today? Davis had thought that he did not care. And then he saw his bête noir, Ann Pullen, preceded by two spearmen and followed by two more. The crowd gave way for her. When she reached the dais, she stopped and turned around and smiled with lovely white teeth set in bright rouged lips.

Though Davis loathed her, he admitted to himself that she was beautiful. Those long wavy yellow tresses, the strikingly delicate and fine-boned face, the perfectly formed and outthrust breasts she was so proud of, the narrow waist and hips, and the long slim legs made her look like a goddess. Venus as she would be if Praxiteles had happened to dream of Ann Pullen. But she was such a bitch, he thought. However, Helen of Troy probably had been a bitch too.

The guards marched her toward the door of the room in which the Inca waited for her. A moment after she had entered the room, the guards admitted the little big-eyed priest who observed the virility of the Incan during his matings. When the king was done, and God only knew when that would be, the royal witness would step outside and announce the number of times the Inca had mounted his woman.

The crowd would rejoice and would congratulate their fellows. The kingdom would continue to flourish; all was well with its citizens' world.

Beware, though, if the Inca failed once.

Davis had never cursed. At least, not on Earth. But he did now.

"Go-o-o-od damn her!"

She had given herself to the Inca and now would become one of his wives, perhaps the favorite. But why? Had she quarreled with Ivar since he had been on the sentinel tower? Or had the Inca tempted her with such offers that she could no longer refuse him? Or had she, the Scarlet Woman, an abomination in the nostrils of the Lord, just decided that she would like to lie with the Inca before she left the kingdom tonight? The man was said to be extraordinarily virile.

Whatever the reason, Ivar would not ignore her infidelity. Though he had done so now and then in the past, that was because Ann had been discreet and he had been lying at the same time with another woman. For Ann to copulate with the Inca in public view, as it were, was to insult Ivar. Though he was usually self-controlled, he would react as surely as gunpowder touched with a flaming match.

"What's gotten into that woman?" Davis mumbled. "Aside from a horde of men?"

Ann Pullen was a late-seventeenth-century American who had lived—and she had lived to the fullest—in Maryland and Westmoreland County, Virginia. Born in a Quaker family, she had converted to the Episcopalian Church along with most of her tobacco planter family. She had married four times, a man by the name of Pullen being her final husband. Just when she took her first lover and when she took the last one even she did not know. But they had been coming and going for at least forty years during her turbulent life an Earth.

As she had declared—this had been in a public record—she saw no reason why a woman should not enjoy the same liberty and privileges as a man. Though that was a dangerous sentiment in her time, she had escaped arrests for harlotry and adultery. Twice, though, she had come close to being whipped by the court flogger because she was charged with attacking women who had insulted her.

Perhaps the isolation of the Maryland and Virginia counties in which she resided had enabled her to avoid the severe punishment she would have gotten in the more civilized Tidewater area. Or perhaps it was the fiery and pugnacious nature and the wild ways and free spirit of the Westmorelandians of her time. In any event, she had been a terrible sinner on Earth, Davis thought, and on the Riverworld she had gotten worse. His Church of Christ beliefs made him scorn and despise her. At the same time, he was grieved because she would surely burn in Hell. Sometimes, though he was ashamed of himself afterward, he gloried in the visions of her writhing and screaming in the torments of Inferno.

So, now, the Jezebel had suddenly decided to couple with Pachacuti. There was not much more she could do to make trouble than this. Except for telling the Inca that Ivar, Davis, and Faustroll were planning to leave the kingdom. Not even she would be so low.

Or would she?

He wished to slip away from the court, but he did not dare to anger the Inca. He was forced to listen to the cries and moans of ecstasy from the emperor and Ann Pullen. The courtiers and soldiers had quit talking to hear them, which made it worse for Davis. Especially since they were not at all disgusted. Instead, they were grinning and chuckling and nudging each other. Several men and women were feeling each other, and one couple was brazenly copulating on the floor. Savages! Beasts! Where was the lightning stroke to burn them with a foretaste of Hell? Where the vengeance of the Lord?

After several hours, the priest came out of the room. Smiling, he shouted that the Inca still had the virility demanded by the gods and his people. The state would prosper; good times would continue. Everybody except Davis and the man and the woman on the floor cheered.

Presently, slave women carried in bowls and pitchers of water and towels to bathe and to dry off the Inca and Ann. When they came out, the chief priest went in to perform a cleansing ritual. After he was done, a servant told Davis that the Emperor was ready for him. Gritting his teeth, but trying to smile at the same time, Davis entered the chamber of iniquity. Despite the bathing, the two still reeked of sweaty and overly fluidic sex.

Ann, naked, was lolling on a couch. She stretched out when she saw Davis and then flipped a breast at him. One of her chief pleasures was to flaunt her body before him. She knew how disgusted that made him.

The Emperor, also naked, was lying on the massage table. Davis went to work on him. When he was done, he was told to massage Ann. The Emperor, after getting off the table, was clothed by his dressers in some splendid ceremonial costume, splendid by Riverworld standards, anyway. Then he left the chamber and was greeted with loud cheers by the crowd.

Ann got onto the table and turned over on her front.

She spoke in the Virginia dialect of her time. "Give me a very good rubdown, Andy. The Emperor bent me this way and that. I taught him many positions he did not know on Earth, and he used them all. If you were not such a holy man, I'd instruct you on them."

Two female attendants remained in the room. But they did not understand English. Davis, trying to keep his voice from trembling with anger, said, "What do you think Ivar is going to do about this?"

"What can he do?" she said flippantly. Nevertheless, her muscles stiffened slightly. Then, "What business is it of yours?"

"Sin is everybody's business."

"Just what I'd expect a smellsmock fleak preacher to say."

"Smellsmock? Fleak?" Davis said.

"A licentious idiot."

Davis was kneading her shoulder muscles. He would find it very easy to move his hands up, close there around her neck, and snap it. Though he was not a big man, he had very powerful hands. For a moment, he almost realized the fantasy flashing through his mind. But a true Christian did not murder, no matter how strong the provocation. On the other hand, he would not be really killing her. She would appear somewhere else tomorrow and bedevil others. Far from here, though.

"Licentious," she said. "You hate me so much because, deep down, you would like to tup me. The Old Adam in you wants to ravish me. But you shove that down into the shadows of your sinfulness, into the Old Horny crouching clown there. I say that because I know men. Down there, they are all brothers. All, all, I say!"

"Whore! Slut! You lie! You would like to have carnal knowledge of every man in the world, and..."

She turned over abruptly. She was smiling, but her eyes were narrow. "Carnal knowledge? You mealy-mouth! Can't you use good old English? You wouldn't say tit if you had one in your mouth!"

Though he was not done massaging, he walked out of the room. The snickering and giggling of the servants followed him through the bamboo walls. They had not understood a word, but the tones of his and Ann's voices and her gestures were easily read.

Having recovered somewhat, he came back into the room. Ann was sitting up on the table and swinging her long shapely legs. She seemed pleased with herself. He stood in the door and said, "You know what Ivar intends for us to do tonight?"

She nodded, then said, "He's told me."

"So you had to have one last fling?"

"I've done the double-backed beast with kings but never with an emperor. Now, if I could only find a god to take me as Zeus took Leda. Or the great god Odhinnr whom Ivar claims he's descended from. A god who has the stamina to keep going forever and no storms of conscience afterward and is always kind to me. Then my life would be complete."

"I could vomit," he said, and he walked out again.

"That's one form of ejaculation!" she said loudly.

He climbed down hundreds of steps, wondering meanwhile why these crazy pagans built such an inconvenient city. When he got to the ground, he searched for Faustroll along the Riverbank until he found him fishing from a pier. The Frenchman's bamboo basket held seven of the foot-long striped species known as zebras. He was describing to his fellow fishers the intricacies of the science he had invented. He called it pataphysics. Davis understood little of it. So, evidently, did the people around him. They nodded their heads at his remarks. But their puzzled expressions showed that they were as much at sea as most of his listeners. That Faustroll's Kishwa was not very good certainly did not help their comprehension.

3

"Pataphysics," Faustroll intoned, "is difficult to define because we must use nonpataphysical terms to define it."

He had to use French words interspersed with Kishwa, because "pataphysics" and many other terms were not in the Incan language. Thus, he bewildered his audience even more. Davis decided that Faustroll did not care deeply whether or not these listeners comprehended him. He was talking to himself to convince himself.

"Pataphysics is the science of the area beyond metaphysics," Faustroll continued. "It is the science of imaginary solutions, of the particular, the seeming exception. Pataphysics considers that all things are equal. All things are pataphysical. But few people practice pataphysics consciously.

"Pataphysics is not a joke or a hoax. We are serious, unlaughing, as sincere as a hurricane."

He added in English for some reason Davis could not figure out, "Pataphysics is synaptic, not synoptic."

Apparently, he had given up on the Incans. He switched to French.

"In conclusion, though nothing is ever concluded in the full sense of 'conclusion,' we know nothing of pataphysics yet know everything. We are born knowing it at the same time that we are born ignorant of it. Our purpose is to go forth and instruct the ignorant—that is, us, until we all are illuminated. Then, mankind as we unfortunately know it now will be transformed. We will become as God is supposed to be, in many respects, anyway, even though God does not exist, not as we know it, its backside is chaos, and, knowing the Truth, we in our fleshly forms will pupate ourselves into a semblance of the Truth. Which will be close enough."

Now here, Davis thought, is one who truly fulfills Ann's definition of a "fleak." And yet...and yet...Faustroll made some kind of sense. Remove all the folderol, and he was saying that people should look at things from a different angle. What was it that that late twentieth-century Arab he had met so many years ago had said? Abu ibn Omar had quoted...what was his name...ah! a man named Ouspensky. "Think in other categories." That was it. "Think in other categories." Abu had said, "Turn a thing over, look at its bottom side. A watch is said to be circular. But if its face is turned at right angles to you, the watch is an ellipse.

"If everybody were to think in other categories, especially in emotional, familial, social, economic, religious, and political areas, human beings would eliminate most of the problems that make their lives so miserable."

"It didn't happen on Earth," Davis had said.

"But here it may," Abu had said.

"Fat chance!" Davis had said. "Unless all turn to the Lord, to Jesus Christ, for salvation."

"And were truly Christian, not the narrow-minded, bigoted, selfish, power-hungry wretches which most of them are. I will offend you when I say that you are one of them, though you will deny it. So be it."

Davis had come close to punching the man, but he had turned away, trembling with anger, and walked off.

He still got indignant when he thought about Abu's accusation.

"Faustroll!" Davis said in English. "I must talk to you!"

The Frenchman turned around and said, "Commence."

Davis told him about Ann and the Emperor. Faustroll said, "You may inform the Boneless about this delightful situation if you care to. We do not wish to be in his neighborhood when he hears of it."

"Oh, he'll hear of it, though not from me. This area is a lava flow of rumor and gossip. Are you still willing to escape from this place tonight, as agreed?"

"With or without Ivar or Ann or you."

He pointed past Davis, then said, "Someone has already told him."

Davis turned around. The city proper, the towering skeleton city, began a half-mile from the Riverbank. The Viking was striding on the ground toward an entrance to a staircase. He gripped in one hand the shaft of a big stone ax. He was also carrying a very large backpack. Davis supposed that Ivar's grail was in it. It bulged so much, however, that it had to contain something else. Even from this distance, Davis could see that Ivar's face and body were bright red.

"He's going to kill the Inca!" Davis said.

"Or Ann, or both," Faustroll said.

It was too late to catch up with him. Even if they did, they could not stop him. Several times before, they had seen him in his insane rages. He would smash in their skulls with the ax.

"He'll not get through the Inca's bodyguards," the Frenchman said. "I believe that the only thing we can do is to follow our plan and leave tonight. Ann and Ivar won't be there. You and I must go without them."

Davis knew that Faustroll was deeply upset. He had said "I" instead of "we."

By then, the Viking had reached the third level and crossed over on it. For a moment, he disappeared behind a translucent wall formed by a lightweight sheet of dragonfish intestine.

"I feel as if I'm deserting him," Davis said. "But what can we do?"

"We have changed our mind, which is the prerogative, indeed, the duty, of a philosopher," Faustroll said. "The least we can do is to follow him and determine what happens to him. We might even be able to aid him in some way."

Davis did not think so. But he would not allow this cuckoo to show more courage than he.

"Very well. Let's go."

They put their grails in their shoulder bags and hurried to the city. After climbing up staircases and ladders, they reached the level on which were the Inca's quarters. They saw many people running around and very noisy about it. From a distance came a hullabaloo that only a large crowd could raise. At the same time, they smelled smoke. It had a different odor from the many cooking fares in the dwellings. Following the direction of the noise and sidestepping people running toward the staircases and ladders, they came out onto a small plaza.

The buildings around this, mostly two-story bamboo structures with half-walls, were government offices. The Inca's "palace" was the largest building, three stories high but narrow. Though it had a roof, its exterior had few walls. Its far side was attached to the main scaffolding of the city.

The odor of smoke had become stronger, and there were more men and women running around. The two men could make no sense out of the shouts and cries until Davis caught the Kishwa word for "fire." It was then they realized the commotion was not caused by Ivar. Or, perhaps, it was. Davis thought of the huge bulging bag on Ivar's back. Had that contained pine torches and an earthen jar of lichen alcohol?

The strong wind was carrying the clouds to the south, which explained why the smoke stink had not been so detectable in the lower levels. Getting to the palace would be dangerous. By now, the bamboo floor of the plaza was burning swiftly and they would have to go around the plaza. For all they knew, the floor on its other side was also ablaze. Near them, a crew was working frantically hauling up big buckets of water from the ground on six hoists. Through the many open spaces among the rooms and the levels, Davis saw lines of people passing buckets of water from the river.

It had all happened very swiftly.

Now Davis smelled the distinctive odor of burning flesh. And he could see several bodies lying in the flames. Several seconds later, a corpse fell through the weakened floor to the one below it.

It did not seem possible that one man could wreak all this.

"Will you go now?" Davis said. "Ivar is doomed, if he's not already dead. We'd better get down to the ground before we're caught in the fire."

"Reason does not always prevail," the Frenchman said. "But fire does."

They retreated, coughing, until the smoke thinned out enough for them to see. The exterior of the building was a few yards from them. Nearby were a staircase and several openings in the floor for descent by ladder. But they could not get to them because of the crowd surrounding them. The staircase and the ladders were jammed with a snarling, screaming, and struggling mob. Several fell off onto the heads of the refugees on the floor below.

"It is possible to climb down on the beams of the outer structure!" Faustroll yelled. "Let us essay to escape via those!"

By then, others had the same thought. But there was enough space for all. When Davis and the Frenchman got to the ground, they were shaking with the effort and their hands, bellies, and the inner parts of their legs were rubbed raw. They worked through the crowds until they were close to the River.

"Now is the time to appropriate a small sailing vessel and go up-River," Faustroll said. "No one is here to object."

Davis looked at the skeletal structure and the people swarming around it and still coming out of it. By then, the bucket brigades had done their work, though he would have bet a few minutes ago that the entire city was doomed. The smoke was gone except for some wisps.

He and Faustroll still had their grails. And a fishing vessel anchored a few yards out contained poles and nets and spears. That would have to be enough.

When they waded out to the boat, they saw a man, dark-skinned, black-haired, eyes closed, lying face up on the floor. His jaw moved slowly. He was not chewing a cud.

"Dreamgum," Faustroll said. "He is now somewhere in Incan Peru, his mind blazing with visions of the land he once knew but that never really existed. Or, perhaps, he is flying faster than light among the stars toward the limits of the limitless."

"No such splendid things," Davis said disgustedly. He pointed at the man's erect penis. "He dreams that he is lying with the most beautiful woman in the world. If he has the imagination to do so, which I doubt. These people are crude and brutal peasants. The apex of their dreams is a life of ease and no obligations, no masters to obey, plenty of food and beer, and every woman their love slave."

Faustroll hauled himself aboard. "You have just described Heaven, my friend—that is, the Riverworld. Except for the masters to obey and every woman being a love slave, as you so quaintly describe the velvet-thighed gender. Get rid of the masters and accept that many women will scorn you but that there are many others who will not, and you have the unimaginative man's ideal of the afterworld. Not so bad, though. Certainly, a step up from our native planet.

"As for this fellow, he was born among the poor, and he stayed among them. But the poor are the salt of the earth. By salt, we do not mean that excretion made by certain geological phenomena. We mean the salt left on the skin after much labor and heavy sweating, the salt accumulating from lack of bathing. That stinking mineral and the strata of rotting flaked-off skin cells is the salt of the earth."

Davis climbed onto the boat, stood up, and pointed at the man's jetting penis. "Ugh! Lower than the beasts! Let's throw the ape overboard and get going."

Faustroll laughed. "Doubtless he dreams of Ann, our local Helen of Troy. We, too, have done so and are not ashamed of it. However, how do you know that he is not dreaming of a man? Or of his beloved llama?"

"You're disgusting, too," Davis said. He bent over and clutched the man's ankles. "Help me."

Faustroll put his hands under the man's arms and hoisted him. "Uh! Why does gravity increase its strength when we lift a corpse or a drunk or a drug-sodden? Answer us that, our Philistine friend. We will answer for you. It is because gravity is not an unvarying force, always obeying what we call the laws of physics. Gravity does vary, depending upon the circumstances. Thus, contrary to Heraclitus, what goes up does not always come down."

"You chatter on like a monkey," Davis said. "Here we go! One, two, three, heave!"

The man splashed into the water on his side, sank under the surface, then came up sputtering. Waist-high in the River, he began walking to the bank.

"Thank us for your much-needed bath!" Faustroll said, and he laughed. Then he began hauling up the anchor-stone.

But Davis pointed inshore and said, "Here they some!"

Ten soldiers, wooden-helmeted and carrying spears, were running toward them.

"Someone's reported us!" Davis said, and he groaned. Two minutes later, they were being marched off to jail.

4

IVAR AND ANN had not been killed. The Viking had fought through many soldiers, slaying and wounding many, yet had somehow reached his goal though he was bleeding from many wounds. His bloodstained ax had crashed down upon the head of the Inca, and Pachacuti had ceased to be the emperor. Ivar had made no attempt to kill Ann. That he was knocked out just after smashing the Inca's skull in may been the only reason he did not slay her.

Under the law of the Western Sun Kingdom, Ivar should have been kept alive to be tortured for days until his body could take it no longer. But the man who seized power had another idea. Tamcar was the general of a regiment but was not next in line for the throne. He immediately launched his soldiers against Pachacuti's, killed them, and declared himself the Inca. His assassins murdered the other generals, and, after some fighting, the survivors of the regiments surrendered to the new Inca. So much for the tradition of an orderly succession.

Though Tamcar publicly denounced Ivar, he must have been secretly grateful to him. He sentenced him to the Leap of Death, but that gave Ivar a thin chance to win his freedom and exile from the kingdom. Ann Pullen, Faustroll, and Davis had had no part in slaying Pachacuti, yet they were judged guilty by association with the Viking. Actually, the new Inca was just ridding himself of all those he considered dangerous to him. He rounded up a score of high-placed men and sent them out onto the gangplank. All but two fell. This pleased the people, though some were disappointed because not all failed. Tamcar sought out others whom he suspected might want to take the throne away from him. They, along with criminals, were forced to make the heap. The mob loved the spectacles. After these warm-ups, the main event came. Ivar and his companions now had their opportunity to thrill the populace. Not to mention themselves.

Two weeks after Pachacuti's death, Davis and his fellow prisoners were taken to the tower at high noon. They had been held in a stockade, thus had had the space in which to exercise vigorously. Also, they had practiced long jumping on the runway and the sand pit provided for those who lead to make the Leap of Death. The Emperor wanted his gamesters to come as near as they could to the receiving gangplank before falling. The people loved a good show, and the Emperor loved what the people loved. He sat on a chair on the platform from which projected the "freedom" plank.

The drums beat and the unicorn-fish horns were blown. The crowd below cheered at the announcement of the first jump.

Faustroll, standing behind Davis, said, "Remember, our friend. The degree of force of gravity depends upon the attitude of the one defying it. If there were such a thing as good luck, we would ask that it be given to you."

"Good luck to you, too," Davis said. He sounded very nervous, even to himself.

The captain of the royal guards shouted that he would begin the count. Before the two minutes were up, Davis had sped down the thirty-foot-long plank, brought his right foot down hard on its end, and soared up. It was then that the rapture seized him. Afterward, he believed that that was the only thing that bore him to safety. It had been given to him by God, of course. He had been saved by the same Being who had saved Daniel in the lion's den.

Nevertheless, he fell hard forward as his feet, just behind the toes, were caught by the end of the plank. His chest and face slammed into the hard yew wood near the edge of the plank. His hands gripped the sides of the plank, though he was not in danger of falling off. He lay for some time before getting up. Cheers, jeers, and boos rose from the mob on the ground. He paid no attention to them as he limped along the plank to the platform and was taken to one side by guards. His heart beat fast, and he did not quit trembling for a long time. By then, Faustroll was running down the gangplank, his face set with determination.

He, too, soared, though Davis doubted that the Frenchman was caught in the ecstasy he had felt. He landed with no inch to spare but managed to make himself fall forward. If he had gone backward and thus sat on the air, he would have fallen.

He was grinning when he got to Davis's side. "We are such splendid athletes!" he cried.

The drums beat, and the horn blew for the third time. Ann, as naked as her predecessors, her skin white with fear, ran along the gangplank. Bent forward, her arms and long slim legs pumping, she sprung over the void without hesitation.

"What courage! What audacity!" Faustroll cried. "What a woman!"

Davis, despite his dislike for her, admitted to himself that the Frenchman was right. But her bravery and strength were not enough to propel her to a good landing. The end of the plank struck her in her midriff and her elbows slammed onto the wood. Her breath whooshed out. For a moment, she hung, legs kicking over the emptiness. Her efforts to catch her breath were agonizing. Then she stretched out her arms, moving her hands along the edge of the plank. Her face was against the wood. She began to slip backward as her grip weakened.

Ivar bellowed, his voice riding aver the clamor of the mob and the cries of the men on the platforms. "You are a Valkyrie, Ann! Fit to be my woman! Hang on! You can do it! Pull yourself up and forward! I will meet you at the platform! If I should fall, I will meet you again somewhere on the River!"

That surprised Davis. During the two weeks of their imprisonment, Ivar had not spoken a word to Ann. Nor she to him.

Ann grinned then, though whether it was with despair or pain or with joy at Ivar's words was a question. Sweating, her face even whiter, struggling hard, she pulled herself forward until her legs were no longer dangling. Then she rolled over and lay flat on her back while her breasts rose and fell quickly. Her midriff bore a wide red mark from the impact. Two minutes later, she got on all fours and crawled several feet. Then she rose and walked unsteadily but proudly to the platform.

Faustroll embraced her, perhaps more enthusiastically than modesty permitted, when she joined him. She wept for a moment. Faustroll wept too. But they separated to watch Ivar when again the drums rattled and the horns blared.

The huge man, his bronze-red hair shining in the sun, stepped onto the gangplank. As the other jumpers had done, he had been bending and flexing and leaping up and down in a warm-up. Now he crouched, his lips moving counting the seconds along with the captain of the guards. Then he came up out of his crouch and ran, his massive legs pumping. The plank bent down under his weight, and it quivered from the pounding. His left foot came down just a few inches from the end. He was up, legs kicking.

Down he came, a foot short of the end of the victory plank. His hands shot out and gripped the sides of the wood near the end. The plank bent, sprang up a little, and sank down again. It cracked loudly.

Davis cried out, "Get on the plank! It's going to break!"

Ivar was already swinging himself backward to get momentum for a forward swing so he could get his leg up on the plank. Just as he did come forward, a sharp snapping noise announced that the wood had broken. Ann shrieked. Davis gasped. Faustroll yelled, *"Mon dieu!"*

Roaring, Ivar hurtled out of sight. Davis rushed forward and pressed his stomach against the railing. The plank was turning over and over. But the Viking was not in sight.

Davis leaned far out. There, thirty feet below him, Ivar was hanging by his hands from a slanting beam. His towerward swing had carried him far enough to grab one of the horizontal beams projecting beyond the main structure. Hanging from the beam with only his hands, he had managed to work closer to the building. But he must have slipped, and he had fallen. But, again, he had saved himself by clutching a cross beam slanting at a forty-five-degree angle in the exterior of the city structure. His body must have slammed hard against it, and his hands were slipping down along the slanting wood, leaving a trail of smeared blood.

When they were stopped where another angled beam met the one he was clinging to, he strove to pull himself up. And he succeeded. After that, he had to climb back up until he got to the platform on which Davis stood. If he did not do that, he would not be freed.

By then, Tamcar had left his throne to look over the platform and down at the Viking. He grimaced when he saw Ivar slowly but surely making his way up the outside of the structure. But even Tamcar had to obey the rules of the ordeal. No one was allowed to interfere with Ivar. It was up to him to get to the platform or to fall. Ten minutes or so passed. And the bronze-red hair of the Viking appeared and then his grinning face. After he hauled himself over the railing, he lay for a while to regain his strength.

When he arose, he spoke to Tamcar. "Surely, the gods favor us four. They have destined us for greater things than being your slaves."

"I do not think so," the Emperor said. "You will be freed, as the gods decree. But you will not go far. The savages just north of our state will seize you, and you will no longer be free. I will make sure of that."

For a moment, it looked as if Ivar were going to hurl himself at the Emperor. But the spears of the royal guard were ready for him. He relaxed, smiled, and said, "We'll see about that."

Davis felt drained. The ordeal had been terrible enough. Now, after having survived it, they would again fall into the hands of evil. Here, at least, they had plenty of food. But, just beyond the upper boundary of the Kingdom of the West Sun, the land on both sides of the River was occupied by people whom it was best to avoid. They gave their slaves just enough food to keep them working; they enjoyed crucifying slaves and tying them up in agonizing positions for a long time; they relished eating them. If you were their captive and you suddenly were given much food, you knew that you were being fattened to be the main course.

Davis thought that he would have been better off if he had fallen to his death. At least, that way, he would have had a fifty-fifty chance to rise again far north of here.

He was still downcast when the boat carrying them brought them within sight of what the Incans called the Land of the Beasts. The two crewmen were starting to haul down the lateen sail. He was sitting with the other captives in the middle of the vessel. Their hands were bound before them with thin cords of fish-gut. They were naked and possessed only their grails. On both sides of them stood guards with spears.

The captain of the guards said, "Within minutes, you will all be free." He laughed.

Apparently, the Emperor had sent word to the Beasts that they would soon have slaves as a gift. A group of dark-skinned Caucasians stood at a docking pier on the right bank. They waved flint-tipped spears and big clubs while they danced wildly, the sun flashing on the mica chips inset in their flaring, light-gray, fish-scale helmets. Davis had heard that they were supposed to be a North African people who lived sometime in the Old Stone Age. Seeing them made him sweat and sick at his stomach. But, so far, they had not put out on boats to meet them.

Ivar, sitting close to him, spoke softly. "We are four. The guards are ten. The three sailors are not worth considering. The odds favor us. When I give the word, Faustroll and I will attack those on the sternside. You, Red-Hair, and you, Ann, will attack the others. Use your grails as hammers, swing them by the handles."

"The odds favor us!" Faustroll said, and he laughed softly. "That is a pataphysical view!"

Ivar bent over and strained to separate the cord securing his hands together. His face got red; his muscles became snakes under the skin. The guards jeered at his efforts. Then their mouths dropped open as the cord snapped, and he shot up, roaring, his grail swinging out. The hard lower edge caught a guard under his chin. Ivar grabbed the man's falling spear with his other hand and drove it into another guard's belly.

The Incans had expected no resistance. If they did get it, they were certain that the handicapped slaves would be easily subdued. But the Viking had removed two guards from the fight seconds after it had started.

Davis and Ann swung their grails with good effect. His came up and slammed into the crotch of the nearest guard. After that, he had no time to see what his companions were doing. A spearhead gashed the front of his thigh, and then the man who had wounded him dropped when Davis's grail smashed into the side of his head.

It was all over within five seconds. The sailors leaped into the water. Ivar ran toward the steersman, who jumped overboard. Following the Viking's bellowed commands, the woman and the two men hoisted the sail. A great shout went up from the savages on land, and they immediately manned boats. Drums sounded, apparently signaling those farther up the River to intercept the slaves' boat.

They came close to doing it. But Ivar, a consummate sailor, evaded them and then left them behind. They sailed northward, free for the time being.

5

Eighteen years had passed since the flight from the Land of the Beasts. They had fought much, been imprisoned a few times, and had suffered several hundred mishaps and scores of wounds. But they had lived in this state, Jardin, for seven years with relative tranquility and content.

Andrew Davis's hutmate was Rachel Abingdon, a daughter of an American missionary couple. He had converted her to his belief that the Redeemer had been born again on the River and that they must find him someday. Meanwhile, they had preached to the locals, not very successfully, but they did have a dozen or so disciples. Materially, Davis thrived. Many men and women came to him daily to be massaged or manipulated osteopathically. They paid for their treatments with artifacts which he could trade for other goods, if he so desired, and with the gourmet foods their grails delivered. Life was easy. The citizens were not power-hungry, at least not politically. The days passed for Davis as if he were in the land of the lotus-eaters. Golden afternoons fishing and happy evenings sitting around the fires and eating and talking merged one into the other.

Ivar the Boneless was general of the army, which was organized solely for defense. But the neighboring states for a thousand miles up and down the River were nonbelligerent. Militarily, he had little to do except keep the soldiers drilled, inspect the boundary walls, and hold maneuvers now and then.

Ann had long ago quit living with Ivar. To Davis's amazement, she had gotten religion. If, that is, the Church of the Second Chance could be called a religion in any true sense. The missionaries he had talked to and heard preach claimed to believe in a Creator. But they said that all Earth religions were invalid in stating they were divinely inspired. The Creator—they avoided the word "God"—had made a being superior to man shortly before the great resurrection of the Earth dead. These were a sort of flesh-and-blood angels, called Makers, whose mission was to save all of humanity from itself and to raise it to a spiritual level equal to that of the Makers. The man or woman who was not so raised was, after an indeterminate length of time, doomed. He or she would wander the void forever as conscious matterless entities without will.

"The Chancers' ethics are very high," Davis had sneered one day while talking to Ann. "They pay no attention to sexual morality as long as no force or intimidation is involved."

"Sexual mores were necessary on Earth," she had answered, "to protect the children. Also, venereal disease and unwanted pregnancies caused great suffering. But here there are no such diseases, nor do women get pregnant. Actually, the largest, the most powerful element of sexual morality on Earth was the concept of property. Women and children were property. But here there is no such thing as property, no personal property, anyway, except for a person's grail and a few towels and tools. Most of you men haven't absorbed that idea yet. To be fair, a lot of women haven't either. But all of you will learn someday."

"You're still a slut!" Davis had said angrily.

"A slut who doesn't desire you at all, though you desire me. The day you realize that, you'll be one more step closer to true love and to salvation."

As always, Davis, teeth and hands clenched, body quivering, had strode away. But he was unable to stay away from her. If he did not talk to her, he could never bring her to the true salvation.

Faustroll, two years ago, had declared that he was God. "You need look no more, our friend," he said to Davis. "Here before you is the Savior. The fleshly semblance of a man that we have adopted should not deceive you. It is needed to prevent you and the rest of us from being blinded by our glory. Accept us as your God, and we will share our divinity with you.

"Actually, you are already divine. What I will do is reveal to you how you may realize this and how to act upon the glorious realization."

Faustroll was hopeless. His philosophy was blather. Yet, for some reason, Davis could not help listening to him. He did not do so for amusement, as he had once thought, or because he might make Faustroll see the Light. Perhaps it was just that he liked him despite his infuriating remarks. The Frenchman had something, a je ne sais quoi.

Davis had not seen Ivar for months, when, one day, Ivar hove into his view. "Hove" was the appropriate word; the Viking was a huge ship, a man-of-war. Behind him was a much smaller man, a tender, as it were. He was short and thin, black-haired and brown-eyed. His face was narrow; his nose, huge and beaked.

Ivar bellowed in Esperanto, "Andrew the Red! Still dreaming of finding the woman who gave birth to a second Christ? Or have you given up that quest?"

"Not at all!"

"Then why do you sit on your ass day after day, week after week, month after month, year after year?"

"I haven't!" Davis said indignantly. "I have made many converts to people who had rejected Christ! Or who had never heard of Him, who had not been in a state of grace!"

Ivar waved his hand as if dismissing their importance. "You could put them all under the roof of a small hut. Are you going to be satisfied with hanging around here forever when, for all you know, your Jesus is up-River and waiting for you to appear so that he may send you forth to preach?"

Davis sensed a trap of some sort. The Viking was grinning as if he were ready to pounce on him.

"It makes better sense to wait here for Him," Davis said. "He will come someday, and I will be ready to greet Him."

"Lazy, lazy, lazy! The truth is that you like to live here where no one is trying to kill or enslave you. You make feeble efforts to preach, and you spend most of your time fishing or tupping your wife."

"Now, see here!" Davis said.

"I am here, and I see. What I see is a man who was once on fire, has cooled, and is now afraid to dare hardship and suffering."

"That's not true!"

"I reproach you, but I also reproach myself. I, too, had the dream of going up the River until I came to its mouth. There I expected to find the beings who made this world and who brought about our resurrection. If they would not answer my questions willingly, they would do so under duress. I say that though it would seem that they are immeasurably more powerful than I am.

"But I forgot my dream. To use your own phrase, I was at ease in Zion. But this place is not Zion."

Davis nodded to indicate the man with Ivar. "Who's that?"

Ivar's large hand pushed the little man forward. "His name is Bahab. He's a newcomer. Bahab the Arab. He was born in Sicily when his people held that island. I do not know when he lived according to your reckoning, but it does not matter. He has an interesting tale, one that reminded me of what I had forgotten. Speak, Bahab!"

The little man bowed. He spoke in a high voice and in a heavily accented Esperanto. Though some of his words were not in local usage, Davis figured out their meaning from the context.

"You will pardon me, I trust, for such an abrupt approach and possible intrusion. I would prefer sitting with you and having coffee and getting to know you before beginning my story. But some people are barbaric or, I should say, have different customs."

"Never mind all that!" Ivar said loudly. "Get on with your story!"

"Ah, yes. Some years ago, I was up-River a long way from here. I talked to a man who had the most amazing news. I do not know if it was true or not, though he had nothing to gain from lying to me. On the other hand, some men lie just for the pleasure of it, sons of Shaitan that they are. But sometimes, if the lie is merely for amusement's sake..."

"Are you going to make me regret bringing you here?" Ivar shouted.

"Your pardon, Excellency. The man of whom I spoke said that he had a curious tale. He had wandered far, up and down this Valley, but had never encountered anything so wondrous. It seems that he was once in an area where a certain woman, who claimed to be a virgin, conceived."

"Oh, my Cod!" Davis said. "Can it be true?"

Bahab said, "I do not know. I did not witness the event, and I am skeptical. But others who had been there at the time swore that what the man said was indeed true."

"The baby! The baby!" Davis said. "Was it a boy?"

"Alas, no! It was female."

"But that couldn't be!" Davis said.

Bahab paused as if he were wondering if Davis had called him a liar. Then he smiled. "I merely tell you what the man and his fellows, actually, five in number, told me. It does not seem likely that all would be conspiring to lie to me. But if I offend you, I will say no more."

"Oh, no!" Davis said. "I'm not insulted. On the contrary. Please continue."

Bahab bowed, then said, "All this had happened years before I came to that area. By now, the baby would be fully grown, if there was such a baby. The woman may not have been a virgin, as she claimed, and some man might be the father. But that would be miracle enough since all men and women seem to be sterile."

"But a baby girl?" Davis said. "That's can't be!"

"I have talked to wise men and women of the late twentieth century, by Christian reckoning, scientists they call themselves," Bahab said. "They told me that, if a woman could be induced to conceive by chemical methods, the child would be female. I did not understand their talk of 'chromosomes,' but they assured me that a virgin female can conceive only a female. They also said that, in their time, this had never happened. Or in any time before theirs."

"They leave God out of their science," Davis said. "It happened once... when Jesus was born."

Bahab looked incredulous, but he said nothing.

"What you think should happen," Ivar said, "and what does happen are often not the same. You still do not know the truth. The only way you can find that is to venture forth again and determine for yourself. Surely, you can't be uninterested because this child was female? There were women goddesses, you know."

"God does what He wishes to do," Bahab said.

"You are right, Ivar," Davis said. "I must search out this woman and her daughter and talk to them. You are also right, I confess, in that I have let sloth and peace lull me to sleep."

"We go! I, too, have been asleep! But I am tired of this purposeless life. We will build a boat, and we will take it up the River! "

"Rachel will be pleased," Davis said. "I think."

Rachel was eager to go, though she also was disappointed that the Savior was a woman.

"But then, we don't know that this story is true," she said. "Or it may be a half-truth. Perhaps the child was male. But evil people have distorted the story, changed it to make the baby a female. It's a lie which the Devil beget. He used many devices to lure the faithful into error."

"I don't like to think that," Davis said. "But you could he right. Whatever the truth, we must try to find it."

Faustroll said that he would go with them. "This virgin birth could be a pataphysical exception. Pataphysics, as we have remarked more than once, is the science of exceptions. We doubt that it happened since we do not remember having done it. We will be pleased to expose the charlatans who claimed that it did happen."

Ann Pullen said that she was staying in Jardin. No one, however, had asked her to accompany them. Davis thought that he should have rejoiced when he heard the news. But he felt a pang. He did not know why he was disappointed or why he felt a hurt in his chest. He detested the woman.

A month later, the boat was complete, a fine ship with a single mast and twenty oars. Ivar had picked the crew, brawny men and their battle-tested women, all eager to put the soft life behind them. Only two of Davis's disciples had been allowed to go on Ivar's boat, and that was because they did not object to fighting in self-defense. The others, pacifists all, would follow in a smaller vessel.

At dawn of the day set for their departure, they gathered at a grailstone. After the stone had shot its thundering and white flash upward, they removed their grails, now filled with food of various kinds, beer, cigarettes, and dreamgum. Davis would pass out the tobacco, beer, and gum to the crew, though he would have preferred to throw them into the River. Since they would eat breakfast on the vessel later in the morning, they began boarding from the pier. The air was cool, but Davis was shivering with excitement. For a long time, he had been aware that something was missing from his life. Now he knew that it was the desire to explore and to find adventure. On Earth, he had been a traveler over much of the United States, lecturing and founding colleges of osteopathy. He had been faced with the hostility of local doctors and of the crowds provoked by the M.D.s. He had charged head-on into the jeers, boos, death threats, and rotten eggs thrown at him. But he had persisted in a campaign he and his colleagues had finally won.

On the Riverworld, he had seldom stayed long in one place except when detained in slavery. He was a walker-to-and-fro of the earth and a far-venturing sailor, too. Real happiness was not his unless he had a quest beckoning him to far lands.

Ivar stood on the rear deck by the steersman and bellowed orders. He, too, was happy, though he complained of the crew's slowness and clumsiness.

Two burly Norsemen began to loosen ropes securing the vessel to the pier. They halted when Ivar bellowed at them to wait a moment. Davis heard a man shouting, and he looked shoreward. The top of the sun had just cleared the mountains; its rays swept away the grayness and shone on the stranger. He was running across the plain, waving his arms and yelling in Esperanto.

"Don't go yet! Wait for me! I want to go with you!"

"He'd better have a good reason for delaying us," Ivar said loudly. "Otherwise, into the water he goes!"

Davis was curious about the mysterious stranger, but he also felt something unaccountable. Was it a premonition of dread? Did this man bring unsettling news? Though Davis had no reason to suspect this, he felt that he would be happier if the man had never showed up.

The fellow reached the pier and halted, breathing hard, his grail dangling from one hand. He was of middle height and rangy. His face was strong and handsome, long, narrow, though partly obscured by his black, wide-brimmed, high-crowned hat. Under the shadow of the hat were dark eyes. The long hair falling from under the hat was glossy black. A black cloak covered his shoulders. A black towel was around his waist. His jackboots were shiny black fish-hide. His black belt supported a wooden scabbard from which stuck the fish-hide-bound hilt of a rapier. If the weapon was made of iron, it was unique in this area.

"What brings you croaking like a raven of ill omen to us?" Ivar yelled.

"I just heard that you were leaving for up-River," the man said in a deep voice. His Esperanto was heavily tainted by his native language, which must have had many harsh sounds. "I've run all the way down from the mountains to catch you. I would like to sign up. You will find me handy. I can row with the best, and I am an excellent archer, though recent events have robbed me of my bow. And I can fight."

He paused, then said, "Though I was once a peaceful man, I now live by the sword."

He drew out his rapier. It was indeed of steel. "This has pierced many a man."

"Your name?" Ivar shouted.

"I answer to Newman."

"I expect and get immediate obedience," Ivar said.

"You have it."

"What is your mission?"

"The end of the River, though I am in no hurry to get to it."

Ivar laughed, then said, "We have something in common, though I suppose that many are also trying to get there. We have room for you as long as you pull your weight. Come aboard. You will take your turn at the oar later."

"Thank you."

The boat was pushed from the pier, and the two Norsemen jumped onto the vessel. Presently, it was making its way up the River. When the morning breeze came, the rowers shipped their oars, and the fore-and-aft sail and the boom sail were hoisted. The crew sat down to eat from their grails.

Ivar came down from the deck to talk to people amidships. He stood above the newcomer. "What tale of interest do you bring?"

The man looked up.

"I have many."

"We all do, Ivar said. "But what have you found most amazing?"

Newman half-lidded his eyes as if to shut out the light while he searched his inner darkness. He seemed to be feeling around for some treasure.

Finally, he said, "Perhaps the most amazing is a man who claimed to be Jesus Christ. Do you know of him or did you live in a time and a place on Earth where he was unknown?"

"My gods were Odin and Thor and others," Ivar growled. "I have sacrificed many Christians to him on Earth. But, near the end of my life, I became a Christian. More from a desire to hedge my bets, you might say, than from true faith. When I came to this world and found that it was neither Valhalla nor Heaven, though much more like Valhalla than Heaven, I renounced both beliefs. But it is hard not to call out for my native gods when I need them."

"Those who had never heard of Jesus on Earth have heard of him here," Newman said. "But you know enough about him so that I do not have to explain who he is."

"I could not escape knowing more of him than I care to hear," Ivar said. He pointed at Davis. "That man, Andrew the Red, is constantly prating about him."

Davis had been inching closer to Newman. He said, "I'm eager to hear your story, stranger. But this man who claimed to be Jesus cannot be He. He is in Heaven, though He may have been reincarnated as a woman on this world. Or so some say. My wife and I are going up-River to find her."

"Good luck, what with all the many billions here and the chance that she might now be down-River," the man said. "But you will not be offended, I hope, if I say that you will be disappointed even if you find the woman."

"Enough!" Ivar said. "The tale!"

"I came to a certain area shortly after the man calling himself Jesus was crucified by a fanatical medieval German monk. He was called Kramer the Hammer. The crucified man was still living, so you will see how soon after the event I arrived. The short of it is that I talked to him just before he died. And then I talked to a man who had lived in the dead man's time and place on Earth and knew him well. This man confirmed that the dead man had indeed been Yeshua, as the witness called him.

"I was very near him when he spoke his last words. He cried out, 'Father! They know what they're doing! Do not forgive them!' He sounded as if his experiences on this world had stripped him of the faith he had on Earth. As if he knew that mankind was not worth saving or that he had failed in his mission."

"Impossible!" Davis said.

Newman stared coldly at Davis, "I'm lying?"

"No, no! I don't doubt your story of what happened. What I don't believe is that the man on the cross was really Jesus. He's not the first nor the last of those who said that they were the Savior. Some may have genuinely believed that they were."

"How do you account for the testimony of the witness?"

"He was lying."

Newman shrugged. "It makes no difference to me."

Rachel touched Davis's shoulder. "You look troubled."

"No. Angry."

But he was also downcast, though he knew he should not be.

That evening, the boat was moored near a grailstone. After the stone thundered, the crew ate the offerings of the grails. They also devoured the freshly caught and cooked fish offered to them by the locals. Davis sat in a circle around a bamboo wood fire. Faustroll was at his side.

The Frenchman said, "Your wife was correct when she said you seemed troubled by Newman's tale. You still seem so."

"My faith is not broken, not even shaken," Davis said.

"You say so. Your body, your voice declare that you are plunged into black thoughts."

"The Light will clear away the darkness."

"Perhaps, friend," Faustroll said. "Here, have some fish. It's delicious. It's something you can have faith in."

Davis did not reply. The sight of Faustroll's greasy lips and the thought of Faustroll's shallowness sickened him. Or did the sickness come from another cause? He was far more disturbed than he had admitted to Rachel or the Frenchman.

"'The stranger, he talked as if with authority," Faustroll said.

"Of course, all crazies do."

"Crazies?"

"There is something deeply disturbing in that man, though he has much self-control. Did you not perceive it? He is dressed in black as if he is in mourning."

"He just seemed like one more mercenary adventurer," Davis said.

Faustroll put his hand on Davis's shoulder.

"There is something we must tell you. Perhaps our timing is wrong, seeing that you are so melancholy. But, sooner or later, you who seek the Light must face it, though the Light may not be the color you expect."

"Yes?" Davis said. He was not very interested.

"We speak of the time when you leaped across the void between Pachacuti's gangplanks. You said that you were seized by a spiritual rapture as soon as your foot left the gangplank. The rapture lifted you as if it were a gas-filled balloon. You soared higher than you should have, higher than you were capable of leaping. It was, you said, given by God. But…" Davis sat up straighter. Some interest flickered in him.

"Yes?"

"You crossed the gap and landed upon the plank. But your feet struck its end. As a result, you landed hard and painfully. You might have fallen off the plank then if you had not grabbed its sides."

Faustroll paused. Davis said, "What about it?"

"Rapture is fine. It carried you across safely. But then you struck the plank. Reality entered; the rapture was gone."

"What about that?"

"We are making an analogy, perhaps a parable. Think about that leap, friend, while you journey in a quest for what may be imaginary. Rapture is nontangible and temporary. Reality is hard and long lasting and often painfully crippling. What will you do if you find that the woman did not conceive and that there is no child?

"Reality may be a club which shatters your ability to ever feel that rapture again. We hope, and it is for your own good, that you never find that child.

"Think about that."

Coda

First I found Rabi'a. Then I found the artifact, which I think of as The Artifact. Which is more precious, Rabi'a or The Artifact? Rabi'a says that I do not have to choose between The Way or The Artifact. There is no choice in this matter between The Way and a machine.

I am not so sure.

My mind, the only truly time-traveling machine, goes back. And then back. And then it goes ahead of this very moment.

HERE I SIT on the rock that rims the top of the monolith. The sun burns the right side of my head and body. My mind burns too, but all over, burns to its center.

I am on the top of a two-thousand-foot-high granite monolith. It rises from the plain not more than a hundred feet from the Riverbank. The last hundred feet of the monolith flares out like a glans with the end cut off. That the monolith is phallus-shaped is, I think, accidental. But I am not sure that anything about this world is accidental. Even the contours of the mountains, which form the Rivervalley, and the course of the River may have both practical and symbolic meaning.

I wish that I could discern the meaning. There are times when I almost have grasped it. But that is as elusive as the water that forms the River.

The top of the monolith, my living space, my physical world, flares out to make a rough circle six hundred feet in diameter. Not much. But it is enough.

You cannot see it from the ground, but that circle is a cup. Within it is a deep and fertile soil, fast-growing bamboo, bushes, and earthworms that eat rotting vegetable matter and human excrement.

In the center of this cup grows a giant oak. At the foot of the tree is a spring, the water brought up through the monolith from the ground-level source by whatever devices the makers of this world concealed in the stone. The water flows northward from the spring in a shallow creek. This broadens out into a lakelet and then cataracts through a narrow gap in the stone of the cup. Rainbow-colored fish live in the creek and the lake. They are about eight inches long and are delicious when fried or baked.

Not far from the tree is a grailstone.

I never needed much on Earth. Here I need even less, though, in a spiritual sense, I require more.

I am like the Dark Age Christian hermits who sat alone on high pillars for years in the African desert. They meditated most of the time, or so they claimed. They seldom moved from their sitting position. If so, they must have had running sores on their asses. I often get up and walk and sometimes run along the very limited circumference of my world. Other times, I climb this three-hundred-feet-high tree, leap from branch to branch, and run back and forth on the largest branches.

Mankind, it is claimed, is descended from the apes. If so, I have, in a sense, regressed to the apes, What of it? There is deep joy in playing on a tree. And it seems fitting to complete the circle from ape to man to ape. It also symbolically matches the circling of the River from North Pole to South Pole and back to the North Pole. What comes out must go back in. In a different form, perhaps. But its essence is matter. Spirit forms from matter. Without matter, spirit has no vessel. Of course, I do not mean The Spirit. Then the time comes when matter dies. Does the spirit also die? No more than a butterfly dies when it changes from pupa to imago. The spirit must go to a place where, unlike this universe but like The Spirit, matter is not necessary.

Or is this kind of thinking born of hope fathered by fear of death? Therefore, without validity.

Ten wishes do not make one piece of pie.

It seems, now and then, strange to utter "I," the first person singular. For so many years on this world, I called myself Doctor Faustroll, and everybody I met thought that was my true name. Many times, I truly forgot that my natal name was Alfred Jarry. The literary character I had created on Earth became me. And I had no individuality. Faustroll was just a piece of the all-embracing "we." But here, at this place on the River, somewhere in the north temperate zone of this planet, "we," which had been "I" in the beginning and then became "we," metamorphosed back into "I." It's as if the butterfly had regressed into the pupa, then again became the butterfly.

Is the second "I" superior to the first one?

I don't know.

Is any one place along the River better than any other place?

I don't know.

But I do know that we, my companions and I, traveled and fought for many years along many millions of miles of the River, going ever upstream, though often that way was from north to south or east or west as the River wandered and wound and writhed. But always, we went against the current.

Then we stopped to rest for a while, just as we had done throughout the journey when we were weary of the fighting and of sailing and of each other's company. Here, I met Rabi'a. Here, I stayed.

Ivar the Boneless, our leader, the huge bronze-haired Viking, did not seem surprised when I told him that I would not sail out with him in the morning.

"Lately, you seem to be thinking much more than is good for a man," he said. "You were always strange, one seemingly touched by the gods, a man with his brain askew."

He cocked an eyebrow at me, grinned, and said, "Have you become faint-hearted because of the allure of this hawk-nosed, doe-eyed, dark-skinned woman you met here? Has she fired up your passion for woman? Which, I have observed, has never been fierce. Is that it? You would abandon our quest for a pair of splendid breasts and hot hips?"

"The physical has nothing to do with it," I said. "In fact, Rabi'a was a celibate all her life on Earth, a virgin, a saint. Resurrection here did not change her mind about that. No, it is definitely not passion for her body that keeps tree here. It is passion for her mind. No, not really that. It is passion for God!"

"Ah!" the Viking said, and he spoke no more of the matter. He wished me good luck, and he walked away.

I watched his broad back, and I felt some regret and some sense of loss. But it seemed to me that his loss was far greater than mine. Many years ago, he had experienced what I can only call a mystic moment. Out of the dark sky, while we were fleeing on a boat from enemies bent on killing us, something bright had seized him. That was evident though he would never talk about it. But, from that moment on, he lost his desire to conquer a piece of the Riverworld, rule it, and expand his holdings as far as his wits and his weapons would allow him. Nor did he ever attack a man or an entire state again. He fought only in self-defense, though there was much aggression in that.

His soul and body drove him always up the River. Someday, so he boasted, he would get to the sea at the North Pole and would storm the great tower that many said was there. And he would squeeze the throats of the tower dwellers until they told him who they were, why they had made this planet and its River, and how they had resurrected all of Earth's dead and brought them here and why they had done it.

His vow to do this made him sound simpleminded. In many ways, he was. But he was not just a cruel, bloodthirsty, and loot-hungry savage. He was very shrewd, very curious, and very observant, especially about those who professed to believe in the gods. Having been a priest and a sorcerer of the Norse religion, he was skeptical of all faiths. Near the end of his life, while he was the king of Dublin, he had converted to Christianity. He was playing it safe just in case that religion might be the true one. It would not cost him anything.

He died in A.D. 873. After his resurrection in his youthful body on the Riverbank, he abandoned the Cross and became an agnostic, though he kept calling on Odin and Thor when he was in a tight spot. Lifelong habits die hard. Sometimes you have to die more than once before the habits die. That might be one of the messages of the Riverworld.

Ivar's character had changed somewhat. Now, instead of physical and temporal power, he wanted the power of knowledge of the truth. A step forward, yes. But not far enough. How was he going to use his knowledge? I suspected that he would be mightily tempted to wield the knowledge torn from the masters of this world—if he ever got it—for his benefit only. He wanted the truth, not The Truth.

Then there was Andrew Davis, the American physician, osteopath, and neuropath. He had died in A.D. 1919. But awakening on the River, though it had confused him, had not made him abandon his fundamentalist Church of Christ religion. Like so many believers, he had rationalized that the Riverworld was a testing ground that God had provided for those who professed to be Christians. That it was not mentioned in the Bible was only another proof of God's mysterious ways.

When he heard rumors that a woman had conceived and borne a male child, he became convinced that God's son was born again. And he had set out up-River to find the woman and the child. A few years ago, he had met a man who had known Jesus on Earth. This man told Davis that he had encountered Jesus again on the Riverbank. And he had witnessed the execution of Jesus by fanatical Christians.

Did Davis then admit that Jesus was just another madman who had believed that he was the Messiah? No! Davis said that his informant had lied. He was a tool of the Devil.

I believe that it was possible that, somewhere on this world, a woman did have a false pregnancy. And that the story of this somehow became twisted during the many years and the many millions of miles it traveled. Result: the tale goes that a woman has given birth in a world where all men and women are sterile. And, of course, the child must be the Savior.

Thus, Davis went with Ivar on his boat, leaving me behind. Davis did not care much about getting to the supposed tower in the supposed North Polar Sea. He hoped—longed—to find the son of the virgin somewhere north of here and to cast himself in adoration at the feet of the son. Who by now should be approximately thirty years old if he exists. And he does not, of course.

After Ivar and his crew sailed off, seven years passed. During this time, I met many dozens of groups of men and women who were going up-River to storm the tower. They were questioners and seekers after the truth, for which I honor them. One of them was a man who claimed to be an Arab. But some of his followers talked, and I found out that he was really an Englishman who had lived in the nineteenth century. My contemporary, more or less. His name was Burton, well known in his time, a remarkable man, a writer of many books, a speaker of many tongues, a great swordsman, a fabled explorer of many lands in Africa and elsewhere. His followers said that he had accidentally awakened in a pre-resurrection chamber made by those mysterious people who had made this planet. They had put him back to sleep, but he had had encounters with these beings since then, and they were out to find him. For what purposes, I do not know. I suspect that this story is one of many tales of wonder floating through the Riverworld.

If any man could get to the tower through the many seemingly insurmountable obstacles and seize the owners of the tower by the throat, this man could. At least, that was the impression I got. But he went on up the River, and that was the last I heard of him. Other questers followed him.

All this time, I was the disciple of Rabi'a, the Arab woman who had lived A.D. 717 to 801. She was born in Basra, a city on the Shatt-al-Arab, a river born of the meeting of the Tigris and Euphrates rivers. This was in the area of ancient Mesopotamia where the Sumerian civilization came into being and was followed by the Akkadian, the Babylonian, the Assyrian, and many others that rose and fell and were covered with the dust. Rabi'a's native city, Basra, was not distant from Baghdad, which some people tell me was the capital of a Muslim nation called Iraq in the middle twentieth century.

Rabi'a was a Sufi and well-known throughout the Muslim world in her time and later. The Sufis were Muslim mystics whose unconventional approach to religion often brought about persecution from the orthodox. That did not surprise me. Everywhere on Earth, the orthodox have hated the unorthodox, and there has been no change here. The not-so-strange thing is that, after the

Sufis' deaths, they often became saints to the orthodox. They were no longer a danger.

Rabi'a told me that, for a long time, there have been Jewish and Christian Sufis, though not many, and these are accepted as equals by the Muslim Sufis. Anyone who believes in God may become a Sufi. Atheists need not apply. But there are other qualifications for becoming a Sufi and they are very hard. Also, unlike the orthodox, the Muslim Sufis genuinely believe in the equality of women with men, a belief unacceptable to the orthodox.

My many friends in late-nineteenth-century, early-twentieth-century Paris (Apollinaire, Rousseau, Satie, and many others, they were legion and legend, great poets, writers, and painters, leapers from the orthodox into the future, where are they now?) would be nauseated or would laugh scornfully if they knew that I aspire to be a Sufi. I sometimes laugh at myself. Who is better qualified to do so?

Rabi'a says that she has traveled The Path upward until she knows the utmost ecstasy, seeing the glory of God. I might be able to do so. No guarantee. She is my teacher, but only I, through my own efforts, can achieve what she has achieved. Others have done it, though they are very few. And then she adds that my strivings may be for nothing. God chooses those who will know The Way, The Path, The Truth. If I have not been chosen, *tant pis, je suis dans un de ces merdiers, quel con, le bon Dieu!* Why am I, Alfred Jarry, once calling himself Doctor Faustroll, mocker and satirizer of the hypocrites, the Philistines, the orthodox and the self-blinded, the exploiter and persecutor of others, the dead of soul, the steadfast and stick-in-the-mud people of faith...why am I now seeking God and willing to work as I have never worked before, to become a slave of God, eat to mention a slave of Rabi'a? Why am I doing this?

There are many explanations, mostly psychological. But psychology never explains anything satisfactorily.

I had heard about Rabi'a for some time, and so I went to hear her directly. I was the student and portrayer of the absurd, and I did not wish to miss out on the particular absurdity she represented...I thought. I hung around the fringe of the crowd of her disciples and the eager to learn and the idly curious. What she said seemed no different from what others of many different faiths had preached. Talk of The Way and The Path is cheap, and only the names of. those who founded the sects and of their disciples differ.

But this woman seemed to radiate something I had never detected in the others. And her words seemed to make sense even if they were, according to logic, absurd. And then she gave me a sidelong glance. It was as if lightning fastened us, as if positive and negative ions had joined. I saw something undefinable but magnetic in those black deerlike eyes.

To shorten the tale, I listened, and then I talked to her, and then I became convinced that what she was talking about was the essence of absurdity. But I recalled that it was Tertuallian who had written about his Christian faith. "I believe because it is absurd." That saying doesn't stand up to logical analysis: But then, it wasn't meant to do so. It appeals to the spirit, not the mind. There's a layer of meaning to it that is as hard to grasp as wine fumes. The nose smells them; the hand cannot hold them.

There is also a method of discipline which the Sufi master requires his initiates to obey. This is designed to lead the initiates upward physically, mentally, and spiritually. Part of it is taking nothing for granted just because it is traditional and conventional. The Sufi never accepts "everybody knows," "They say that..." Neither had I done that, but the Sufi evaluation method was different from mine. Mine had been to expose to ridicule. Theirs was to instill in the initiate an automatic method of looking at all sides of anything and, also, to teach the non-Sufi if that were possible. I had never believed that my satiric poetry, novels, plays, and paintings would illuminate a single person among the Philistines. I appealed only to minds that already agreed with me.

Thus, my schooling progressed under Rabi'a, though not very swiftly. I was her physical servant, bound to fetch and carry for her, attentive to her every waking moment. Fortunately, she liked to fish, so we spent many hours at my beloved pastime. I was also her spiritual servant, listening to her lectures and observations, thinking on them, answering her many questions designed to test my comprehension of her teachings, to see if I was making any progress. I was in bondage until I quit or I, too, attained the highest mastership and burned ecstatically with the flame of The One.

On the other hand, what else important did I have to do?

When Rabi'a heard me make that remark, she reproached me. "Levity has its place, but it too often indicates a giddy mind and a lack of seriousness," she said. "That is, a serious lack in the character. Or fear of the thing laughed at. Meditate about that."

She paused, then said, "I think you believe that you can attain a glimpse of The One through my eyes. I am only our teacher. You alone can find The Way."

It was not long after that that she decided to climb to the top of the monolith. There, if the top was inhabitable, she would stay for a long time. She would take along three of her disciples if they wished to accompany her.

"And how long, vessel of the inner light, will we remain there?" I said.

"We will let our hair grow until it reaches our calves," she said. "Then we will cut it off next to the scalp. When, after many cuttings, we have saved enough hair with which to make a rope long enough to descend from the top to the ground level, then we will leave the monolith."

That seemed a long time, but four of her disciples said that they would follow her. I was one. Havornik, a sixteenth-century Bohemian, wavered. He admitted that, like those who refused to go with her, he was afraid of the climb. But he finally said that he would try to overcome his lack of courage. He regretted that decision on the way up because he could use only his fingers and toes to cling to juts or ledges or holes in the rock, and many of these were small. But he made it to the top. He lay on the ground, quivering for an hour before he got the strength to stand up.

Havornik was the only one who was afraid. But he conquered his fear. Thus, he was the bravest of us all.

I wish that he had been as brave in his climbing out of his Self as he had been in climbing the mountain.

Or do I? After all, he might have saved me from my Self.

Three days after we got to the top, I found The Artifact. I was on my way to the little lake to fish when I saw something sticking out of the dirt at the base of a large bush. I don't know why I discerned it, since it was smeared with mud and protruded slightly from the ground. But I was curious, and I went to it, Bending down close to it, I saw the top of something bulb-shaped. I touched it; it was hard as metal. After digging in the soft earth around it, I pulled out something man-made. Made by sentiments, anyway. It was a cylinder about a foot long and three inches in diameter. On each end was an onion-sized bulb.

Very excited, I cleaned it in the creek water. It was black metal and bare of pushbuttons, slides, rheostats, and any operational devices. I didn't, of course, have the slightest idea who had made it or what it did or why it had been left or lost on this near-inaccessible peak. That day, I forgot about the fishing.

After an hour of touching it all over and turning it over and over and squeezing it, hoping to find a way to activate it or to open a section that would reveal controls, I took it to Rabi'a and the others. She heard my story, then said, "It may have been left here by accident by the makers of this world. If so, the makers are not gods, as many suppose. They are human beings like us, though they may differ in bodily form. Or it may be that the device was left here for some purpose in their plan. It does not matter who made it or what its function is. It has nothing to do with me or you. It can only be a deterrent, an obstacle, a stumbling block in The Path."

I was flabbergasted at this appalling lack of scientific curiosity—or any other kind. But, on reflection, I admitted that, from her viewpoint, she was right. Unfortunately, I have always been very interested in mathematics, physics, and technology. Not to brag (though why not?), but I am well-versed in these branches of science. In fact, I once designed a timetraveling machine that almost convinced many people that it was workable. Almost, I say. No one, including myself, ever built one to test its validity. That was because time travel seemed impossible according to the science of my day. Sometimes, I wonder if I should have built the machine. Perhaps time travel is impossible most of the time. But there may be moments when it is highly possible. I am a pataphysician, and pataphysics is, among other things, the science of the exceptional.

Rabi'a did not order me to get rid of The Artifact and forget about it. As her disciple, I was bound to obey her no matter how reluctant I was to do so. But she knew me well enough to realize that I would have to experiment with it until I gave up the search to determine its function. And perhaps she hoped to teach me a valuable lesson because of my willingness to veer from The Path for a while.

The third day after I had found the mysterious device, I was sitting on a branch of the great oak and staring at the device. Then I heard a voice. It was a woman's speaking a language I didn't know and had never heard before. And it came from one of the globes at the end of the cylinder. It startled me so much that I froze for a few seconds. Then I held the end near to my ear. The gibberish stopped after thirty seconds. But a man spoke then from the bulb at the other end.

When he stopped, a green ray bright enough to be seen in the daylight shot out. But it faded after four feet from the source, the bulb. It gave birth at the termination to a picture. A moving picture in which three-dimensional actors moved and spoke audibly. There were three strikingly handsome people in it, a Mongolian man, a Caucasian woman, and a Negro woman, each in a flimsy ancient-Greece-like robe. They were seated at a table the legs of which were curved and beautifully carved into the semblance of animals unknown to Earthly zoology. They were talking animatedly to each other and, now and then, into devices exactly like the one I held in my hand.

Then the images faded into sunlight. I tried to bring them back by duplicating the series of finger pressures on the cylinder just before they had appeared. Nothing happened. Not until at night three days later was I able to activate the device. This time the images were no brighter, the device apparently automatically adjusting itself to the exterior illumination. The scene projected was of some place along the River and seemed to be during the day. There were the usual men and women in their towels, fishing and talking. They spoke in Esperanto. Across the River were round bamboo huts with thatched roofs and many people. Nothing of any great interest. Except that one of the men nearby looked remarkedly like a man in the projection of the first scene, the meeting at the table.

From this I deduced that the makers of this world—I had no doubt that they were the makers—walked among the River-dwellers disguised as such. Whatever machine was recording this scene must be set in a boulder or perhaps in one of the indestructible and unmeltable irontrees everywhere on this world.

At the moment the scene was projected, Rabi'a and Havornik were present. She was interested, but she said, "This has nothing to do with us." Havornik, the Bohemian, however, was excited, and he was greatly disappointed when the scene faded out. I let him try his hand at reactivating the device after I had failed to do so. He also failed.

"There's some way to operate this," I said. "I'll find out what it is if I have to wear it out pressing on it."

Rabi'a frowned, then she smiled and said, "As long as playing with it does not interfere with your walking on The Path. It does no harm to have fun if you remain basically serious."

"All fun is basically serious," I said.

She thought for a moment, then smiled again and nodded.

But I became obsessed with operating The Artifact. When my mind should have been on Rabi'a's words, I thought of the device. Whenever I could, I retreated to the great tree or sat on the rim of the peak. Here, I experienced moments when I seemed to be on the brink of what I had written on Earth about God. That was the formula I had arrived at. Zero equals infinity. That was the formula for God, and, sometimes, it seemed that my soul—if I had one—was bereft of flesh and bone. It was close to realizing directly the truth behind that equation. I almost ripped off the mask of Reality.

When I told Rabi'a that, she said, "God is a mathematical equation. But God is also everything else, though The Spirit is apart from Himself."

"I can't make any more sense out of what you say than what I said," I replied.

She only said, "You may be approaching The One. But it is not with the help of that machine. Do not confuse it with The Way."

That night, while my companions slept, I sat on the rim and watched the bonfires far below. They were sitting or dancing around the flames or falling drunkenly on the ground. And then I thought of my years on Earth and here, and I felt pity mingled with despair for them. For myself and for my Self, too.

I had written many plays, stories, and poems about the stupid, the hypocritical, the savage, the unfeeling, and the exploiters of the wretched and doomed masses. I had jeered at all of them, the masters and the masses, for their failings and their low intelligence. Yet was it their fault? Were they not born to be what they became? Was not each one acting in accordance with what he could not surmount? Or, if a few did have perception and insight and the courage to act on these, were these not born to do that?

So how could anyone justly be praised or condemned? Those who seemed to lift themselves by their bootstraps to a higher plane were only doing so because their natal characters created their destinies. They deserved neither blame nor praise.

It seemed to me that there was no such thing as genuine free will.

Thus, if I, too, attained the ecstasy and the bliss of Rabi'a, it was because I was set on my course by my fleshly inheritance. And because I had lived so long. Why should Rabi'a or I be rewarded because God, in a manner of speaking, had willed it?

Where was the fairness or justice in this?

Those boobs and yahoos cavorting down below could not help being such. Nor could I or Rabi'a claim a superior virtue.

Where was the fairness and justice?

Rabi'a would have told me that it was all God's will. Someday, if I reached a certain plane of spiritual development, I would understand His will. If I did not, I was elected to be one of those doomed wretches who had filled the Earth and now filled the Riverworld.

On the other hand, she would say, all of us are capable of attaining union with God. If He so wills it.

At that moment, my restless gropings along the device seemed to have activated it. A green ray sprang from both bulbs, curved—it could not be true light—and met twelve feet beyond me. At the junction appeared a man's face. It was huge and scowling, and his words seemed to be threatening. After several minutes, while I sat motionless as if hypnotized by Doctor Mesmer, a woman's voice interrupted the tirade. It was very pleasant and soothing, yet somehow forceful. After another few minutes, the wrathful face relaxed. Presently, it was smiling. And then the emanations ceased.

I sighed. I thought, What did that mean? Does it have any special meaning for me? How could it?

Rabi'a's voice startled me. I turned and rose to face her. Her face looked stern in the bright light of the stars. Havornik was behind her.

"I saw; I heard," she said. "I can see where this is taking you. You are considering following the mystery posed by this machine instead of The Mystery posed by God. That will not do. It is time for you to choose between the Artifact and The Artificer. Now!"

I hesitated for a long time while she stood unmoving in body or face. Then I held the device out to her. She took it and gave it to Havornik.

"Take this and bury it where he will not find it," she said. "It is of no value to us."

"I will do so at once, mistress," the Bohemian said.

He disappeared into the bushes. But that dawn, as I was walking along the rim, weary from sleeplessness and wondering if I had decidedly rightly, I saw Havornik. He was climbing down through the gap in the stone through which we had entered this little world above the world. His grail was strapped to his back. The Artifact dangled on his chest at the end of a hair rope hung around his neck.

"Havornik!" I cried. I ran to the edge of the rim and looked down. He was not very far from me. He looked upward, his eyes huge and wild, and he grinned.

"Come back up," I shouted, "or I'll drop a rock on you!"

"No, you won't!" he shouted. "You have chosen God! I have chosen this machine! It's real! It's hard and practical—and is the means to getting answers to my questions, not the imaginary being Rabi'a convinced me for a while actually existed! It is of no value to you, no consequence! Or have you changed your mind?"

I hesitated. I could follow him down to the ground and wrest it from him there. I longed for it; I felt crushed with a sense of loss. I'd been too hasty, too awed by Rabi'a's presence, to think clearly.

I stood there, looking down on him and at The Artifact, for a long time. If I tried to take the machine from him, I might have to kill him. Then I would be among many who would desire the machine and would kill me to get it, if they could.

Several times, Rabi'a had said, "Killing for the sake of material things or for an idea is evil. It is not The Way."

I struggled with myself as Jacob struggled with the angel at the foot of the ladder. It was no fixed match; it was hard and desperate.

And then I shouted down at Havornik, "You will regret that choice. But I wish you good luck in finding the answers to your questions! They are not my questions!"

I turned, and I started. Rabi'a was ten feet behind me. She had not said a word because she did not want to influence me. I, I alone, must make the choice.

I had expected a compliment from her. But she said, "We have much work to do," and she turned and walked toward our camp.

I followed her.